BEYOND
THE
HERO

BEYOND THE HERO

Classic Stories
of Men
in Search of Soul

Allan B. Chinen, M.D.

A Jeremy P. Tarcher / Putnam Book
published by
G. P. Putnam's Sons
New York

A Jeremy P. Tarcher/Putnam Book
Published by G. P. Putnam's Sons
Publishers Since 1838
200 Madison Avenue
New York, NY 10016

Requests for such permissions should be addressed to:
Jeremy P. Tarcher, Inc.
5858 Wilshire Blvd., Suite 200
Los Angeles, CA 90036

Library of Congress Cataloging-in-Publication Data
Chinen, Allan B., date.
Beyond the hero: classic stories of men in search of soul
Allan B. Chinen
p. cm.
Includes bibliographical references and index
ISBN 0-87477-737-2
1. Men—Folklore.   2. Fairy tales—Psychological aspects.
3. Masculinity (Psychology).   4. Psychoanalysis and folklore.
I. Title.
GR469.C45 1993   92-31732 CIP
398.2'081—dc20

Design by MaryJane DiMassi

Printed in the United States of America
1 2 3 4 5 6 7 8 9 10

This book is printed on acid-free paper.
∞

*To Glenn and all brothers
who have gone before.*

This book draws on the experiences of many men, nameless and forgotten, who have handed down their male wisdom through folktales. To them go my deepest respect and gratitude. Yet the book would not have been possible without the insights of men today, too, and I wish to acknowledge my debt to those I have worked with as a therapist. Together we journeyed deep into men's issues, and from them comes the wisdom in this book. I would also like to thank several colleagues for their invaluable advice, reflections, and critique on earlier versions of this manuscript: Art Johnson, Ed McCord, John Martin, Larry Peters, Bruce Scotton, Miles Vich, and Michael Lidbetter. Their expertise as historians, psychologists, psychoanalysts, anthropologists, and editors has enriched this book immensely. Finally, I want to express my appreciation to Robert Bly, poet laureate of the men's movement, for his generous and thoughtful critique of the manuscript; to Connie Zweig, my editor at Tarcher, for her enthusiasm and straight-to-the-point insights; and to my agents, Jim and Rosalie Heacock, whose support, friendship, and guidance have brought this book and its two predecessors to fruition.

Contents

Prologue

A question haunts men today. In weekend retreats and men's groups, through books and solitary musings, men ask what it means to be a man. Old standards change, the heroic ideal falters, and men grope for a new paradigm of manhood. In Robert Bly's *Iron John*, Sam Keen's *Fire in the Belly*, and Robert Moore and Douglas Gillette's *King, Warrior, Magician, Lover*, men raise painful questions about masculinity. The fairy tales in this book, gathered from around the world, offer answers.

The claim is grandiose and I do not make it lightly. But the stories demand such a strong assertion. Where most familiar fairy tales concentrate on gallant young men, the stories in this book focus on *mature* males. The protagonists here have taken the hero's path and in the middle of life seek something deeper and more substantial. What they find is seasoned manhood, a masculinity beyond the hero's.

Men today desperately need these tales. Writers like Mark Gerzon in *A Choice of Heroes*, Aaron Kipnis in *Knights Without Armor*, and Keith Thompson in *To Be a Man* have described the collapse of heroic and patriarchal ideals, the traditional models of manhood. Feminists have revealed the violence inherent in the heroic paradigm and the secret contempt of patriarchs for all things feminine. Pacifists warn that the hero's glorification of war threatens human survival in a nuclear age. Ecologists denounce the hero's dream of conquering nature and his habit of ravaging the earth. Meanwhile, minorities and ethnic groups rise up against the patriarch and dispute his insistence on one law, one culture, and one doctrine for everyone.

In this tumult some men yearn for a simpler time, when heroes were honored by all, and patriarchs ruled over women and nations. Yet deep in their souls, most men know they cannot turn back time, any more than they can believe that the earth is flat or that Apollo and Zeus still live on Olympus. Without any alternative to the warrior or the king, though, men are tempted to return to old ways, striking back against feminists, pacifists, ecologists, and minorities. Yet the earth *is* round, and Apollo and Zeus are long gone. This is the importance of the fairy tales in this book: they reveal the path beyond the hero and the patriarch.

ON MEN'S TALES

The notion that fairy tales might have something serious to say to grown men might seem ridiculous. Such stories, we think today, are only for children. Yet this has been true only in the last few centuries. For most of history and for many traditional cultures today, fairy tales were told by adults and for adults. The stories are folktales, passed down by word of mouth over centuries, and they contain the distilled wisdom of many generations. In the "olden days," fairy tales were taken seriously and even used in healing ceremonies and initiation rites. Unfortunately, most publishers today aim fairy tales at children and either delete or denigrate adult roles. This makes stories about mature men— what I call "men's tales"—uncommon and relatively unknown. I found the men's tales in this book only by reading through some 5,000 fairy stories and picking out the ones whose protagonists are seasoned men, somewhere in the middle third of life. The vast majority of fairy tales are about children and adolescents. The stories of mature men were buried deep in old anthologies and forgotten.

Men's tales are long and complex. When I initially came across them, they baffled me. I put them aside to work on other fairy stories: tales about midlife and the issues that confront both men and women, which I discuss in *Once Upon a Midlife,* and stories about old age, contained in *In the Ever After.* When I returned to men's tales several years later, the stories slowly began to make sense. By comparing the tales with each other, their common themes became apparent. Men's tales, in fact, are astonishingly similar across the world, suggesting that the stories reveal basic elements of the masculine soul. In interpreting the tales, I tried to remain true to the dramas. I began with my collection of men's stories from around the world and then searched for psychological concepts that fit all the tales. I wanted to avoid starting with a favorite theory and forcing the tales to fit it. After all, men's tales were told for millennia and probably will be around for millennia more—long after today's psychological theories have been replaced by new ones. I initially interpreted the stories with concepts from Jungian psychology and research in adult development, since they were most familiar to me. But neither discipline was powerful enough to unravel the meanings of the stories. So I explored unfamiliar fields from anthropology to paleontology, tracking down descriptions of secret male societies, the folklore of hunting tribes, and the art of prehistoric man. A novice in new disciplines, I stumbled about in confusion and often felt like a fool. But I soon realized that this is a major theme in men's tales: the dramas show men venturing into the unknown and bumbling their way toward a deeper understanding of manhood. My research repeated the drama of men's tales!

In meditating on the stories, I also found their themes uncannily familiar. Similar motifs had surfaced in my own dreams and fantasies over the years. My exploration of men's tales soon became an intensely personal undertaking. More important, the same themes appeared in the dreams and fantasies of men with whom I worked as a psychotherapist: painful struggles with fathers, secret doubt about one's manhood, fear and fascination for the feminine, above all, a search for the masculine soul and a yearning for deep, life-giving male energy. Men's tales reflect these raw issues, while men's lives illustrate the stories. The one illuminates the other. The stories offered advice and hope to me and the men with whom I traveled on inward journeys. But the experience and reflections of men in therapy also made the meaning of the stories clear. Without their courage and insight, this book could not have been written. Men's tales are the stuff of men's lives.[1]

If I cite anecdotes from the lives of men I worked with and from my own life, I do not claim that we resolved the issues portrayed in men's tales, much less arrived at the wisdom in the stories. This is the advantage of the tales: they contain more experience than any one man can gain in a lifetime. The tales are a legacy from men who have gone before, providing a map for all who peer anxiously ahead.

MEN'S TALES AND THE DEEP MASCULINE

Men's stories portray what Robert Bly has aptly christened "the deep masculine." This is the part of the male psyche that is normally buried under conventional male roles, heroic ideals, and patriarchal ambitions. In fact, men's tales break dramatically with traditional masculine values and poke fun at heroes and patriarchs. The satire is startling because the myths and legends of most cultures extol the virtues of warriors and kings. Men's tales escape this conformity for several reasons. First, they are fairy tales and are not meant to be believed. Men's tales can mock anything and speak the unspeakable simply by saying, "Once upon a time," meaning, "This is only a fairy tale." Myths and legends, by contrast, claim to be true, so they are forced to obey prevailing heroic and patriarchal conventions.

Men's tales also specifically address mature men who have already mastered traditional male roles and who now need help in breaking free. Here men's tales differ from fairy stories about youth, like "Cinderella" or "Tom Thumb." The main function of "youth tales" is to indoctrinate children and adolescents in heroic ideals and patriarchal rules. Freed from that burden, men's tales explore alternative images of manhood. This is why the stories offer men a post-heroic and post-patriarchal vision of masculinity.

Men's tales speak directly from the unconscious in the original voice of the male psyche. This is because the stories were probably told by men privately, among soldiers or in secret male lodges. Without women and children present, men put aside heroic pretenses and reveal their secret fears and dreams. Men also undoubtedly recounted their tales after much drinking. Such altered states of consciousness foster the spontaneous emergence of unconscious material. So men's tales are like dreams: they bring up issues ignored in conscious life, or suppressed by social convention. Unconscious themes appear in myths, legends, and literature, too, but they have been censored and edited by priests or writers. Men's tales, by contrast, speak in the primordial voice of the male psyche.

WOMEN, YOUTH, AND THE DEEP MASCULINE

Men's stories link the deep masculine specifically with midlife. This is because men traditionally pursue heroic dreams in youth without questioning those ideals. Only in the middle years, after divorce, illness, and career setbacks, do men question the heroic and patriarchal paradigm, and seek something beyond it. So the deep masculine usually becomes an issue at midlife. In today's culture, though, the timing has started to shift. As feminism takes root, many men reject heroism in youth, not midlife. Young men often grapple with the deep masculine in high school and college, seeking alternatives to the hero. Stories about the deep masculine are not just for men at midlife, but for any man caught in the middle—after the hero dies and the patriarch falls, but before their successor appears.

If men's tales are about men, they are also for women: for wives, mothers, daughters, lovers, and co-workers, bewildered and infuriated by the men around them. Men's tales help explain the deeper reasons behind stereotypical male behavior, such as men's barbed put-downs of each other or their silence about emotions. The stories also challenge men to move beyond traditional male chauvinism. Yet men's tales do not advocate a gentle, domesticated, "feminized" or "soft" male. The stories portray fierce and passionate men. The tales affirm feminism *and* celebrate masculine vitality. This is not a "New Age" invention, either, because the stories come from traditional societies across the world. Men's tales reflect the original image of manhood.

HOW THE BOOK IS ORGANIZED

Men's tales are too rich for any single explanation to suffice. To accept only one interpretation would return us to the way of the hero and patriarch, who habitually insist that there is only one truth, namely theirs! I therefore encourage individuals to make their own interpretations and include the stories themselves for readers to reflect on, with comments to facilitate the process. I retell the tales because the original versions often used old-fashioned, flowery language that does not speak to men today. Moreover, fairy tales are meant to be told and retold, and only after I recounted the stories many times to myself and to friends did the tales make sense.

I chose the stories for this book based on how typical they are of men's tales. Where several versions were available, I chose the one that seemed the most complete and gripping. Each story addresses only a few aspects of mature masculine psychology. However, when assembled together the tales portray a larger picture, like the piece of a mosaic. I have arranged the book so that each tale builds on previous ones, adding new themes and insights. The stories can be read and enjoyed individually, but when placed in sequence, they reveal men's journey beyond the hero.

The first tale, "The Wizard King," hails from France and features a powerful patriarch battling his son, a heroic Prince. The story dramatizes how the hero and patriarch are really two aspects of one masculine archetype. The hero is the patriarch-to-be, the patriarch, an aging hero, and the two fight for dominance. Their ancient struggle will be familiar to many fathers and sons and to their wives and mothers. As the story makes clear, tragedy results if the father cannot give up his patriarchal power.

Chapter 2 presents a Moroccan tale, "The Sultan's Handkerchief," in which a monarch *does* break free from heroic and patriarchal traditions. He succeeds by listening to his wife and learning feminine skills from her, such as acting on intuition, understanding emotions, and valuing relationships. The Sultan's drama highlights two major tasks for men venturing beyond the hero: reclaiming their own feminine side and respecting the women in their lives. Several aboriginal cultures in Africa and

New Guinea formalize the two tasks with a unique rite of passage in which mature men are initiated into the service of a goddess.

In "The King's Ears," the third chapter, a mighty monarch hides a shameful secret: he has goat's ears instead of human ones. In trying to accept his deformity, the King dramatizes an essential task for maturity. This is confronting "the shadow," Carl Jung's term for the faults and failings in ourselves that we normally hide, deny, or avoid. For men, these hidden elements include wild, animal instincts that they inhibit as they grow up. After years of repression, the primal energies leap out. The process is often frightening, but "The King's Ears" offers practical advice on how men and women can survive this tempestuous phase in men's lives.

"The North Wind's Gift," an Italian tale, expands on the hidden wildness in men's souls. The story focuses on what Robert Bly, poet laureate of the men's movement, calls "the wild man." Normally repressed by social etiquette, when the wild man emerges he often seems savage, so men and women fear him. Yet the tale emphasizes that the wild man is not a barbarian or a primitive backlash against feminism. He is ultimately nurturing and healing.

The fifth story, "The Little Peasant," exposes a scandalous secret about the male psyche: the deep masculine is personified by the Trickster. Found in mythologies around the world, the Trickster is an archetypal male figure who plays pranks, lies, and steals. He is commonly thought to be a criminal, sociopath, or barbarian, but new findings in folklore and anthropology show that this negative image is mistaken. The Trickster actually is a creative, positive, life-giving, and uniquely masculine figure who reveals the deeper meanings of manhood.

In Chapter 6, the Hindu story "The King and the Ghoul" introduces a new aspect of the deep masculine. This is the Spirit Brother who appears in dreams and fantasies to aid and advise men in the midst of a midlife crisis. He is a Trickster and uses riddles and paradoxes to pry men away from conventional thinking and masculine logos. The Spirit Brother also frees women from men's unhealthy dependence on them: where young men habitually seek comfort from women in times of trouble, the

Trickster Brother offers mature men an alternative—a masculine source of camaraderie and wisdom. Ultimately, the Spirit Brother leads men to a divine male power and uncovers the sacred face of the deep masculine.

The hilarious story "Brother Lustig," in Chapters 7 and 8, demonstrates that men's midlife encounter with the Trickster is really an initiation. Just as puberty rites move young men from the world of their mothers and families into the realm of heroes and patriarchs, men's midlife experience takes them beyond the hero into the deep masculine. Many secret fraternities around the world still celebrate these mature male initiations. Men's tales preserve the tradition, and the stories were probably told long ago in male rites of passage. "Brother Lustig" reveals that the initiations are ultimately shamanic and that the Trickster is close kin to the shaman. Trickster and shaman, in fact, are really two aspects of one masculine archetype, just as the hero and patriarch are part of one masculine ideal.

The final story, in Chapters 9 and 10, "Go I Know Not Whither," explores the divine face of the deep masculine. Although Russian, the tale has striking parallels to the Celtic legend of Parsifal and the Holy Grail, emphasizing the cross-cultural depth of men's tales. The Russian story also links the deep masculine to hunters.

Anthropology confirms that the archetype of the shaman-Trickster animates hunting cultures, the way the warrior-king dominates patriarchal societies. Significantly, hunting cultures precede both goddess societies and patriarchal civilizations. Images of the shaman-Trickster appear in Stone Age art from the dawn of the human race. This means that before men were warriors or kings, they were hunters, shamans, and Tricksters. The shaman-Trickster is the original archetype of the masculine, antedating the hero, the patriarch, and the great goddess. He is literally the deep masculine—hidden in the depths of time. Chapters 11 and 12 explore these themes and their practical implications for individuals and society today.

THE CENTER OF MEN'S SOULS

Men's tales have a startling message. Beyond the hero and the patriarch lies the deep masculine, personified by the hunter, the shaman, and the Trickster. This threefold archetype of manhood is the core of the male soul. It is "deeper" or "beyond" the hero in several ways. First, the archetype of the Trickster normally appears after the hero in men's lives. Only men who have mastered the hero's way can deal with the primordial energies of the unconscious and the deep masculine. The Trickster is post-heroic. The deep masculine also comes before the hero in a historical sense, because the hunter-Trickster arises at the dawn of human civilization, many millennia before the warrior-king. Patriarchal society covered up and repressed the hunter-Trickster, keeping him hidden in the unconscious. The Trickster is therefore beyond the hero in a third sense: he is "behind" or "beneath" the hero. Finally, the hunter-Trickster offers a vision of manhood for the future, beyond today.

The hunter, the shaman, and the Trickster personify a masculine fierceness that avoids warfare, honors the feminine, and recognizes the balance of nature. In an egalitarian, post-industrial age in which women insist on their rights, war means nuclear holocaust, and the continuing "conquest" of nature leads to ecological disaster, a return to the original archetype of manhood is deeply healing. Astonishing as it may seem, the Trickster offers a positive new model for men in their roles as husbands, fathers, lovers, laborers, and leaders. And the Trickster emphasizes healing instead of heroism, communication rather than conquest, and exploration over exploitation.

These conclusions surprised me. I knew only a little about the Trickster when I started looking at men's tales, hardly anything about the men's movement, and virtually nothing about hunting or prehistory. So I could not guess where the stories would lead. Yet this is the underlying message in men's tales: they force men to explore the unknown, wandering in a realm beyond the warrior and the king. Through sorrow and laughter, ashes and ambrosia, insight and instinct, the stories lead to a richer, more sacred manhood and ultimately to a fuller, more authentic humanity.

CHAPTER ONE

The Wizard King:
Father/Son, Hero/Patriarch

---

the WIZARD KING

(FROM FRANCE)

Long ago, there lived a mighty King, who ruled a great and prosperous land. The King was a wizard, and his knowledge of magic was vast. In his youth, the monarch married a beautiful Queen, and he counted himself the happiest man in the world. His wife soon bore him a son, and the Queen took the newborn Prince to her fairy godmother. The fairy bestowed on the baby Prince both charm and wit, the ability to delight everyone and to learn anything with ease.

Tragedy struck a few years later. The Queen took ill and died. With her last breath, she advised her son to consult his fairy godmother on any weighty matter. The Prince promised, and the Queen died in peace. The Prince was heartbroken, but he was young and resilient, and time healed his grief. Not so with his father. The Queen's death threw the King into despair, and nothing could draw him from his wild sorrow.

Finally, the King decided to travel the world, hoping the distraction would relieve his anguish. He used his magic to visit fabulous realms, and one day he took the form of an eagle and flew to a palace by a beautiful lake. The King saw a Queen and her grown daughter sitting together, and the Princess was more beautiful than the moon and stars together. The King fell in love with her, and his grief vanished for the first time. Moved by his passion, the King swooped down on eagle wings, snatched the Princess in his talons, and flew off.

The Princess screamed with terror and struggled mightily, so the King landed in a beautiful meadow and resumed his human shape. "Do not fear me," he told the Princess. "I am a King and have fallen in love with you. I want to marry you and give you all the happiness in the world."

"If you love me," the Princess exclaimed, "return me to my home!"

The King could not bear to give up the Princess, so he created a magnificent palace for her, filled with gold, flowers, and countless servants. "All this, and anything else you desire, is yours," the King promised, gesturing to the palace, "if you marry me."

"All I desire," the Princess replied, "is to return to my home."

"That I cannot allow," the King exclaimed. With more magic, he created wondrous gifts and diversions for the Princess, including a parrot that spoke and recited poetry. Still the Princess insisted on returning home. So the King surrounded the palace with a magic cloud to prevent anyone from entering or leaving, and he returned to his own castle.

The King told no one of the Princess, but he visited her every day. He gave her gifts, each more costly than the other, yet the Princess still repudiated him. At last a terrible thought struck the King. "Perhaps," he thought, "the Princess refuses me because she has heard about my son!" From that day on, the King became jealous of the young man, and to make sure the two would never meet, the King sent his son on a long voyage.

The Prince journeyed in distant lands, until he came to a realm where everyone grieved. The Prince asked the reason, and the King and Queen explained that their daughter had been carried off by a monstrous eagle. The Queen showed a portrait of the Princess to the young man. The Prince fell in love with the maiden at once, and vowed to search for her. So the Queen gave him a locket with the Princess's picture, and the gallant young man set off on his quest. But the first thing he did was visit his fairy godmother and ask her advice. She consulted her magic books.

"Ah," the fairy godmother exclaimed, "I see where the Princess is. But your own father is the one who has kidnapped her!"

"My father!" the Prince exclaimed. Then he paused and asked pensively, "Does the Princess stay willingly with him?"

"No," the fairy godmother said. "She is imprisoned by his magic, and yearns to return home."

"Well, then," the Prince said, "father or not, I will rescue her!"

"That is easier said than done," the fairy godmother said. "Your father is a powerful wizard, and surrounds the palace of the Princess with a magic cloud." The fairy godmother looked through more books. "I have an idea," she said finally. "The Princess has a parrot which talks to her, and the bird often flies over the magic cloud into the countryside. If we can capture the parrot, I can turn you into one just like it, so you can fly back and speak to the Princess. Then I can help both of you escape."

The Prince soon caught the parrot, and the fairy godmother changed the young man into an exact twin of the bird. The Prince flew over the magic cloud into the enchanted palace, and when he found the Princess, he was struck dumb by her beauty.

"Why are you silent?" the Princess asked the parrot in alarm. "Are you ill? You always talk and recite poetry so well!" She took the bird, and stroked its feathers gently. The Prince recovered his speech, and began praising the beauty and kindness of the Princess. She laughed, reassured the parrot was well. At that moment, the King entered, and the Princess scowled. She refused to speak to the wizard, despite the gifts he brought. The Prince was relieved to see that she despised the King, and when the wizard departed, the Prince spoke to the Princess.

"Do not be alarmed," the parrot said, "I am really a Prince, sent here by your mother, the Queen. I have come to rescue you." The Prince took his normal form, and showed the Princess the locket the Queen had given to him.

The Princess recognized the jewelry and rejoiced. "You speak the truth! I am saved!" A commotion outside the window interrupted the young couple, and the fairy godmother arrived with a chariot drawn by two eagles.

"Quickly," she said, "climb into the chariot. We must escape before the King finds out." They flew off, heading straight for the home of the Princess.

Back in his palace, the King suspected something was wrong. He changed himself into an eagle, and hurried to his enchanted palace. He found the place empty and the Princess missing, so he mustered all his magic, and discovered that his son had stolen the Princess from him! "I will kill my son!" the King vowed, "along with the Princess, and the meddling fairy!" With that, the King changed into a harpy, with a ferocious beak and bloody talons, and he pursued the fairy godmother.

The fairy knew the King was after them, so she raised a storm to delay the wizard, and they reached the land of the Princess safely. Her mother and father rejoiced to see their daughter again.

"We have no time to lose!" the fairy godmother warned. "The wizard king still pursues us and will soon be here. The only way to save the Princess and Prince is to have the two marry at once."

The King and Queen agreed, and the wedding was celebrated on the spot. Just as the young couple exchanged vows, the wizard King appeared. In his rage and despair, the King threw poison at the Prince and Princess to kill them, but the fairy godmother used her magic to fling it back at him, and the deadly potion struck the wizard. He fell into a deep sleep, and the King and Queen ordered the sorcerer thrown into prison.

The Prince pleaded for his father's release. "He cannot harm us now that we are married," the Prince said. "And he is my father, after all."

The King and Queen relented, and released the wizard King.

But he changed himself into a bird and flew off. "I'll never forget this!" the wizard King shrieked at his son and the fairy godmother. "I'll never forgive you!" Then he vanished in the distance and was never seen again.

As for the Prince and Princess, they settled down to a new life together, and lived happily for the rest of their days.

Father/Son, Hero/Patriarch

FATHER AND SON

The story starts with a King who has married and is somewhere in the middle third of life. But the tale is not just about the King, because the drama also stars his son, the Prince. The tale has two leading men, father and son, and the story is deeply insightful. By the middle years, many men have married and become fathers. Or they have taken positions of fatherly responsibility, supervising younger men. Yet men remain sons to their own fathers and obedient to higher bosses. So men move back and forth between seeing themselves as powerful father-figures and subordinate son-figures. The story captures men's dual roles by using two protagonists.

The tale focuses on the battle between the wizard King and his son, each vying for the beautiful Princess. This is the Oedipal drama, made famous by Freud, who thought that the competition between father and son was the core of masculine psychology. Freud's original notion can be broadened, because male mentors often compete with apprentices, men teachers with students, and bosses with employees, each man trying to best the other. Father-figures fight with son-figures, and fairy tales around the world reflect the battle, like the Grimms' story "The Devil with Three Golden Hairs," the Serbian drama "Three Wonderful Beggars," or the Arabian tale "The Man Who Would Be Stronger Than Fate."

The present story does not stop with the Oedipal contest, but introduces other elements in the psychology of fathers and sons.

After the Queen dies, the King cannot recover from his grief, and he seeks solace in long journeys. In the process, the King neglects his son. The situation will be painfully familiar to most men. In today's society, the usual relationship between father and son is distance or absence. Preoccupied with work, fathers spend little time with their sons and offer less emotionally. Sons hunger for their fathers and often recognize the depth of their yearning only in midlife. Until then, young men are usually too busy rejecting their fathers to notice their "father hunger." (Something similar applies to fathers and daughters, but I focus on men in this book.)

In neglecting his son, the King acts out of grief, not malice or indifference. When the Queen dies, the King suffers a catastrophic midlife crisis. He is deeply wounded and has little to offer his son psychologically. The same happens in real life, because the painful distance between fathers and sons is usually the result of a wound in the father's soul. Some fathers are alcoholics, some workaholics, others are tyrants, or overly timid. Whatever the overt failing, an inner injury prevents the father from nurturing his sons. The father *cannot* give more to his sons, rather than *will* not.

The King's wound helps explain his excesses in the story. When he sees the beautiful young Princess and falls madly in love with her, his misery vanishes for the first time, and he imagines he will be happy again if the Princess will marry him. This is a common drama for men at midlife. Troubled by the crises of the middle years, many men seek solace in the arms of younger women. Sometimes this works, but more often it fails, as "The Wizard King" illustrates.

The story also shows how the King's suffering fuels the Oedipal conflict between father and son. The King kidnaps the Princess and then fights his son for her, because he is desperate and needy. Like an injured lion, the King seizes whatever promises relief and lashes out at anyone who opposes him, even his own son. This image of the wounded father haunts many men's tales. The medieval story of Parsifal is dramatic and portrays the Fisher King, the guardian of the Holy Grail, suffering from an injury that never heals. (I discuss Parsifal's drama more fully in Chapters 3 and 10.) The ailing father symbolizes a double task for men at midlife—coming to terms with the wounds of their fathers and with their own injuries. These are the underlying problems for many men who seek therapy, and the story offers healing insights about both issues.

When the Prince goes on his quest to save the Princess, he consults the fairy godmother and learns that it is his father who kidnapped the beautiful maiden. The Prince's reaction is typical of young men. He considers his father a villain, condemns the older man, and battles his father for the Princess in a classic Oedipal rebellion. By doing so, the Prince avoids facing his father's pain and grief. He sees his father as evil and powerful, rather than as wounded and tormented. Like other young men, the Prince also denies his own suffering and his yearning for a good father.

By the end of the story, the Prince marries and symbolically moves from youth to maturity. He also shifts in his attitude toward his father. When the wizard King is captured and imprisoned, the Prince forgives his father and asks for his release. Many men will identify with the Prince here, because by midlife, most sons outgrow their adolescent rejection of fathers. Many sons have become fathers themselves and recognize the difficulty of the job. Accepting their father's shortcomings, grown sons long for reconciliation. Not all fathers are ready for this, as the wizard King illustrates: the monarch rejects his son's expression of love and flies off in anger. In real life, fathers often die without resolving differences with their sons, leaving the younger man with a festering wound.

HERO AND PATRIARCH

Many writers, such as Sam Osherman in *Finding Our Fathers,* and Michael Gurian in *The Prince and the King,* offer eloquent reflections on fathers and sons. Certainly the issue is prominent for most men in therapy. But coming to terms with father-son problems is only the first step on a much longer journey. Manhood involves more than being a father or a son and "The Wizard King" quickly introduces other facets of masculinity. The story is not simply about a father and a son, but a King and a Prince. The King acts the part of a patriarch, while his son plays the role of the hero. They are an archetypal pair in myths around the world, the patriarch and the hero. Between the two, a consistent drama takes place, where the young man succeeds the older patriarch, either by peaceful means or violent overthrow. Hero and patriarch are really two phases in one life cycle, different aspects of a single, underlying masculine archetype. The hero is the patriarch-to-be, and the patriarch, a former hero. "The Wizard King" illuminates the typical relationship between the two.

When the wizard King kidnaps the Princess, he personifies the patriarchal principle taken to an extreme. He becomes a ruthless tyrant abusing his power, ignoring the rights and wishes of the Princess. The story reinforces the point by saying that the King took the form of an eagle when he seized the Princess. The eagle is a bird of prey, killing and devouring what it wishes, and a traditional symbol of patriarchal authority, handed down from Imperial Rome to the American republic.

The King's patriarchal excess is a major reason why his part of the story is tragic. As Joseph Campbell noted in *The Hero with a Thousand Faces,* aging patriarchs typically become tyrants, enslaving everyone around them. Greek myths are graphic about this pattern, starting with one of the first patriarchal gods, Ouranos. According to the myth, Ouranos feared that one of his sons would overthrow him, so he buried every child that his wife Gaia bore, pushing the children back into the earth, Gaia's body. But one son, Chronos, escaped the oppression. When he grew up, Chronos overthrew his father, only to hear a prophecy that one of his sons would dethrone him. So Chronos started devouring his children as soon as they were born. Zeus escaped his father, Chronos, and later deposed the older god. After Zeus became the new patriarch, he heard yet another prophecy saying that a son of his would eventually overthrow him!

The ancient battle between patriarch and hero will be familiar to men of the Baby Boom generation who played out the drama in the 1960s. Protesting the Vietnam war and mistrusting anyone over thirty, the young men of the Baby Boom battled patriarchal figures, only to become, thirty years later, patriarchal authorities themselves. Women will also recognize the battle. As mothers and wives, many struggle to settle fights between fathers and sons without lasting success. This is because the conflict is a normal phase in masculine development. It helps the son develop strength of character, and the father, wisdom. Problems arise only when the father clings to the patriarch's role and refuses to move on. By definition, within a patriarchy, only one man can be patriarch. All others, including his sons, must be subservient. So the hero-son must wait until his patriarch-father vacates the throne or dies. If the senior man refuses to give up his position, the son must overthrow the father.

Anthropology confirms that the more patriarchal and heroic a culture is, the greater the hostility between fathers and sons. The more a society emphasizes male dominance, the more intense the Oedipal conflict.[1] Much of the pain and competition that divides fathers from sons springs from the patriarchal paradigm of manhood. Here we arrive at a deeper meaning of the wounded father in "The Wizard King." The father's injury symbolizes a basic fault within patriarchal tradition. The patriarchy wounds men by forcing them to bow to male authorities, to compete with peers, and to be wary of their sons. Wounded men then become wounding fathers, who rear another generation of wounded men.

The conflict between patriarch and hero also occurs *within* each man and not just between men. In psychological terms, the patriarch can be interpreted as the ego, the center of conscious will, planning, and action. In youth, most men learn to control their impulses so that by midlife the ego dominates a man's conscious life, like a king ruling over his realm. At this time, new elements arise in men's lives, such as unfamiliar feelings, baffling dreams, and vague yearnings. The fresh young hero personifies these emerging aspects of a man's personality, but the temptation for mature men is to suppress them, and to have the inner patriarch destroy the inner hero.

BEYOND THE HERO/PATRIARCH

If the wizard King fails to move beyond the patriarchal paradigm, his son is more successful and the story explains why. Notice first that the younger man is helped by a fairy godmother, to whom he was introduced by his mother. The fairy represents a maternal figure, contrasting with the King's patriarchal power. The story thus suggests that a feminine influence is needed for men to move beyond the hero. The Prince also contacts the Princess by disguising himself as a parrot. Parrots are highly intelligent and can mimic speech. They often appear in fairy tales as messengers and go-betweens and make a good symbol for communication. So the parrot contrasts with the eagle, who symbolizes power. In this detail, the story hints that men must exchange the eagle's domination for the parrot's communication. Other men's tales develop the metaphor in greater depth, like ''The Child and the Eagle'' from Africa. Moving from eagle to parrot, from conquest to communion, is not easy for men raised in the heroic tradition. The transition is usually frightening or confusing, and men often turn to therapy for assistance. Men also find help from women, but not in the traditional way, where women do all the communicating for men. The task for men here is to learn vital skills, like expressing emotion, from women.

''The Wizard King'' sums up two traditional images of manhood: father-son and hero-patriarch. The two paradigms constitute the opening scene, the starting point, in any man's search for the meaning of manhood. Yet the story also separates the two models of masculinity. All men have fathers and begin as sons. But not all men need to be heroes or patriarchs. In fact, the tale warns that tragedy results if men do not outgrow their heroic and patriarchal ideals. The remaining tales in this book describe the long, arduous, frequently hilarious, always surprising journey beyond the hero and the patriarch.

CHAPTER TWO

The Sultan's Handkerchief: Men's Initiation into the Feminine

---

the sultan's handkerchief

(FROM MOROCCO)

Long ago and far away, there lived a great Sultan in a palace of gold. His Grand Vizier had a daughter named Zakia, and one day, the Sultan met her for the first time. Zakia was so beautiful that the Sultan fell in love with her instantly. The next day, the monarch summoned his Grand Vizier and offered to marry Zakia. The minister was pleased with the proposal and agreed. But when he told his daughter about the marriage, she refused.

"I do not even know the man," Zakia insisted. "How can I marry him?"

The Grand Vizier turned white. "If you refuse, the Sultan can have my head cut off! You cannot reject a royal request!" He pleaded with Zakia and the two argued all day. Finally Zakia consented, but she insisted on one condition for the marriage.

"The Sultan must learn a trade," she said. "If he lost his throne, how would he earn a living!"

The Grand Vizier exclaimed with horror, "How can I tell the Sultan to learn a trade? He will throw me into the dungeon!" But Zakia would not change her mind. So the next day, with trembling knees, the Grand Vizier told the Sultan about Zakia's demand.

The monarch thought a moment and smiled. "I accept," the Sultan declared, "and now I know your daughter is as wise as she is beautiful!"

The Sultan called all the tradespeople in his land and asked them to show him their crafts. He watched their demonstrations, and then decided to learn the art of weaving. From that day, the Sultan arose earlier than usual each morning and sat alone weaving. Then he attended to his royal duties, and returned later in the evening to his loom.

The Sultan was surprised to find that he had a talent for weaving. After some time, he decided to weave a handkerchief for Zakia as a token of his love, and to show her that he had mastered a craft. So he wove a beautiful cloth, with a red rose in the center and a dark forest in the background.

When Zakia received the gift, she realized that the Sultan truly loved her, so she kept her agreement, and their wedding was celebrated with great fanfare. After they married, the Sultan found Zakia's advice to be wise and practical, so he consulted her on many matters of state. One day, he turned to Zakia and mused, "I wonder what my people really think and feel? I cannot tell from my officials, because they agree with everything I say."

Zakia reflected a bit and replied, "It is said that to understand someone, you must walk in his shoes and eat at his table. Perhaps you should go in disguise and mingle with our people."

The Sultan liked the idea, and so the next day, he took his chamberlain and another minister, and they ventured into the city, dressed like ordinary citizens. The Sultan marveled at the bustling bazaar and the crowded alleys, fascinated by all the bargaining and arguing. But the chamberlain and minister soon tired of the adventure, not used to plain clothes or walking in the streets.

"It's time for lunch," the chamberlain said.

"Yes," the minister chimed in, "let's return to the palace."

"Why don't we eat like ordinary people?" the Sultan asked. "There's a cafe I'd like to try. People at the market talked about how good the food is." The Sultan pointed to the restaurant, and the two officials reluctantly agreed to go. They went up to the cafe, and paused to open the door. Just then, the threshold gave way beneath them, and they fell into a deep pit.

"What happened?" the three men exclaimed in shock, groping in the dark. A few minutes later, a trapdoor opened high above them, and an evil-looking man poked his head in.

"Look who fell into my trap today!" the man exclaimed. "You probably came to my cafe because we are famous for our food. Well, you will soon learn the secret of my recipe, because my butcher will slaughter you and serve you up to my customers!"

The Sultan and his officials were horrified. The chamberlain and minister cried out indignantly. "Release us at once! Do you know who we are?"

The Sultan immediately clapped his hands over the two men's mouths.

The evil man laughed hideously. "It does not matter who you are, you'll still end up in a pot!" The man cackled and closed the trapdoor.

"What a monster!" the chamberlain exclaimed. "We must tell him the Sultan is here! He will free us instantly."

"No," the Sultan replied, "if he knew who we are, he would have to kill us for sure! What are we to do?"

The chamberlain and minister realized the wisdom of the Sultan's words. The two men sat miserably on the ground, while the monarch paced back and forth. Then the Sultan had an idea.

Some time later, the evil man opened the trapdoor and lowered some food and water. "I want you nice and plump when I slaughter you," he declared.

"My good man," the Sultan pleaded, "I realize you cannot let us go now that we know your secret, but I have a proposal for you. If you spare our lives, we can earn you a good sum of money. You see, I am a weaver, and my work is valued at the Sultan's court. I can weave for you, and you can sell my cloth to the palace. We would rather labor for you in this cellar the rest of our lives than be butchered like cattle."

The evil man paused a second. "I'll think about it," he said and closed the trapdoor.

A little later, the villain opened the hatch, and lowered a loom and some thread down to the Sultan. "Let me see what you can weave," the evil man demanded, with a greedy glint in his eye.

The Sultan sat down and began weaving. He worked all that night, and by the next morning he finished a handkerchief, just like the one he had given Zakia, with a red rose in the center and a dark forest in the background. When the evil man saw the handkerchief, he gasped, never having seen anything so beautiful.

"Go to the palace," the Sultan suggested, "and give this handkerchief to Zakia, the Queen. She will pay you handsomely for it!"

The evil man lost no time and rushed off. The palace was in turmoil when he arrived, since the Sultan had been missing for a day. Guards and ministers hurried hither and thither. In all the commotion, the evil man went up to Zakia, and presented her with the handkerchief.

"I am a merchant," the evil man explained, "and I have for sale the work of the best weaver in the land." He showed Zakia the Sultan's handkerchief, and she recognized her husband's handiwork immediately. Zakia quickly deduced the evil-looking man had something to do with the Sultan's disappearance.

"How beautiful this handkerchief is!" Zakia exclaimed, concealing her suspicions. "I will buy it." Then she gave the evil man a bag of gold, more than he had ever dreamed. The villain ran off, delirious with his wealth. Zakia ordered soldiers to follow him, and when the villain arrived at the cafe, the soldiers overheard him talking to the Sultan.

The soldiers returned to Zakia, told her the news, and she ordered the cafe surrounded by troops. She oversaw the operation herself, mounted on her dark stallion. The soldiers rushed into the cafe, captured the villain and his henchmen, and freed the Sultan. When the monarch emerged from his prison, he ran to Zakia and they embraced. He was overjoyed at his rescue, and moved by his wife's great wisdom in locating him. And Zakia, who had worried over her husband, realized how much she loved him. So the two returned to the palace, arm in arm, and spent the rest of their days together, in wisdom and joy.

Men's Initiation into the Feminine

THE ENCOUNTER WITH THE FEMININE

This charming story has a monarch as the main character, like ''The Wizard King'' in the last chapter. Men's tales frequently feature Kings, and the monarchs symbolize the honor and success most men seek in youth. The tale begins when the Sultan falls in love with Zakia and proposes marriage. When Zakia insists that the Sultan first learn a trade, he agrees, and his consent is extraordinary. As a monarch, learning a menial craft would be demeaning to the Sultan, and as an absolute ruler, he could probably force Zakia to marry him. (Although not mentioned, the Sultan may have a harem of wives.) In obeying Zakia, the Sultan puts aside his royal pride and prerogative, and voluntarily gives up his patriarchal role. The Sultan differs dramatically from the wizard king in the last chapter, who kidnapped the princess and tried to force her to marry him. The wizard insisted upon his patriarchal authority, and tragedy resulted.

The Sultan specifically chooses to learn weaving, a craft usually associated with women. This is again surprising, since the story comes from a strongly patriarchal culture, in which men disdain ''women's work.'' However, the same event surfaces in other tales, like ''Stubborn Husband, Stubborn Wife'' from Persia, ''The Wife Who Became King'' from China, and ''The Lute Player'' from Russia, as I discuss in *Once Upon a Midlife*. These stories consistently show men embracing feminine roles and values at midlife. What is the meaning of this amazing motif?

Carl Jung offers an interpretation. Based on his own life and his clinical work as a psychiatrist, Jung observed that young men normally suppress their fear, pain, and neediness, dismissing these emotions as "feminine." Cast out of conscious awareness, the feelings go underground. But they are too powerful to be eliminated, so they surface at midlife, demanding their due. Research from around the world confirms Jung's insights.[1] As men age, they become more emotionally expressive, sensitive to relationships, and open about their fears and needs. Men move away from heroic stoicism and learn to honor the feminine. This is exactly what the Sultan does in agreeing to Zakia's request. In real life, giving up heroic habits is rarely so easy. Expressing emotions is difficult for men, admitting fears and doubts even more painful, and acknowledging feelings of dependence and the need for nurturing, downright shameful. Not suprisingly, many men seek therapy to sort out the confusing issues that arise when they grapple with their feminine side.

In the story, Zakia is remarkably strong-willed in insisting that the Sultan learn a trade. Like the monarch, she breaks with patriarchal tradition. Furthermore, she illustrates how mature women develop: women typically suppress their assertiveness and autonomy in youth to fit traditional feminine stereotypes, but after midlife, they reclaim their long-neglected "masculine" traits. In the process, they often force their husbands to grow. Many men today begin their journey beyond the hero when their wives discover feminism!

THE INNER WOMEN: THE ANIMA

Zakia is so wise and strong that she is really larger than life, and this brings up a second point about her. She symbolizes feminine mystery and power. Her name, "Zakia," for instance, resembles the Arabic word for "sweet," reflecting the tender, nurturing aspect of the feminine. Yet Zakia is also fierce and leads the soldiers to the Sultan's rescue at the end of the story. Zakia thus resembles Athena, the Greek goddess of war and wisdom, and the story reinforces Zakia's divine nature in her name: "Zakia" is similar to a traditional Islamic term for God. Zakia is thus like Sophia, the Judeo-Christian symbol of God's sublime wisdom.

As a fascinating, powerful, divine woman, Zakia is typical of the female figures that appear in men's dreams at midlife. Jung was one of the first to notice this phenomenon, and called the mysterious women "anima" figures. ("Anima" is the feminine form of the Latin word for "soul.") Jung suggested that anima figures symbolize a man's emerging feminine side, and Zakia provides an excellent example. She does not just represent a strong woman in real life, she also personifies a man's feminine side in his inner life.

Psychotherapists like Murray Stein in his book *In Midlife,* Daryl Sharp in *The Survival Papers,* or John Sanford and George Lough in *What Men Are Like* have confirmed the importance of the anima in men's midlife experiences. Since Jung introduced the notion of the anima and first described men's midlife struggle with the feminine, his personal experience is of interest. He provides an eloquent account in his autobiography, *Memories, Dreams and Reflections.* In his late thirties Jung broke painfully with his mentor, Sigmund Freud, and in the schism, Jung lost all the prestige and authority he had gained from his youthful work. Jung understandably suffered a midlife crisis. During this painful period, Jung noticed a whole series of mysterious women in his dreams and fantasies. In one episode, Jung encountered Elijah and a beautiful blind woman named Salome. Jung readily recognized Elijah as the archetypal wise old man, prominent in myths and fairy tales, but Salome baffled him. Only later did Jung realize that she symbolized his feminine side, his emotional, erotic, and aesthetic impulses. These were still very much undeveloped and unconscious for him, so Salome appeared to him as a *blind* woman.

Significantly, Jung's anima figures appeared after he abandoned the heroic ideals of his youth. A "big" dream early in his midlife crisis symbolized Jung's break with heroism. A "big" dream is a pivotal, deeply moving, and profoundly meaningful dream. Jung adopted the term from his study of dreams among African and Native American tribes. In his big dream, Jung ambushed and murdered Siegfried, the archetypical hero of Germanic tradition. The dream was deeply disturbing to Jung, but he soon realized that assassinating Siegfried symbolized killing the hero within himself and abandoning his heroic ambitions. Only after taking this step did anima figures spring up freely from Jung's unconscious. The anima reflects a post-heroic period in men's lives. "The Sultan's Handkerchief" repeats the pattern: the monarch learns a menial trade, voluntarily setting aside his heroic and patriarchal prerogatives, and only then does Zakia, the anima, marry him and enrich his life.

THE PRACTICAL WISDOM OF THE FEMININE

After their marriage, the Sultan consults Zakia about running his government. On a literal level, he respects his wife's wisdom and takes her opinions seriously. Again, this reverses patriarchal tradition, which imagines women incapable of public affairs. On a symbolic level, in consulting Zakia the Sultan turns to his feminine side for help in solving problems. In psychological terms this involves men paying attention to their emotions, sometimes for the first time in their lives. For many men today, this occurs when they take an active role in raising their children. Men also may reclaim feeling through psychotherapy. Peter provides an example. A minister in his early forties, he came to me for therapy, troubled by depression and doubts about his religious vocation. During the course of therapy Peter had a series of vivid, healing dreams. In these nocturnal adventures, Peter returned to his all-boys boarding school and wandered through hallways and playing fields he had not remembered in many years, talking with classmates and teachers he had not seen for even longer. But unlike what happened in real life, Peter felt intense fear, longing, loneliness, anger, and uncertainty in his dreams, all the emotions he had suppressed in adolescence, in order "to be a man." Through therapy, he relived his past and regained his emotional life. As he did so, his depression lifted, and Peter discovered a long-lost sense of joy and playfulness in his work.

As part of consulting the anima, men also reclaim their intuitions. Because "gut feelings" are traditionally considered feminine, most young men avoid hunches in favor of facts and logic.[2] Yet at midlife, men return to their intuitions. Jacques Monod and Jonas Salk, for instance, each won Nobel Prizes in Medicine for rigorous, scientific work early in their careers. Later in life, they turned to intuitive, philosophical reflections.

When the Sultan asks Zakia for advice about what his people really think, she suggests he walk among them. She tells him to relate to them on a practical, human level. This is a traditionally feminine perspective, which contrasts with the more abstract approaches men prefer, like fact-finding commissions, opinion polls, and official hearings. Zakia's advice highlights a vital task for men at midlife, embracing mundane forms of the feminine and especially practical feminine skills like empathy. This affirmation of the feminine contrasts with the melodramatic attitude of young men who unconsciously treat women as divinely beautiful or horribly ugly. Fairy tales capture the youthful male spirit by having the young hero rescue the loveliest princess in the world from the clutches of the most hideous witch. This youthful spirit often takes a new form at midlife in therapy: men hope that the anima will offer a bit of numinous wisdom, and that a few dramatic insights will resolve their problems. But understanding rarely resolves the issues—what is required is living through and grappling with the thousand small emotions of everyday life.

A detail emphasizes the practical nature of the anima. When the Sultan weaves a handkerchief for Zakia, he portrays a red rose, superimposed on a forest. The rose is an archetypal symbol, usually associated with the feminine and true love. Roses also symbolize divine wholeness and integration, for example, in the rose windows of Gothic cathedrals. If the rose is a mystical symbol, though, it appears on something used to wipe one's nose! The handkerchief is feminine and magical, but also highly practical.

ENCOUNTER WITH THE SHADOW

Following Zakia's advice, the Sultan walks incognito among his people. Then he and his companions fall into the trap of an evil man, who plans to butcher them and serve them as meat in his café. The Sultan's misfortune is surprising, since he is kind, open-minded, and genuinely concerned for his people. He does not deserve such a calamity, so why would it happen to him?

Jung offers an interpretation. At midlife, men (and women, too) grapple with "the shadow." This is Jung's poetic term for the dark side of life, for everything that we would rather not see in ourselves, and especially our vices and failings. The cannibal cook personifies the shadow and represents the opposite of what the Sultan consciously strives to be. The villain embodies the greedy, murderous, sneaky impulses in every human heart, which adults normally repress. These dark instincts cannot be ignored forever, and surface in maturity, as Connie Zweig and Jeremiah Abrams vividly explain in the anthology *Meeting the Shadow*. Figures like the cannibal chef appear frequently in men's dreams at midlife, demanding that men face their faults and failures. Disaster happens if they fail the task, as the wizard king demonstrated in the last chapter: the sorcerer refused to confront his rage, envy, and hatred, and tragedy resulted. The Sultan, fortunately, succeeds in facing the shadow.

Notice that the Sultan falls into the pit while following Zakia's advice. This suggests that heeding the feminine is often painful and arduous for men. Other fairy tales confirm the hint, like "Three Strong Women" from Japan. The reason for the difficulty lies in men's early training. In heroic and patriarchal cultures, boys are taught to reject the feminine: "Don't be a sissy!" boys are warned. Later, young men are told, "Real men don't cry—only women and wimps do!" So when a man's feminine side emerges at midlife, it threatens his masculine identity, and many men dream about falling into pits, or floundering in water as they struggle with their feminine traits.[3]

Two types of anima figures become prominent here. The first is the wounded anima. She symbolizes a man's incomplete, injured connection to his feminine side. Jung's dream of the blind Salome is one example. In his book *Men's Dreams, Men's Healing*, Robert Hopcke offers another illustration with a "big" dream of a man at midlife. In the dream, the man met a deformed woman in an iron lung, undergoing an excruciating operation to help her recover from an illness. Upon awakening, the man realized the woman represented his unhealthy connection to his own feelings. She was a wounded anima and dreaming of her jolted the man into paying attention to his emotions.

The anima also can be wounding. She attacks or otherwise coerces men into giving up their heroic ways and honoring the feminine. The story of Parsifal provides a graphic example. He was one of the foremost knights of King Arthur's Round Table, but at the peak of his heroic glory, a dreadful woman denounced Parsifal before all of Camelot. She listed his shortcomings and faults, berated him for wronging many women in his life, and demanded that he seek the Holy Grail as penance. Attacking his pride and prestige, the dreadful damsel epitomizes the wounding anima.

In my own life, the wounding anima appeared in a deeply moving dream. In the drama, I fled from a terrible war in which many people were killed or injured. A woman with a gun pursued me, and I ran away faster. Then she shot me and I fell down in great pain. As she approached, she aimed her gun at me once more. I stood up and turned toward her and the battlefield. At that moment, I was filled with grief and compassion for the people dying in the war, and I knew I had to return to them. I took a step toward the battleground, and a voice declared, ''This is the first stage of enlightenment.'' The woman looked in my eyes, lowered her gun and turned away, a satisfied expression on her face.

In my dream, fleeing the war symbolizes how I, and other men, typically run away from feelings and emotional conflicts. An anima figure pursues me, presumably to make me deal with my feelings. So I naturally run away faster, until she finally shoots me. She literally is the wounding anima. From my pain comes compassion for others, and I return to my fellow people. A voice declares the action to be the first step in enlightenment. Illumination, the dream voice reveals, is not a sublime, abstract, metaphysical insight, as men are inclined to think. It begins with simple empathy. When I realize this, the wounding anima turns away, having accomplished her job for the moment.

MEN'S RESCUE BY THE FEMININE

If the encounter with the anima precipitates a crisis for many men, paradoxically, she also rescues them, the way Zakia frees the Sultan from the cannibal. Yet the feminine also helps men in subtle ways. For instance, the Sultan sends a message to Zakia by using a feminine skill, weaving a handkerchief. Even more important, the Sultan relies on feminine wisdom to outwit the cannibal cook: the monarch realizes that invoking his authority would be futile, but appealing to the villain's greed might work. Learning feminine talents, the story emphasizes, is serious business for men at midlife. Weaving and understanding human psychology may have started out as hobbies for the Sultan, but when he falls into the cannibal's pit, they become lifesaving. Until trapped by the cannibal, in fact, the Sultan relied on Zakia the way many men depend on their wives to handle feelings and manage relationships. In the cannibal's pit, the Sultan cannot ask for his wife's advice, but must think for himself. The task is vital for men in maturity—learning to do their own emotional work. This clears up men's unhealthy psychological dependence on women, while freeing women from a traditionally feminine but onerous chore.

When Zakia rescues the Sultan, the story reverses the usual plot of youth tales, where a hapless princess is saved by a gallant hero. Here a helpless King is rescued by his Queen! Other men's tales repeat the drama, like "The Lute Player," from Russia. The theme is archetypal and emphasizes how men's tales break with patriarchal tradition. The stories also demand that men do the same.

The Sultan's tale specifically says that the cook planned to butcher him and his officials. The image of being dismembered appears in other men's tales, and one of the earliest examples comes from the Egyptian god Osiris. At the height of his power and glory, Osiris was murdered by his evil brother Set, who cut up Osiris' body and strewed the pieces all over the earth. Isis, the wife of Osiris, searched for the body parts, assembled them, and then resurrected Osiris from the dead. Great god though he was, Osiris had to be rescued by the feminine. Similar motifs emerge in men's dreams and therapy at midlife. In fact, the image of dismemberment sums up men's passage through the middle years. Dismantling familiar heroic habits is painful and feels like being butchered. Yet only then can men fully experience and honor the feminine. The process reverses the archetypal drama of young men: in myths around the world, the young hero kills a great goddess, and like Marduk, the Babylonian warrior-god, often dismembers the goddess. In maturity, by contrast, men feel as if they are torn apart by the goddess.

MEN'S INITIATION INTO THE FEMININE

Men's painful encounter with the anima constitutes an initiation into the feminine. A few aboriginal cultures explicitly celebrate such a rite of passage for mature men, although the ceremonies are less common and less familiar than male puberty rites.[4] The Bimin-Kuskusmin people of New Guinea provide a valuable example. In the tribe, induction into manhood occurs in several stages, beginning with adolescence and extending into maturity. The adolescent initiation, like male puberty rites in general, inflicts terrible ordeals on young men, which they endure to prove their manhood. The elders of the tribe also teach the adolescents the basics of men's lore, which centers around distrusting, rejecting, and avoiding anything feminine. The boys are told how Yomnok, the primal god of the tribe, wrested control from Afek, the primal goddess. Ever since then, the boys learn, men must keep control of women. Indoctrinated in this tradition, the boys are welcomed as men in the tribe.

As Bimin-Kuskusmin men move into midlife, they are initiated into a higher level of manhood, and the new rite of passage reverses the lessons of the puberty initiation. Mature men are told that women are good, and that it is important to have cordial relationships with them. The new initiation does not involve heroic ordeals like puberty rites, but rather the consumption of special foods that are considered "female," such as marsupial meat. (The emphasis is on eating and nurturing, rather than passing painful tests.) The older initiates also learn an amazing chapter in the story of Yomnok and Afek, kept secret from young men. The expanded myth describes the period before the male Yomnok dominated Afek. Yomnok was too weak then even to impregnate the goddess, so he put his head temporarily in one of her many vaginas. Nurtured by her, Yomnok gained the strength to impregnate Afek. The goddess then gave birth to the various creatures of the world. Later, separated from Afek, Yomnok grew weak again, so he had to put his head periodically in Afek's vaginas. The new chapter in the myth clearly tells men that strength and energy come from the goddess. After despising and rejecting the feminine in youth, mature Bimin-Kuskusmin men honor the goddess.

From Africa, there are more examples of men's mature initiation into the feminine. Among the Yoruba, successful middle-aged men join the Ogboni cult, which focuses on the worship of Onile, a Great Mother Goddess.[5] Only men who have done well in life and have mastered the way of the hero and patriarch can join the order. (A few select women are also initiated, but the cult is predominantly male.) The initiation ceremony is secret, but involves honoring the earth mother, with such ritual exclamations as "Mother! Powerful! Old!" (Although several Western anthropologists were initiated, they refused to disclose further details.) When initiated men enter the Ogboni house, they kiss the ground three times, and say, "The mother's breasts are sweet," dramatizing their devotion to the goddess.

The Endo tribe of Kenya provides a third instance of men's initiation into the feminine with the "tum nyohoe" ritual.[6] This ceremony constitutes the last major rite of passage for a man and marks his transition into full maturity. The ceremony is celebrated with the man's wife and lasts several days. The first phase involves men making beer, a traditionally masculine activity, and women grinding grain, a feminine endeavor. On the third day, the women gather secretly at dawn and sacrifice a goat. Later that morning, the men meet by themselves, and then in the afternoon, men and women join together in a dance ceremony. In the ritual, the husband dances in a woman's goatskin dress. He gives up being a young warrior and symbolically adopts more feminine traits.

Western society does not formally celebrate men's midlife initiation into the feminine, but mythology and literature portray the process symbolically. In *The Odyssey,* for instance, Odysseus engineered the final Greek victory over Troy, and at the peak of his heroic triumph set sail for home. On the way, he lost all his ships and was forced to deal with a series of magical women, from Calypso the beautiful nymph, to Circe the beguiling sorceress, on to the enchanting Sirens and the goddess Athena herself. These women are anima figures, and Odysseus' encounter with them dramatizes men's midlife confrontation with the feminine in its positive and negative aspects. Dante's *Divine Comedy* repeats the drama. At midlife, Dante loses his way in a wilderness and descends into Hell. In this midlife crisis, Dante's beloved Beatrice sends him help, consolation, and comfort from her place in heaven. Like Zakia, she plays the role of the anima and rescues Dante from many disasters.

Lacking formal rites of passage into the feminine, men today experience the transition privately, inwardly. By default, psychotherapy has become a major vehicle for men's midlife introduction to the goddess. Here women therapists play a crucial role and many men gravitate toward them. Authors like Robert Lawlor in *Earth Honoring,* John Rowan in *The Horned God,* and Edward Whitmont in *Return of the Goddess* have written extensively about men serving the feminine, so I will not discuss the subject further. I want to emphasize only one point. Though vital, the initiation into the feminine is not the final task for men at midlife. Indeed, it is only the first of three initiations for men, the preliminary step in a longer journey.

CHAPTER THREE

The King's Ears:
The Shadow of the Patriarch

the king's ears

(FROM EUROPE)

There once lived a mighty King who had everything a man could desire. Only one thing troubled him—he had the ears of a goat! The King carefully hid his deformity beneath a beautiful crown, fearing that if his people discovered his secret, they would laugh at him and defy his authority. But like any other man, the King needed his hair cut. The same thing happened every time a barber came to the palace. The King would remove his crown, revealing his goat's ears, and the astonished barber would exclaim, "Your Majesty, you have goat's ears!" The King would scowl mightily, but let the man cut his hair. When the barber finished the King would ask, "How do I look?" Every barber blurted out, "Your Majesty, you look handsome—except for the goat's ears!" And whenever a barber said that, the King drew his sword and killed the man on the spot.

Soon all the barbers dreaded the summons to the palace, fearing for their lives. They worried so much that they became thin and stopped singing. This was a great misfortune, because the barbers were the best musicians in the land.

One day, a master barber received the summons to cut the

King's hair. Overcome with terror, the man took to bed, trembling in every limb. He called his apprentice and asked the young man to go in his place. The master barber was loath to send the youth to an early death, but he had no desire to die himself. The apprentice reluctantly gathered the tools of his trade and went to the palace, determined to stay alive.

The King greeted the young barber, and took off his royal crown. The goat's ears popped up, and the young man was tempted to exclaim, "Your Majesty, you have goat's ears!" But the apprentice bit his tongue, and kept silent. The King was surprised. The youth trimmed the King's hair, and the King looked at himself in the mirror. Then he asked his question, "Young man, how do I look?"

The apprentice bit his tongue again, and said simply, "Your Majesty, you look handsome." The King was delighted with the reply.

"I am pleased with your skill," the King told the young barber. "From now on, you will cut my hair." The King gave the young barber a bag of gold and sent him home.

The young man had never seen so much money before in his life! He ran home and told his master about cutting the King's hair. But the apprentice said nothing about the monarch's ears. Every few weeks, the youth trimmed the King's hair, returning home with another purse filled with gold. But as time went on, the apprentice became thin and drawn. His master noted the young man's poor health and called a physician.

The doctor examined the novice and then declared, "If I am not mistaken, you have a secret eating away at you. You must tell it to someone, or you will die."

"But I cannot tell anyone!" the apprentice exclaimed.

"If you will not tell me," the doctor said, "perhaps you can tell your master, or a priest."

"I cannot!" the poor man insisted.

"This is serious," the doctor pondered. He thought for a moment, and then said, "You must dig a hole in the earth, and tell the secret to the earth. That will cure you."

When the doctor left, the apprentice went into the wilderness, dug a deep hole, and then whispered, "The King has goat's ears!" Immediately, the youth felt his anxiety vanish. So he said a little louder, "The King has goat's ears!" The young man felt his strength revive, and so he shouted into the earth, "The King has goat's ears!" He felt positively light-hearted, and he returned home, completely cured.

Reeds sprouted from where the youth had revealed his secret. One day, a group of young shepherds passed by, tending their flocks. "Those reeds will make perfect flutes!" the children exclaimed. They gathered several stalks, whittled them into flutes, and blew on them. But the only sound that came out was, "The King has goat's ears! The King has goat's ears!" After a moment of surprise, the children blew on the reeds again, and the same words came out. "The King has goat's ears! The King has goat's ears!" The children rolled on the ground with laughter and ran home, playing their strange flutes for everybody. Soon all the people were laughing, and the King quickly heard about it.

In a rage, the King summoned his barber. "How dare you reveal my secret!" the King bellowed. "Prepare to die!" The King drew his sword.

"But I told nobody!" the youth protested.

"Then how is it that everybody laughs at me?" the King demanded.

"I do not know!" the apprentice said miserably. "I became sick from keeping your secret, and my doctor told me to share it with someone else, or I would die. I told him I could not reveal the secret to anyone, so he suggested I tell it to the earth. So I did. I dug a hole in the wilderness, and said, 'The King has goat's ears.' Then I covered the pit!"

The King paused. He had a quick temper, but he was also a just man. So the King summoned some of the townspeople, and demanded why they talked about his ears. "Several children," the people explained, "are playing flutes in town, and the flutes say, 'The King has goat's ears!'" The King ordered the children brought to him, and the young shepherds demonstrated their strange flutes. "We cut the reeds in the wilderness," they explained, describing the location.

"But that is where I told my secret!" the barber cried out. The King rode out to the forest with the barber to see the place himself. The young man pointed to a spot where reeds grew, and the King cut a stalk and whittled it into a flute. He blew through the reed, and out came, "The King has goat's ears! The King has goat's ears!"

"The children's story is true!" the King exclaimed. Then he sighed. "Even the earth reveals my secret!" But the monarch also smiled. He felt relieved that his secret was out. And if the people laughed at his ears, everyone still obeyed his laws. So the King started to joke about his ears, too, and he made the young man the Royal Barber. So both the King and the barber lived long and happy lives.

The Shadow of the Patriarch

THE PATRIARCH'S SHAME

The tale begins with a powerful monarch as its protagonist, and the King once again represents the authority and honor men typically seek in youth. Yet the story also reveals a shameful secret behind the King's power and glory. Beneath his golden crown, the monarch has goat's ears! The King's humiliating secret symbolizes a profound truth about men in patriarchal cultures: men suffer from hidden shame, a point Francis Weller makes eloquently with his essay in *To Be a Man*. To fit the heroic ideal, men deny their fears and pain, minimize the dangers of their endeavors, and overestimate their abilities. The result is the familiar machismo of young men and the lofty pride of patriarchs. Yet few men can truly live up to the ideal of the hero, and men feel ashamed of their failure. The King's deformed ears, hidden by his crown, dramatize this secret male shame. In extreme cases men suffer from the "impostor syndrome," where an outwardly successful man fears that he does not deserve his recognition and will be discovered as a fraud. More commonly men have dreams of being caught naked in public or taking exams for which they are not prepared.

The King specifically has goat's ear, and the animal is symbolic. Christian tradition associates the animal with the Devil and witchcraft. So goats represent the dark side of life. (The Christian symbolism was presumably known to the listeners of this European tale.) Other versions of the story say that the monarch has donkey's ears, but the donkey, too, is linked in European folklore with the Devil. In hiding his goat's ears, the King conceals his demonic side. Psychologically, he struggles with his shadow, just like the Sultan who confronted the cannibal cook and the wizard king who wrestled with rage and envy.

The King initially denies his shadow and kills any barber who mentions his ears. He uses violence to defend his pride. The story is perceptive, because heroes and patriarchs habitually use force to defend their "honor." Literature traces this bloody theme far back in history. In *The Iliad,* the ancient Greeks sacked Troy to avenge their honor after Paris, a Prince of Troy, eloped with Helen, the wife of the Greek King Menelaus. A millennium afterward, medieval tales romanticized knights and their deadly battles over honor, while American gunfighters repeated the drama centuries later. Feminists already have pointed out the violence lurking within the heroic and patriarchal ideal of manhood. What "The King's Ears" adds is that the violence comes from injured pride, fueled by men's secret shame. Men do not relish violence nor are they brutal by nature. Men become violent out of desperation, when their hidden humiliation is exposed.

The King spares the young barber because the apprentice remains silent about the King's ears. But the young man starts to waste away. The King's secret is destructive to him, and the detail is symbolic. Men's habit of hiding their fear and vulnerability is unhealthy not only to themselves, but to those around them. This is particularly true in families. Many sons know the shadowy, shameful sides of their fathers, but like the young barber, they keep silent about it. The secret may be that the father is an alcoholic, or has terrifying temper outbursts, or is under his wife's thumb. The unspoken knowledge erodes the son's confidence in his father and damages the young man's sense of manhood. Sons waste away psychologically, like the young barber in the story.

CONFRONTING THE SHAME

The King's secret eventually comes out. Children play flutes which proclaim, "The King has goat's ears!" The ensuing laughter humiliates the mighty King, toppling him from his lofty, patriarchal position. We saw something similar in the last two chapters, where the wizard king is defeated and thrown into prison, and the Sultan is captured in the cannibal's pit. Other men's tales repeat the theme, like the Jewish story "The King's Dream," or the Russian tale "The Tsar and the Angel." These stories show powerful men thrown down from the pinnacle of fame and authority and dramatize how men's heroic dreams and patriarchal ambitions collapse at midlife. The calamity forces men to confront their fears and vulnerability, and a midlife crisis commonly results. The process can be subtle, though, because heroic ideals and patriarchal traditions often decay slowly in men's lives, through burnout and disillusionment.

Humiliated by the magic pipes, the King threatens to kill the young barber. This repeats the Oedipal drama we saw in "The Wizard King," in which the enraged father vowed to kill his son. The barber is not the son of the King, but the conflict is still between a father-figure and a son-figure. Happily, "The King's Ears" portrays a successful resolution to the Oedipal battle. Instead of succumbing to his rage, the King realizes the error of his ways, recognizes the foolishness of his pride, stops killing barbers, and even rewards the youth richly. The King reforms and gives up his patriarchal pride. He confronts his shadow and comes to terms with it.

Other men's tales like "The King Who Would Be Stronger Than Fate" from India, the Jewish story "The Miser," or "Dreams" from China, emphasize the point: self-confrontation and self-reformation are essential if men are to mature and grow wise with age, rather than become rigid and bitter. Men who acknowledge the shadow at midlife are more psychologically stable and satisfied with life than men who do not.[1]

Significantly, there are no women in "The King's Ears." Unlike "The Sultan's Handkerchief," where the ruler is rescued by his wife, the King with goat's ears is helped by a young man, not a woman. The story focuses on men and the masculine, rather than on women and the feminine, and the point is insightful. When men struggle with their innermost shame, they do not accept help from women. At this stage, if wives, mothers, daughters, or lovers ask men what is the matter, men become touchy, moody, and angry, just like adolescents. To reveal their secret shame to a woman is intolerable for men of any age. Only other men can heal the secret male shame, and women must often simply wait out this phase in men's lives. "The King's Ears" specifically shows a younger man redeeming the King, and other men's tales repeat the theme. The drama is archetypal and involves a wounded father-figure being healed by a son-figure. We touched on this motif in Chapter 1 with the legend of Parsifal. There the Fisher King, the guardian of the Holy Grail, suffers from a wound that will not heal, but is finally cured by Parsifal, the innocent young knight. Here the King with goat's ears is wounded by secret shame and finds relief through the young barber. The theme reappears in the *Star Wars* movie trilogy, where the evil Darth Vader is redeemed by his son, Luke Skywalker. The young man helps his father turn away at the last moment from the powers of darkness.

The motif is psychologically insightful. Fathers are often rejuvenated by their sons (or grandsons). Inspired by their sons' admiration and need for them, many men rise to the occasion, work out personal problems, and become more integrated individuals. These men give their sons what they missed from their own fathers—support and affection. In the process the men heal their own wounds. Something analogous happens to mentors and teachers, who are revitalized by the youthful enthusiasm of their pupils. Before a middle-aged man can be healed, though, he must swallow patriarchal pride and be open to the convictions and criticisms of younger men. The King with goat's ears dramatizes the point. Despite his rage, the King stops himself from killing the young barber, gives the youth a chance to explain, and then rides out into the wilderness to investigate for himself. He contrasts with the wizard king in the first chapter, who could not bear to learn from his son.

BEYOND THE PATRIARCH

We can interpret the King and the young barber in another way. The monarch can also be a symbol of the mature male ego, accustomed to commanding the psyche. The young barber would then personify a new masculine energy arising from the unconscious. In fact, "The King's Ears" suggests that the barber represents a new type of male vitality, distinct from the heroic and patriarchal image of manhood. The tale gives several intriguing clues about what this new male energy involves.

The first hint comes from the fact that the King's secret is exposed by flutes whittled from reeds growing in the wild. Although different versions of the tale come from various parts of Europe, all contain this detail, indicating that the motif is significant. Patriarchs, of course, are linked to cities and states, so it is not surprising that alternatives to him would come from the wilderness and nature. The combination of music, goat's ears, and the forest also brings up the image of Pan, the goat-legged satyr in Greek mythology. Living in the woods, Pan symbolizes a wild masculine energy hidden in the unconscious. Does he represent an alternative to the patriarchal ideal of manhood? A third clue suggests that he does. The young man who helps the King is specifically a barber who cuts men's hair and deals with men's hairiness. But hairiness symbolizes men's link to wild animals and instinct, as Robert Bly highlights in *Iron John*. The word "barber," I might add, derives from the Latin, "barba" or beard, and is linked to "barbarian," a wild, hairy man like Pan. A final clue about the new image of masculine energy revolves around another meaning to the King's goat's ears. In European tradition, fools or jesters wore caps with animal ears, and the practice was probably familiar to tellers of the tale. The story thus hints that the archetype of the fool or jester hides behind the patriarch, the way the King's goat's ears were concealed behind his crown!

From "The King's Ears" alone, we can draw no definite conclusions about a new nonpatriarchal type of male energy. The story provides only a few hints, but when we compare it with other men's tales, a more complete—and astonishing—picture emerges.

CHAPTER FOUR

The North Wind's Gift: Men's Oppression and the Wild Man

---

the north wind's gift

(FROM ITALY)

a farmer was once so poor that he could barely feed his wife and three children. He worked from dawn to dusk, but at every harvest, the North Wind blew across the fields, spoiling the crops. One day, the peasant had had enough. "The North Wind is ruining me!" he cried out in anger. "I am going to demand justice!"

The peasant left home and walked on and on. He came to the castle of the North Wind and knocked on the door. The Wind's wife let him in and explained that her husband was not home, but would return momentarily. Soon enough the North Wind appeared, and the farmer greeted him. "Good day, sir," the peasant said.

"Good day to you, too," the North Wind replied. "And who are you?"

"I am a farmer and you blow across my fields every harvest-time, ruining my crops," the peasant said. "Because of you, my family starves. So I have come to ask you to put things right."

The North Wind took a liking to the man and asked, "What do you want me to do?"

The farmer bowed. "That is for you to decide."

The North Wind thought a moment, brought out a box, and gave it to the farmer. "This box is magic. It will give you food when you open it. But tell no one about the magic, otherwise you will lose the box."

The farmer was overjoyed, thanked the North Wind, and started back home. On his way, he stopped beside the road, wished for lunch, and opened the box. Instantly, a table appeared, laden with cheese, bread, sausages, and wine. The farmer ate happily, then closed the casket. The food vanished, and the farmer resumed walking.

When he returned home, the farmer's family ran out to meet him. They asked him about his journey and he told them about the North Wind and the magic box. The peasant wished aloud for some dinner, opened the coffer, and their kitchen table was suddenly covered with roasts and salads, cakes and cheeses. The farmer told his wife not to mention the magic box to anybody. "And especially don't tell the prior!" The priest was their landlord and a greedy man.

The next day, the prior summoned the farmer's wife and asked about her husband's journey. The priest was charming and cunning. Soon enough, the wife mentioned the magic box. The prior immediately sent for the farmer and demanded the casket.

"But if I give you my magic box, I will have nothing!" the farmer protested. "My family will starve again."

The prior made veiled threats about evicting the peasant and promised the farmer loads of grain in exchange for the box. Finally, the farmer handed over the magic coffer. The next day the prior sent a few bags of rotten seed to the peasant, and so the poor man was no better off than before.

After a time, the peasant gathered his courage, and returned to the castle of the North Wind. "It is you again!" the North Wind exclaimed, when he saw the farmer. The peasant explained how he lost the magic box, but the North Wind only frowned.

"I told you to keep the casket secret. Now go away, because I will not give you anything else."

The poor farmer pleaded. "You are my only hope!" he exclaimed. "Besides, it is you who ruin my crops!"

The North Wind relented, went inside and returned with a magnificent golden box. "I will help you one more time," the North Wind said. "But do not open this case until you are starving."

The farmer thanked the North Wind and went on his way. Halfway home, he felt hungry, wished for a fine meal, and opened the box. Instantly, a ruffian leaped out, brandishing a club, and started beating the farmer. The peasant ran to and fro but could not escape his assailant. Finally, the farmer managed to close the golden coffer, and the thug vanished. Bruised and limping, the farmer returned home.

His wife and children gathered eagerly around him, asking what he received from the North Wind. "It is something even more wondrous than the last gift!" the farmer said. Then he told everyone to sit around the table. He opened the gold box and quickly stepped outside the room. Two brigands leaped out of the magic casket, and began thrashing the wife and children. After a few moments, the farmer stepped into the room, closed the lid of the box, and the ruffians vanished.

The farmer turned to his wife. "Tomorrow you must go to the prior and tell him that I have an even better gift than the last one. But say nothing else!"

The wife understood. The next day, she visited the priest and boasted of the new gift her husband had received from the North Wind. The prior sent for the farmer, and asked for the golden chest.

The farmer protested. "If I give you my new magic box, I will have nothing for my family again!" But the farmer showed the prior the golden case.

"I must have it!" the prior exclaimed greedily. He promised to give the peasant back the other box, and anything else the farmer desired.

With a great show of reluctance, the farmer consented. "But don't open the golden box unless you are starving!" the farmer warned.

The two exchanged boxes and the prior gloated over his new treasure. The prior's bishop was to visit the next day, so the priest decided to wait and use the magic box then. "When we are all ravenous," the prior thought, "I will open the magic box. What a fine meal I will serve the bishop! I may even be promoted!"

The next day the bishop arrived with his retinue. After all the Masses were said, the hungry prelate and his retinue gathered in the dining room. The prior brought out his golden box, and opened it. Instantly, six men with clubs leaped out and began beating the priests. They howled for mercy and prayed for help, but the ruffians went on hitting them. The farmer, who was watching from a window, slipped into the room, and closed the lid on the magic case. The thugs vanished and the farmer returned home with his golden box.

The prior never bothered the peasant from then on, and the peasant guarded his magic treasures carefully. And so he and his family lived in ease and comfort the rest of their days.

Men's Oppression and the Wild Man

MEN'S OPPRESSION

Unlike the monarchs in the first three chapters, the protagonist in this story is a peasant at the bottom of society, oppressed on all sides. The North Wind freezes the farmer's crops, his wife ignores his warnings, and his landlord intimidates him. The story brings up an important theme. Not all men become heroes and patriarchs by midlife. In fact, very few can. Most men labor under bosses and many are exploited just like the poor farmer. Like women, men experience their own forms of oppression in patriarchal society, something emphasized by Aaron Kipnis in *Knights Without Armor* and Mark Gerzon in *A Choice of Heroes*.

In lacking masculine fierceness and confidence, the peasant symbolizes three groups of men today. The first are those who have been wounded in life. These men come from deprived childhoods, suffer from depression or alcoholism, doubt their own worth, and never assert themselves. They lacked models of masculine strength in childhood because their fathers were usually absent or weak. As adults, many men also endure crippling social or economic hardship and have no opportunity to develop their talent. This is especially true for men of minority groups, "men of color." Hobbled by childhood traumas, assailed by prejudice, or demoralized by poverty, wounded men struggle to survive, just like the poor farmer.

The peasant also represents a second group of men. These individuals consciously reject traditional masculine roles and consciously favor their feminine side instead, embracing feeling, intuition, nurturing, and sensitivity. Artists, pacifists, healers, and gay men often fall in this group. Many are influenced by modern feminism, which reveals the chilling history of men's abuse of women and the secret link between war and masculine psychology. These men explicitly extol the importance of the goddess, honor the feminine, and often lose touch with their masculine instincts.

The third category of men is probably the largest. These are "gentle men" brought up to avoid fistfights, refrain from profanity, and work hard at their jobs. They dress neatly, drive their children to school, and control their anger with bosses. They reject the old warrior ideal. Recent Hollywood films trace the shift to gentler, more "civilized" male roles. Early on, actors like Clark Gable and John Wayne were leading men, reflecting the heroic image of self-confident, aggressive males. But a new generation of male protagonists replaced the earlier macho figures. William Hurt, Woody Allen, Kevin Costner, and other "new men" are typically sensitive, self-questioning, and some would say even wimpish.

Wounded men, nontraditional men, and gentle men have one thing in common with the poor peasant: they have lost contact with their male energy. Robert Bly eloquently describes this problem. Although he enthusiastically embraced the search for a gentler form of manhood some years ago, Bly now questions the effects of men's "domestication." Men today, he argues, have become desperate and angry precisely because they have given up their masculine fierceness. Other writers agree, like Sam Keen in *Fire in the Belly*, Eugene Monick in *Phallos: Sacred Image of the Masculine*, and James Wyly in *The Phallic Quest*. They insist that men need to reclaim their native male vitality and "The North Wind's Gift" shows how.

MEN'S LIBERATION

After many years of suffering, the peasant finally becomes angry with his situation and searches for the North Wind. The peasant's goal is symbolic. In mythology around the world, wind spirits are virtually always male. In seeking the North Wind, the peasant searches for an archetypal masculine power—exactly what he needs. The Wind responds positively and gives the poor man a magic box that produces food. The gift may seem to be mere wish-fulfillment, the dream of an unsuccessful man finally having a stroke of luck. But if only wish-fulfillment were involved, the story would end here, and the tale goes on to even more important events.

The North Wind warns the peasant to keep the magic box a secret, but the farmer tells his wife, she tells the prior, and the peasant loses the box. The peasant cannot keep a secret. He lacks masculine self-discipline. Worse, when the priest threatens to evict the farmer and demands the magic box, the peasant capitulates. Yet with the North Wind's gift, the farmer no longer needs to work, so the prior's threats are empty. Unfortunately, the peasant is too meek to realize this. The story is psychologically accurate. In real life, many men find treasures—perhaps concluding a difficult deal at work, or inventing improved factory procedures—only to have the credit stolen by unscrupulous bosses. A more subtle but equally destructive form of this oppression occurs *within* individual men. Many carry a toxic superego, an internalized parent, who criticizes and harasses them endlessly, the way the prior intimidates the peasant. Such a superego steals all joy from a man's life, so that his labor and success bring him little satisfaction. Like the poor peasant, these men suffer from an oppressive landlord, but an internal one.

Happily, the farmer does not despair over losing his magic food box. Perseverance is a virtue he has from the beginning. He keeps planting his crops year after year, even when the North Wind ruins each harvest. The farmer plucks up his courage and returns to the North Wind with a second request for help. This time the North Wind plays a trick on the farmer, giving him a box that looks even more magnificent than the last. The peasant ruefully discovers that the cask contains ruffians, not food. The thugs are profoundly symbolic.

THE WILD MAN VS. THE SAVAGE

After being beaten by the ruffians, the peasant goes home and releases the bullies on his family. This is brutal, but the story is painfully honest. The ruffians make a good symbol for a man's anger, and the peasant has many reasons to be furious. He has been oppressed for years by his landlord and the North Wind, with little hope of change. Like many men in dead-end jobs or unhappy marriages, the farmer also bottles up his frustration. So when his anger first appears, it is explosive: the thugs leap out and mercilessly beat the peasant and his family. In real life, many men do something similar and take out their anger with the world on the nearest and easiest targets, their wives and children.

The ruffians' violence makes them wild and savage figures, so they may initially resemble what Robert Bly christened "the wild man" who personifies the deep masculine. As Bly describes the wild man, he is a primordial masculine energy that is normally inhibited by layers of social etiquette and buried deep in men's unconscious (hence he is the *deep* masculine). Concealed in a golden box, the thugs appear to fit Bly's definition. They are primitive brutes suppressed by social convention, hidden behind a pretty façade. Certainly, many people fear that brutality lurks at the core of the male psyche and that men are inherently violent, despite superficial male chivalry. Many feminists express this fear eloquently and identify men as the prime agents of war, rape, and murder. Men themselves often fear their own anger. And many men's tales show meek males suddenly becoming violent after years of silent frustration, like "Animal Talk and the Nosy Wife" from Italy, "The Animal Languages" from Germany, "The Man and the Snake" from Africa, and "Shemiaka the Judge" from Russia. These stories are disturbing because they apparently extol male violence. A closer look at the tales, though, reveals something entirely different, as "The North Wind's Gift" illustrates.

In the story, the peasant lets the thugs beat his family only for a short time. Then he closes the lid on the box and controls the violence. Most important, the farmer turns his aggression upon the greedy priest, a more appropriate victim. (The priest's bishop is also soundly beaten and this may seem excessive, but the prelate is not an innocent party. As the prior's superior, the bishop failed to curb the priest's abuses as a landlord.) The ultimate message of the story is that men must direct their anger against justified targets, like abusive bosses, oppressive institutions, and suffocating patriarchal traditions. The tale does not encourage men to simply explode with rage and become savages. In fact, after the first time, the peasant stops inflicting the thugs on his family, and he even spares the prior after the priest learns his lesson. The story insists that men harness anger and aggression in constructive ways. Once the peasant learns this, he lives happily ever after with his family.

The peasant's tale dramatizes an important point that Robert Bly makes: the wild man is *not* a savage. Critics of the men's movement often confuse the two and regard the wild man as a primitive and violent barbarian. Here the peasant's story is important, because it distinguishes the wild man from the savage and clarifies the relationship between the two. The thugs in the golden box are clearly savages, since they mindlessly beat up anybody around them. The North Wind, by contrast, is not barbaric. In fact, he is helpful, caring, and generous, trying to aid the poor peasant with the two magic boxes.

The relationship between the North Wind and the violent thugs is revealing. The ruffians derive from the North Wind and constitute his second gift to the peasant. So the thugs and their savagery represent part of the North Wind. Yet it is only a small aspect of the Wind's more complex character, since he is also helpful and nurturing.

THE NURTURING MALE

The order in which the North Wind gives his presents to the farmer is deeply symbolic. The magic food box is first and the violent ruffians second. This suggests that the Wind is primarily nurturing and secondarily violent. Moreover, in giving the peasant the box with ruffians, the Wind was trying to teach the man a lesson about standing up for himself. Behind the Wind's violent second gift lies a generous and helpful attitude. Other men's tales repeat this symbolic sequence. Stories like "The Wishing-Table, the Gold Ass and the Cudgel in the Sack" from the Grimms' collection, "Brother Lustig" from Germany (discussed in Chapters 7 and 8), and "Go I Know Not Whither" from Russia (discussed in Chapters 9 and 10) portray men receiving magical treasures from powerful male figures, and the first gifts are nurturing, while the second ones are violent.

The fact that the North Wind is primarily nurturing seems surprising, since the stereotype of primitive masculinity is that of the savage. In Italian folklore, in fact, the North Wind is usually considered destructive because of its association with winter storms and barbarians to the north. The present story defies the stereotype of primitive male violence by having the North Wind be kind and nurturing. Robert Bly refers to such nourishing male figures as "male mothers." This phrase is somewhat unfortunate, because it implies that nurturing is the domain of the mother, and, in fact, the caring, generous male is ancient and archetypal.

Across cultures and throughout most of history, men's first and foremost role is that of provider, as anthropologist David Gilmore emphasizes in his book *Manhood in the Making*. Men labor long hours and undertake risky ventures to provide food for their families, hunting dangerous game or fishing on the open ocean. The warrior role, by contrast, is episodic and secondary. Aboriginal societies make the point clear. In many tribes of New Guinea and the Amazon jungle, village life centers around a "Big Man," who is the tribal leader chosen by virtue of his talent and competence. He organizes the defense of the village when necessary and acts as warrior-chief if needed. But the majority of his time and effort is spent coordinating the village's agricultural and hunting activities. He is responsible for accumulating food and redistributing it, making sure that no one goes hungry. He is provider first and warrior second. Moreover, he uses his authority to gather resources only to give them away to his people. His power and prestige depend on how generous he is.

The nurturing foundation of the masculine psyche is overlooked in modern culture, partly because men's role as provider has become abstract and intangible. Men bring home only a paycheck today with numbers scribbled on a piece of paper. They do not return with deer or bison that they hunted themselves. So children have little concrete evidence of their father's nurturing vitality.

In emphasizing the provident and caring aspect of masculine energy, "The North Wind's Gift" allays fears that men are inherently violent and brutish. The story points out that men become violent when they are oppressed, like the little peasant exploited by his landlord. Yet the core of the masculine soul is nurturing, like the North Wind with his helpful, clever gifts to the farmer.

THE NORTH WIND AND THE DEEP MASCULINE

Generous and caring though he is, the North Wind remains a wild masculine force. This point becomes clear if we remember that the North Wind is a spirit of wild stormy, winter weather. He is a wild man.

Furthermore, as Joseph Campbell and Mircea Eliade noted, storm spirits like the North Wind represent ancient masculine figures, *from whom patriarchal gods evolved*. In the Greek pantheon, Zeus, the ruling patriarch, started out as a storm god with lightning as his weapon. Among the ancient Peruvians, Viracocha was a paramount deity who also began as a storm god, like Zeus. The same holds for Odin, the chief Norse god; Nyame, the creator god of the Ashanti in Africa; and Yahweh in Jewish tradition.

While the violence of storm gods is obvious, their nurturing power is equally important. In both Greek and Hebrew creation stories, a divine wind moved over the primordial waters, generating life. Similarly, in Native American lore, a divine wind often fertilized the earth or the first woman, bringing forth plants, animals, and people. Wind spirits are generative and wild, nurturing yet aggressive, just like the North Wind.

Older than patriarchal gods, the North Wind represents a forgotten, wild masculine force. This is the definition of the deep masculine. (The tale emphasizes the "deep" nature of the North Wind by saying he lives far, far away, beyond the peasant's normal world. Metaphorically, the North Wind resides in the unconscious.) A similar image of the deep masculine surfaced earlier in Chapter 3 with "The King's Ears." There the monarch hid his goat's ears under his crown, and the ears allude to Pan, a primordial masculine force like the North Wind. Pan is wild but not savage. He makes music, not mayhem.

In the peasant's tale, the North Wind, not the thugs, represents the wild man and the deep masculine. The ruffians personify anger, aggression, or violence, and reflect only a small aspect of the male psyche. An analogy may help here: the thugs are like the monstrous gargoyles that surround medieval Christian cathedrals or the statues of demons that guard the entrances to Buddhist temples. The brutes protect the sanctuary and serve the deity within. Only those who push beyond the terrifying images find the divine vitality inside.

As a wild man, the North Wind is simultaneously nurturing and aggressive, and he helps men reconcile two apparently conflicting tasks of midlife. The first, as discussed with "The Sultan's Handkerchief," is for men to honor their long-neglected nurturing side, initially represented by the anima. The second, as the present story emphasizes, is to reclaim the wild man and the aggressive powers he controls. Combining the power to nourish and to attack, the North Wind breaks with traditional, patriarchal stereotypes, which sharply separate men from women, the masculine from the feminine, aggression from nurturing. The

North Wind is able to do this because he is older than patriarchal gods and offers an alternative to the patriarchal paradigm.

THE WILD MAN IN MEN'S LIVES

"The North Wind's Gift" shows how an oppressed man makes contact with the deep masculine and changes his life. The drama is not merely the stuff of fairy tales because the same process occurs in the lives of men today. In his book *The Survival Papers*, Daryl Sharp, a Jungian analyst, offers a good example with the case of Norman. A dutiful husband and father, at midlife Norman discovered that his wife was involved in an affair with another man. Devastated by this revelation, Norman came to therapy and struggled to rebuild his life. During this painful period Norman had a "big" dream. In it, a timid man was trying to subdue a horse, but the animal ran wild through the streets. Another man appeared, riding a motorcycle, and he offered to lend his leather jacket and boots to the meek man.

Upon awakening, Norman identified the horse as his wife, whom he perceived as totally out of control. The meek man, of course, was Norman himself. The man on the motorcycle was in real life a powerful, ruthless colleague Norman knew from work. Playing the role of an intimidating "biker" in the dream, Norman's co-worker represents a modern version of the wild man, personifying the aggressiveness and fierceness Norman felt lacking in himself. When the biker offers his boots and jacket to Norman, he symbolically gives Norman a bit of primordial masculine power. After this dream, Norman became more assertive and self-confident. He decided to leave his wife and started a new life on his own. Like the meek peasant helped by the North Wind, Norman found advice and support from a powerful male figure, representing the wild man and the deep masculine.[1] (Norman, however, did not beat his wife or children!)

Another example of reclaiming the deep masculine comes from Eugene Monick, a Jungian analyst and Christian minister. At the age of forty, Monick was appointed the pastor of an important parish, succeeding a nationally prominent preacher. Monick feared he would fail in his enormous new responsibilities and thought of declining the job. Then he had a "big" dream which changed his mind. In the dream, Monick was part of a group of men gathered around a huge stone phallus which emanated a powerful, divine presence. The dream was brief, but when he awoke, he felt a new sense of self-assurance. He was confident for the first time in his leadership abilities. Through his dream Monick felt that he had made contact with a deep source of masculine power, symbolized by the sacred phallus. This phallic energy is the archetypal masculine "cockiness" that is one part aggression, one part arrogance, and one part whistling in the dark. ("Cockiness," as might be expected, derives from "cock.") It is the primordial masculine energy that Monick named "phallos" in his book with that title.

As a minister, Monick had spent most of his life developing his gentle half, his nurturing, feminine side. His midlife dream of the sacred phallus introduced him to a primordial masculine force equivalent to the North Wind. The wild male energy did not make Monick a savage. Instead, it gave him the strength to carry out his new responsibilities and be nurturing in a wider sphere.

Monick's dream depicts a rite celebrating male energy. There are few such rituals in today's society, which leaves men to fend for themselves. Fortunately, the men's movement experiments with various ceremonies, from sweat lodges to vision quests, creating new initiation rites specifically dealing with the deep masculine. Psychotherapy also provides an important opportunity for men to reclaim male vitality. Therapy is particularly important because it provides a place where men can wrestle with the anger and violence often confused with the wild man. Here male therapists are often needed, just as women are helpful when men wrestle with anima issues. In reclaiming primordial masculine energies, men need the assistance of males who have separated the wild man from the savage in their own lives.

BEYOND THE HERO AND PATRIARCH

Before concluding this chapter, two points are worthy of comment. First, the peasant's journey to the North Wind overtly resembles the hero's quest, so familiar in myths and tales of youth. However, there are important differences between the peasant's odyssey and the hero's adventure. The peasant does not battle dragons, witches, or tyrants, which is the usual task of the young hero. Nor does he seek a fabulous treasure or want to become King. The farmer seeks reparation rather than glory. Compensation is his goal, not conquest, therapy instead of triumph. Like most men in midlife, he has given up the ambitious dreams of youth and will settle for healing rather than heroism. The peasant's journey is post-heroic. Significantly, the peasant goes to the North Wind to ask for *help*. The farmer realizes that he cannot solve his problems by himself. He contrasts with the young hero, who typically rides off alone on his quest, supremely confident in his own abilities. Learning to ask for help is perhaps the hardest task for men in the middle years. Many men want to try psychotherapy or join a male support group but feel ashamed to start. Here the peasant's story offers reassurance: once he asks for aid, the North Wind provides it. But the peasant has to seek help first.

The last point is that the North Wind is tricky. When he gives the peasant the second box, the North Wind plays a prank on the farmer and leads him to think that the box will give him food just like the first. (The North Wind even tells the peasant not to open the box until famished.) The peasant is rudely surprised when the thugs appear and attack him. Wind spirits like the North Wind are typically tricky. They are elusive and unpredictable, just like the wind. Moreover, the peasant learns to be tricky himself and dupes his landlord at the end of the story. This raises an intriguing suggestion: Could the deep masculine be tied up with trickiness? The next tale answers the question in a surprising way.

CHAPTER FIVE

The Little Peasant:
Shadow and Trickster

---

the little peasant

(FROM GERMANY)

far away and long ago, a poor peasant and his wife lived in a village where everyone else was wealthy. One day, the peasant had an idea. "I shall ask the carpenter to carve us a wooden calf," the little peasant told his wife, "and if we take care of it, the calf will grow into a cow. Then we will have all the milk and butter we need."

The carpenter made the wooden calf, and the next day the peasant asked the cowherd to take care of the animal. "But it is such a little calf," the peasant said, "you will have to carry it to the pasture." The cowherd obliged, hauled the calf to the meadow, and set it down to graze.

That evening, when the cowherd called the animals together, the calf stayed in the meadow. The cowherd became vexed. "If you won't come," he shouted at the calf, "you can stay there all night!" And the cowherd returned home.

When the peasant asked for his calf, the cowherd told him the animal refused to come home. "But I want my calf back!" the peasant exclaimed. The two returned to the pasture, and found the calf missing. Someone had stolen it. So the little peasant dragged the cowherd before the mayor and demanded justice.

The mayor awarded a cow to the peasant as compensation, and the peasant returned home overjoyed. "Our fortune is made!" the peasant told his wife.

Alas, the peasant could not afford to feed his cow, and he was forced to slaughter it. He walked to the next village to sell the cowhide, and on the way he came across a raven with a broken wing. The little peasant picked up the wounded bird, wrapped it in his cowskin and resumed his journey. A storm broke out, and the peasant ran to the nearest shelter, which was the miller's house. The miller was not home, but his wife was, and she grudgingly let the peasant in. She offered him a slice of stale bread and dry cheese to eat, and brusquely pointed to a pile of straw he could lie on. The little peasant thought her inhospitable, but said nothing, lay down on the straw, and closed his eyes.

A few minutes later, the parson came knocking on the door. The miller's wife stole a glance at the peasant, who pretended to sleep. Then she opened the door. "Come in, come in! I've been waiting for you," she told the minister. She took out a roast, a salad, a cake, and a bottle of wine, and soon she and the parson ate, laughed, and carried on. The little peasant watched everything through half-closed eyes.

Suddenly, the miller called out from outside. "I'm home!"

"Good heavens!" the miller's wife exclaimed. "My husband has returned early!" In an instant, she hid the roast in the oven, the wine under the pillow, the salad beside the bed, and the cake beneath it. Then she told the parson to climb into the closet on the back porch.

The miller walked in, and his wife smiled nervously. "Thank God you have returned!" she said. "I worried about you in the storm!"

The miller shook the rain off his coat, and noticed the peasant sleeping on the straw. "Who is that?" the miller asked his wife. "A peasant, caught in the storm," she explained. The miller nodded, and asked for some food.

"I only have bread and cheese," the wife replied, and set it out.

"That's good enough," the miller grunted and turned to

awaken the peasant. "Come," the miller told the peasant, "eat with me if you like."

The peasant quickly joined the miller, and the two started talking about this and that. The miller noticed the raven wrapped in the hide. "What is that?" the miller asked.

"Oh," the peasant replied, "that is my soothsayer."

The miller was surprised. "Can it tell my fortune?"

"To be sure," the peasant answered. "It gives four prophecies, but the fifth it keeps for itself."

"Let me hear one," the miller asked. So the peasant pinched the raven until it made a noise.

"What did it say?" the miller inquired.

"My soothsayer," the peasant interpreted, "said there is a salad next to the bed."

"That's ridiculous," the miller insisted.

"My soothsayer is never wrong!" the peasant declared, so the miller went to look. And there beside the bed was a salad!

"Upon my word!" the miller exclaimed. "Can your soothsayer tell me something else?"

The peasant pinched the raven again. "The second prophecy," the peasant said thoughtfully, "is that there is a bottle of wine under the pillow."

"That couldn't be true!" the miller exclaimed, but he went to look anyway, and sure enough, there was the wine! The peasant pinched the bird a third time.

"What did it say?" the miller asked.

The peasant scratched his head. "My, this is strange," he said, "the soothsayer says there is a roast in the oven!" So the miller looked inside, and found the beef. The raven croaked a fourth time, and the peasant exclaimed, "Now the soothsayer says there is a cake under the bed!"

By this time the miller's wife had turned pale. She retired to the bedroom, taking the key to the closet on the porch. "I like your soothsayer," the miller said, munching on the salad and roast. "And what would its fifth prophecy be?"

"Let us eat our meal first," the peasant answered, "because

the last one is always bad." So the two men ate heartily, and bargained over what the miller would pay for the final prophecy. They agreed on three hundred gold pieces, and the little peasant pinched the raven. It croaked and the peasant stood up in surprise. "This could not be!" he exclaimed.

"What is it?" the miller asked, somewhat alarmed.

"The soothsayer says that the Devil is hiding in the closet on your porch!"

"That I will not have!" the miller exclaimed. He took the keys from his wife, and unlocked the closet door. The parson burst out and ran away so quickly, he looked like a fleeting shadow.

"Bless me!" the miller exclaimed. "So that was the Devil, the scoundrel!" The miller thanked the peasant for ridding his home of the demon, and paid the peasant three hundred gold coins.

The little peasant returned home, bought a new house, and lived a comfortable life with his wife. His neighbors became curious about his newfound wealth, and they badgered him until he told them his secret. "I slaughtered my cow and sold the skin in the next town for three hundred gold coins!"

When the villagers heard this, they rushed home, butchered all their cows, and ran to the next town. When they arrived, the tanner was perplexed. "I do not need so many skins!" he exclaimed, and he paid them only a trifle for each hide.

The villagers were furious. "We have been tricked by the little peasant!" they cried out. They ran home, hauled the peasant before the mayor, and everyone condemned the innocent man to death. The mayor himself pronounced the sentence. "You will be sealed in a barrel full of holes, and thrown into the river to drown!"

The villagers shoved the little peasant in a cask and carried him toward the river. Then they called for a parson to say the last rites, and left the peasant alone with the minister. The peasant looked out through a hole in the barrel and recognized the parson.

"I let you go from the miller's house," the peasant told the minister, "so you must set me free now." The parson hesitated and then nodded in agreement. At that moment, a shepherd walked by herding his sheep. The little peasant knew the shepherd had always dreamed of being mayor, so the peasant cried out noisily, "I refuse! No matter how much you ask me, I will not be mayor!"

"What are you talking about?" the shepherd asked, coming up to the peasant.

"The villagers want me to be mayor," the little peasant explained. "But to become mayor, I have to roll around in this barrel, and I have no desire to do that!"

"I will take your place!" the shepherd volunteered. The two men switched places, and the little peasant walked away with the shepherd's flock.

The parson called the villagers back to the barrel, and they proceeded to push the cask into the river. They returned home triumphantly. To their surprise, they saw the little peasant in town with a herd of sheep.

"How did you survive?" the villagers asked the peasant.

"The barrel sank deep into the water," the peasant explained, "and finally hit bottom. I stepped out and found a beautiful meadow on the riverbed, with sheep just waiting to be taken!"

As soon as the villagers heard this, they ran to the river and looked in. They saw the clouds reflected in the water and cried out, "Look, look! There are the sheep, just like the peasant said!" The mayor and all the villagers jumped into the river to gather animals for themselves, and every one of them drowned. Since the little peasant and his wife were the only people left in the village, they inherited the whole place. And so they lived in wealth and ease for the rest of their lives.

Shadow and Trickster

MEN AND THE SHADOW

In this Grimms story, the little peasant lies, cheats, steals, and murders his neighbors—and then lives happily ever after. He con-

trasts sharply with the familiar young hero in fairy tales who
succeeds because he is honest, brave, and virtuous. How are we
to understand the peasant's shocking behavior and the fact that
he is rewarded for it? A theme from previous chapters helps. The
peasant resembles a shadow figure and has many unsavory criminal tendencies. He demonstrates how men's dark side emerges
at midlife, just like men's feminine traits. The peasant also seems
savage, breaking every rule of civilized life. He causes so much
mayhem and mishap, he resembles the violent thugs in "The
North Wind's Gift."

Young men normally control criminal temptations and barbaric
impulses with heroic ideals and patriarchal rules. As men move
beyond the hero and patriarch in maturity, the shadow often leaps
out. Jung described a poignant example.[1] He knew a pious
churchwarden who became increasingly rigid, moralistic, and intolerant of other people in his forties. Then, at age fifty-five, the
minister awoke one night, saying, "Now at last I've got it. I'm
just a plain rascal!" The pastor spent the rest of his life in scandalous pursuits. All the desires and impulses that the minister
suppressed in youth broke free, and riotous living replaced righ-
teous life. Like the little peasant, Jung's middle-aged acquaintance started acting out the shadow.

Other men's tales repeat the theme, such as "Buying Loyalty"
from China, "Davi Dal" from Wales, "Harisarman" from India, "The Peasant Astrologer" from Italy, and "Husband Pour
Porridge on My Shoulder" from Yugoslavia. The stories portray
mature men starting to lie, steal, and murder innocent people.
The tales dismayed me. I had hoped that as men aged, they moved
from heroism to wisdom, coming to terms with the feminine and
the shadow. Instead, middle tales suggest that men become ruffians, savages, psychopaths, and delinquents!

Here we come to a puzzle. In reality, men do not become
criminals at midlife. Men's delinquent behavior normally declines with age.[2] If newspapers tell lurid tales of middle-aged men
embezzling, taking bribes, or cheating on their wives, the men usually started much earlier and are only caught in the middle years.
The majority of outlaws and rogues are young men, and by midlife
most delinquents and criminals settle down and straighten out. If

men do not really become savage or criminal at midlife, how are we to interpret fairy tales like "The Little Peasant"?

As I wrestled with the question, I was struck by how much the little peasant resembles an archetypal figure in mythology—the Trickster. Around the world, Tricksters lie, steal, cheat, and murder people, just like the little peasant. In researching Trickster mythology, I also discovered that Tricksters are almost invariably male, like the Native American Coyote, the Siberian Raven, the Green Hermes, the Polynesian Maui, the African Eshu, and the Australian Bamampana, among others. The majority of Tricksters are also married men with children. So Tricksters are typically mature males.[3] This suggests that Tricksters like the little peasant symbolize the psychology of mature manhood!

The notion is disturbing because Tricksters are usually considered unsavory or even evil.[4] In Christian lore, the chief Trickster is Satan, the source of lies and betrayal. The same applies to Ogo-Yuguru, the Trickster for the Dogon of Africa, and Loki of Norse mythology. Similarly, the Zuni of Southwest America link their Trickster with death, murder, and mayhem. Modern psychology continues the negative view and usually interprets Tricksters as primitive figures, acting out wild instincts and sociopathic impulses. Jung and Jungians, for instance, generally equate the Trickster with juvenile delinquents, schizophrenics, alcoholics, psychopaths, and savages.[5]

The idea that Tricksters such as the little peasant symbolize the male psyche will disturb men, but many women may feel the point is self-evident. Most women have struggled at some time with unreliable men who wander in and out of their lives, robbing them emotionally. Many women secretly suspect that men are scoundrels at heart, just like the Trickster.

A closer look at "The Little Peasant" and Trickster folklore, however, reveals something startling.[6] The peasant and other Tricksters are not criminals or barbarians, but complex figures with creative, life-giving powers hidden beneath their shadowy exterior. Indeed, "The Little Peasant" shows how the Trickster differs in basic ways from the sociopath and the savage. The story also gradually reveals that the Trickster offers a new vision of masculine energy, distinct from the hero and the patriarch.

THE TRICKSTER VS. THE CRIMINAL

Perhaps the most dramatic feature of the little peasant is that he is something of a con man. He fools the cowherd into giving him a real cow for a wooden calf, dupes the miller into paying three hundred gold coins for a ''prophecy,'' and later tricks the shepherd into being executed in his place. The peasant steals a cow, a pile of gold, and the shepherd's life. Yet he is far from a simple criminal.

First of all, the peasant is actually less shadowy and criminal than his neighbors. When the villagers slaughter all their cows, it is because of their own greed. Yet they blame the peasant for their misfortune. In a rage, they condemn the little peasant to death, although he does not deserve such a harsh sentence. (The original version specifically says the peasant is innocent.) So the villagers act out the shadow more than the peasant. In many ways, the peasant's victims also deserve their misfortunes. The cowherd, for instance, was lax in leaving the peasant's calf behind in the meadow at night. The cowherd also should have noticed the difference between a wooden calf and a real one, since he deals with cows all the time! Similarly, the shepherd who substitutes for the peasant acts out of blind ambition. He foolishly believes the peasant's tale about becoming mayor by being rolled in a barrel. Later, when the villagers jump in the river and drown, it is because of their lust for the ''sheep'' on the river bottom. Surrounded by greedy, impulsive, and violent neighbors, the little peasant survives only with clever schemes. His deceptions are motivated more by necessity and desperation than avarice or sociopathy. Nor does the peasant plan his tricks in advance. He stumbles from one predicament to another, improvising on the spot, simply trying to survive.

The peasant also does not run away or hide from the consequences of his actions the way a criminal would. After the peasant makes up his tale of selling a cowskin for three hundred gold pieces, his neighbors slaughter all their cows, ruin themselves, and then come looking for him, seeking vengeance. The peasant does not flee, which would be the smart thing to do, but lets the villagers seize him and condemn him to death. Even more dramatically, when the peasant escapes execution by having the shepherd take his place in the barrel, the peasant later reappears in town instead of hiding. Unlike a sociopath, the peasant does not evade responsibility for his actions.

These two traits—resorting to trickery out of necessity and not denying responsibility for one's actions—are characteristic of Tricksters across cultures. Tricksters are thieves and steal things through deceptions, just like the little peasant. Hermes, the Greek Trickster, was the patron of robbers, while Legba of Africa, Coyote of North America, and Maui of Polynesia prided themselves on their clever thievery. Yet behind the Trickster's deceptions is harsh necessity. Odin, the Norse god, provides an example particularly relevant to our German fairy tale. Less familiar as a Trickster than the infamous Loki, Odin qualifies as one, because of his many deceits and ruses.[7] Odin frequently lied, cheated at riddle games, and even broke sacred oaths. But he did so for one purpose: to defend the gods against the frost giants who threatened to destroy the world. Odin had to be shrewd, cunning, and often cynical, like the little peasant, because he lived in a harsh, competitive world.

Odysseus offers another example. Called "the wily Greek" by Homer, Odysseus resorted to tricky deceptions out of necessity, as his encounter with the Cyclops dramatizes. When the Cyclops trapped Odysseus and his crew in a cave, the monster proceeded to eat a few men for dinner. To escape, Odysseus and his sailors secretly made a giant spear, tricked the Cyclops into becoming drunk, blinded the monster when he fell asleep, and then fled to safety. Odysseus resorted to trickery in order to survive, just like the little peasant. After escaping, however, he taunted the monster. "If anyone asks who outwitted you," Odysseus yelled from his ship, "tell them it was Odysseus." This turned out to be a terrible mistake, because the Cyclops appealed to his father, the god Poseidon, to wreak vengeance on Odysseus. Poseidon obliged, delaying the wily Greek's return home with many calamities. In revealing his name, Odysseus acted partly out of pride, but there is also a deeper truth here. Like the little peasant, Odysseus is not a simple criminal, whose goal is to remain unknown and escape punishment. In general, after stealing, Tricksters do not flee and try to evade responsibility for their actions. They typically stay around to see the results of their ruses and suffer the consequences. In African lore, Eshu habitually stirred up trouble, watched what happened, only to be attacked by his victims. The same applies to other Tricksters, like Coyote and Wakdjunkaga of North America.

HIDDEN WISDOM

In accepting the consequences of their actions, Tricksters like the little peasant or Odysseus consciously acknowledge the shadow. Here they offer a vital lesson for men: indulging the shadow in small ways and accepting the consequences, the way the little peasant does, is therapeutic. It prevents more-violent eruptions which result from denying the shadow completely, as happens with the peasant's neighbors. The peasant's tricks and the scandalous deeds of Tricksters function like vaccinations. A mild bout with the shadow prevents a more dangerous infection. In mythological terms, making offerings to the shadowy gods of the underworld keeps them happy and prevents disaster. In psychological language, the Trickster makes the shadow conscious, so that men do not blindly enact their dark impulses. This, I think, is why men's tales like "The Little Peasant" show men becoming criminals at midlife. The stories bring up the shadow *in fantasy,* so that men do not need to act it out *in reality.* The tales are therapeutic.

In acknowledging the shadow, the Trickster contrasts with the hero and the patriarch who claim to be virtuous, noble, and just. Yet heroes and patriarchs steal and lie. They take booty from those they kill in war and dominate the survivors. In peace they hoard wealth and power, exploiting those beneath them. Heroes and patriarchs justify their actions with ideological explanations. They claim to "liberate" their wartime enemies and cite property rights for peacetime privileges. The Trickster dispenses with all rationalizations. By openly stealing, he explicitly brings up the shadow.

In ignoring their dark side, heroes and patriarchs usually project it on other people. They see themselves as good, virtuous, and honorable men, while they denounce their enemies as evil, sneaky, and barbaric. Typically, patriarchal cultures project the shadow on the Trickster (and women, too), the way the villagers blame the peasant for their misfortune. This helps explain the Trickster's unfairly odious reputation. He brings up issues that the hero and the patriarch try to hide, so patriarchal traditions suppress him. As "The Little Peasant" illustrates, conventional society also tries to kill off Trickster figures.

Besides bringing up the shadow, the Trickster's stealing conceals a very specific and profound insight. By stealing, the Trickster emphasizes that whatever he gains comes only at the expense of another person. This reflects a "zero-sum" view: one person's profit means another's loss, so that gain and debit add up to zero. The little peasant dramatizes the point when he gains a cow at the cowherd's expense, escapes execution by having the shepherd killed in his place, and inherits the village when all his neighbors perish. The peasant gains from other people's losses. The story emphasizes the zero-sum theme with a small detail: there is no magic in the drama. The little peasant rescues the raven with its broken wing, and in most fairy tales of youth such an animal would turn out to be magical. It would help the protagonist find a wonderful treasure and bring new wealth into society. No such thing happens to the peasant. He has to manufacture his own luck, and what he gains must come from someone else.

The zero-sum motif is characteristic of Tricksters. Odysseus' encounter with the Cyclops is again instructive. The wily Greek's plan to blind the Cyclops required some time to carry out. Meanwhile, the Cyclops killed and ate more men, just as Odysseus knew would happen. Odysseus accepted the cruel fact that a few crewmen had to die so that the rest might live. This is the zero-sum attitude in its bleakest form. Nor did Odysseus glorify the dead men. He wept for them. Death was a loss and a tragedy, not a triumphant sacrifice, as it is to young heroes. In Norse mythology, Odin also followed the zero-sum game. In one episode, Odin went on a quest to gain the power of prophecy, and he learned that to succeed he had to gouge out one of his eyes and hang himself on the branches of Yggdrasil, the World Tree. Odin made the dreadful sacrifice. Although he was chief of the gods, he still had to obey the zero-sum rule, paying a steep price to win the power of prophecy.

By midlife most men will identify with the Trickster's zero-sum realism, having encountered their own Cyclops, perhaps in the form of a destructive marriage, an abusive boss, or a devouring father. Escape is possible from the monstrous situation, but only with costly ransom. Like Odysseus, men must kill off some of their "inner crew," for example, suppressing artistic sensibility in order to be competitive and tough. Like Odin, men also suffer grievous wounds to win insight and wisdom. Midlife itself forces the zero-sum philosophy on men, because by then men have only a limited number of years in which to accomplish their goals and pursuing one dream means giving up others.

The Trickster's zero-sum outlook also applies to relationships. Many women feel that men are psychological thieves, asking for emotional support from them at home but offering little in return, or expecting women co-workers to fetch coffee without reciprocating the favor. This emotional stealing and exploitation reflects the heroic and patriarchal tradition, not the spirit of the Trickster. The hero and the patriarch expect others to do their bidding and feel entitled to many privileges, but they ignore the costs of their prerogatives to other people. The Trickster reckons *all* costs and benefits, not just to himself but to people around him. This is the essence of his zero-sum perspective, which the Trickster exaggerates by his emphasis on stealing. He dramatizes the sacrifices and costs inherent in any relationship. The Trickster's insight is particularly relevant today, when women reject the patriarchal assumption that they will sacrifice themselves for family and children. As women pursue careers, their husbands grapple with a zero-sum situation: there is only so much time and energy to handle career, family, and parental responsibilities, so husband and wife must juggle multiple demands, and devotion to one area requires stealing time from the others.

THE TRICKSTER'S GENERATIVITY

The zero-sum attitude easily leads to selfishness. In a ruthless world, why not cheat as much as possible? Here "The Little Peasant" adds a subtle warning. The original version of the story specifically says the peasant lived in a village where everybody else was rich. So when the peasant dupes the cowherd into giving him a real cow for the wooden one, the peasant steals from someone better off than himself. Later, the peasant takes three hundred gold coins from the miller, who also seems well able to afford it. (The miller has cakes and roast beef all over his house!) At no time in the story does the peasant steal from those less fortunate than he. In particular, he does not trick any children and adolescents.

The theme is subtle, but becomes clearer in other men's tales, like "The Fisherman and the Mermaid" from Wales, "Master Francesco-Sit-Down-and-Eat" from Italy, "Three Wonderful Beggars" from Serbia, and "The Devil With Three Golden Hairs" from Germany. These tales show that mature men can lie and cheat their peers or superiors with impunity, but if they take from younger people or those less fortunate than themselves, the men are destroyed. Behind all the trickery and cheating, a fundamental rule holds—generativity. As Erik Erikson defined the term, generativity is a spirit of protecting, nourishing, and cherishing the next generation, one's children, students, and protégés. More broadly, generativity is generosity to those less fortunate. "The Little Peasant" reveals that men can cheat those better off than themselves, but not those worse off. This is the ethic of the legendary Robin Hood.

The generativity of Tricksters is often hidden. Robert Pelton emphasized this in his analysis of Tricksters: they often seem selfish and evil, but they are fundamentally on the side of life and creativity. Loki, the shadowy Norse Trickster, dramatizes the point. Through his deceits, Loki caused the death of Baldur, the beloved son of Odin. Through further ruses, Loki foiled the gods' attempt to retrieve Baldur from the land of the dead. According to Norse tradition, Loki would also provoke the ultimate battle between the gods and demons in which the world would be destroyed. But, and this is crucial, a new world would arise from the ruins of the old, and one of the leaders of the dawning age would be Baldur. He would survive the wholesale destruction of the old gods because he was imprisoned and protected in the land of the dead. Loki's machinations seem shadowy and criminal at first, but they ultimately lead to renewal. It is this hidden generativity which separates the Trickster from a simple shadow figure or a mindless savage. The point surfaced earlier in "The North

Wind's Gift," which distinguished the Wind from the savage thugs. The Wind tricked the peasant into opening the golden box, releasing the ruffians, who beat him. But behind the Wind's brutal prank lay a desire to help the peasant. Underneath the violence was generativity.

THE WISDOM OF HUMOR

Other traits of Tricksters help explain many details in "The Little Peasant." Indeed, the Trickster archetype illuminates tales of mature men, just as the hero archetype explains fairy tales about youth. Humor, for instance, is prominent in "The Little Peasant." Such comedy is also typical of men's tales and Trickster stories. Behind the humor lies profound insight into mature manhood. The Trickster's humor is satirical, as the peasant demonstrates when he makes the philandering parson bolt from the closet like a demon out of hell, poking fun at priests and ministers. A more subtle parody occurs later in the tale, when the peasant tricks the shepherd into taking his place in the barrel and the shepherd drowns. In Christian tradition, the preeminent example of a self-sacrificing shepherd who saves the lives of others is Christ. (Since the story comes from a Christian culture, we can assume that the storyteller and the audience would be familiar with the theme.) Instead of revering the martyred shepherd, "The Little Peasant" makes fun of the man and portrays him as a buffoon. Sacrilegious humor like this is characteristic of Tricksters. From Ananse in Africa, to Wakdjunkaga in North America, Tricksters make fun of authorities and dogmas, and the purpose behind their humor is to break up rigid conventions for the sake of creative, new alternatives.[8] The Trickster's humor helps men laugh themselves beyond the hero and patriarch. (The King with goat's ears did exactly that in Chapter 3, when he learned to laugh at himself.)

The humor in "The Little Peasant" borders on the macabre because so many people lose their fortune and their lives. The story threads a very narrow path between cruelty and comedy. This black humor surfaces repeatedly in men's tales and in Trickster stories around the world, like "One Trick Deserves Another'' from the Kikuyu in Africa, "Just Deserts" from Tunisia, and "The Woodcutter with a Brain" from Morocco. The black humor is archetypally masculine, and many women find it distressing. They deplore men's habit of putting each other down with witty, cutting remarks. Yet the dark, biting comedy reflects an important task for mature men—transforming aggression, anger, envy, jealousy, and frustration into something useful and enjoyable. The Trickster's humor does this by neutralizing or "sublimating" shadowy impulses. As students of humor have noted, biting wit allows us to be nasty and polite at the same time, letting us speak the unspeakable. Sublimating aggression and anger through humor is particularly important for men at midlife. In youth, men channel their aggression into competition at work or sports, romantic "conquests" of women, or attacks on "the establishment." By midlife, many men have become part of the establishment, so they cannot rail against it. At the same time, victory at work becomes less likely as the prospect of further promotions recedes. Competitive sports also become more painful with an aging body, and most men, particularly if they have dealt with the inner feminine, abandon the "conquest" image in their relationships with women. So men's traditional outlets for aggression fail. Yet men have more reason to feel frustrated and trapped in the middle years. In this situation, the Trickster's wit offers an invaluable outlet. His black humor is therapeutic and helps men come to terms with their anger, frustration, and aggression.

Macabre humor also transforms and redeems tragedy, as Sigmund Freud emphasized. Wit, he observed, allows individuals to triumph over misfortune. Freud specifically had gallows humor in mind, the amusement of a man who can see the absurdity of the human situation and laugh at his own death. "The Little Peasant" reflects this humor, for example in having all the villagers drown trying to catch sheep on the bottom of the river. The situation is ludicrous, allowing us to laugh at both greed and death, two unfortunate constants of the human condition. The wit of Tricksters helps mature men come to terms with tragedy and death.

A recent Trickster tale highlights the point. It is the story of a Hopi man who belonged to the society of sacred clowns in his tribe, a secret fraternity.[9] A variant of the Trickster, Hopi clowns do outrageous things at religious ceremonies. They usually appear by suddenly jumping down from high buildings, and then parody tribal priests and officials. The clowns poke fun at marriage and funerals and make light of love or death to prevent people from taking religious dogmas—or life itself—too seriously. This particular Hopi clown was highly respected among his people, and when he died his tribe gathered to honor him. To everyone's horror, the man's closest friends carried his corpse to the roof of a tall building and threw the body to the ground! The clown had arranged beforehand for the gruesome rite to make fun of his funeral and to appear one last time the way sacred clowns usually do, by jumping from rooftops and disrupting solemn rituals. He made his funeral into a wild comedy and scandalized everybody. At the same time, like the little peasant, he helped transform tragedy and loss into humor and laughter.

One final point is important about the humor in "The Little Peasant." The peasant plays pranks on other people, but he also suffers many setbacks himself. He is not a detached observer, immune from the drama. He is entangled in the mess with everybody, and if he were not, the story would be sadistic, not funny. This is true of Tricksters in general. They are the victims of hilarious pranks as often as they are the perpetrators. More important, Tricksters mock themselves as much as they poke fun at others. Such self-deprecating humor is characteristic of mature individuals, in contrast to the wit of young men who usually mock other people.[10] The young hero, after all, aims to surpass everybody else, and for him humor is merely one more means of winning. To the Trickster, wit makes everybody equal: humor reveals everyone's foolishness and the absurdity of the human condition.

Wakdjunkaga, the Winnebago Trickster, offers an excellent example of the Trickster's self-deprecating humor. He fell into trouble so often that he developed a ritual exclamation, "Ah, for this I am called 'Wakdjunkaga,' meaning 'the foolish one'!" Heroes and patriarchs, by contrast, hardly ever laugh at their errors, and fairy tales of youth, dominated by these two archetypes, are rarely funny. Wakdjunkaga's exclamation, I might add, has become a great comfort to me. After doing or saying something particularly stupid, I simply repeat his words silently to myself, like a mantra or prayer, "Ah, for this I am like Wakdjunkaga, the foolish one!" and it relieves the pain of wounded male pride.

In mocking people, society, and themselves, Tricksters accept and tolerate human foibles. The little peasant pokes fun at the miller's wife by revealing where she hid all her food, but he does not denounce her to her husband. The peasant also lets the parson escape from the closet, rather than expose him and have him punished. The peasant's tolerance is lifesaving because the minister later lets him escape from the barrel. The peasant's actions convey an acceptance of human faults, rather than a lofty condemnation of it. His attitude symbolizes another task for mature men—giving up the demanding, often rigid, moral idealism of youth in exchange for a more humane and humble moral stance. The Trickster helps men with the task because his wild antics strain conventional ethical notions, stretching men's moral muscles to make them more flexible.

TRICKSTERS IN MEN'S LIVES

This lengthy discussion of the Trickster may seem esoteric. However, Tricksters are the stuff of men's lives and not merely creatures of theory or fairy tale. Tricksters commonly appear in men's dreams and fantasies at midlife, and Robert Moore and Douglas Gillette offer a poignant example in their book, *King, Warrior, Magician, Lover*. During an exercise of guided imagery, a man in his middle years was astonished to find a Trickster figure materialize. The Trickster threatened the man and said he was setting the man up for a disastrous fall. When the man asked the reason for this, the Trickster explained that he was the voice of the man's true feelings, and that he wanted wine, women, song—a break from work and achievement. The Trickster demanded the man give up his heroic ambitions and patriarchal discipline to explore new ways of life.

Accepting the Trickster is not always easy, as illustrated by a dream I had some years ago. In the episode, I watched a group of men gambling, drinking, and cavorting in a huge underground sewer, laughing and having a good time. Although brief, the dream was powerful and I was scandalized by it. The men represented all the unruly, wild, hedonistic and Tricksterish energies I had suppressed in my youth, like other men. Such a negative reaction is typical when men first encounter the Trickster in their lives.

Fortunately, the Trickster also takes more appealing forms. For Nathan, who came to me for therapy, a positive Trickster figure prompted a midlife career change. A business executive, Nathan had risen steadily on the corporate ladder as a result of hard work and dedication. When offered a promotion to be his company's president, Nathan was ecstatic and proud. Then he realized that the new position would require extensive travel away from his family, and he began to have doubts about his career for the first time. In this midlife quandary, Nathan started psychotherapy, and we struggled to sort out the deeper issues behind his indecision—his youthful dream of running his own business, the desire to be more successful than his father, his fear of neglecting his children the way his father neglected him, and his growing awareness of how much he depended emotionally on his wife. Then Nathan had a "big" dream. In it, he was the groom at a wedding, standing at the altar with his bride. A large crowd was gathered in the church, with many dignitaries from Nathan's company. Just as the minister was about to begin the marriage vows, a man came dancing up the aisle, dressed in a costume with bright yellow feathers, like Big Bird on the television program "Sesame Street." The commotion interrupted the ceremony, and everyone began clamoring loudly.

Nathan associated the wedding with his pending promotion because he feared his new position would require so much time and effort from him that it would be like a marriage. This reflected a new zero-sum perspective on his part. He had previously ignored the cost of his career to his family, but now he worried about the effect of frequent business trips on his wife and children. Profit to his career now meant loss to his family. As if to confirm the point, a Trickster figure pops up, the outrageous Big Bird figure. Tricksters, as discussed before, personify the zero-sum outlook. Nathan readily identified Big Bird as a part of him that wanted to do something wild and crazy. He also realized just how tired he was of his long hours and heavy responsibilities at work. He had been a conscientious individual from childhood, working from an early age, and he rarely took long vacations. The dream changed all that. Nathan declined the promotion to president, moved to a smaller company, worked fewer hours, bought a vacation property in the wilderness, and began spending much of his free time fishing or hiking with his family.

In Nathan's dream, Big Bird plays a role similar to that of the Hopi clowns mentioned earlier. The feathered creature interrupts a serious ceremony, demanding attention for all the "scandalous" impulses Nathan had repressed in youth, his wild, playful, indulgent, fun-loving side. Opposed to work, responsibility, power, and achievement, the Tricksterish Big Bird helped Nathan break free from the heroic and patriarchal ideal of manhood. Nathan felt rejuvenated as a result.

CONCLUSIONS

"The Little Peasant" suggests that Tricksters personify the psychology of mature men. The assertion is initially surprising, baffling, and distressing because the little peasant seems to be a criminal and Tricksters generally have a bad reputation. A closer look at both, though, reveals that their shadowy appearance conceals a new and positive vision of manhood, distinct from heroic and patriarchal ideals. The peasant's stealing, for instance, reflects the sobering insight that one person's gain often comes from another's loss. Heroes and patriarchs deny this zero-sum reality by focusing only on their personal profits and ignoring the cost to others. Women have traditionally paid the price for heroes and patriarchs, sacrificing themselves for husbands and sons. The Trickster demands that men become conscious of such psychological thievery. Age also forces the zero-sum insight on men, as the boundless optimism of youth gives way to the finite realities of midlife. By making shadowy realities explicit through stories and fantasy, the Trickster helps men deal with the dark side of life, with envy, frustration, and despair. Tricksters use humor to detoxify men's anger and aggression, unlike the hero and patriarch who glorify both. The Trickster also uses wit to transform the tragedies of human life. Instead of despairing over old age and death, the Trickster laughs, celebrating the craziness of the human condition. Ultimately, the Trickster is therapeutic for men. He helps men deal with painful midlife issues and introduces them to a new, more mature masculine vitality.

At the same time, the Trickster pokes fun at the hero and the patriarch, the way the peasant mocked the parson and the Church. This helps men break free from traditional male roles, but it also provokes the enmity of patriarchal culture. Society therefore suppresses the Trickster, calls him a criminal, and tries to kill him, the way the peasant's neighbors attempted to execute him. This is why the Trickster suffers from a bad reputation and why his wisdom is not immediately obvious. Patriarchal society rejects him, forcing him to hide. The Trickster represents a positive, male archetype normally concealed in the unconscious. This is the definition of the deep masculine, hinting that the Trickster is the spirit behind the wild man and the deep masculine. If the suggestion came from only "The Little Peasant," the interpretation would be tenuous, but other men's tales make the conclusion inescapable. Beneath the Trickster's apparently criminal behavior lies a rich, paradoxical, and profound male energy. Indeed, when men venture beyond the hero and stumble in confusion, the Trickster appears in the nick of time to become mentor, therapist, teacher, and companion, as the next tale shows.

CHAPTER SIX

The King and the Ghoul: The Trickster Teacher

---

the king and the ghoul

(FROM INDIA)

O nce upon a time, there lived a great and noble King. Each morning he sat in his audience hall, hearing the petitions of his people. One day, a hermit approached the King, gave the monarch a beautiful fruit, and then departed. The King handed the gift to his minister without further thought. Years went by, and each day the sage presented the King with a fruit and departed without a word.

One morning, the holy man gave the King his usual gift and departed. A pet monkey grabbed the fruit from the King's hands, ate it, and spat out the pit. The King stared in astonishment—the seed was a priceless jewel! The King turned to his minister. "What did you do with the other fruit?"

"I threw them in the treasury room," the minister replied. The two men hastened there and found a mound of rotting fruit. And hidden within the refuse lay a pile of glittering gems.

The next day, the hermit approached the King with another fruit. The monarch exclaimed, "Venerable sage, how can I thank you for your priceless gifts? I am deeply in your debt. If you need anything of me, ask what you will, and I shall help you."

The holy man bowed. "I gave you the precious fruit because you are the noblest and bravest man on earth," the ascetic told the monarch. "In my spiritual labors, I need the assistance of a man like you."

"Name what you need. I will help," the King replied.

The holy man bowed again. "Meet me tomorrow at midnight, at the cremation grounds in the cemetery. I will explain everything to you then."

"I will be there," the King declared. The next night, the King went alone to the graveyard, and to where the dead were cremated. The place was frightful, filled with the smell of burnt flesh. Human bones lay scattered everywhere, and ghosts prowled about. But the King was a brave man and did not turn back. He searched for the sage and found him in the middle of the cemetery, sitting beside a makeshift altar.

"I have come to help you," the King announced.

The ascetic nodded with approval. "You are truly brave and noble," the hermit said, "to keep your word and come to so frightful a place."

"What do you wish of me?" the King asked.

The holy man replied, "I am conducting an important religious ritual, and for this ceremony, I require the body of the criminal, hanging from the gallows tree there." The hermit pointed in the distance. "Cut the corpse from the tree and bring it to me. That is the only help I require."

The King nodded. The task sounded grisly, but he had promised to aid the ascetic. The King walked to the gallows tree, climbed up, and cut the corpse down. He put the body on his back and started toward the hermit.

The cadaver spoke up. "I greet you, royal sir!"

The King dropped the body in astonishment, and the corpse flew back into the tree, laughing like a demon. "A ghoul!" the King exclaimed, realizing the cadaver was inhabited by a demon. But the King was determined to bring the body to the holy man. So he climbed into the gallows tree again, picked up the corpse, hoisted it on his back, and started toward the mendicant.

The ghoul laughed. "The way is long, and your burden is heavy. So I will tell you a riddle to while away the time. If you know the answer and do not speak, you will die. But if you say the answer, I will fly back into the tree with the corpse."

The ghoul began his tale. Long ago, a beautiful woman was wooed by three men. Before she could choose her husband, she died and was cremated according to the custom of her people. Overcome with grief, one suitor sat in her ashes, weeping and lamenting. The second suitor gathered her bones and carried them wherever he went. The last man wandered the land, despairing of life. One day, the third man learned how to resurrect the dead. So he hastened back to the other two men and told them how they could revive the woman they loved. The first suitor gathered the ashes in which he had sat. The second man produced the woman's bones. And the third took the ashes and bones and resurrected the woman. When she was restored to life, the three men argued over who should marry her.

The ghoul turned to the King, and asked, "Which of the three suitors should be the woman's husband?" The King pondered a moment, and then said, "The man who raised the woman from the dead is like her father who brought her to life. The suitor who carried the woman's bones and cherished them is like a son, who takes care of his mother. But the man who sat in the ashes was like a husband, remaining faithful to her. So he should marry the woman." The ghoul cackled and flew back to the gallows tree with the corpse.

The King clenched his teeth, returned to the tree, retrieved the cadaver, and lifted it on his back. The ghoul laughed wickedly. "You are a patient man," the ghoul said. "So let me tell you another riddle."

Once upon a time, a demon killed a man's wife. The husband was heartbroken because he loved her deeply, so he gave up his worldly belongings and became an ascetic, wandering the land and begging for food. One day, he came to a noble residence, and the mistress of the house gave him a bowl of rice to eat. The man left the food under a tree while he washed in a stream. A snake ate some of the rice and accidentally dripped its venom in the bowl. When the man consumed the rice, he became sick. He accused the nobleman of poisoning him, and the man in turn blamed his wife.

The ghoul whispered in the King's ear, "My good friend, tell me who is responsible for the poisoning?" The King paused a moment, and then replied. "Nobody is, and it is wrong to blame anyone." The ghoul laughed and vanished into the night, taking the corpse with him.

The King turned around, returned to the gruesome tree, and found the body hanging there. He took it down, and carried it once more on his back. "Dear friend," the ghoul said, "I see you do not give up. So I will tell you another tale."

Long ago, the ghoul began, a thief plagued a city, and nobody could catch him. Finally the King himself went to search for the robber. They met, and the King pretended to be a thief. The two joined together to rob several houses. Then the thief took the King to his home in the underworld. When the King was alone in the robber's house, a servant warned the monarch that the thief planned to murder him. The King escaped, returned to his palace, mustered all his troops, and captured the thief. The ruler then sentenced the robber to die. As the felon was led to the gallows, a maiden saw him and fell in love with the thief. She ran up to the King and pleaded for him to spare the criminal. The King refused, so the maiden vowed to kill herself. Hearing this, the outlaw wept, and then he laughed.

The ghoul paused and said, "This is my question. Why did the convict weep and laugh?" The King thought about the matter for several minutes, and then he answered, "The thief wept because he was moved by the woman's love, and he knew he could not return her sacrifice with any comparable gift. But he laughed, seeing the absurdity of his fate—to have a beautiful woman fall in love with him just before he died!" Instantly, the ghoul flew up into the dark sky, taking the corpse with him.

Over and over that night, the King returned to the gallows tree, retrieved the dead body, answered another riddle from the ghoul, lost the corpse, and had to start all over again. Finally, the ghoul told a riddle the monarch could not solve.

Long ago, the demon said, a King and his son went hunting. The King was a widower, and the Prince a bachelor. In the forest, the two men found two sets of human footprints, one large and one small. With their skill as trackers, the two men deduced that the footsteps came from a highborn woman and her daughter, who were fleeing in haste for some reason. Father and son agreed that when they met the two women, they would propose marrying them. The King would wed the woman with the big footprints, since she would be the older woman, the mother, while the Prince would marry the woman with the small footprints, who would be younger, and thus the daughter. They soon found the two women and learned that they were a widowed Queen and a Princess, fleeing their homeland because of an invasion. The King and Prince offered them refuge in their country, and proposed marriage. The women accepted, but it turned out that the Queen had small feet, and the Princess, big ones. The father and son still kept their agreement. So the King married the woman with the bigger feet, namely the Princess, and the Prince married the woman with the smaller feet, namely the Queen. Each woman then had a son.

The ghoul cackled with anticipation. "And what, my good King," the ghoul asked, "is the relationship these children will have to each other?"

The King turned the thought over in his head, and became baffled. So he said nothing. Finally the ghoul spoke up. "You are wise," the ghoul said, "to remain silent. And you are brave to persevere in carrying the corpse. I salute you." The demon flew up in the air and bowed to the monarch. "I have grown fond of you in our time together," the ghoul continued, "so I will tell you a terrible secret. The man you are helping is not a holy sage, but an evil magician. He is a necromancer who plans to murder you and use you as a human sacrifice when you bring him this corpse. By doing this, the necromancer will gain power over all spirits." The ghoul paused. "Yet there is a simple way to foil his wicked plans, if you have the courage." The ghoul whispered in the King's ears. "And now," the ghoul concluded, "carry this corpse to the necromancer! And we shall see what destiny has in store for you."

The King hoisted his grisly burden on his back and went to the "holy man." The "sage" was delighted. "You are the bravest man who has ever lived," the necromancer declared. He asked the King to set the corpse up before the altar and bow down before it, prostrate on the ground, as if to worship it. The necromancer secretly drew a sword, with which to behead the King.

"Alas, my dear friend," the King replied, remembering what the ghoul advised. "I was born a prince, and I have never bowed down before to anyone or anything. So I do not know the proper way to do this ritual. If you show me, I will follow your example."

Impatiently the necromancer said, "It is simple. Just do this." The evil magician prostrated himself on the ground before the corpse, and touched his face to the earth. At that moment, the King drew his sword, and struck off the villain's head. Then he completed the necromancer's nefarious ritual, using the magician's corpse the way the villain had planned to use his body.

In the next moment, a thousand spirits and gods materialized in the cemetery, and they exalted the King for his courage and honor. The great god Shiva appeared and praised the King. "You will have unlimited glory," Shiva promised the monarch, "in this world and the next. If there is any further boon you wish, ask it now, and it will be granted."

The King paused thoughtfully, and then said, "I desire only one thing—that the stories the ghoul told me tonight will be known to all men, so that everyone may benefit from their wisdom."

"It is done," Shiva declared.

And that is how you know this tale!

The Trickster Teacher

THE SHADOW AND THE TRICKSTER

This story is long and complicated. Fortunately, the tale repeats many motifs from previous stories, and the old themes help make sense of the new drama. The protagonist is a King, as commonly occurs in men's tales. Yet the story really starts when the King surrenders his royal prerogatives by leaving his palace and going alone to the cemetery. Symbolically, he abandons the patriarchal paradigm, just like the monarch in "The Sultan's Handkerchief," who walked incognito among his people.

The King specifically goes to a crematorium at midnight. The setting is grisly and demonic and brings up a familiar theme—men's midlife encounter with the shadow. The King's journey to the cemetery is equivalent to the Sultan falling into the cannibal's pit in Chapter 2: both men come face-to-face with evil, death, and tragedy. The present King needs a lesson about the shadow because he is so naive about it. At the beginning of the tale, the King feels grateful to the "holy man" for the priceless jewels, rather than suspicious. Yet why would the "sage" give jewels to the King? Large bribes, after all, usually mean an illicit favor will be requested. The King ignores the warning and blithely promises to help the ascetic without knowing what "the sage" wants. The King compounds his indiscretion when he agrees to meet the "holy man" on the cremation grounds at midnight, a time and place more properly the domain of demons, ghosts, and evildoers.

The necromancer makes a good shadow figure. Where the King strives to be just, kind, and noble, the magician is devious, cruel, and villainous. (The two men parallel the Sultan and the cannibal cook in Chapter 2.) Moreover, we later learn that the necromancer desires dominion over all spirits, seeking power over the dead and not just the living. He represents the patriarchal principle carried to an extreme and reflects the shadow side of the patriarchy. (The necromancer thus resembles the wizard king in

Chapter 1, who abused his power to kidnap the beautiful princess.)[1] Significantly, the necromancer is something of a Trickster and deceives the King throughout the story. The fruit he gives the King seems ordinary but really conceals priceless jewels. The beautiful gems in turn disguise the hermit's evil purpose, because he is not really a holy man but a necromancer who plans to murder the King.[2] As a tricky shadow figure, the magician reiterates a theme from "The Little Peasant": the Trickster is closely linked to the shadow.

The King encounters the shadow in another form when he grapples with the corpse of a criminal, something horrible and repugnant. Pacing back and forth in the cemetery with the dead body on his back, the King dramatizes a difficult phase for men in the middle years. At this time, men struggle with the grief and pain they avoided or denied in youth, carrying the corpses of past loves, murdered dreams, and childhood traumas. The torment and timing differ for each man, but the process is similar. For one individual, the corpse might be a shameful deed committed in youth, for another a marriage dissolved in bitterness, and for a third a talent never developed which then withered away. Often there is a real cadaver, because aged fathers die, leaving their middle-aged sons to labor with painful memories and lingering regrets. In carrying corpses, men walk what Robert Bly eloquently calls "the road of ashes," and many men start therapy for the first time when they reach this dark inner place.

In such a painful situation, men may be tempted to seek solace from women, turning to the anima or more commonly to wives, daughters, and mistresses for support. Women, for their part, will feel an urge to rescue their men, the way Zakia did in "The Sultan's Handkerchief." Yet men's challenge is to bear their burden and walk back and forth in the cemetery. Women's task is to wait, painful though it may be to watch husbands, sons, and lovers suffer. This leads to a problem. As discussed earlier, at midlife men must turn to the feminine for help. So when should men do this, rather than take the road of ashes? A man's history offers the answer. If he still fears the feminine and denigrates women even in subtle ways, a man's task is to learn about the anima and honor the feminine. But if a man has befriended his anima and developed good relationships with real women, his next task is to carry a corpse in the inner graveyard.

The ghoul makes his appearance in the cemetery and initially seems to be another shadow figure. Yet he is far more. (There are many versions of this Hindu tale, but all make clear that the ghoul is male.) For one thing, the ghoul is a Trickster figure. He tells the King tricky riddles and puts the monarch in an impossible situation. If the King answers the riddles, the ghoul steals the corpse and returns it to the gallows tree. If the King does not answer, but knows the solution, the ghoul threatens to kill the King. Either way, the King loses, and this is typical of the dilemmas that Tricksters foist on people. Because he harasses the King, the ghoul seems to be an enemy of the monarch. As the story proceeds, though, the ghoul reveals his helpful, healing side. In fact, he teaches the King important lessons through riddles, as the details of the ghoul's stories show. He functions as therapist, teacher, and mentor.

THE GHOUL AS TEACHER

The riddles vary in different versions of the epic, but there are usually twenty-four.[3] I retell only four for the sake of brevity and choose the most typical ones. In general, the ghoul's riddles do not portray romantic adventures, with a young hero riding off on a quest, battling an enemy, and then living happily ever after. The stories involve stealing, cheating, and murdering—the plot of ''The Little Peasant'' and the stuff of Tricksters, not heroes. The ghoul's tales also have specific lessons for the King and for men at midlife.

In the first story, a woman is raised from the dead. The ghoul asks which of the woman's three suitors should marry her, and the King solves the problem by comparing the actions of the men to basic family roles. The suitor who brought the woman back to life is like a father who begets a daughter; the man who carried her bones with him is like a son taking care of his mother; but the suitor who sat in her ashes is like a husband remaining with his wife for better or worse. Two points are noteworthy here. First, the riddle focuses on human relationships which are traditionally considered the domain of the feminine. So the ghoul's puzzle reiterates a central task for men at midlife, coming to terms with the feminine. Second, in answering the riddle, the King resorts to social conventions about family roles. He does not have to think for himself, but relies on traditional male roles of son, father, and husband. The ghoul soon forces the King to abandon such conventional thinking.

In the next story, a man is poisoned by a snake which accidentally dripped venom onto the man's rice. The ghoul asks who is guilty of the man's poisoning, and the King answers that no one is. He even insists that blame is not the real issue. This may seem to be mere common sense, but there is a deeper message here. The King explicitly accepts a *tragic* view of life. He acknowledges that there are circumstances beyond human control, and that bad things often happen to good people without reason or blame. In accepting chance and tragedy, the King gives up the faith of heroes and patriarchs, the belief that with enough effort, courage, and skill, everything can be conquered and controlled. Surrendering this youthful optimism is a difficult task for men at midlife, because it forces them to confront their vulnerability.

The third riddle falls into two parts, each with a distinctive theme. In the first half, a thief plagues a city until the ruler personally searches for the brigand, befriends the felon, and goes to the villain's home in the underworld. This is analogous to what happens in the main tale where the King offers to help the necromancer and meets the magician at the cemetery. In the ghoul's riddle, a servant warns the ruler that the brigand plans to murder him, so the ruler escapes and later captures the thief. In the main drama, the King does not yet know that the necromancer plans to murder him, but the ghoul tries to warn him by telling him the story of the murderous thief. (As a Trickster, the ghoul naturally uses tricky, indirect communication.) The ghoul reveals himself to be the King's ally and not his enemy.

The riddle about the thief then shifts to a new theme. A beautiful woman falls in love with the felon and vows to kill herself if he is not pardoned. The villain weeps and laughs, and the ghoul asks the King why the condemned criminal would do so. The King explains that the convict wept out of grief and gratitude, moved by the woman's love. Then the criminal laughed at the absurdity of having a beautiful maiden fall in love with him just before his execution. The King's explanation demonstrates that he has a relatively good understanding of human emotions and relationships. In other words, he has access to his feminine side. The King's answer also reveals that he understands gallows humor. He appreciates how laughter transforms tragedy into comedy, and this is another important lesson from the Trickster, as discussed in "The Little Peasant."

BEYOND OEDIPUS AND LOGOS

The ghoul's last story, the tale of the father and son marrying a mother and daughter, stumps the King. Although different versions of "The King and the Ghoul" present various riddles in changeable order, all end with the same puzzle. Clearly it is significant. Perhaps the most obvious aspect of the riddle is that it reeks of Oedipal themes. The father marries the daughter, and the son marries the mother. The father, of course, does not marry his own daughter, or the son, his own mother. The Oedipal themes are displaced, but the motifs are too prominent to ignore.

The ghoul notes that the Queen and Princess each bear a son and asks what kinship the newborn boys will have to each other. The King is baffled. His confusion with this riddle contrasts with his confidence in solving the problem about the dead woman with three suitors. In the earlier tale, the King used traditional definitions of fathers, sons, and husbands. These conventions fail miserably with the final riddle about the newborn sons. Tracing out the family trees reveals that the two boys are uncle to each other. From the King's side, his newborn son is brother to his already-grown son, the Prince. (Technically, the King's baby boy and the adult Prince are half brothers.) As brother to the Prince, the King's newborn son will be uncle to any children the Prince has. Looking at the Queen's side, her infant boy is brother to her first, grown daughter, the Princess. As brother to the Princess, the Queen's new son will be uncle to the Princess's children. Hence, the two newborn infants are simultaneously uncle and nephew to each other! The situation is mind-boggling because convention demands that one person be the uncle and the other, the nephew. The confusions arise because the children's kinship can be traced through the King's side, *or* the Queen's, through the father or the mother. So the blood ties can be understood in what anthropologists call a "patrilineal" or a "matrilineal" way, that is, through the father's line, or the mother's line. The former is typical of patriarchal societies, yet the King does not automatically choose it. Symbolically, he breaks once more with the patriarchal paradigm.

In presenting two valid, competing viewpoints, the ghoul attacks one of the foundations of patriarchal thinking, the assumption that there is only one right answer to any problem (namely, the patriarch's). The patriarchal pattern of thinking is often called "logos" and can be seen in males from boyhood onward. When boys play games, for instance, they often spend more time arguing about the rules and who is right than actually playing together.[4] Later, young men seek the meaning of life, always assuming there is one answer, the absolute truth. In attacking patriarchal logos, the ghoul reveals the hidden purpose of his riddles. Although the stories seem to wander from topic to topic, they gradually stretch the limits of logos until masculine logic finally snaps.

Only when the King gives up and remains silent with the ghoul's last story does the demon stop stealing the corpse. The story contains an important message here. The King, like most men at midlife, relies on logos to solve his problems. But this only perpetuates his dilemma: the King has to keep retrieving the corpse, the way Sisyphus had to push his stone uphill. Psychologically, when men use only logos, ignoring emotions, and insisting on one right answer to every question, life becomes sterile and repetitive. For men in therapy, one of the biggest challenges is to silence male rationality and to step outside the intellect. Only then do men directly experience their problems—and resolve them. Tricksters like the ghoul help in the process by forcing paradoxes and ambiguities on men, and breaking up the structure of logos. Men then deal with the "irrational" side of life, and especially with feeling and intuitions.

In undermining the King's logos, the ghoul plays a traditional role of Tricksters, who poke fun at fundamental social conventions, sacred dogmas, and basic taboos. As we saw in "The Little Peasant," Tricksters try to dismantle basic rules of thought and action so that people can experiment with new forms of life. Eshu, the Yoruba Trickster, emphasizes the point. Asked why he told lies, Eshu explained, "I like to make people think."[5] The ghoul accomplishes the same task with his riddles, "deconstructing" the King's rational, masculine world view. Indeed, the ghoul's riddles are reminiscent of Zen koans, which paralyze logos, allowing the individual a deeper and more direct experience of the world.

In opposing any single "right" answer and fostering many competing views, the ghoul and other Tricksters are pluralists. Their pluralism is vital to men at midlife and helps men become open to new elements within themselves. By maturity, men discover that they are masculine *and* feminine, strong *and* weak, good and bad, creative and destructive, loving and hateful, all at the same time. To understand and accept this inner complexity, men must tolerate contradictory views of themselves. This mature pluralism contrasts with the heroic self-concept of young men, who suppress any part of themselves that conflicts with their conscious identity. Young men try to rule their psyches like a King over his kingdom. By the middle years, most men give up the effort and settle instead for being the chairman of a raucous, inner committee. The shift is invigorating, because pluralism correlates with creativity, generativity, and greater psychological maturity.[6]

Pluralism also helps men deal with their children and the next generation. At home, middle-aged fathers confront outrageous and provocative opinions from teenage offspring, and at work men encounter new ideas from junior colleagues. In the heroic and patriarchal spirit, men try to suppress these novel views and impose their opinions on others. With the Trickster's pluralism, men listen, experiment, and explore. Pluralism, in fact, resolves the Oedipal competition between father and son. Within patriarchal tradition, there can be only one authority and one truth, so father and son vie for that position. With pluralism, there are many truths and many authorities, so father and son need not compete.

Giving up patriarchal logos is frightening to most men, and

the original myth of Oedipus reveals why. While a young man, Oedipus became King of Thebes with the power of logos: he figured out the riddle of the Sphinx and won the Theban throne. The mature Oedipus, however, was ignorant of the fact that he had killed his father and married his mother. (Both Oedipus and the King in the ghoul's saga are stumped by the same situation, the triangle between mother, father, and child.) When the mature Oedipus learns the truth about his parents, he realizes how blind he has been all his life, and his faith in logos is destroyed. He puts out both his eyes and flees Thebes. Psychologically, when his logos collapses, so does his whole life. Even the city of Thebes disintegrates, falling into a terrible civil war. Logos is a fundamental principle of the patriarchy, so attacking logic raises the specter of chaos. This is another reason men initially see the Trickster as an enemy. Yet he is not an adversary of men, only of heroes and patriarchs. The ghoul, after all, assaults the King's *logos,* not the King himself. Moreover, when logos collapses, calamity results only if men have no alternative. But the Trickster's pluralism provides a new approach to life. In the ghoul's saga, the King does not blind himself, flee, or despair like Oedipus, because the King has the ghoul as a teacher and therapist.

Although he undermines logos, the ghoul uses gentle, indirect ways to do so. This is pragmatic. A direct assault on logos makes men defensive and less likely to change. Women know this instinctively, and tread lightly in challenging male logic. Logos, after all, is a sanctuary of patriarchal tradition, and women's criticism of it will unconsciously feel like sacrilege to many men. As a male, the Trickster can question logos with greater impudence. (This is one reason why male therapists can be particularly helpful with men struggling to break free from logos. But the therapist must be "initiated" and have already ventured beyond traditional masculine reasoning.)

BECOMING A TRICKSTER

When the King remains silent with the last riddle, the ghoul is impressed and tells the monarch what the "holy sage" is really up to. The ghoul shifts from tormentor to teacher, and reveals his true colors: he is an ally, not an enemy. Notice the twists here. The necromancer appears to be friendly and helpful to the King, but really plots to destroy him, while the ghoul initially seems to be evil, and turns out to be the King's teacher. The theme of a helpful Trickster surfaced earlier in "The North Wind's Gift," in which the Wind tricks the poor peasant with the golden box for the peasant's benefit. The present tale elaborates on the motif.

The necromancer asks the King to fall prostrate before the corpse, intending to kill the monarch. Following the ghoul's advice, the King claims to be ignorant of how to bow down, so the magician demonstrates. The King then beheads the magician. The King thus becomes a Trickster. He deceives the necromancer the way the magician deceived him! At the same time, the King becomes a murderer. He does not act in self-defense in beheading the necromancer, since the monarch could have simply left the cemetery when he discovered the magician's plot. The King also kills the necromancer when the villain is prostrate upon the ground and defenseless. No chivalrous hero would strike a helpless man in this way. By heroic standards, the King acts shamefully. He becomes a bit shadowy himself, and his next action reinforces the theme.

After killing the magician, the King completes the necromancer's ritual, using the magician's corpse the way the villain would have used the King's. The monarch becomes a necromancer himself. The distinction between an all-good King and an all-bad necromancer vanishes. The King now includes both good and evil, light and dark. Here the tale dramatizes an important task for men at midlife. Heroes, patriarchs, and young men characteristically split the world into good and bad, identifying themselves with the former and denouncing their opponents as the latter. The challenge to mature men is to recognize both sides within themselves, acknowledging the darkness in their own hearts. The Trickster helps in this task because he is open to his shadow and even boasts about it.

After completing the grisly ritual, spirits and gods materialize and praise the King. In psychological terms, he gains greater access to the unconscious and its powerful archetypes. This is a direct result of the King becoming a Trickster. In giving up logos and adopting the Trickster's pluralism, the King no longer needs to repress or deny shadow elements in himself. He stops trying to dominate the psyche like the hero and patriarch, and his greater psychological openness allows powerful new elements to arise from the unconscious.

When the spirits and gods praise the King, chief among them is Shiva. Significantly, Shiva is a Trickster god in the Hindu pantheon. The King thus meets a divine male Trickster, just the way the oppressed peasant in "The North Wind's Gift" met the North Wind. Both stories depict a mature man gaining access to a sacred and tricky masculine energy. Shiva offers the King any boon as a reward, but the monarch asks for something very simple. He requests that the stories the ghoul told him be known to all people so that everyone can learn from them. The King's request is generative, not selfish, and aims at passing on the wisdom he has received. He does not crave power or glory, emphasizing once more that he has gone beyond the hero and the patriarch.

THE TRICKSTER TEACHER IN MEN'S LIVES

"The King and the Ghoul" portrays an extraordinary saga in which a man meets a Trickster figure who initially appears to be demonic. Yet the Trickster turns out to be an ally, and teaches the man a whole new perspective on life. The same drama frequently emerges in therapy with men today. The ghoul, in fact, plays the role of a wily therapist, but he uses an unorthodox and uniquely masculine approach. The ghoul relies on paradox rather than sympathy and imposes tests instead of offering support. He contrasts with the empathic, nurturing anima.

Therapeutic Tricksters also appear spontaneously in men's inner world, through dreams and fantasy. An example took place in my own life several years before my research on fairy tales. I had a series of almost visionary experiences then, which were not quite dreams but more than fantasies. I could not make sense of these inner adventures, so I wrote them down and put them away. When I worked on this chapter, I remembered a particular episode in these "visions" which repeats the themes of "The King and the Ghoul."

In the imaginary adventure, I went on a journey through many lands, seeking wisdom. Along the way, I met "the Stranger," a mysterious man who rescued me in several dangerous incidents. When the Stranger made his way into a desert, I followed, expecting the best. But there was no food in the wilderness, and after some time I thought I would die of hunger. The Stranger then walked into an ancient ruin and I followed. I found a room filled with roasted meat and impelled by hunger I ate heartily. To my horror, I discovered a human hand in one dish and a human head in another! The banquet was a cannibal's feast! I vomited and fled from the room, only to trip and fall into a chasm. I caught the edge of the abyss just in time and cried for help, unable to pull myself out. The Stranger approached, deliberately stepped on my fingers, and made me plunge into the pit. I fell in terror for a long time, hit water, and descended deeper. Spirits of the dead crowded around me, and I shuddered at their clammy touch. Then I burst out of the darkness into a luminous realm. In that moment, I saw that the world was a hollow sphere, and that I had spent my life journeying on the inner surface of the ball. When I fell into the chasm, I plunged through the thin rind of the world, reaching the true outer surface for the first time, glimpsing the celestial light surrounding the globe.

After working with men's tales, my "vision" made more sense. The imaginary experience began with the appearance of a mysterious Stranger who offered to guide me on a search for wisdom. The Stranger led me into the wilderness until I was famished and then tricked me into eating a cannibal feast. Like the ghoul, the Stranger represents a Trickster figure who acts in an apparently demonic way. The descent to the cannibal feast is analogous to the King's journey to the cremation ground. The cannibal feast itself offers a concrete symbol of integrating the shadow, dramatizing a phrase from Robert Bly, "eating the shadow." As a vile crime, the cannibal feast is also similar to the King's murder of the necromancer and the King's completion of the necromancer's grisly ritual.

In my "vision," the Stranger threw me into the pit and I fell into the world of the dead. Ultimately, I broke through into a transcendent, luminous realm, where I discovered that the world I knew was really the inside of a hollow sphere. My perspective was literally turned upside down and inside out. This is precisely the function of the Trickster teacher, who overthrows logos and conventional reasoning. The mystical experience at the end of the vision also matches the conclusion of "The King and the Ghoul," when the King meets Shiva and all the gods. The parallels between my fantasy and the fairy tale may not be immediately apparent, but this is to be expected: the Trickster loves disguises and takes unexpected forms in men's lives.

THE TRICKSTER AND HATE-TO-BE-CONTRADICTED

The themes in "The King and the Ghoul" cut across cultures. To emphasize this point, I conclude the chapter with a tale of Ananse, the Ashanti Trickster from Africa. This is the story of how Ananse dealt with a villainous character named "Hate-to-be-Contradicted,"[7] and it parallels "The King and the Ghoul" in an amazing way.

Hate-to-be-Contradicted habitually provoked people into disagreeing with him and then killed them. One day, Ananse decided to teach Hate-to-be-Contradicted a lesson and invited the man to his house for a meal. When Hate-to-be-Contradicted arrived, Ananse was absent. The Trickster, however, had instructed his children in what to do.

Hate-to-be-Contradicted asked the children where Ananse was, and they told him that their father had broken his penis in seven pieces the day before and had gone to the blacksmith to have the organ repaired. Hate-to-be-Contradicted said nothing about this preposterous tale, but asked the children where their mother was since she was also absent. The youngsters answered that she went to the stream to catch her waterpot. They explained that she had gone for water the evening before and accidentally dropped her pot. The container would have broken, except she caught it just in time. Unfortunately, their mother did not completely catch the pot, so she had to return in the morning to finish the job! Hate-to-be-Contradicted fumed at the ridiculous story, but he kept silent once more.

Ananse appeared, greeted Hate-to-be-Contradicted warmly, and served his guest a stew filled with peppers. Hate-to-be-

Contradicted soon asked for some water, and a child went out of the house only to return with an empty cup. Hate-to-be-Contradicted asked again for water, the child left, and once more returned empty-handed. Finally, Hate-to-be-Contradicted demanded why the child did not bring water. The boy repeated the story his father had told him to say.

The boy explained that the family waterpot was filled with water, but he could not remove any. This was because the top layer of water belonged to his father, Ananse, and the boy could not touch that. The middle layer belonged to Ananse's first wife, and the boy did not want to disturb it. The bottom layer belonged to Ananse's second wife, who was the child's mother, so the boy wanted to use only that water. But he dared not mix up the different layers of water because that would cause great trouble in the family.

The child's preposterous tale was too much for Hate-to-be-Contradicted, and he accused the boy of lying. Ananse immediately attacked Hate-to-be-Contradicted, exclaiming, "You hate people who contradict you, and you kill them when they do, yet you contradict my son!" The Trickster beat Hate-to-be-Contradicted to death, cut up the villain's body, and scattered the pieces over the earth. And that is how contradiction spread throughout the world!

In the Ashanti tale, Hate-to-be-Contradicted kills anyone who disagrees with him. He makes a good symbol of patriarchal logos, which rejects contradiction and assumes there must be one right answer to any issue, namely the patriarch's opinion. As a nasty, evil character, Hate-to-be-Contradicted is also a shadow figure, just like the necromancer in "The King and the Ghoul." To provoke Hate-to-be-Contradicted, Ananse presents him with progressively more preposterous tales, which are similar in spirit to the ghoul's riddles. Ananse's tales also poke fun at logos. Ananse's wife, for instance, supposedly dropped her water jar, but did not finish catching the pot and returned the next day to finish the job. The story mocks the focus of logos on abstract distinctions, like separating the beginning and end of an action as two independent things. Ananse's final tale about drawing water from the water pot is particularly symbolic. The idea that different people own distinct layers of water in a vessel is ridiculous, so Ananse parodies the discriminating function of logos again. Ananse's story also contains implicit Oedipal themes. The boy says he can draw water only from his mother's portion at the bottom of the pot. To do so he has to disturb the top layer of water, which belongs to his father, Ananse, and the middle level which belongs to Ananse's first wife. So a boy wants something from his mother but dares not obtain it, because his father (and another of his father's wives) stand in the way. The situation sums up the Oedipal drama, adjusted for the polygamy of Ashanti culture.

The final tale is too much for Hate-to-be-Contradicted. He blows up, contradicts the boy, and is killed by Ananse. Symbolically, patriarchal logos explodes when confronted with an Oedipal paradox, the way the King cannot solve the ghoul's final riddle in the Hindu tale. By killing Hate-to-be-Contradicted, Ananse becomes exactly like his victim, intolerant of anyone who disagrees with him. So Ananse becomes Hate-to-be-Contradicted for the moment, and this parallels what happens in "The King and the Ghoul" when the monarch kills the necromancer and becomes a black magician himself. The similarity between the two stories, one from Africa and one from India, is clear. The parallels reveal the deep structure of the male psyche and what men have in common despite cultural differences.

Both stories also confirm important themes from "The Little Peasant" in the last chapter. The three tales portray Trickster figures who initially seem shadowy or criminal. The little peasant steals from his neighbors, the ghoul harasses the King, while Ananse abuses his guest. Yet behind their shadowy actions lies a positive masculine energy opposed to patriarchal conventions and personified by the Trickster. The peasant mocks the patriarchal figure of the parson, while the ghoul and Ananse attack logos, a fundamental principle of the patriarchy. These assaults on patriarchal tradition seek to liberate men from conventional masculine roles. As a result, men ideally become pluralists, open to differences of opinion, new ideas from the next generation, and to their own inner complexity—to being weak and strong, kind and cruel, masculine and feminine. The Trickster also teaches men to laugh at themselves, to see the humor in apparently tragic situations, and to experiment with life. The peasant, the ghoul, Ananse, and other Tricksters, in short, offer an alternative to the heroic and patriarchal paradigm of masculine power. This new vision of male energy is specifically post-heroic and post-patriarchal, as "The King and the Ghoul" demonstrates: the King gives up his patriarchal prerogatives before the ghoul pops up and teaches the monarch a new way of life.

Only a close look at men's tales reveals the wisdom of Tricksters. These elusive male figures normally hide behind shadowy appearances and conceal themselves in the unconscious. As a powerful masculine archetype hidden in the male psyche, the Trickster fits the definition of the deep masculine. This confirms the scandalous suggestion from "The Little Peasant" that the Trickster *is* the deep masculine. The next tale elaborates on the theme and shows that the Trickster is the master of initiation in a male rite of passage specifically for mature men.

CHAPTER SEVEN

Brother Lustig:
Part 1. The Spirit Brother

BROTHER LUSTIG

(FROM GERMANY)

a man, known as Brother Lustig, once served in the King's army. After many years of war, Lustig's King signed a peace treaty and dismissed all the soldiers. Lustig was sent on his way with only a loaf of bread and four silver coins. "A fine way to treat a loyal soldier!" Lustig muttered, but he was not one to bear grudges, so he whistled a jaunty tune and set out on the road. A beggar came up to Lustig and asked for food and alms. Brother Lustig exclaimed, "This small loaf and four coins are all I have. Still," he went on, "I shall give you something." So Lustig broke his loaf into four pieces, and gave one to the poor man. Then he counted out his four coins and gave one to the beggar.

"God bless you," the beggar said, and the two men parted. The pauper was none other than St. Peter, walking the earth, and he hurried away to disguise himself as a cripple. Then he limped back to Lustig and begged for food and money.

"I have little enough for myself!" Lustig complained. "Still, you have less than me." So Lustig gave the cripple a slice of bread and a coin.

"God bless you," the cripple declared, and hobbled on his way. As soon as he was out of sight, St. Peter took the form of an old, sick man, and met Lustig down the road. "Have you alms for an old beggar," the apostle asked, "or a slice of bread for the hungry?"

"You're the third man who's asked from me this morning," Brother Lustig exclaimed. "What has the world come to! But I have a little I can share." So the soldier gave the old man a slice of bread and a coin. Then Lustig hurried to the nearest inn. "If I don't eat my last piece of bread and spend my money now," he thought, "I shall have nothing for myself!" The ex-soldier bought a beer, ate his bread, and set out on the road once again.

A little later, Lustig ran into a soldier, who was St. Peter in one more disguise. "Good day, brother," the apostle said, "have you alms or bread for a penniless man?"

"Ah no, good fellow," Lustig replied. "I have nothing to eat or spend. If you have no money, too, we can go begging together."

"No need for that," St. Peter smiled. "I know something of healing, and if you come with me, I'll give you half of what I earn." Lustig readily agreed and the two set off on the road again, singing old army tunes. They came to a farmhouse where everyone wept because the farmer lay deathly ill. "I can cure your husband," St. Peter told the farmer's wife. The apostle anointed the farmer with a salve, and in a trice, the man arose from bed, whole and healthy. Out of gratitude, he offered St. Peter anything on the farm as a reward. "I need no reward," the apostle declared.

"Psst! Psst!" Brother Lustig whispered in his companion's ear. "We have to eat, don't we?" But St. Peter would take no gift. "Don't be a fool!" Lustig poked his comrade in the ribs. "At least take some food!" St. Peter still refused, but the farmer and his wife saw that Lustig wanted something, so they fetched a lamb and gave it to the soldier as a reward.

"If you want it so much," St. Peter told Lustig, "you must carry the lamb yourself."

"Easy enough!" Lustig declared, and the two departed together.

"What a queer fellow he is," Lustig mused about his companion, "saving the farmer's life and taking no reward!" As they traveled, the lamb became heavier and heavier, until Lustig could carry it no further. "Look, friend," Lustig said, stopping beneath a tree, "this seems a nice enough place to rest. I will make a fire and cook the lamb, then we can have a proper meal."

"As you wish," the saint replied, and he gave a pot to Lustig for cooking. "But I leave everything to you. I will walk by the river and come back later. Mind you don't start dinner without me!"

"Certainly not!" Brother Lustig exclaimed. He built a fire, boiled some water, slaughtered the lamb, threw it into the pot, and stirred it round and round. The stew smelled delicious, and Lustig licked his lips, waiting for his companion to return. The minutes become hours, and each time the pot bubbled, it seemed to say, "Taste me!" And each time Lustig looked away, his stomach rumbled, "Now!"

"What could be keeping him?" Lustig thought impatiently. Finally Lustig fished around in the pot and plucked out the heart. "That's supposed to be the best part," he thought to himself, and nibbled a bit of it. One bite led to another and the heart was soon gone. At that moment St. Peter returned. Lustig hastily replaced the lid on the pot. "Well, it's about time!" Lustig reproved his companion. "The stew's been ready for hours."

"I'm not hungry now," St. Peter said. "Just give me the lamb's heart and you can have the rest."

Lustig gulped nervously. Then he fished around in the pot, pulling up chunks of meat. "Is this the heart?" he asked St. Peter. "No," the apostle replied. "How about this?" "No, it's not that." "This one?" "Not that either." Suddenly Lustig exclaimed, "How foolish of us! Of course we can't find the heart in here! Lambs have no hearts!"

"Eh?" the apostle asked in surprise. "Lambs have no hearts?"

"Yes. How silly of us to forget!" Lustig went on quickly.

"But how could that be?" St. Peter asked. "All creatures have hearts."

"All creatures except lambs," Brother Lustig replied.

"Well," St. Peter said, "if lambs have no hearts, then I don't want any of this stew. You can have it all." So Lustig ate the meal with gusto.

The next day the two men set out on the road and came to a broad stream. "We can ford the river here," St. Peter said. "Why don't you go first?"

"No, no," Lustig replied hastily, "you lead and I'll follow." Privately, Lustig told himself, "If it's too deep, I don't want to drown!" St. Peter started off across the river, and the water came up only to his ankles. In no time at all he was on the other side, beckoning for Lustig to follow. The ex-soldier hoisted his pack and waded into the river. With the first step, the water came up to his knees, with the second, to his waist and before he knew it, Lustig was floundering in the river.

"Help! Help!" Lustig sputtered. "I can't swim!"

"I will help you," St. Peter said, "if you confess you ate the lamb's heart!"

"I don't know what you're talking about!" Brother Lustig cried out. "Help! I'm going to drown!"

"Confess you ate the lamb's heart!"

"What are you saying at a time like this! Help me!"

St. Peter could not bear to let his companion drown, so he made the water recede, and Lustig stumbled out of the river. When he recovered, the two resumed their journey. They soon came to a land shrouded in gloom because the King's daughter lay deathly ill. "This is our chance, friend!" Lustig exclaimed. "We can win a fortune by healing the Princess!" He wanted to rush to the castle, but St. Peter kept walking more and more slowly.

"Don't be a sluggard!" Lustig urged his companion. "The Princess might die at any moment!" But the apostle only dragged his feet all the more. When they came to the palace, they learned the Princess had just expired. "Now you've done it, slowpoke!" Lustig accused his companion.

"No need to shout," the apostle replied calmly. "I can raise the dead, too!" St. Peter went up to the King and Queen and told them he knew the secret of reviving the dead.

"Bring my daughter back to life," the King declared, "and you shall have half my kingdom!" St. Peter requested that he and his friend be left alone with the body of the Princess. Once by themselves, the apostle told Brother Lustig to build a fire and boil some water. Then St. Peter cut up the body of the Princess and threw the pieces into the pot. When the flesh boiled off, the apostle gathered the bones and laid them on the bed, carefully putting each bone in its proper place. St. Peter stood back, and said, "Arise, dead Princess, in the name of the most Holy Trinity!" Once, twice, three times he said this, and the Princess arose, as if she had just awakened from a nap.

The King and Queen were overjoyed when their daughter walked out of the room. "Name what you will," the King told the two soldiers, "and it is yours!" St. Peter refused any reward, but Lustig kept poking the apostle and whispering in his ear. The King saw that Lustig wanted something, and ordered the soldier's knapsack filled with gold. Then St. Peter and Lustig set off once more.

In the middle of a forest, St. Peter stopped and turned to his comrade. "Let us divide the gold equally."

"Ah," Lustig exclaimed, "so you have come to your senses. I took you for a fool back there, refusing a fortune." Lustig handed the gold to St. Peter. The apostle carefully counted out the coins and put them in three piles. "Three piles?" Lustig asked. "But there are only two of us here!"

St. Peter explained, "This pile is for you," and he pushed one heap of coins to Lustig. "This one is for me," he pulled one pile to himself. "And the third is for the person who ate the lamb's heart!"

"Why, that was me!" Brother Lustig said quickly, sweeping the extra gold into his knapsack.

"But I thought lambs have no hearts?" the apostle said in surprise.

"No hearts?" Lustig exclaimed incredulously. "How could you think such a thing? All creatures have hearts!"

"So be it," St. Peter said. "The gold is yours, and this too," pushing his share to Lustig. "But I will no longer travel with you. You must go on alone."

"I'm sorry for that," Lustig replied, "because I like you and enjoy your company." But Lustig took comfort in his new wealth. After the two men parted, Lustig went his way, and in no time at all, he spent his fortune and was penniless once more.

By then, Lustig found himself in another kingdom, shrouded in gloom. The reason, Lustig learned, was that the daughter of the King had just died. "Aha!" Lustig thought to himself, "I shall earn myself some money." He hurried to the palace, presented himself to the King and Queen, and offered to bring the Princess back to life. The King and Queen promised Lustig any reward he wanted if he succeeded.

Lustig asked to be alone with the dead Princess. He lit a fire, boiled water in a pot, cut the body of the Princess up, and threw all the pieces into the cauldron. After the flesh boiled away, Lustig fished out the bones and laid them on the bed. Then he scratched his head. "Ah, this is a problem! How do the bones go together?" He arranged the skeleton as best he could, stepped back, and then said, "Arise dead Princess, in the name of the most Holy Trinity!" Once, twice, three times he said this, with no results. Lustig rearranged the bones and tried again. Still nothing happened. "Confound you, girl, get up!" he cried out at last. Lustig started to worry. If the King learned his daughter was boiled to bits, what would he do to Lustig?

At that moment St. Peter appeared at the window, still disguised as a soldier. "Scoundrel," the saint said, "what are you doing with the dead?" Brother Lustig looked sheepishly at his former companion and explained the situation. The apostle studied the bones and then said, "This will not work at all! You have jumbled everything up! Just this once I will help you out. But never again try to raise the dead!" He shook his finger at Lustig. "And I warn you not to ask for any reward from the King!" Lustig nodded meekly.

St. Peter rearranged the bones, stepped back, and commanded three times. "Dead Princess, arise in the name of the Most Holy Trinity!" The Princess arose, whole and healthy. St. Peter went on his way, and Lustig eagerly led the Princess to her parents.

The King and Queen rejoiced. "Name your reward," the King declared. Lustig hemmed and hawed, never quite asking for a reward, but the King took the hint. He ordered Lustig's knapsack filled with gold. The soldier jubilantly went on his way, only to run into St. Peter, still in disguise.

"A fine man you are," the apostle declared. "I told you not to ask for a reward, and here you are with a pile of gold on your back!"

"Well"—Brother Lustig smiled weakly—"I can't disobey a King when he commands me to take his gold!"

St. Peter sighed. "So be it. But remember, don't ever try raising the dead."

Lustig laughed. "I won't need to, now that I have *this* reward." He shook his pack and the coins jingled loudly.

The apostle sighed again. "You'll run out of money soon enough, and then you'll be tempted to raise the dead." The apostle thought a moment, then he took the pack from his own back and gave it to Lustig. "Take my knapsack," he told the soldier. "It is magic, and whatever you wish to go into the pack will do so. You will never be wanting again, so you will have no need to raise the dead. And when we part this time, we shall never meet again." St. Peter took his leave, and Lustig resumed his journey, thinking no further about his companion's gift.

The days went by, and Lustig soon found himself with only four coins to his name. So he stopped at an inn, ordered wine and bread, and sat down to eat. In front of him, the innkeeper roasted two geese, and the sight of them made Lustig hungry. He eyed the birds and then remembered the magic knapsack his companion had given him. "Well, well," Lustig thought to himself. "Let's see if there's anything to what that odd fellow promised!"

"Into my pack, the two of you," Lustig muttered at the geese. In a trice, the two birds vanished from the oven, and when Lustig peered in his pack, there they were! Lustig paid for his beer, hurried out the door, tipping his hat at the innkeeper, and went to a nearby meadow. As he settled down and started eating a goose, two workmen came along the road.

"Good day, fine sir," the journeymen said, eyeing the geese hungrily.

"Good day," Brother Lustig replied. Then he paused and thought to himself, "I do not need two geese for myself." So Lustig gave one to the two men. They happily accepted the gift and hurried to the nearest inn for a bottle of wine. "What a stroke of luck!" they congratulated each other.

The innkeeper looked suspiciously at the two youths, eating such a fine goose. So he ran to his oven, opened it, and saw both his birds missing. "Thieves!" the innkeeper screamed at the workmen. "How dare you steal my geese!"

The two men protested, "A soldier gave the goose to us!"

"Liars!" the innkeeper shrieked, and he fetched a stick and began beating the two men until they ran away.

Far from the commotion, Lustig resumed his journey. He came to a castle, but found it strangely empty. Lustig stopped at a small inn next door. "Have you lodging for the night?" Lustig asked the innkeeper.

"Alas, no," the landlord said, "I have none. The lord of the castle has moved in here because his castle is haunted by demons."

Lustig scratched his head. "A man's got to sleep somewhere, and if you have no room, I'll stay in the castle."

"Many men have tried," the innkeeper warned, "but none have returned to tell about it." Lustig would not be dissuaded, so the innkeeper gave the soldier the keys to the fortress and food for dinner. Lustig marched into the main hall of the castle, built himself a fire, and ate his dinner. Then he lay down to sleep.

In the middle of the night, Lustig was awakened by a commotion. Nine devils frolicked in a circle around him, breathing fire and making a racket. "Dance as much as you like," Lustig warned the hideous creatures, "just don't come any closer."

The devils leaped up to Lustig, taunting him. "Enough!" the soldier cried out angrily. "Get away! Otherwise I'll teach you some manners!" The demons only laughed and jostled against Lustig. So Lustig grabbed a stick of wood and hit the devils. He was a hearty fighter, but nine demons are too much for any man, and the ex-soldier was soon getting the bad end of the deal. "Help! Help!" he cried out, as the devils pummeled him unmercifully. Lustig ran to and fro but he could not escape the monsters. Then he remembered his magic knapsack.

"Into my pack, all of you!" Lustig shouted. In the next moment, the devils were trapped in his knapsack and Lustig gleefully tied the bag shut. The demons squealed and smoke poured from the pack, but none of the devils could escape. So Lustig lay back down and went to sleep.

The next morning Lustig awoke and made his way to the inn. The innkeeper was astonished to see Lustig alive, and ran to the lord of the castle. The nobleman appeared and exclaimed, "You're still alive, my good man!"

"Why, yes," Brother Lustig explained, "and I've cleaned out the devils that haunted your castle."

"You're a brave man," the lord said. "Stay in my service, and I shall see you shall never go wanting."

Lustig shook his head. "I want to see the world, so I'll just wander the road." But before he left, Lustig asked a smith to pound his backpack. The smith obliged, and hammered the knapsack. After a while, Lustig opened the pack and shook it out. Eight devils tumbled out, dead as could be. The ninth demon was tiny and had survived the beating, hidden in a corner of the pack. The little devil crept quietly away and ran back to Hell, unnoticed by Lustig.

Lustig continued on his way for many years, until he realized his time in the world would end. He began worrying about what would happen to him after he died. So he asked a hermit for advice. "How do I enter the Kingdom of Heaven when I die?" Brother Lustig inquired.

The hermit pointed to a rocky path in the woods. "The road to Heaven is there, and it is narrow, steep, and hard." The sage pointed to a lovely avenue nearby. "That is the road to hell, and it is broad, easy, and comfortable."

"Only a fool would take the hard road," Lustig told himself. So he set out on the easy avenue. In a short time, Lustig came to a huge black gate. It was the door into Hell, but it was closed for the day. Lustig picked up the knocker and rapped loudly. A window in the door opened and a devil peered out to see who had come calling. The demon gasped in terror when he saw Lustig, shut the window, and ran to the chief devil. The doorkeeper was the little demon who had barely escaped with his life from Lustig's knapsack!

The imp told all the devils not to let Lustig in. Otherwise, the demon explained, Lustig could wish everybody into his knapsack! The devils bolted the door shut and told Lustig to go away.

"Just my luck!" the former soldier grumbled, "turned away from Hell!" So Lustig labored back up the broad, comfortable road, until he came to the hard, steep path. "Well," he said to himself, "it can't be helped. I have to stay somewhere for eternity." So he set out on the narrow trail, and climbed and climbed and climbed. At last he came to Heaven, and there, behind the pearly gate, dozed St. Peter, dressed in beautiful white robes. Brother Lustig recognized him at once as his old friend.

"Oh!" Lustig thought, "so my comrade is here before me. This will surely go well!" Lustig called out, "Old comrade! Here I am again, and I need a place to stay. Let me in!"

St. Peter roused himself and looked at Lustig with surprise. "You came here?" St. Peter exclaimed. "I can hardly believe that! You must try the other road, the broad and easy one."

"I've been there already and they won't let me in."

"Well, I can't let you in here, either." St. Peter shook his head firmly.

"A fine soldier you turn out to be," Brother Lustig retorted, "not helping a comrade in need." Lustig turned to leave, but then paused a moment. He took off his knapsack. "If you won't have anything to do with me, then I don't want anything to do with you either. Take your confounded pack back." Lustig thrust the knapsack through Heaven's gate.

"Eh? Well, all right then," St. Peter said, feeling a little awkward. The apostle hung the magic knapsack on a hook next to his seat, and then Lustig called out, "Into the pack with me!" Instantly, he found himself in his knapsack, and when he popped out, there he stood on the shining streets of Heaven. And once inside, St. Peter let him stay. So there Brother Lustig remains—unless he's wished all of Heaven into his knapsack!

Part 1. The Spirit Brother

POST-HEROIC MAN

This story from the Grimms' collection is long, hilarious, and initially baffling. When I first read the tale, it felt like a "big" dream: it went on and on, seemed very important, and yet I could make little sense of it. Reading and rereading the story only confused the situation more, since the tale is so complex and packed with symbols. Comparing the drama to tales we have already discussed, though, reveals striking similarities between the stories. These commonalities help unravel the symbolism in "Brother Lustig."

Lustig's tale begins when he is discharged from the army with little reward for his years of service. Ex-soldiers like Lustig are often protagonists in men's tales, as in "Three Army Surgeons" from the Grimms' collection, "The Devil's Sooty Brother," also from the Grimms, or "Go I Know Not Whither" and "Clever Answers" from Russia. The plight of former soldiers sums up the collapse of heroic and patriarchal ideals that men suffer at midlife. After working long and hard toward a heroic dream, like

Lustig serving his King, many men find themselves left in the lurch with nothing to show for their devotion. If a man attains his youthful ambitions, he often finds them dissatisfying and meaningless. If he fails in his dreams, he realizes there is no time left for a second attempt. Lustig personifies the post-heroic period in men's lives.

Following his discharge, Lustig realizes that his King exploited him. The monarch welcomed Lustig in war when he needed soldiers, only to send him packing when peace arrived. To the King, Lustig is merely cannon fodder. The story repeats a theme from "The North Wind's Gift": men are oppressed by patriarchs. Even men who *do* become heroes are cast off when they are no longer needed. Victorious athletes are forgotten when past their prime or disabled from injuries, and war heroes succumb to something similar, as Michael Messner and Don Sabo eloquently point out in their essays on former champions.

Although he finds himself in a painful midlife crisis, Lustig does not give up. Like the peasant in "The North Wind's Gift" or the monarch in "The King and the Ghoul," Lustig refuses to despair. He starts traveling the road and soon encounters St. Peter. The manner in which the two men meet is highly significant. St. Peter disguises himself as a cripple, a beggar, an old man, and an ex-soldier, asking for food and money. Lustig can ill afford to give anything away, but he shares what he has, underscoring how generous he is: he has integrated his feminine, nurturing side. For his part, St. Peter plays the role of a Trickster, deceiving Lustig with various disguises. As the story proceeds, in fact, St. Peter more and more resembles the Tricksterish demon in "The King and the Ghoul." The apostle harasses and helps Lustig, the way the ghoul tormented and instructed the King. St. Peter, like the ghoul, turns out to be a therapist, teacher, and mentor.

The Trickster theme is so important, it even appears in Lustig's name. In German, "Lustig" means gay, jolly, funny, amusing, odd, or strange. The name conjures up images of the fool or clown, which is a classical form of the Trickster. Lustig also has many traits typical of Tricksters, and these attributes contain vital insights for men at midlife.

THE TRICKSTER AS WANDERER AND HEALER

After they befriend each other, St. Peter and Lustig travel without any definite destination. (St. Peter remains disguised, like a good Trickster.) Such wandering is typical of Tricksters around the world, like Hermes from Greece, Eshu and Legba of Africa, or Wakdjunkaga and Coyote in America. Indeed, Hermes was the patron of travelers, and shrines were erected to him by the roadside, particularly at crossroads. Legba and Eshu are likewise associated with crossroads and travel. As a wanderer, the Trickster offers an excellent symbol for change, transition, and transformation. He sums up men's plight at midlife, as Murray Stein points out in his book *In Midlife,* focusing on Hermes. Just when men reach some measure of success and comfort and expect to enjoy themselves, their lives are turned upside down. Familiar patterns collapse, forcing them to roam the world, seeking a new way of life, just like Lustig. This confused wandering contrasts with the confident quest of the young hero, who pours all his energies into one or two dreams. When those ambitions disintegrate at midlife, men shift from heroic quests to post-heroic roving.

The Trickster's wandering differs from that of the "eternal youth." The latter is a man who remains an adolescent at heart, no matter what his chronological age, and never makes or keeps commitments. He flits from place to place, job to job, relationship to relationship. Tricksters like Lustig *have* made commitments and kept them. Lustig served twenty-five years in the army before wandering the road! Eternal youths do not tolerate such commitments. They are "pre-heroic" and know little about loyalty, perseverance, or dedication, the traditional virtues of the hero and the patriarch. Lustig has mastered those qualities and now faces new tasks. His wandering is post-heroic, not adolescent.

The Trickster's wandering is often sexual. Lustig's story does not reflect the theme, because most European fairy tales were heavily censored prior to publication. Yet Trickster tales from around the world are graphic about the Trickster's sexual roaming. Wakdjunkaga of North America, for instance, traveled the land, having intercourse with every woman he could. Yet he was married and had a family. He wandered from the marriage bed. Ananse in Africa did something similar, although he returned home more frequently. The Trickster's philandering dramatizes two male traits which women often bemoan—men's frequent aversion to commitments in relationships and men's apparent promiscuity in sex. Behind the Trickster's sexual wandering, though, lies deeper symbolic meanings, the way the Trickster's stealing conceals his zero-sum wisdom. The Trickster's philandering, for example, reflects a restless, exploratory spirit. Tricksters refuse to accept limitations or conventions. Where the patriarch and hero claim one viewpoint, one mate, one family, and one territory as their own, the Trickster crosses boundaries and constantly seeks out new connections. He is at heart an explorer and a pioneer. The Trickster's promiscuity also undermines a romantic ideal in heroic tradition. The young hero supposedly falls in love with a beautiful woman, marries her, and then lives happily ever after. In reality, many husbands and wives have affairs. So the Trickster's philandering mocks a fiction of heroic and patriarchal tradition. Trickster tales exaggerate his promiscuity to make the point, the way dreams dramatize their themes.

As they travel together, Lustig and St. Peter come upon a sick farmer, and the apostle cures him. Such healing is common in fairy tales about midlife, such as "Three Army Surgeons" from Germany, "The Stoning" from Morocco, or "The Bonesetter" from Japan. The importance of the healing theme to men in the middle years is readily apparent. On a literal level, men begin to suffer from various physical ailments. Sprains from weekend athletics take longer to heal, and heart disease exacts a grim toll. The youthful motto, "Victory at any cost!" becomes the midlife worry about simply surviving. Psychological healing also becomes vital because men acknowledge their inner wounds at midlife and walk the road of ashes. Healing is a post-heroic preoccupation. At maturity, therapy replaces triumph as a priority.

Healing is also an attribute of Trickster figures. Although the fact is often overlooked, Tricksters bring vital healing arts to their people.[1] Wakdjunkaga gave humankind important medicines, as did Legba and Eshu in Africa. (Legba also spread diseases to force people to buy his medicines!) Among the Zuni, the Ne-wekwe healing cult was founded by a Trickster figure and provides healing ceremonies for the sick. Hopi Trickster-clowns, similarly, perform their outrageous actions to heal disease and reconcile social conflicts within their communities. Navajo healing ceremonies include tales of Coyote the Trickster as an integral part of the rite. Behind their pranks and buffoonery, Tricksters are healers and therapists, providing exactly what men need in maturity.

THE TRICKSTER VS. THE PATRIARCH

After St. Peter cures the farmer, Lustig takes a lamb as a reward and cooks it. The apostle then plays a little trick on Lustig. St. Peter makes the soldier promise not to eat anything until the apostle returns, but St. Peter stays away so long that Lustig cannot resist his hunger. The ex-soldier eats the lamb's heart and invents the ridiculous story about lambs not having hearts. In effect, St. Peter entices Lustig into breaking a promise and lying. St. Peter even gave Lustig the pot to use for cooking, so the apostle's actions border on entrapment! As the tale continues, the apostle tempts Lustig into further misdeeds. Later, for instance, when St. Peter raises the dead princesses, he insists that Lustig not take any compensation despite the fabulous rewards offered them. This puts Lustig in an impossible situation—imagine turning down a winning lottery ticket! Lustig naturally breaks his word once more and takes a reward. Further in the drama, St. Peter gives Lustig the magic knapsack, which is an invitation to even more mischief. Lustig quickly obliges, using the magic pack to steal two geese from the innkeeper. So St. Peter lures Lustig into lying, cheating, and stealing. He transforms the ex-soldier into a Trickster.

St. Peter's actions are shocking. He is the legendary "rock" upon which the Catholic Church is founded and the theological foundation for the Pope's patriarchal authority. (The Pope rules in Peter's name.) St. Peter, we might expect, would be a wise

old man, an august patriarch. Instead he is a rascal and a prank-
ster, doing the opposite of what a patriarch should. Yet "Brother
Lustig" is not alone in portraying St. Peter as a Trickster, and
many other folk stories repeat the theme.[2]

In playing pranks, St. Peter carries out the role of the sacred
clown. Common in many cultures, like the Hopi discussed in
Chapter 5, sacred clowns represent a variant of the Trickster.
They parody important authorities and religious rituals, mocking
patriarchs and their dogmas. The medieval Feast of the Ass provides a European example. In a rite widely celebrated in France
and England, congregations paraded around the church behind a
donkey, while a mock Bishop played the part of a sacred clown,
reciting the Mass and burning shoes instead of incense. These
festivities even occurred in Notre Dame Cathedral of Paris, but
were eventually suppressed by the Catholic Church. In a similar
spirit, "Brother Lustig" parodies many orthodox Christian doctrines. In the episode with the stew, for instance, Lustig eats the
lamb's heart, yet the lamb is a traditional symbol of Christ. (This
would presumably be known to the listeners of this tale.) The
"sacred heart of Jesus" is also a frequent image in Catholic lit-
urgy. Eating the lamb's heart, then, implies eating the heart of
Christ, a macabre spoof on Christian symbolism. The story also
pokes fun at the Christian sacrament of holy communion. In eating consecrated bread and wine, the worshiper partakes of the
body and blood of Christ. Lustig mocks the doctrine by eating
the lamb's heart. Behind the Trickster's sacrilegious humor lies a
serious purpose. Tricksters attack established dogmas to force
men to explore new possibilities.[3] "Brother Lustig" uses humor
and parody for this purpose, the way "The King and the Ghoul"
relies on riddle and paradox. The aim is the same in both cases,
to "deconstruct" conventional rules. It is also the goal of therapy
with most mature men, who need help in becoming more flexible
and expressive, less judgmental and patriarchal.

Another, subtler meaning lies behind St. Peter's hilarious
pranks. A close look at the Biblical St. Peter reveals that he
originally was something of a Trickster figure. In the New Testament, he bumbles along, makes mistakes, and often disobeys
Jesus. When Jesus walks on water, for instance, Peter tries to

follow and promptly sinks into the ocean, the way Lustig almost drowned trying to cross the river. Before the crucifixion, Peter lied, denying that he knew Jesus. Lustig, similarly, denies that he ate the lamb's heart. Because of his bumbling and faults, Peter is an unlikely choice to be a patriarch in Christian tradition, yet that is what he has become. By portraying Peter as a Trickster, "Brother Lustig" hints at a shocking secret. Peter was originally a Trickster, not a patriarch, more a fool than a hero. The same motif surfaced earlier in "The King's Ears," where the monarch's goat's ears resemble the animal ears that fools wear. Behind his crown, the King has the trappings of a fool, not a patriarch. The fact that the Trickster lurks behind the patriarch may be shocking to men, but it rarely is to women. Wives and mothers often see the fool hiding behind the dignified roles their men put on. Women diplomatically keep this insight to themselves, but the Trickster brings the secret out into the open and celebrates it. There is no shame, the Trickster insists, in being a Fool—rather the opportunity for fun. Having goat's ears, the Trickster reassures men, is no deformity, and every man, he adds, has goat's ears.

THE SPIRIT BROTHER

In their adventures become, Peter and Lustig become comrades, and the title of the story emphasizes their fraternity, *"Brother Lustig."* The tale makes no references to Lustig's being a member of a religious order, and Lustig, probably would not have had time to become one, since he has apparently been a soldier for most of his life. So the term "Brother" is probably not religious, and most likely simply refers to the camaraderie of soldiers. The story reinforces the theme in a subtle detail. Only St. Peter and Lustig have proper names, while everybody else has generic titles, like "the sick farmer," "the Princess," "the innkeeper," "the King," and so on. By naming only the two men, the story focuses on them and highlights the importance of their friendship.

Although St. Peter has magical power, he does not try to dominate Lustig. Their relationship is not that of master and servant, patriarch and vassal, or father and son, but comrade and peer. This is surprising since Peter is an apostle and traditionally a patriarchal authority. In his unexpected fraternal role, Peter introduces an important archetype in men's tales, that of the Spirit Brother, a spiritual being who accompanies, advises, and plays pranks on a man during a midlife odyssey. The theme appeared earlier, in "The King and the Ghoul," where the ghoul, like St. Peter, aids the King during a dangerous midlife passage. Classical literature elaborates on the Spirit Brother, and Dante's *Divine Comedy* offers an example.

As we discussed in Chapter 2. Dante suffers a midlife calamity and describes his metaphorical descent into Hell and Purgatory in his literary classic. The beautiful Beatrice aids him on his journey, but mainly from a distance. It is actually the spirit of Virgil, the classic Roman poet, who accompanies Dante on each step of the way through Hell. Virgil tells Dante how to pass safely through the many perils of the Inferno, and rescues him from trouble, the way St. Peter helps Lustig out. Like the ghoul, Virgil acts as teacher, mentor, and therapist to a man in a midlife crisis. Moreover, Virgil and Dante relate to each other as peers, not as superior and inferior, despite Dante's great admiration for Virgil. Fraternity prevails, not hierarchy. Dante does not present Virgil as a Trickster, like St. Peter in Lustig's tale, but the theme surfaces covertly because poets are closely allied to Tricksters. Communication, after all, is the main goal of poets, as it is for Tricksters such as Hermes and Legba. Tricksters carry messages and are even credited with inventing language itself. Poets also mediate between the archetypal and the mundane, the inner and outer worlds, and combine the sublime with the demonic in their work. These are traits of Tricksters, who shuttle between the gods, humanity, and the underworld. Finally, poets create lovely deceits with their words, no less than Tricksters, and some languages, like Norwegian, use the same term for "poet" as for "liar"![4]

Other men's tales, such as "Go I Know Not Whither" (Chapter 9), elaborate on the theme of the Spirit Brother. Male fraternity, in fact, is an archetypal motif in mythology, deeply healing for men today. Modern culture considers intimacy to be feminine, and so men typically look to women to create and sustain relationships. Historically, though, *male* fraternity was the model of intimacy, not romantic love between man and woman, as it is today.[5] To the ancient Greeks, Eros was a god, not a goddess. In focusing on male fraternity, though, it is vital to distinguish the Spirit Brother from the warrior comrade.[6] The two are easily confused because the brotherhood of warriors is also ancient and appears in one of the earliest written epics, the story of Gilgamesh and Enkidu from Sumeria. The saga focuses on the adventures of the two heroes, battling enemies together. They are warrior-comrades. Similarly, *The Iliad* from ancient Greece celebrates the friendship between Achilles and Patrocles, two warrior-heroes, while *The Song of Roland* from medieval Europe describes the adventures of two knights, Roland and Oliver. Recent literature, such as *All Quiet on the Western Front* or *A Farewell to Arms,* repeats the image of warrior-comrades.

The fraternity of war heroes is the stuff of youth, and the camaraderie fails at midlife. Quite simply, hero-comrades die young. Achilles and Patrocles fell at Troy, while Roland and Oliver perished in the bloom of youth. War buddies never have to grapple with the responsibilities of maturity, the problems of raising a family, and fears of growing old. This is the importance of "Brother Lustig" and other men's tales. The stories address the concerns of aging men and offer a new model of male camaraderie no longer based on youthful heroism. Lustig is an ex-soldier, not a young warrior. The fraternity between Lustig and St. Peter is a matter of sharing new experiences and healing old wounds, rather than fighting common enemies and conquering foreign lands.

Only recently has the importance of men's spiritual camaraderie in maturity been emphasized, for instance by Sam Keen in *Fire in the Belly,* and Keith Thompson in *To Be a Man.* This contrasts with the burgeoning literature on men and the feminine. Yet one of the few factors that correlates with a man's successful transition through midlife is having close relationships with siblings in adolescence. As George Vaillant found in his extensive research on men, the experience of being a brother provides a resource for men to draw on in the middle years. Men also find support and guidance from fraternity in a literal way. A businessman gave an example from his life, during a workshop I presented on men's tales. The man described how he hit bottom in his forties when he went through a painful divorce. He survived only because old fraternity buddies, from whom he had not heard since college, learned about his ordeal, called him, and shepherded him through his crisis. They functioned as his Spirit Brothers.

The brother archetype becomes important at midlife for several reasons. By this time, many men have seen one or both of their parents die. Conflicts with mother and father, so characteristic of youth, begin to fade, either because the disputes have been resolved or because they are no longer relevant. By middle age too, most men have come into positions of authority at work or home. There are fewer superiors to fight with and more peers. Spiritual fraternity is post-heroic, and fairy tales dramatize the point. In many stories about youth, three brothers vie for the hand of a Princess and the right to succeed the old King. When the youngest brother wins the contest, the older ones plot to kill him. Tales of youth emphasize competitiveness between brothers, not camaraderie. The stories reflect the realities of patriarchal society, in which only one man can become the ruling patriarch. The Spirit Brother liberates men from the frantic, fratricidal competition of youth.

The Spirit Brother also helps women by relieving them of a traditional feminine role, providing men with emotional support and intimacy. Mature men can find help from comrades, not just wives and mistresses. This frees women to pursue their own ventures. On the other hand, some women find it threatening when their husbands, fathers, and sons shift attention away from them and toward male comrades. These women often unconsciously undermine men's development. But this occurs mainly when women have devoted themselves exclusively to limited female roles, like that of mother or wife, and neglected their own psychological growth. Women who have developed as individuals in their own right welcome men's shift to masculine camaraderie. Ultimately, what men learn about trust and intimacy from their spiritual comrades, they bring back to their relationships with women. Men's new fraternal skills foster greater depth in male-female intimacy.

The archetype of the Spirit Brother often emerges in men's dreams. As men age, their dreams tend to shift away from a youthful focus on mother images, first to father-figures and then to male groups.[7] Andrew Samuels, a Jungian analyst, offers an example in his book *The Plural Psyche,* with a man who came to analysis suffering a midlife crisis. A social worker by profession, the man was troubled by a male boss at work, whom he saw as tricky and shady, almost bordering on the criminal, just like a Trickster. Yet the man repeatedly dreamed of his boss as a helpful figure, and the dreams echo the themes of "Brother Lustig." In one episode, the boss gave the dreamer a rifle in the middle of a war, rescuing the man from a terrible fix. In another, the tricky boss acted as a tour guide, leading the dreamer out of a confusing situation. The two dreams recall how St. Peter saves Lustig first from drowning in the river and later from bungling the resurrection of the second princess. In a third dream, the man met his boss, who had become an emissary of the Pope. In "Brother Lustig," of course, St. Peter is a Trickster and the predecessor of popes. Although Samuels does not discuss the motif, the man dreamed of his boss in the role of the Trickster Brother.

THE TRICKSTER AS SOURCE OF LIFE

After healing the sick farmer, Lustig and Peter arrive at the kingdom where the Princess just died, and St. Peter resurrects the dead woman. (Recall that "The King and the Ghoul" has a similar episode in which a dead woman is revived: the theme is archetypal in men's tales.) The details of St. Peter's ritual are deeply symbolic. The apostle cuts up the corpse and boils the pieces, until only the bones are left. St. Peter then resurrects the Princess from the skeleton. This gruesome rite provides a metaphor for midlife. Men's youthful convictions and ambitions collapse, leaving them feeling vulnerable and needy, like the dying princesses. Then even this raw, sensitive part of a man is killed and boiled away, leaving only bones, the most basic stuff of the body. Finally new life appears. The theme surfaced earlier in the

Moroccan tale, "The Sultan's Handkerchief." There the Sultan fell into a pit and was threatened with being butchered and eaten, with having his life dismantled completely.

In the Sultan's tale, the monarch is rescued by Zakia, an anima figure. Lustig's story gives no such powerful role to the anima. In fact, the only candidates for anima figures are the two princesses, and they are dead! *Male* vitality is emphasized here, not feminine energy. The life-giving masculine power also comes from St. Peter in his role as a Trickster, not a patriarch. Here we come to an important trait of Tricksters around the world: they represent a male life force.[8]

The theme takes various forms in mythology around the world. Often the Trickster is the original creator of life, as is the case among the Kung of Africa with their Trickster-Creator, Gao, or among the Northwest Native Americans with Raven. Many Tricksters explicitly have the power to raise the dead, and some of them, like Coyote of North America, even resurrect themselves. Frequently, the Trickster's vital force is expressed in sexual ways: he functions as a life-giver in a concrete, biological sense. The Trickster's phallic, procreative energy is well illustrated by Hermes, who was symbolized by phallic symbols called "herms," placed by the wayside in ancient Greece. Shiva of India, another Trickster god, as well as the Tricksters Eshu and Legba of Africa, are also associated with sacred phalluses. The Yoruba tribe explicitly link Eshu to what they call "ase," the primordial life force. Paul Radin, the folklorist, noted that the association is general and that the Trickster symbolizes "the procreating power as such," a life-giving energy that is uniquely masculine.[9]

The Trickster, though, personifies more than sexual vitality. He is a life-giver in a *social* sense, bringing language, fire, and medicines to humanity, as well as vital inventions, like metalworking. These gifts make human life possible. Tricksters, in fact, personify "the raw forces out of which human life is made,"[10] as Robert Pelton concluded after his analysis of Trickster tales. The Trickster's primordial life force is what two Jungian analysts, Eugene Monick and James Wyly, independently called "phallos," a generative sexual, social, *and* spiritual energy.

The image of the Trickster as a primordial source of life is vital to men in several ways. First, he promises healing to men walking "the road of ashes," offering advice, camaraderie, renewal, and rejuvenation. In practical terms, the Trickster Companion is often a male therapist, because men today have few close male friends. Fortunately, with the men's movement, the Spirit Comrade increasingly includes an entire men's group. Second, as a thoroughly masculine image of the life force, the Trickster Brother counteracts the mistaken view that only the feminine and the Great Mother Goddess have the power to give life. Many recent discussions of the Goddess, in fact, make her out to be the sole source of life, as if the ancients were ignorant of sexual biology. But mythologies make clear that the Trickster is at least as old an archetype as the Mother Goddess. (I discuss this point in greater depth in Chapters 11 and 12.) Yet the Trickster is not the Father God of patriarchal tradition. The Trickster represents a nonpatriarchal source of masculine vitality. He is an alternative to both the patriarch and the Great Goddess.

Many men experience the Trickster's primordial masculine power as a purely physical, sexual impulse. Yet the Trickster's energy is social and spiritual as much as it is sexual. It is easy to forget the deeper meaning here. Psychoanalysts do so when they argue that sex is fundamental and that men's social and spiritual interests are only sublimations of erotic drives. The Trickster disputes their claim. In folklore, the Trickster's role as the bringer of fire, language, medicines, and vital foods is as basic as his sexuality. To be sure, many men become stuck in sexual promiscuity and never reach the deeper, generative core of the male psyche. The situation here parallels the Trickster's thievery. Some men become criminals in youth, but the majority do not, and by midlife most men arrive at the Trickster's zero-sum insight, the wisdom hidden behind his kleptomania. Similarly, by midlife most men abandon sexual license and begin to appreciate the Trickster's deeper masculine generativity.

The Trickster's primordial life force appeared in a dream I had several years ago. Because I did not understand the episode, I simply wrote it down and forgot about it. I recalled the dream while working on this chapter and recognized its parallels to "Brother Lustig." In the dream, I was part of a group of men in a spaceship and we landed on an unknown planet. Our ship was damaged in the process, and we could not take off. The planet had breathable air, but was lifeless and lacked water. Fearful we would perish when our supplies ran out, we began searching for food and water. We soon discovered a cave and descended into it, hoping to locate a hidden spring. Using ropes and pitons, we climbed a long way down, but just as the last person reached bottom the rope broke. Without a way up, we were trapped in the cavern, and with supplies sufficient only for a few days we were desperate. Yet as the days went by, miraculously the food and water in our packs never gave out. We eventually discovered why. In our explorations through the cave, we came across the first evidence of intelligent life on the planet. It was a stone wall from which protruded a silver metal rod, about thirty feet long and a foot wide, constantly rotating. I knew in that way peculiar to dreams that this machine was hundreds of thousands of years old, and that it was a generator of some sort. Its power was responsible for our food and water never running out. Soon after coming upon this strange device, we found our way back to the surface of the planet. And with the help of the machine, we were able to make the desert planet fertile and colonize the new world.

In the dream, I start off with a group of men in a spaceship. Being part of a male space crew brings up the theme of masculine camaraderie, and recalls Lustig's situation at the beginning of his tale: he is a soldier in an army. The spaceship emphasizes the masculine theme, since the heavens are usually the province of male deities. In the dream, we are stranded on a barren planet, descend into a cavern, and become trapped there. The episode symbolizes the collapse of the heroic paradigm, analogous to Lustig's being abandoned by his king or Dante's descending into Hell. Stranded in the cavern, we have only limited food and water, but miraculously our supplies never run out. Our backpacks continue to sustain us, the way Lustig's magic rucksack helped him. The source of the magic in my dream turns out to be a massive silver rod rotating deep within the earth. Although placed horizontally rather than vertically, the cylinder is a giant phallic symbol, a high-tech version of the ancient Greek herm, the sacred phallus symbolizing Hermes, or an atomic-age version of the Hindu lingam, personifying Shiva. The silver rod represents a masculine source of life and energy linked to Tricksters. Machinery, I might add, is consistent with the Trickster's role as an inventor, giver of fire, and a patron of metalworking. The space-age dream thus repeats an age-old drama: male comrades descend into the unconscious and encounter the primordial, life-giving masculine energy of the Trickster. The themes are elusive and highly disguised, but that is characteristic of the Trickster!

TRICKSTER TRAITS

To continue with Lustig's tale: After St. Peter resurrects the first princess, Lustig tries to do so on his own and bungles the attempt. St. Peter rescues him and then gives Lustig the magic knapsack to prevent the ex-soldier from trying to raise the dead again. The pack is symbolic. Lustig first uses the bag to steal two geese from the innkeeper. Theft, of course, is typical of Tricksters. But with his magic knapsack, Lustig could presumably have conjured up anything he wanted without stealing. The fact that he steals reiterates the zero-sum theme associated with the Trickster. If Lustig is to gain something, he has to take it from somebody else. Significantly, Lustig does not use the pack to enrich himself. To the contrary, when he steals two geese, he gives one to the young workmen. Lustig's trickery, his zero-sum perspective, is tempered by generativity. And across cultures, Tricksters typically give away what they steal. This confirms a theme from ''The Little Peasant'' in Chapter 5: generativity underlies the Trickster's thievery. Surprisingly, Lustig's gift to the young men backfires, and the two youths are beaten by the innkeeper. The episode emphasizes that there is no such thing as a ''free lunch,'' and that the Trickster's magic is not simple wish-fulfillment.

On his travels, Lustig comes to the castle haunted by demons. He stays there, despite warnings against it, and then battles the devils. This is a typical event in tales of heroic young men, but several factors make Lustig's fight with the demons different. First, he loses. The demons overpower Lustig until he thinks of his magic knapsack at the last minute. Symbolically, fighting and the heroic approach fail him. On the other hand, the Trickster's way, symbolized by the magic knapsack, saves him. Second, Lustig does not battle the demons to win glory or treasure. He simply seeks shelter in the castle. Comfort is his goal, not conquest, something post-heroic men will understand. After clearing the castle of the demons, Lustig even declines a reward from the grateful lord, the first time Lustig refuses one! Lustig prefers to wander the road. He voluntarily chooses what was forced on him at the beginning of the story when he was summarily discharged from the army and had to roam the world.

After trapping the demons in his pack, Lustig asks a smith to beat the devils to death. This brings up an intriguing point. Lustig initially uses the magic pack to obtain food, making it a source of nourishment. Later, he uses the knapsack violently, trapping the demons in it and killing them. The knapsack is nurturing first and only later violent, just like the magic boxes in "The North Wind's Gift." The North Wind's first box provided food, while the second gift released violent thugs. Moreover, the North Wind, like St. Peter, is a Trickster figure. Both stories, otherwise so different, converge on the same theme: they portray the Trickster as a primordial masculine power whose energy is primarily nurturing and only secondarily violent.

One demon manages to survive the smith's beating, and his escape proves to be crucial. At the end of the story, the demon refuses Lustig entry into Hell. The irascible soldier is forced to make his way to Heaven, presumably to his eternal advantage. A similar drama occurs in "The Little Peasant," where the adulterous parson escapes from the miller's house and later allows the peasant to evade execution. In both tales, the escape of what seems to be evil turns out to be lifesaving. The point is subtle but insightful. The youthful hero tends to be a puritanical perfectionist and tries to eradicate evil completely. Tricksters, by contrast, accept human foibles, excuse mistakes, laugh at failures, and tolerate evil. Tricksters personify a more flexible, forgiving superego, which contrasts with the rigid, idealistic morality typical of young males. The transition from one to the other is a challenge for mature men.

At the end of the tale, Lustig wonders where he will stay for eternity and asks a hermit for advice. Lustig, of course, then takes the short, easy road to Hell, rather than the long, hard one to Heaven. He does the opposite of what he is supposed to, having become a first-rate Trickster. Eventually Lustig goes to Heaven and tricks his way into paradise. This is a scandalous way to enter Heaven, but typical of the Trickster's sacrilegious humor. Significantly, St. Peter lets Lustig stay, suggesting divine approval or at least tolerance of Lustig's trickery. The conclusion of the story thus hints at an important theme—there is a spiritual dimension to the Trickster behind all his mischief and misadventures. The theme surfaced earlier in "The King and the Ghoul," where the god Shiva appeared at the end of the tale to bless the monarch. Other men's stories will expand on the motif.

A CASE OF THE TRICKSTER BROTHER

By now, this discussion of "Brother Lustig" may seem long, complicated, and heavy on theory. What we need is an illustration of the Trickster Brother as he appears in a man's life. Jung provides that. As discussed earlier, Jung broke with Freud and fell into a painful midlife crisis in his thirties. During this time, he had a number of dramatic dreams and fantasies which introduced him to the figure of the anima, the inner feminine. After she emerged, Jung encountered a second numinous character, initially in a dream and later in a series of fantasies. The new figure was a man with the wings of a kingfisher bird and the horns of a bull. Jung became fascinated by this man, named him "Philemon," and often carried on imaginary conversations with him while taking walks. Jung considered Philemon his "inner guru" and painted him many times. Jung even hung a portrait of Philemon in his "inner sanctum," the tower Jung built at Bollingen. Barbara Hanna, in her biography of Jung, went so far as to call Philemon "the most important figure in all Jung's exploration."

Philemon was Jung's Spirit Brother, lending him spiritual and psychological aid in the middle of a midlife crisis. While less playful and humorous than St. Peter in "Brother Lustig," Philemon displays deep connections to the Trickster. For one thing,

Jung credited Philemon with introducing him to the unconscious. This is a traditional role of the Trickster: Hermes, Legba, and Eshu all mediate between humanity and the underworld, between conscious and unconscious. In painting Philemon, Jung also portrayed him as a "herm," a phallic column with a man's head on top. As mentioned before, Hermes, Eshu, Legba, and Shiva are traditionally represented by such a sacred phallus. Finally, Jung explicitly considered Philemon to be a primordial masculine energy, which is exactly what the Trickster personifies. Philemon, in short, represents a Trickster Brother, helping a man through a treacherous midlife transition, like St. Peter in "Brother Lustig," Virgil in *The Divine Comedy,* and the demon in "The King and the Ghoul." Philemon was Jung's Trickster-therapist and emphasizes the archetypal reality of the Spirit Brother in men's lives.

MEN'S MIDLIFE INITIATION

One last theme remains to be discussed in "Brother Lustig," that of initiation. The motif becomes clear when we compare Lustig's tale with male puberty rites. Anthropologists from Van Gennep to Victor Turner observed that there are three basic stages in adolescent male initiations—separation, transition, and reintegration. In the first phase, boys are taken away from their mothers, often forcibly, and separated from their childhood way of life. In the second stage, the young men undergo frightening ordeals, which destroy their childish beliefs and throw the youths in a confusing, transitional state. The boys then learn the secret lore of their fathers and forefathers, usually involving the way of the hero. After proving they are tough, cunning, strong, and brave, the youth are welcomed as men among men. They return to society in the final phase of initiation, reintegration.

Lustig's tale recapitulates this three-stage rite of passage. His adventures begin with his forcible separation from a familiar way of life: he is abruptly discharged from the army after twenty-five years of service. In contrast to puberty rites, in which boys are taken from their mothers and learn to be heroes, Lustig is removed from the world of heroes. Lustig starts off where most puberty rites end up: his initiation is *post-heroic.* Lustig next wanders the road without any definite aim, and his transitional situation reflects the second phase of initiation. Having lost his comfortable, heroic way of life, Lustig has not yet found a replacement. At this point, Lustig meets St. Peter, who teaches Lustig the wisdom of the Trickster. As a master of initiation, St. Peter introduces Lustig to a post-heroic and post-patriarchal way of manhood.

"The King and the Ghoul" repeats the initiation process. At the beginning, the King leaves his palace to meet the "sage" in the cemetery. The monarch separates himself from his familiar patriarchal way of life, and this constitutes the first stage of his initiation. The King next enters a transitional period, symbolized by the cemetery, in between the world of the living and the dead. There the King meets the ghoul, who uses riddles to teach the monarch about the shadow, pluralism, and black humor, while dismantling the King's logos and conventional beliefs. The ghoul initiates the King into the way of the Trickster. The culmination of the rite occurs when the King kills the necromancer with a clever ruse, and Shiva, a divine Trickster, celebrates the King's successful initiation.

The two stories reveal that men's middle experience, so painful and confusing, constitutes an initiation into a new mode of manhood. Somewhere in the middle years, men's youthful dreams, hopes, and ideals collapse, leaving them in limbo, like Lustig abruptly discharged by his King. The heroic and patriarchal paradigm of youth is destroyed in this first stage of the midlife initiation. Men then wander, uncertain of direction and purpose, and a new figure arises through dreams, fantasies, friendships, or therapy. This is the Trickster Brother, and he offers men counsel, support, and hope. As the patron of the open road and the enemy of dogmatism, the Trickster helps men break up the heroic habits of their youth. Through humor and scandal, the Trickster entices men into exploring new ways of life. Men learn about healing and resurrection rather than battle or conquest, and they embrace fraternity and equality rather than hierarchy and authority. The change from the hero and patriarch to the Trickster is difficult, since there are few formal rites of passage for mature males today, and many men turn to therapy for help. During the transition, men often feel as if they are boiled alive, until only bones are left. Yet from the skeleton, the Trickster resurrects new life, drawing on a powerful, inner masculine life energy. Usually symbolized in mythology by a sacred phallus, this male vitality is not merely sexual, but also social and spiritual: the Trickster has affairs and begets children, but he raises the dead, too, invents language, and brings fire to humanity. And the Trickster's vitality is as ancient and important as that of the Great Goddess. The Trickster Brother essentially initiates men at midlife into the deep masculine. This mature male initiation is not a product of the recent men's movement, or a ''New Age'' phenomenon. It is an ancient, archetypal experience, honored by many secret men's societies across the world, as the next section reveals.

CHAPTER EIGHT

Brother Lustig: Part 2.
Secret Societies and Men's
Initiation into the Deep Masculine

LEGENDS OF MATURE MANHOOD

Many aboriginal societies separate younger and older men in distinct fraternal orders.[1] In fact, the male puberty rite is often only the first in a series of initiations, and as men mature, they move through different fraternal lodges. The Adelaide aborigines of Australia have five stages of manhood, and men are eligible for the "bourka," the highest degree, only when they are "gray-haired." Similarly, tribes like the Wanika and the Wadai in Africa separate middle-aged men from young males, as did Native Americans like the Sioux and the Blackfoot. Fraternities of young men are typically heroic and warlike, but societies of middle-aged men are not. Mature men's lodges, in fact, revolve around the Trickster, not the hero. The lore of senior fraternities makes the point clear, and the legend of Payatamu from the Newekwe cult of the Zuni offers a good example. His story recapitulates the drama of "Brother Lustig" in an astonishing way.

According to legend, Payatamu was the son of the Sun God. Each morning, Payatamu brought out the solar disc to light up the world. One day, he met a woman who challenged him to a game of hide-and-seek. The wager was their lives and Payatamu lost, so the woman cut off his head and took it home. When

Payatamu's family learned what happened, they retrieved his body and sent out animals to find his missing head. A mole finally brought it back and his family reunited Payatamu's head with his body. Payatamu arose from the dead, but he was drastically changed. From then on, he always said and did the opposite of what he meant. He became the first "contrary" and founded the Newekwe cult as a society of sacred clowns.[2]

The Zuni story begins with Payatamu as a typical hero and the son of a great father, the Sun. Payatamu starts off with all the attributes of a young man initiated into heroic manhood, just like Lustig, who begins his tale as a soldier. Payatamu then meets a mysterious woman who beheads him, and his death reiterates a familiar event in men's tales: a hero is thrown down at the height of his power and glory. Payatamu's calamity resembles Lustig's misfortune in being summarily discharged from the army by his King and left to beg for a living. Both men lose their heroic way of life in maturity. Payatamu is fortunately raised from the dead, recalling the resurrection theme in "Brother Lustig." But after his revival, Payatamu becomes a "contrary." In Zuni society, contraries play the role of Tricksters, violating social conventions and sacred taboos. They do silly, outrageous things at solemn rituals and mock tribal elders. So Payatamu starts off as a hero serving a divine father and ends up as a Trickster, mocking conventional rules. He parallels Lustig, who shifts from being a dutiful soldier serving a King, to a Trickster wandering the world. Payatamu eventually founds the Newekwe fraternity to celebrate and institutionalize the Trickster's way of life. While Lustig does not establish a secret men's society, his friendship with St. Peter brings up the fraternal motif.

A drama similar to Payatamu's and Lustig's appears in a myth from the European Masonic Order, early in its history.[3] When men were initiated into the rank of master mason, the highest rank at the time, they learned a secret story about Hiram, the patron of the order. Hiram was the master mason and architect for the Biblical King Solomon. At the height of his career, he planned a magnificent public spectacle, the creation of a lake of molten metal. Solomon, however, became jealous of Hiram and sabotaged the mason's project, so that the lake of metal overflowed and threatened to kill all the spectators. In his moment of disaster and humiliation, Hiram had a vision of a gigantic man who commanded him to cast himself into the molten metal. Hiram obeyed, leaped into the lake of fire, and fell to the center of the earth. There the giant introduced himself as Tubal-Cain, one of Hiram's forefathers, and revealed the secret of Hiram's ancestry. In the beginning of the world, the giant said, one of the Elohim or divine spirits married Eve, who then bore a son named Cain. Another of the Elohim, named Jehovah, created Adam out of dirt and united him with Eve. She then bore another son, Abel. Using his power, Jehovah raised Abel over Cain and persecuted Cain and all of his descendants. Yet Cain's progeny taught humanity how to build in stone, write, make music, and work with metals. According to prophecy, Tubal-Cain went on, the sons of Cain would eventually overthrow the descendants of Adam and destroy the tyranny of Jehovah. After these revelations, Tubal-Cain returned Hiram to Solomon's city.

This early Masonic initiation myth may seem incomprehensible at first. However, by comparing the legend to "Brother Lustig," the myth makes sense. The drama begins with Hiram, the original Mason, working on a spectacular project at the peak of his career. But Solomon becomes jealous of Hiram and ruins the mason's work. Here the legend reiterates two important themes in men's tales. First, Hiram is thrown down from the pinnacle of glory and his heroic way of life collapses around him, the way Lustig was summarily discharged from the army. Second, Hiram is attacked by Solomon, a patriarch, the way Lustig was betrayed by his King and given hardly anything for twenty-five years of service.

In Judeo-Christian tradition, Solomon is considered a wise man, yet the Masonic legend describes him as a villain. The story is heretical and subversive, just like "Brother Lustig" with its scandalous presentation of St. Peter. The Masonic tale even makes Jehovah out to be a rogue, unfairly persecuting Cain. (The legend repeats Gnostic teachings which were rejected by early Christianity.) In turning sacred dogmas upside down, the Masonic legend reflects the Trickster's irreverent spirit and his insistence that men abandon comforting conventions. According to the story,

Cain and his descendants gave humanity masonry, the alphabet, fire, and metalworking. This reverses Biblical tradition, which describes Cain and clan as criminals. Yet Cain's gifts are characteristic of Tricksters. Hermes, Raven, Coyote, Legba, and Eshu bring language, fire, vital foodstuffs, and metalworking to humanity. This suggests that Tubal-Cain and the Cain progeny are also Tricksters. The Masonic myth elaborates on the Trickster motif in several details. Hiram, for instance, meets Tubal-Cain in the center of the earth after leaping into the molten metal. The fiery, subterranean setting suggests that Tubal-Cain and Cain's descendants are demonic. As "The Little Peasant" and "The King and the Ghoul" make clear, Tricksters initially appear to men in just this diabolical way. This is partly because the Trickster opposes heroic and patriarchal ideals, as discussed before, so patriarchal tradition makes him out to be a villain. The Masonic myth repeats the theme by saying that Cain and his descendants will eventually overthrow Jehovah, the patriarchal god. Like other Tricksters, Cain and company represent a masculine energy distinct from and opposed to the patriarch. The Masonic legend notes that Jehovah is only one of the Elohim or divine beings. This is a Gnostic doctrine and reflects a pluralistic spirit which contrasts sharply with the monotheism of orthodox Judeo-Christian tradition. In the Masonic myth, there is no single god but a number of competing divinities. As discussed in Chapter 6, such pluralism is characteristic of the Trickster, whereas insistence on a single authority defines the patriarch. Finally, the Masonic myth offers a graphic depiction of the Trickster as the deep masculine. Hiram falls into the depths of the earth and there meets Tubal-Cain, a powerful male spirit, concealed and oppressed by patriarchal tradition. Symbolically, Tubal-Cain is a masculine energy who is literally deep—in the earth and in the male psyche.

If the Masonic myth parallels "Brother Lustig," it also echoes the tale of Payatamu. The Zuni story begins when Payatamu is beheaded and his heroic life is destroyed. Similarly, Hiram is humiliated at the peak of his glory and falls into the lake of molten metal. Payatamu is revived as a Trickster and founds the Newekwe cult, a post-heroic fraternity, while Hiram meets Tubal-

Cain, learns the mysteries of the Trickster, and becomes patron of the Masonic Order.

MEN'S SECRET SOCIETIES

Payatamu's legend and the Masonic myth of Hiram typify the lore of secret societies composed of mature men. Besides the early Masonic Order and the Newekwe of the Zuni, such fraternities include the Poro of Western Africa, the Nanga of Fiji, the Cannibal society of the Kwakiutl in Northwest America, some segments of the Triad association in China, and the Rosicrucians of Western Europe, among others. Although their rituals and lore differ, these male societies share many traits which reveal the influence of the Trickster and the virtues of seasoned manhood.[4] Men's tales like "Brother Lustig" faithfully reflect the characteristics of such lodges. This makes the stories invaluable: they preserve the traditions of mature fraternities even after such organizations have withered away in modern society.

Secret fraternities are important because they give precedents for seasoned manhood and practical models for men today. First of all, these lodges are post-heroic. They include only men who have mastered the way of the hero and the patriarch, like Lustig, who was a soldier for twenty-five years. Members of mature lodges are typically successful warriors or chiefs who give up the struggle for power and turn to spiritual activities, such as instructing young men in tribal lore. The fraternities thus demonstrate the difference between mature manhood and youthful heroism. Most senior fraternities also accept *any* man who has proved himself, irrespective of his social status outside the fraternity. Commoners thus mingle with nobles, even in cultures where this is rare outside the lodge. In Lustig's story, the poor soldier travels with no less a personage than St. Peter, the premier apostle. Mature fraternities thus abandon the hierarchy typical of heroic and patriarchal organizations. The lodges embrace the Trickster's spiritual camaraderie, and this new brotherhood cuts across tribal boundaries. Initiates of the Poro, Ukuku, and Mwetyi lodges in Africa, for example, travel safely through different tribal territories, despite warfare between the tribes. The Trickster's fraternity overrides patriarchal boundaries or heroic loyalties to a clan. Lustig symbolizes this aspect in a subtle detail. As a soldier, Lustig fought to defend or expand the boundaries of his country. As a wanderer, he traveled from kingdom to kingdom, ignoring the borders for which he fought earlier.

Related to this defiance of boundaries, mature men's societies habitually do outrageous and scandalous things. They break social borders. The Kwakiutl Cannibal society required ritual cannibalism as part of its initiation, as did higher ranks of the Poro society in West Africa. Both fraternities come from cultures that abhor cannibalism, so the initiation deliberately defies a basic social taboo. This subversive spirit forces men to question comfortable assumptions and explore new perspectives, two goals of the Trickster. Lustig's tale reflects this Tricksterish spirit in the episode with the lamb's heart, where the story pokes fun at the image of the sacred heart of Jesus.

Within the privacy of their secret lodges, mature men become playful and relaxed. They tease each other and play pranks, like Lustig and St. Peter. Temporarily liberated from family and tribal responsibilities, men are free to be themselves and experiment with new roles. With such a playful, scandalous, and outrageous spirit in mature men's societies it is not surprising that their mythic patrons are Tricksters. Payatamu the Trickster is the patron of the Newekwe cult, while Tubal-Cain plays that role for the early Masonic order. Ogo-Yuguru, the Trickster for the Dogon people of Africa, presides over their male Society of Masks; Minabozho the Hare-Trickster established the Medewiwin society of the North American Ojibway tribe; and Wakdjunkaga is the patron of the Medicine Rite of the Winnebagos. The rule of the Trickster in mature fraternities is often very concrete because initiates are taught various tricks to fool fellow tribesmen. Lodge members become Tricksters. The Whare Kura, a Maori secret society, teaches their initiates ventriloquism, while the men's lodges of the Kwakiutl in Northwest America instruct their members in sleights-of-hand. Such trickery recalls how Lustig learned to steal after St. Peter gave him the magic knapsack, and the pack itself is the ultimate tool for sleight-of-hand!

The ruses of mature male lodges have a serious, generative

purpose. The trickery is used, for instance, in puberty rites for young men. The older men pretend to be spirits, gods, demons, and ancestors and terrorize adolescent boys to separate them from their childhood ways and initiate them into the way of the hero. If the youths see only the heroic aspect, the Trickster is the secret patron of the rite. The trickery is also important in other rites of secret fraternities. Lodges like Native American societies of sacred clowns conduct tribal ceremonies to ensure good hunting and fertile fields or to resolve tribal tensions. The fraternities use masks and magic tricks to awe their tribesmen, but behind the deceptions lies a generative purpose. "Brother Lustig" hints at this generativity when he gives one of his stolen geese to two hungry young men and later clears a castle of demons, making it safe for people to live in again. His trickery helps others.

The close parallels between "Brother Lustig," mature male fraternities, Payatamu's legend, and the Masonic story, I suggest, reflect a common origin in the male psyche. Mircea Eliade noted that fairy tales often preserve initiation themes long after the rites have been forgotten. So men's tales may derive from the secret myths of senior fraternities.

While rare in modern society, fraternities of mature men have not disappeared completely. The archetype is too powerful. A contemporary example is the Bohemian Club, a secretive, all-male society based in California.[5] Originally founded by Bret Harte and several other journalists, who were something of Tricksters themselves, the Bohemian Club meets annually in a secluded wilderness. The club consists of highly successful men who have mastered the way of the hero and patriarch. Chief executives of billion-dollar companies and several former American presidents are members. Yet the primary focus of the annual meeting lies in producing ribald skits and hilarious musicals. In these extravaganzas, senators, generals, and millionaires often dress as women, amidst much laughter. The spirit of the Trickster, not the patriarch, inspires these festivities. To be sure, some men use the retreat to make business contacts, but this practice is explicitly discouraged. "No women, no gambling, no business, no arguing" is the informal motto.

Exclusive fraternities like the Bohemian Club are controversial today. Historically such all-male societies were often racist cabals, where a few older men cut deals among themselves and excluded women and minorities. The real problem, I think, lies in the heroic and patriarchal pattern, not the all-male group itself. It is the heroic emphasis on proving one's manhood which leads groups of young men, like tavern buddies, into panty raids or gang rape. The patriarchal obsession with power, in turn, tempts exclusive organizations composed of older men into becoming cabals. Fraternities inspired by the Trickster, by contrast, oppose heroic conquest and patriarchal authority. Trickster societies emphasize equality and exploration instead of exclusion and exploitation. Despite their bad reputation, then, senior male fraternities have many positive potentials. They parallel the Trickster himself, who initially appears to be a criminal, but who conceals hidden male wisdom. To be sure, many mature male lodges remain stuck in shadowy elements of masculine fraternity, the way some men become thieves and never reach the insights behind the Trickster's stealing. Yet the failure and faults of a few men and their lodges should not discredit the Trickster's deeper wisdom.

MEN'S SOCIETIES IN MODERN CULTURE

Men today usually do not have access to or interest in traditional secret societies. So, many spontaneously create their own lodges. Aaron Kipnis offers an amusing and poignant report in his book *Knights Without Armor.* For many years, he and several other middle-aged men met in an ongoing discussion group. Yet the gathering started off informally as a traditional, weekly, all-male poker party! Calling themselves the knights of "the round (poker) table," the patron of their assembly was the Trickster, an inveterate gambler himself.

For other men, the Trickster's initiation occurs individually and especially through therapy. Modern society lacks socially sanctioned rites or fraternities for mature men, so psychotherapy has become a major vehicle for men's initiation into the deep masculine. Joseph Henderson, a Jungian analyst, offers a striking example in *Thresholds of Initiation,* with a forty-eight-year-old man in analysis. The gentleman had a "big" dream which proved to be pivotal in his life. In the dream, the man started off as a youth in the military. He went with a group of young men to a stadium for an Olympic competition. Afterward, the athletes swam in the ocean, and the youths found an enormous rock hidden underwater. Five hundred of the young men lifted the stone up. The dreamer moved away a slight distance, and from this perspective he recognized that the rock was actually a man's head, part of an ancient statue hidden for centuries on the ocean bottom. The scene shifted again, and the gentleman stood next to another man in front of a store window. The dreamer bent over, pulled down his pants, spread his buttocks apart, and looked at his anus reflected in the window, while making a strange expression with his mouth. The other man laughed and followed suit.

The dreamer associated the drama with some sort of initiation rite, but was unsure what it involved. Henderson underscores the initiation theme and discusses the adolescent elements in the dream, like the young men competing for an Olympic prize. We can deepen the interpretation if we relate the dream to men's tales, Tricksters, and men's initiation into the deep masculine. The dream begins with a traditional heroic activity, young men vying for a grand athletic championship. The dreamer participates eagerly in the competition and then, as part of a group of men, lifts up a huge stone from the sea. Here the dreamer shifts to being an observer, and he recognizes that the stone is actually a man's head from an ancient statue. Since the ocean commonly symbolizes the unconscious in dreams, the archaic figure can be interpreted as a masculine element emerging from the unconscious, namely, the deep masculine. Significantly, the dreamer identifies the stone as a man's head because he is some distance away from it and can thus make out the overall shape of the rock. Only when the dreamer distances himself from his heroic activities can he recognize the deep masculine. This separation from the heroic paradigm is the first step in the mature male initiation, as "Brother Lustig" and "The King and the Ghoul" showed.

The next episode in the dream is initially puzzling. The dreamer pulls down his pants, bends over, and looks at his anus reflected in a store window. Henderson interprets this episode as the return of normal, adolescent, autoerotic instincts which the dreamer, like other men, repressed as an adult. This is a form of confronting the shadow: young men suppress their crude impulses in order to take a place in society, but those instincts return at midlife. Yet there is a deeper layer of meaning to the anal episode, because scatological themes are typical of Tricksters. A few Trickster tales illustrate the point.[6]

Wakdjunkaga, the Winnebago Trickster, once left his anus to guard some roasted ducks while he went on an errand. (Wakdjunkaga had detachable body parts.) When he returned, Wakdjunkaga found someone had stolen the ducks, so he became furious with his anus for failing to watch his food. Wakdjunkaga sat in the fire to punish his anus—and burned himself! Coyote, for his part, once made a number of young maidens pregnant. Chased by irate tribe members, he hid in a hollow log, but the people sealed both ends off. Trapped inside, Coyote escaped only by cutting himself into small pieces and pushing them out a little knothole. Then he reassembled himself, but he misplaced his anus. As might be imagined, the oversight led to endless embarrassing problems until Coyote used a carrot as a plug. From Africa comes a kindred tale about Ananse the Ashanti Trickster. Ananse learned a magic trick that allowed him to remove his head at will and then reattach it. Unfortunately, he accidentally stuck his head to his buttocks, producing a whole series of hilarious misadventures until he found the countermagic. Many more tales specifically associate anal humor with the Trickster, and there are several reasons for this. The Trickster likes to shock people and make fun of conventional propriety, so scatological humor fits him perfectly. He also insists that individuals acknowledge the shadowy, "shitty" side of life. In classical Freudian terms, anal themes relate to issues of control and self-control, and the Trickster naturally mocks such self-discipline.

The anal theme in Trickster tales casts new light on the dream of the man staring at his anus. The drama introduces the archetype of the Trickster through a highly disguised and appropriately scandalous form. (The Trickster, of course, loves disguises and scandals.) The Trickster theme also helps explain the presence of the second man in the dream. He is a Trickster Brother. By mimicking the dreamer and laughing, while looking at his own anus, the second man makes the shocking exhibitionism a hilarious farce. The event also become symbolic. When the two men look at the reflections of their rear ends, they make funny expressions with their mouths. Pursed the right way, the mouth can look just like the anus. The dream thus links the mouth, with its refined connection to language and food, to the anus, with its unsavory link to feces and wastes. Such a scandalous union of opposites is the Trickster's delight. The second man thus transforms a crude, shadowy event into a shocking, symbolic action. Without the Trickster Brother, in fact, the dream would simply seem auto-erotic and perverse.

The man's dream dramatizes a shift from the archetype of the hero, which animates young men, to the path of the Trickster, characteristic of mature manhood.[7] This is the pattern portrayed in "Brother Lustig," the tale of Payatamu, and the Masonic myth of Hiram: mature men turn from the hero's virtue and glory to the Trickster's humor and scandal. My interpretation of the dream may seem convoluted, but Trickster motifs usually appear in small details that can be easily overlooked. Heroic and patriarchal imagery is more obvious, familiar, and dramatic. The hero and patriarch, after all, love fame and glory, so when they appear in dreams and fantasies, they demand center stage. The Trickster prefers disguises and prowls the outer boundaries. He is therefore easy to miss. The problem is complicated by the fact that many men still have heroic tasks to complete and unfinished business from youth to resolve. How is a man to know whether to remain on the hero's path or seek the Trickster's? Fortunately, a man's inner Trickster will give clues. If he clings too long to heroic ways, his life will be stagnant and sterile: the inner Trickster will keep him walking back and forth in a cemetery, the way the ghoul harassed the King in the last chapter, until the man finally proceeds to the next step. When a man is ready, though, the Trickster emerges in dreams and fantasies, usually in an unexpected or shocking form.

One further aspect of men's initiation into the mature manhood remains to be discussed—the connection between the Trickster and the shaman. "Brother Lustig" highlights the point when St.

Peter resurrects the dead princesses by boiling their bodies until only the bones are left.

SHAMAN AND TRICKSTER

St. Peter's ritual differs markedly from how the New Testament portrays resurrection: Jesus simply commands a newly dead person, like Lazarus, to arise. As the premier apostle, we would expect St. Peter to follow suit, and the fact that he does not forces us to look for symbolic meanings. We discussed one interpretation already: dismembering the bodies dramatizes how men's convictions are dismantled at midlife. But there is a deeper level of meaning, and the key lies in the gruesome nature of the apostle's procedure. St. Peter even uses a cauldron like those traditionally associated with witches and black magic in European folklore. The apostle's resurrection rite thus seems demonic. This is blasphemous, because Christian tradition makes God the source of resurrection and healing, not the Devil. The peculiarity of Peter's actions demands a closer look.

An explanation of the macabre resurrection can be found in shamanism, because St. Peter's procedure is remarkably similar to shamanic initiations. In a tradition found among aboriginal cultures from Australia to Siberia and in both North and South America, an individual is initiated as a shaman when he has a visionary experience in which he is boiled alive, dismembered, or destroyed in some way, until only his skeleton remains.[8] Then demonic spirits resurrect the initiate, giving him a new body and the power to heal. "Brother Lustig" elaborates on the shamanic theme in a small detail: Lustig travels to both Hell and Heaven at the end of his tale. But such journeys are a traditional function of shamans, who visit the underworld and the world above, communicating with demons and gods.

An earlier allusion to shamanism appeared in "The King and the Ghoul." There the monarch goes to the cemetery, contends with the shadowy ghoul and the evil necromancer, and returns with great blessing and power. His drama recapitulates what shamans practice in their healing rituals. When a shaman treats a patient, he goes into a trance and experiences a descent into the underworld. There he confronts the demons of disease and death and negotiates with them, the way the King and the ghoul converse; or the shaman battles the underworld spirits, the way the King kills the necromancer. The successful shaman returns with a cure for his patient.

Other fairy tales refer to shamanism even more explicitly, like "The Godfather" from Germany, "The Bonesetter" from Japan, "The Angry Wife" from Russia, and "The Stoning" from Morocco. As Mircea Eliade pointed out, shamanic themes were incorporated into fairy tales, even though formal religions like Christianity suppressed shamanic practices. What is significant about "Brother Lustig" is that it portrays St. Peter being a Trickster *and* a shaman at the same time. This suggests the two roles are linked, and many scholars, such as Carl Jung and Joseph Campbell, have confirmed the association. Tricksters are divine versions of shamans, what Campbell calls "super shamans."[9] The shaman, conversely, is a human version of the Trickster. Shamans and tricksters can be considered part of the same archetype, two aspects of a single mythic image, just the way the hero and the patriarch are two aspects of one archetype. The traits of the shaman-Trickster also sum up the themes of men's tales and the major tasks men face in midlife. Indeed, the shaman-Trickster offers an alternative to the hero and patriarch as a paradigm of manhood. This becomes clear if we consider a few basic traits common to the shaman and the Trickster, as portrayed in "Brother Lustig" and the other men's tales.

COMMUNICATION

First of all, shamans and Tricksters are communicators and mediators. Tricksters like Hermes, Legba, and Eshu are messengers, linking humanity and the gods, as well as the living and the dead. Shamans do the same thing in their trances, carrying petitions and prayers from their fellow tribesmen to spirits and gods. "Brother Lustig" conveys the theme in the person of St. Peter. The apostle's historic mission was to communicate God's word to humanity, and in Catholic lore, St. Peter and his successors, the Popes, mediate between humanity and God. Even earlier,

"The King and the Ghoul" introduced the communication motif with the ghoul who tried to teach the monarch through clever riddles.

In emphasizing communication, the shaman-Trickster differs sharply from the hero-patriarch. The latter seeks conquest rather than communication and domination instead of discussion. The contrast is clear in "The Wizard King," where the autocratic King takes the form of the predatory eagle, while his conciliatory son adopts the guise of a poetic parrot. The eagle symbolizes the power and glory of the hero-patriarch, while the parrot represents the communication and cleverness of the shaman-Trickster. The contrast resurfaces in "The King and the Ghoul," where the ghoul differs drastically from the necromancer. The ghoul tries to communicate with the King, while the necromancer seeks to dominate and exploit the monarch.

As mediator and messenger, the shaman-Trickster symbolizes a major task for mature men—shifting from a youthful focus on conquest and domination to a new spirit of negotiation and communication. Miguel Cervantes, the Spanish writer, offers a dramatic example of this transition. A professional soldier in his youth, Cervantes started writing only at midlife and published his classic book, *Don Quixote,* at fifty-eight years of age. Cervantes moved from warrior to storyteller, from hero to communicator. An acquaintance of mine experienced a similar transformation. I met John through my work on fairy tales, after he started a new career as a storyteller. Curious about his dramatic life-change, I asked him about his experience, and he described an extraordinary saga. A highly successful entrepreneur and a former Marine, while he sat in his office one day, John literally heard a voice commanding him to tell stories. He feared he might be going crazy, but the voice did not let up until he obeyed. He sold his business and started telling tales, first to friends, then as a professional storyteller. Like Cervantes, John gave up the hero's path for communication and the way of the shaman-Trickster. Telling stories, I might add, is characteristic of Tricksters. In Ashanti lore, the Sky God awarded Ananse the Trickster custody of all tales and named the stories after Ananse.

As a male spirit, the shaman-Trickster personifies *masculine* communication. This is vitally important today when communication is often considered "feminine," and men are encouraged to emulate women, for example in verbalizing feelings. From Hermes to Ananse, the shaman-Trickster embodies a male mode of communication. Instead of talking things over and sharing emotions, which is emphasized in feminine conversation, the shaman-Trickster jokes, teases, and tells tall tales—an archetypally masculine style of communicating. Feminine connection also emphasizes ongoing relationships and continual contact between people. Male connection, by contrast, tends to be episodic. Men may not talk to each other for years at a time, yet when a crisis occurs, brothers and comrades often join together and support one another as if no time had passed. "Brother Lustig" illustrates this when Lustig bumbles his attempt at resurrecting the second dead Princess, and St. Peter rescues him. The apostle offers to help even though the two men had parted over irreconcilable differences some time before. By coming and going unpredictably, the Trickster symbolizes a uniquely masculine spirit of communion, which is intermittent, unspoken, and intangible—until needed. Men and women must respect these deep, archetypal differences in communication. If men need to learn more about expressing their emotions, women must also recognize the profound meanings in men's actions, jokes, and silences.

As a communicator, the shaman-Trickster carries messages between the gods and humanity. In psychological terms, he communicates between the inner and outer worlds, between conscious and unconscious. The shaman-Trickster provides men with a *masculine* link to the unconscious. He corrects the misconception that the anima is a man's only connection to the inner depths. If that were true, men would be forever dependent upon the feminine to guide them into their own psyches, and would have to lean on wives, mothers, lovers, and daughters to understand themselves. The shaman-Trickster relieves men and women of this error. This is another factor which makes male therapists particularly helpful to men in therapy. (But this is true only if the therapist has moved from hero-patriarch to shaman-Trickster, and learned both feminine and masculine modes of understanding.)

INTEGRATING OPPOSITES

Because of his capacity to mediate, the shaman-Trickster balances opposites and paradoxes. In fact, he is a mass of contradictions. Mercurius, the Trickster in European alchemy, was said to be good and evil, beautiful and ugly, old and young, creator and destroyer, all at once. The same applies to Native American Tricksters, like Wakdjunkaga and Coyote, and African Tricksters like Eshu or Legba. The Yoruba of Africa even say that after the High God created good and evil, he sent Eshu specifically to balance the two sides. Shamans, in turn, are full of opposites and contradictions. They are considered both profoundly wise and wildly foolish, akin to gods with their power to heal, but also like demons with their ability to cast evil spells. Many male shamans wear female clothing, combining masculine and feminine traits. Lustig and St. Peter reflect the contradictory nature of the shaman-Trickster. The apostle demands that Lustig be virtuous and yet entices the soldier into lying and stealing. For his part, Lustig steals, but gives generously to the poor. Similarly, the ghoul in "The King and the Ghoul" is demonic, but also healing. He harasses the King while teaching the monarch vital lessons.

In integrating opposites, the shaman-Trickster diverges from the hero-patriarch. As we discussed with "The Little Peasant," the hero-patriarch chooses one side of a duality and suppresses the other. He typically divides the world into male and female, good and bad, light and dark, strong and weak, sublime and dirty. Then he claims the former camp as his, denying any trace of the latter in himself. Men's task in maturity is to integrate the two sides. Jung was perhaps the first modern psychologist to notice that balancing dualities is a major task for mature men, but Daniel Levinson confirms the point in *The Seasons of a Man's Life*. At midlife, men struggle with the polarities of youth and old age, creation and destruction, love and hate, male and female, good and bad, power and vulnerability, triumph and tragedy. To survive, men must transcend dualities, and hold several conflicting views at once.[10] This is a talent the shaman-Trickster offers to teach.

One particularly dramatic polarity that the shaman-Trickster balances is life and death: the shaman-Trickster is intimately linked to death and resurrection. As mentioned earlier, shamans are typically initiated by visions of dismemberment and revival. For their part, Tricksters like Wakdjunkaga and Coyote of North America, Fox from South America, or Kaggen from Africa, are regularly killed, dismembered, and resurrected. Tricksters can even resurrect themselves, like Coyote, who cut himself into little pieces to escape from a log and then reassembled himself.

The fact that shamans and Tricksters are repeatedly killed and resurrected is profoundly symbolic. In contrast to the hero-patriarch, who denies his pain and fear and tries to maintain a façade of invincibility, the shaman-Trickster accepts his vulnerability and woundedness. The hero-patriarch sees injury and suffering as defeat and humiliation, something to be avoided, denied, or repressed. The shaman-Trickster sees woundedness as an opportunity for transformation and insight. He mocks the stereotype of the "strong, silent" hero. Yet the shaman-Trickster is no weakling. In aboriginal cultures, shamans are typically robust individuals who can dance or drum for hours on end, longer than other men in their tribe. As Roger Walsh points out in *The Spirit of Shamanism,* shamans are also confident, flexible, creative, intelligent, and healthy psychologically. So if the shaman-Trickster acknowledges his vulnerability and woundedness, he remains fierce and strong. He combines power and weakness, life and death. He provides a new model of manhood for men struggling with their vulnerability and neediness at midlife—for men in therapy, in recovery, or on an inward quest. Most important, the shaman-Trickster promises help and healing when men take the road of ashes, as they inevitably do in the middle years.

A final polarity that the shaman-Trickster integrates is particularly important for men today—individuation vs. the common good. The individualism of the shaman-Trickster is clear. Shamans do not conform to conventional religious dogma, but rely upon their own visions for guidance. The Trickster, for his part, consistently opposes orthodoxy and loves to break rules. Like the little peasant, the ghoul, and Lustig, the Trickster favors individual innovation over collective conformity. Here the shaman-Trickster contrasts dramatically with the hero-patriarch, who insists that everyone follow the same rules, namely his own. Where the patriarch codifies and formalizes laws, such as the ancient Code of Hammurabi, the Ten Commandments, or the Napoleonic Code, the shaman-Trickster thumbs his nose at convention. He personifies another major task for men at midlife—breaking free from conformity to seek one's own inner vision. At the same time, the shaman-Trickster works for the common good and not simply his own profit. The Trickster gives humankind gifts essential to civilization. Prometheus, Raven, and Maui gave fire to humanity, while Hermes, Eshu, and Legba brought language and speech. Ogo-Yuguru, an African Trickster, laid down the basic customs for the Dogon people, and so did Ananse for the Ashanti and Coyote for many Native American tribes.[11] For their part, shamans use their rituals to heal the sick, guarantee plentiful game for hunters, and ensure fertility for mothers. Shamans also help resolve conflicts between individuals, and they make prophecies to aid tribal decisions. As a giver of culture and a helper of humanity, the shaman-Trickster reminds men of two important lessons at midlife. First, he insists that private experience and individual development are not enough. Men must take action within their communities. The shaman-Trickster seeks the common good and not just his own enlightenment. He is not simply a therapist to individuals, but to society in general. For men today this means that personal therapy or recovery can only be the first step of a longer journey. Initiation into the deep masculine is complete only when men return to the concerns of their communities.

Second, the shaman-Trickster specifically offers a *nonpatriarchal* approach to society. His unique perspective becomes clear if we compare the attitudes of the patriarch and the Trickster toward a central issue in society—power. The patriarch uses power as a weapon to control other people, while the Trickster sees power as a tool for everyone to use. The Trickster, for instance, brought language to humanity so that people could communicate with each other and speak their minds. The patriarch, on the other hand, uses language as "logos" or law, with which he enforces his will. Moreover, the patriarchal image of power is a pyramid with the hero-patriarch at the top and everybody underneath. The Trickster's image is a road which anyone can use. Eshu the African Trickster is called "roadmaker," and many shamans are known as "pathfinders." The shift from domination to generativity, from the hero-patriarch to the shaman-Trickster, is a major difference between men who become tyrants with age and those who grow in wisdom.

INITIATION INTO THE SHAMAN-TRICKSTER

The parallels between shamans and Tricksters confirm that they are really two aspects of one mythic pattern, just as the hero and patriarch are two facets of one archetype. Furthermore, men's initiation into the shaman-Trickster occurs only after men surrender the heroic and patriarchal paradigm. Mircea Eliade suggested something like this after his review of initiation rites. He concluded that there are three basic types: puberty rites, induction into secret societies, and shamanic initiations.[12] The latter two were so similar, he felt, that they were variations on a single form. So there are really two forms of initiation for men: puberty rites dominated by heroic themes, and initiation into secret societies inspired by the shaman-Trickster. The second passage is men's midlife immersion in the deep masculine.

The shaman-Trickster and the hero-patriarch represent two distinct models of the male psyche. The traditional heroic concept depicts the ego fighting off unacceptable impulses, controlling instincts, sublimating drives, and forging a coherent sense of identity. Like a patriarch, the ego tries to subdue the unconscious and rule the psyche. The shaman-Trickster personifies negotiation and mediation with the unconscious instead of battle or conquest. Integration is his goal, not domination. This helps explain why the Trickster is a post-heroic archetype. Direct contact with the unconscious can be overwhelming, and so younger men repress it. With maturity and the strength of experience, men learn to withstand a face-to-face encounter with the unconscious. Older men therefore stop repressing the unconscious.

Writers like Sam Keen in *Fire in the Belly* and Robert Bly in *Iron John* have decried the lack of male initiations in modern society. The result, they argue, is that teenage boys have little guidance in becoming men. Yet there is another, equally serious problem. There are many heroic initiations still available for young men today, as Aaron Kipnis in *Knights Without Armor* and Michael Gurian in *The Prince and the King* point out: earning a million dollars, joining the army, going on wilderness treks, or finishing a doctorate. The deeper problem, I think, is the lack of initiation for *fathers*, for mature men. Without these midlife initiations, older men remain stuck in heroic and patriarchal roles and do not make way for their juniors. So father and son, mental and apprentice, senior and junior, battle for position. The Oedipal combat is often to the death. Neither side can imagine anything besides sweet victory or intolerable defeat. When fathers are initiated into the mysteries of the shaman-Trickster, they move on and allow their sons to move up. The shaman-Trickster resolves the Oedipal rivalry inherent in the heroic and patriarchal paradigm. This mature male initiation helps women, too, because older men also make room for younger women. Moreover, under the guidance of the shaman-Trickster, men abandon the patriarch's patronizing attitude toward women and the hero's love-hate relationship toward the "fairer sex."

The ultimate result of the shaman-Trickster's initiation is contact with the divine. In "Brother Lustig," the soldier enters Heaven, while in "The King and the Ghoul," the monarch meets Shiva face-to-face. The two tales bring up the spiritual tasks of men at midlife. The next story elaborates on the issue, at the same time it summarizes all the themes discussed so far.

CHAPTER NINE

Go I Know Not Whither: Part 1.
From Inner Feminine to
Deep Masculine

GO I KNOW NOT WHITHER,
BRING BACK I KNOW NOT WHAT

(FROM RUSSIA)

Long ago, there lived a soldier named Fedot, who was a marks-man in the army. He went hunting for his King every day in the forest and returned laden with game, so the King favored him over other soldiers. One day, Fedot ventured deep into the wilderness, saw a dove sitting on a branch, and shot it. When Fedot picked up the bird to wring its neck, it spoke.

"Spare my life, and you will be rewarded!" the dove exclaimed. Fedot was astonished. "Take me home," the dove went on, "put me on your windowsill, and when I fall asleep, strike me with the back of your right hand. Then you shall see what you shall see."

The soldier followed the dove's advice. He went home, put the bird on his windowsill, waited until it went to sleep, then struck it with the back of his hand. Instantly, the dove turned into a beautiful woman. "You have won me," the maiden said in a lovely voice, "and now I shall be your wife!" Fedot rejoiced in his good fortune, and married the maiden.

Some time later, Fedot's wife said, "You hunt every day in the forest with little reward. But I have an idea which will make us rich." She asked Fedot to buy two hundred rubles' worth of silk, and when he returned with the thread, his wife told him, "Sleep, my husband, and in the morning we shall see what we shall see." The marksman went to bed, and his wife opened a magic book she owned. Two spirits materialized.

"What do you wish?" they asked her.

"Take this silk," she said, "and weave me a beautiful carpet, with pictures of the kingdom on it." The spirits bowed and set to work. By morning they finished the carpet, and it was so beautiful, it lit up the room like the sun.

When Fedot awoke, his wife gave him the tapestry. "Take this to the market," she said, "and sell it. But do not set a price yourself, just take whatever is offered." When Fedot showed the cloth at the marketplace, a crowd of merchants quickly gathered, astonished at the beauty of the weaving.

"What is your price?" the merchants asked.

"You are merchants," Fedot answered, "so you tell me how much it is worth." The merchants murmured among themselves, but they could not set a price, so marvelous was the carpet. At that moment, the King's steward rode by. He saw the tapestry and offered 10,000 rubles for it. Fedot agreed, and the steward returned to the palace. "Majesty," the minister told his King, "look at the magnificent tapestry I bought today!"

When the King saw the cloth, he desired it for himself. He took it from his steward and paid the man 25,000 rubles. The chamberlain accepted the money and rode off to Fedot's house. "I shall order myself another one!" he thought. When Fedot's wife appeared at the door, the minister was struck dumb by her beauty. He forgot what he came for, and from then on, he could neither eat nor sleep.

The King inquired about his steward's ailment. "It is Fedot's wife!" the chamberlain sighed. "Never have I seen such beauty!"

The King went to look for himself, and when he saw her, he fell in love with her at once.

"I am the King, but I have no Queen," the monarch muttered to himself. "How could a lowly soldier have such a beautiful wife? She should be mine!" The next day, the King summoned the steward. "You told me about the soldier's wife. Now tell me how to get rid of Fedot so I can marry his wife! If you fail," the King threatened, "I will have your head cut off!"

Try as he might, the chamberlain could not think of a way to eliminate the soldier. Then he ran into Baba Yaga, the witch. "I know your troubles," Baba Yaga declared, "and I can help you."

"If you do," the steward said hopefully, "I will pay you in gold!"

Baba Yaga cackled. "You want to get rid of the marksman, Fedot, so the King can marry his wife. The soldier is simple, and easily done in, but his wife is cunning. So this is what you must do." The witch whispered to the steward. The minister nodded eagerly, gave her a bag of gold, and ran back to the palace. The next day the monarch summoned Fedot.

"Marksman," the King declared, "I have a task for you. Beyond thrice nine lands, in the thrice tenth kingdom there lives a stag with golden horns. Bring this creature back to me alive. If you fail, it will cost you your head! I will provide you with a ship and sailors." The King ordered up the oldest ship in his navy, sure to sink in a short time, and sent his steward to gather up fifty drunks and ruffians to serve as Fedot's crew. The soldier saw all this and returned home troubled.

"What is the matter?" his wife asked him. Fedot explained the problem, and his wife smiled. "You have nothing to fear. Just sleep tonight. The morning is wiser than the evening." When Fedot went to bed, his wife opened her magic book, and the two spirits materialized. "Find me this golden stag," she commanded, "in the thrice tenth kingdom, beyond thrice nine lands." The spirits vanished, and before dawn they returned with the golden stag.

When Fedot awoke, his wife told him, "Take this stag on board your ship. Sail away for five days, and then turn back." So the soldier put the animal in a cage, covered it up, and loaded it on the ship. The King came to bid Fedot farewell, and the monarch smiled malevolently.

When the ship sailed out of sight, Fedot gave his crew all the wine they wanted, so they remembered nothing of the trip. On the fifth day, Fedot turned the ship around and sailed back home.

The King was furious. "You dare return without the golden stag?" the monarch demanded.

"But here it is," Fedot replied, taking the cover off the cage. The King was enraged at Fedot's success, but he could not do anything to the marksman. So the monarch summoned his steward.

"You failed!" the King shouted. "Your head is forfeit unless you find another way to get rid of this soldier!"

The frightened steward ran off, seeking Baba Yaga. He found her and asked for her help again. She nodded and said, "As I told you, the soldier is a simple man and easily disposed of. But his wife—she is another matter. Still, you have nothing to fear. I have a task that not even she can succeed at!" The witch whispered in the chamberlain's ear. The steward brightened, paid her more gold, and rushed back to the King. When the minister told the King the plan, the monarch grinned maliciously.

That very day the King summoned Fedot. "I have another task for you," the monarch told the soldier. "Go I know not whither and bring back I know not what, and if you return before you succeed, I will have your head!"

Fedot went home, full of woe. His wife asked what the problem was and he explained the King's demand. "Ah," she murmured, "it takes nine years to get there and nine more to return. But go to sleep. The morning is wiser than the evening." When Fedot went to bed, his wife opened her magic book, and the two spirits appeared. She asked them, "Can you go I know not whither, and bring back I know not what?" The spirits shook their heads and replied, "We do not know where that place is." So the wife sadly closed her book.

The next morning, she awoke her husband, gave him a golden ball, and told him, "For eighteen years you must wander, but this ball will show you the way. And wherever you go, use this handkerchief to wash your face. I made it myself." She and Fedot sadly took leave of each other, and Fedot set off on his journey.

Soon afterward, the King went to Fedot's wife. "Marry me!" he commanded her. "I am married to Fedot," she replied, "and he still lives." "If you do not agree," the King threatened, "I shall force you." The beautiful wife laughed, struck her foot on the floor, turned into a dove, and flew into the forest.

Meanwhile, Fedot walked on and on, following the ball as it rolled in front of him. Finally, the ball rolled up to a palace and vanished. The soldier scratched his head a moment and walked inside. Three beautiful maidens appeared and besieged the marksman with questions. "Who are you?" "From where have you come?" "Where are you going?"

Fedot brushed aside their queries. "My ladies, I have journeyed far. You should give me food and rest first, and then ask me questions." So the three women set out a meal and showed Fedot to a room. He collapsed on the bed and slept the night. The next morning, the maidens awoke the marksman and brought him towels and water for washing.

"I have my own towel," Fedot said, and drew out the handkerchief from his wife. The maidens cried out, "Where did you find such a cloth?"

"My wife made it," the soldier said proudly.

"Then you are the husband of our sister!" the maidens exclaimed, and they fetched their mother. The old woman took one look at the handkerchief and nodded. "Yes, my daughter made that."

Fedot told his story, describing how he met his wife, and explaining the King's evil plans to separate them. When Fedot finished, he asked the women, "Do you know how to go to I know not whither and bring back I know not what?"

The maidens shook their heads, and the old woman sighed,

"Alas, even I do not know where you might find such a thing. But my servants may know." The old woman went outside, clapped her hands, and from all sides, birds and beasts appeared. "Dear friends," she cried out, "you see everything on land and in the air. Do you know how to go to I know not whither and bring back I know not what?" The beasts and birds talked among themselves, and then said, "No, we do not know."

The old woman went to a cupboard and drew out an enormous book. She opened it, and two giants appeared. "What do you wish, madam?" they asked.

"Take me and my son-in-law to the middle of the ocean," she commanded. In the blink of an eye, Fedot found himself floating above the waves with his mother-in-law. The old woman clapped her hands, and all the inhabitants of the sea appeared. "Dear servants," she asked them, "you swim through the oceans and rivers of the world. Do you know how to go I know not whither and bring back I know not what?" All the creatures of water talked among themselves, and then they shook their heads. "No, we do not know how to go there and bring back that marvel."

Fedot became discouraged, but an old frog came forward, limping painfully. "Croak! Croak!" the frog whispered. "I know the way!" The old woman picked up the frog, and they all returned to the palace. "What you seek," the frog told Fedot, "is at the end of the world. I would lead you there myself, but I am too old to walk. I have been retired for thirty years, and it would take me fifty more to make the journey."

The mother-in-law thought a moment, filled a jar full of milk, and put the frog in it. "Carry this jar," she told Fedot, "and let her show you the way." The marksman quickly set forth with the frog.

Fedot traveled far and wide, guided by the frog, until they came to a river of fire, circling a great mountain. The frog crawled out of the jar. "Sit on my back," the frog said, "and I will leap over the fire. Do not fear for me." Hesitantly, Fedot sat on the tiny creature, worried he would squash her. Beneath him the frog swelled up until she was as big as a barn. Then she leaped over the river of fire, and shrank back to her normal size.

"You must go on alone," the frog told the soldier. "Enter that door"—the frog pointed to a portal in the mountain—"and you will find yourself in a cave. Hide yourself. Two men will appear. Watch what they do and when they leave, do exactly what they did. I will wait for you here."

Fedot walked through the door and found himself in a great cavern. He hid in a cupboard, and a few moments later, two old men came into the cave. They yelled out, "Shmat Razum, set us a meal!" Instantly, candles were lit, and a feast set out. The two old men sat down, ate their fill, and then said, "Shmat Razum, clear everything away!" The dishes vanished, and the two old men departed.

Fedot crawled out of his hiding place, sat at the table, and cried out, "Shmat Razum!" A voice replied, "What do you wish?" The soldier answered, "Give me some food." Before Fedot could take another breath, a sumptuous meal appeared before him. The marksman paused, and said, "Shmat Razum, brother, why don't you sit down and eat with me?"

The invisible being replied, "I thank you, good man. For thirty years I have served these two old men, and not once have they invited me to join them." Another plate and fork appeared beside the soldier, and soon the utensils began to move and food disappeared. Fedot marveled at his invisible companion, and the two began talking. Finally Fedot asked, "Shmat Razum, why don't you journey with me and be my servant?"

The voice replied, "Why not? I see that you are kind, and I have toiled too long for the old men. I will go with you." Fedot left the cave, but when he turned around, he saw nobody following him.

"Shmat Razum!" Fedot cried out. "Are you still with me?"

"Of course!" the voice said, "I will not desert you!"

The soldier returned to the frog, and sat on her back. She swelled up once more, leaped across the river of fire, and shrank back to normal size. Fedot put her in the jar of milk, picked up the vase, and marched off toward his mother-in-law's home.

When Fedot arrived at the palace, Shmat Razum set out a feast and entertained everyone with music. The old mother and her daughters laughed and danced and never felt happier. Finally the festivities came to an end, and Fedot bid the women farewell. He set out for home with Shmat Razum. Fedot walked and walked, and then gasped, "Whew! I can walk no more today, I am too tired!"

"Tired?" the invisible servant answered. "You should have told me sooner." In the next moment, the soldier was lifted up in a great wind. Beneath him, the land rushed by. Fedot cried out, "Shmat Razum, stop a moment, my hat fell off!" "It's too late," the invisible servant replied, "your hat is five thousand leagues behind us." After a while, Shmat Razum slowed down over the middle of the ocean, and said, "If you like, I will make a beautiful island for you. You can rest there a moment, and I will tell you how to win a fortune." The soldier agreed, and before his very eyes, an island emerged from the sea, with golden sand and stately trees.

Shmat Razum put Fedot down on the island and said, "Three merchants will sail by in their ship. They each have a magic talisman, so invite them to dine with you and bargain with them. Then exchange me for all their magic charms, and I will return to you later." Soon afterward, a ship sailed into view with three merchants on board. When they saw the island, they landed, and Fedot greeted them warmly.

The merchants exclaimed, "We have traveled over this ocean for years, and never saw this island before!"

"My servant made it," Fedot explained, and clapped his hands. "Shmat Razum," Fedot commanded, "set a meal for us." A sumptuous feast appeared, and the three merchants stared with amazement.

"We have magic of our own," they told the soldier. "If you give us your servant, you can take any talisman you want!" The first merchant brought out a magic box. When he opened the casket, a beautiful garden appeared all around them, complete with scented flowers and shady trees. When the merchant closed his box, the garden vanished. The second merchant took out an ax, hit a piece of wood with it, and a ship appeared on the ocean, filled with sailors and soldiers. The merchant struck the ax a second time, and another ship appeared, its banners flying and its cannons booming. Then the merchant covered his ax, and the navy vanished. Finally the third merchant drew out a horn and blew on it. A whole regiment of men appeared, with horses and muskets. The merchant blew a second time, and more soldiers appeared, until an army stood before them. When the merchant breathed into the other end of his horn, the army vanished.

"Choose which magic you like," the merchants offered, "and we will trade it for your servant."

Fedot laughed. "I am only a simple man. What use would I have for gardens, an army or a navy? Still, if you want to trade, give me all three charms for my servant."

The merchants talked among themselves. "He asks a high price! But if we have his servant, we can live in ease, eating and drinking all we wished!" So they agreed to Fedot's terms, and gave him the box, the ax, and the horn.

"Shmat Razum," the merchants asked the servant, "will you serve us faithfully?"

A voice answered, "Why not?" The merchants boarded their ship, and told their new servant to set out a banquet for them. Wine, meat, bread, and cakes appeared, and the merchants ate and drank until they fell asleep.

Back on the island, Fedot became worried. "Where is Shmat Razum?" "Right here!" the invisible servant said. Fedot rejoiced. "Well," the soldier went on, "it's time we made for home." Scarcely had he spoken when a great wind lifted the marksman into the air, and bore him swiftly homeward.

Back on the ship, the merchants woke up. "Shmat Razum, bring us food!" they commanded. But no matter how they yelled and threatened, nothing happened. "We have been cheated!"

they wailed. They sailed back looking for Fedot, but the island and the soldier were gone. So the merchants gnashed their teeth and resumed their journey.

Meanwhile, Fedot flew over mountains and seas, until he saw his own country. He pointed out a pretty spot near the ocean. "Shmat Razum, let us stop there. Can you build me a castle?"

"Why not?" the invisible servant replied, and before Fedot put his feet on the earth, a magnificent castle appeared. The marksman picked up his magic box, and opened it. Instantly, a beautiful garden graced his castle, full of fountains and streams and blooming trees. A blue dove flew by, landed on the earth, and turned into Fedot's wife. The two embraced passionately, and Fedot told her the story of his adventure.

"As for me," the wife explained, "I spent the time living in the forest as a dove." They embraced again, and Shmat Razum set out a feast to celebrate their reunion.

Across the way, Fedot's King looked out from his palace, and saw the castle. He flew into a rage. "How dare anyone build a castle without my permission! And a castle better than my own!" The King sent soldiers to investigate, and they told the monarch that Fedot had returned safely, built the castle, and now lived there with his wife. The King turned purple with rage. "Send out my army! Send out my navy! Tear down that castle, and kill that wretched soldier and his wife!"

The King's army and navy sallied forth. Fedot saw them, and drew out his magic ax and horn. He struck the ax once, twice, a hundred times, until the sea was filled with his own navy. Then he blew on the horn once, twice, a hundred times until then ground shook with his own army. Fedot's men routed the King's forces, and the King himself was slain in the battle. When the fighting stopped, Fedot hid his ax, and blew on the far side of his trumpet. His navy and army vanished.

Without their old King, the people of the kingdom gathered together to decide what to do. They consulted among themselves and then asked Fedot and his wife to become their new King and Queen. The soldier and his wife accepted, so they were crowned amidst great celebrations. And for the rest of their days, they ruled the land in wisdom, peace, and grace.

From Inner Feminine to Deep Masculine

MEETING THE ANIMA

This fairy tale is long, complicated, and fraught with symbolism, like men's tales and Russian literature in general. I shall therefore approach the story step by step, starting with motifs which appeared in previous tales. The drama begins when Fedot shoots a magic bird while hunting, and the creature turns into a beautiful, wise, and powerful woman. She provides an excellent example of the anima, reminiscent of Zakia in "The Sultan's Handkerchief." Fedot's dove-wife also dramatizes how men usually come to terms with the inner feminine: the anima often appears first in men's dreams in the form of a magic animal. The subhuman state of the anima (the animal anima) reflects a man's relative ignorance and unconsciousness of his feminine side. (The anima is not always a benign animal like a dove. She can take the form of a shark, a wolf, or a tiger, and the more a man ignores his feminine side, the more terrifying a form the anima often assumes!) Fedot initially intends to kill the dove since he hunts for the King, and this detail sums up men's first reaction to the inner feminine: men denigrate, suppress, or exploit the feminine, following traditional patriarchal attitudes. In Fedot's drama the dove speaks to him, revealing her magical nature, and he heeds her advice. Fedot's action epitomizes a crucial step for men—being open to the voice of the inner feminine when it first appears in therapy, dreams, or fantasies. In practical terms, the challenge for men is to attend to faint stirring of emotions and intuitions which they are trained in youth to suppress. Eventually men learn to integrate their feminine side, which Fedot symbolizes by marrying the dove-maiden.

After the wedding, whenever Fedot has a problem, his wife

uses her magic book to solve the difficulty, first weaving the tapestry that made them rich, and then fetching the golden stag. But she uses her magic only when Fedot sleeps. So her power makes a good symbol for the creative energy of the unconscious. Fedot literally "sleeps on his problems," and his anima-wife solves them for him. This is the classic role of the anima for men, maintaining a fruitful, helpful connection to the unconscious.

A subtle detail underscores the importance of the feminine in Fedot's life. When Fedot's wife weaves the beautiful carpet, she tells him to sell it in the marketplace, but not to set a price on it himself. He obeys her, reflecting his openness to the anima. By not setting a price on the carpet, Fedot also adopts an accommodating, receptive attitude, a trait traditionally considered feminine. Fedot's actions reverse the stereotypically active spirit of heroes, and for this he is richly rewarded. He receives 10,000 rubles for his carpet, a princely sum!

Here we come to a small problem. Fedot has married well and become rich without struggling much or suffering greatly. He seems to have succeeded too easily. There are several reasons for his easy victories. Dramatic struggles are the stuff mainly of youth tales, where a young man must prove his heroism. Fedot has already done this: he is specifically a soldier, implying that he has mastered the way of the warrior-hero. The story also notes that Fedot goes into the forest every day, hunts wild animals, and returns with game for the King's table. His actions recapitulate the archetypal quest of the young hero, who ventures into the wilderness, battles beasts or villains, and returns with a trophy. Fedot does this on a daily basis, signifying that he has mastered the heroism of youth and even made it routine. Moreover, Fedot is flexible, changes his ways, and learns quickly, like the monarch in "The Sultan's Handkerchief." Both Fedot and the Sultan have a relatively easy time precisely because they attend to the tasks of midlife. Fedot's tale underscores this point by saying he is an expert marksman. He presumably hits his target every time he goes hunting, and he does the same thing psychologically, consistently doing the right thing the first time around. Fedot's drama presents an *ideal* portrait of men's development, what happens when everything goes right. His name repeats the theme, because in Russian "Fedot" is short for "Theodor," which means "gift of God." His successes are blessings of Heaven. In real life, men stumble, lose their way, or give up. Men also struggle with unfinished business from childhood, grappling with mother and father issues, all of which Fedot has apparently resolved. Yet Fedot's story of success is vital to men because he shows the way ahead. He reminds them that there is more to life than simply recovering from childhood. Fedot's tale, in fact, reveals men's spiritual calling, which is easy to overlook or forget in the press of personal problems and past traumas.

After the King sees Fedot's wife, the monarch plots to kill him and steal his wife. The King's conspiracy brings up three familiar themes. First, Fedot is persecuted by a patriarch, just like Lustig in the last chapter. The plight of the two soldiers dramatizes men's oppression within patriarchal society. Second, Fedot's monarch is a particularly nasty character and represents a shadow figure. Throughout the tale, the King tries to possess and control everything around him. When he first lays eyes on the wonderful carpet, he takes it from his chamberlain. Later, when the King sees Fedot's wife, he covets her, too. In seeking power beyond all bounds of decency, he resembles the necromancer in "The King and the Ghoul" and the Wizard King in Chapter 1. Finally, the contest between the King and Fedot represents a battle between a father-figure and a son-figure over a beautiful woman. This is the familiar Oedipal struggle. Fortunately, Fedot's tale offers an alternative to the competition between father and son or patriarch and hero, and presents a new vision of manhood.

The earliest hint of the new paradigm appears when Fedot seeks the stag with golden antlers. Living in a land far away, in the "thrice tenth kingdom," the stag represents something hidden in the unconscious. As a male animal, the stag symbolizes the masculine, and as a wild beast, the creature points to a primordial form of male power, not yet shaped by civilization and patriarchal tradition. Possessing golden antlers, the stag is also magic and archetypal. So Fedot's search for the stag is a quest for an archetypal image of the masculine, separate from patriarchal tradition, and concealed in the unconscious. It is a search for the deep masculine.

THE QUEST FOR THE UNKNOWN AND
THE GREAT GODDESS

When Fedot returns with the stag, the enraged King sends him on a second journey, to "go I know not whither and bring back I know not what." The destination is unknown, and the goal unspecified, making for a confused voyage at best. But this is men's situation at midlife! After the heroic dreams of youth collapse or fade away, men wander in limbo, like Lustig in the last chapter, seeking new meaning and purpose. The title of Fedot's drama sums up the painful situation of men who venture beyond the hero.

Fedot discovers that his wife cannot figure out his second quest. Neither she nor her magic spirits know how to "go I know not where and bring back I know not what." This suggests that the inner feminine can help a man only so far in his development: the anima has limits. Fedot's wife nevertheless provides him with a magic ball and a handkerchief. Following the ball, Fedot eventually meets three beautiful women, and by means of his handkerchief the women recognize him as their brother-in-law. They introduce him to their mother, and she turns out to be an extraordinary person. She calls all the creatures of air, land, and water her "servants," and this can mean only one thing—she is the mistress of nature, the Great Mother Goddess herself. Fedot thus moves from his own inner feminine, symbolized by his anima-wife, to the realm of the archetypal feminine, personified by the Great Mother.

The tale contains a subtle bit of advice for men and women here. As men wrestle with their inner feminine side, they commonly ask women for advice and help, particularly in dealing with feelings. But this can quickly degenerate into traditional patriarchal roles, in which men expect women to take care of their emotional needs. Moreover, as the anima appears in men's dreams and fantasies, men often confuse her with a real woman. Men then have affairs, mixing up the magical, fascinating, inner anima with alluring, intriguing women in the outer world. Men's task at midlife is to deal with archetypes of the feminine, with inner female figures, not flesh-and-blood women. Fedot's story emphasizes the point by shifting from Fedot's wife to his mother-in-law, the Great Goddess herself. As an archetypal figure, the Great Mother is not to be confused with a real woman. The goddess is an inner figure, not someone with whom a man can have an affair!

As Fedot encounters progressively more powerful feminine archetypes, he does not lose his male identity. When he first meets his three sisters-in-law, for instance, he acts in a typically masculine fashion. The three women besiege Fedot with questions about who he is and where he comes from, but he dismisses their inquiries and tells them to fetch him food. He insists upon his own needs, a stereotypically masculine trait. The point is important: although Fedot honors the feminine, he does not lose his male energy.

When Fedot asks his in-laws about going "I know not where" and bringing back "I know not what," even the old woman cannot answer. Her limitation is amazing, since she is the Great Goddess. The story confirms that the feminine can help men only up to a certain point on their journey. Fortunately, the Great Mother does not hinder Fedot, either, and here his story reverses the usual plot of youth tales. When the young hero meets a Mother Goddess, a battle typically ensues in which the hero kills or subjugates her. These battles reflect the psychology of young men, struggling to free themselves emotionally from mother complexes. Fedot's encounter with the Great Mother is peaceful, presumably because he has already completed the tasks of the young hero, and separated psychologically from his mother. In real life, of course, most men still struggle with some mother issues at midlife. Fedot's drama skips over this process, as mentioned before, in order to illuminate what lies beyond, focusing on the challenge of entering mature manhood and not simply leaving childhood.

When Fedot's mother-in-law asks all her servants for help, only an old female frog responds, and she is deeply symbolic. As a creature who changes from an aquatic tadpole to an air-breathing animal, the frog makes a good symbol of transformation. As an animal rather than a human, the frog also symbolizes something unconscious. And as a female animal, the frog points specifically to a feminine element in the unconscious. So the story shows Fedot encountering yet a deeper level of the feminine, moving from the anima personified by his wife, to his in-laws and the Great Mother, symbolizing the archetypal feminine, and now to a nonhuman, primordial female symbol.[1]

When the frog becomes Fedot's guide, she takes the place of his wife as his helper. The story scrambles the usual pattern in youth tales, in which the gallant hero rescues a beautiful maiden from an ugly monster. Here an ugly creature replaces the beautiful maiden and rescues the male protagonist![2] The message is important for men at midlife because the inner feminine often takes unexpected forms, and if a man expects the anima or real women to be all beauty and virtue, he is in for a rude shock. Feminine wisdom and power are far deeper than superficial appearances, despite the hero's worship of beautiful women.

Guided by the frog, Fedot arrives at a mountain surrounded by a river of fire. The frog carries Fedot over the flames and then tells him to go into the mountain alone. Apparently, the frog cannot help Fedot any further, and the reason quickly becomes evident.

THE TRICKSTER COMPANION

When Fedot enters the mountain he sees two old men. They are the first males he encounters on his quest and suggest that Fedot will now be dealing with masculine issues, not feminine ones. The story confirms the hint in several ways. The mountain itself provides an archetypally masculine image. Mountains are usually associated with male deities, like Yahweh on Mt. Sinai and Zeus on Olympus. In European folklore, moreover, mountains were the abodes of dwarves, who were usually male. Many mythologies also designate a special mountain as the "axis mundi" or "world axis," around which the world turns and which is usually interpreted as a masculine symbol, akin to phallic symbols. To underscore the male focus, the story introduces Shmat Razum, an invisible spirit. Shmat turns out to be male, since Fedot addresses him as "brother." (Presumably Fedot could tell from Shmat Razum's voice.) Shmat Razum also appears to be a wind spirit, since he later transports Fedot on gusts of wind. As discussed in Chapter 4 with "The North Wind's Gift," wind spirits are typically masculine in mythology.

The story's new emphasis on the masculine helps explain why the frog could not take Fedot into the fiery mountain, and why Fedot's wife and mother-in-law did not know how to "go I know not whither." Fedot's final quest involves masculine mysteries. For this task, he needs male helpers, not females. And here Shmat Razum is profoundly symbolic. On first appearances, Shmat Razum might seem to involve simple wish-fulfillment. He magically feeds people and gratifies wishes. The story refutes this interpretation in the episode involving the three merchants. They barter their magic treasures for Shmat Razum, specifically so he can gratify all their wishes. Shmat Razum responds by deserting them. He refuses to indulge self-indulgent men.

In promising to serve the three merchants and then abandoning them, Shmat Razum acts like a Trickster. This is not surprising, since he seems to be a wind spirit, and wind spirits are usually Trickster figures. The story confirms Shmat Razum's identity as a Trickster when he hovers over the ocean and creates an island. The same event occurs in Trickster tales from various cultures. The Ostyaks of Siberia, for example, describe how Doh, their great shaman and Trickster, flew over the primordial sea, found no place to land, sent diving birds to fetch mud from the bottom, and created the world from mud. Similar tales are told about Raven, the Northwest American Trickster.

Shmat Razum also teaches Fedot to be a Trickster, telling the soldier how to defraud the three merchants. Shmat Razum thus resembles St. Peter, who enticed Lustig into lying and cheating. Indeed, the parallels between "Go I Know Not Whither" and "Brother Lustig" are extensive and deep. Fedot and Lustig are both soldiers betrayed by their monarchs, while Shmat Razum and St. Peter are Trickster Brothers, male spirits who befriend men in midlife crises. Despite their magic powers, Shmat Razum and St. Peter also treat their mortal companions as comrades and peers. The Tricksters emphasize fraternity and equality in their relationship with the soldiers, not heroic hierarchy or patriarchal authority. In addition, St. Peter and Shmat Razum share a demonic aspect. St. Peter uses a gruesome resurrection ritual in which he boils bodies in a cauldron, while Shmat Razum lives in a mountain surrounded by fire, suggestive of the underworld. (Many mythologies depict the land of the dead surrounded by a river of fire.)

Shmat Razum's name deepens the parallels to Lustig's tale. Like St. Peter and Lustig, only Shmat Razum and Fedot have proper names, highlighting the importance of their friendship. Moreover, "Shmat" recalls the Russian word "shmatka," meaning "bit" or "piece," as in a "piece of cloth" or "rag."³ "Razum" means "reason" or "understanding" and is closely related to Logos, the archetypally masculine principle. In Christian tradition, presumably familiar to Russian storytellers, logos is identified with God, the divine Word that created the world. So the name of the invisible servant thus means something like "a bit of reason" or "the rag of Logos" and directly links him to a masculine deity. Analogously, St. Peter, as the premier apostle, is directly linked to the masculine God of Christian theology.

In addition to its parallels to "Brother Lustig," Fedot's tale resembles "The King and the Ghoul," and the similarities between the Russian, German, and Hindu tales underscore the archetypal nature of men's tales. "The King and the Ghoul" begins when the monarch agrees to help the "sage" without knowing what the magician wants. The King leaves his patriarchal role and commits himself to go he knows not where and do something he knows not what! In this confusing state, the King meets the ghoul, who plays the role of the Trickster Companion, like Shmat Razum with Fedot and St. Peter with Lustig. The ghoul uses riddles to force the King to give up logos, throwing him into an even more confused state where he seeks he knows not what. Eventually, the ghoul teaches the King how to be a Trickster and helps the monarch deceive the necromancer. This recalls the way St. Peter taught Lustig how to steal and lie, and how Shmat Razum helped Fedot defraud the three merchants. Finally, the ghoul helps the King defeat the necromancer, the way Shmat Razum enabled Fedot to overthrow his evil monarch.

One important difference separates the three men's tales. "Brother Lustig" and "The King and the Ghoul" focus almost exclusively on the masculine, while Fedot's story also attends to the anima and the inner feminine. Indeed, Fedot's tale clarifies the relationship between heroic manhood, the anima, and the deep masculine, central issues in the lives of mature men. The three themes appear in exactly that order: after men give up the heroic and patriarchal paradigm, the anima appears, and only later does the deep masculine emerge in the form of the Trickster Brother. Men move through the three issues in a developmental sequence.

FROM MASCULINE TO FEMININE TO MASCULINE

The first shift, from conventional manhood to the inner feminine, appears early in Fedot's tale. He begins the story as a soldier, hunter, and marksman, three stereotypically masculine roles. Then he turns to the feminine, starting with his anima-wife and moving to her mother, the Great Goddess. In embracing the feminine, Fedot parallels the monarch in "The Sultan's Handkerchief," who gave up his patriarchal prerogatives to honor Zakia.

Fedot's tale then introduces a second transition, from inner feminine to deep masculine. The shift is clear when Fedot leaves his guide, the frog, and ventures alone into the fiery mountain to meet Shmat Razum. He shifts from his feminine in-laws to masculine figures. Several details foreshadow this shift. At the beginning of the tale, Fedot's wife obtains two magic objects for him, the beautiful carpet and the stag with golden horns. As something woven and used in the home, the tapestry belongs to the feminine realm, while the stag is clearly masculine. So the masculine follows the feminine. An even subtler example of the sequence involves the handkerchief Fedot receives from his wife. A feminine symbol, the handkerchief is replaced later by a masculine cloth, namely Shmat Razum. As mentioned before, "Shmat Razum" means "a rag of reason," or "a cloth of logos." So Shmat Razum represents a masculine version of a handkerchief! Finally, the merchant's three magic treasures recapitulate the feminine-to-masculine shift. Their first charm is a magic box that creates lush gardens, conjuring up feminine images of domestic beauty and bliss. The second and third magic treasures are quintessentially masculine, an ax and a horn which create a navy and an army. Close attention to these details may seem like overinterpreting the story. But the particulars are so consistent with each other, they cannot be ignored. (Recall that in "The North Wind's Gift" the first box contained food and the second, thugs with clubs. Again a shift from more feminine imagery to masculine themes occurs.)

The transitions from conventional manhood to the inner feminine, and from inner feminine to deep masculine appear in classical literature. *The Odyssey* provides an excellent example and closely parallels Fedot's tale. Odysseus begins his drama with a military triumph at Troy, a conventional heroic, masculine achievement analogous to Fedot's being the best marksman in the army. Odysseus was delayed for many years on his journey home from Troy and forced to wander he knew not where, just like Fedot. On his voyages, Odysseus encounters numerous feminine figures, from Circe to the Sirens, and they represent anima figures, paralleling Fedot's wife and her family. Odysseus thus moves from the heroic masculinity of the Trojan war to the realm of the inner feminine.

The second shift, from anima to deep masculine, occurs when Odysseus meets the spirit of Teresias, the famous Greek seer. Teresias predicts that Odysseus will reach his homeland safely, but also warns him to make a special sacrifice to Poseidon upon his return. As a powerful masculine force hidden within the ocean, Poseidon makes an excellent symbol of the deep masculine. Teresias also tells Odysseus specifically to sacrifice a bull, a ram, and a boar to Poseidon. The animals are all male and notable for their aggressiveness. So Odysseus' final task, after many years of dealing with the anima, is to honor the deep masculine.[4]

The same double shift surfaces several centuries later in *The Golden Ass,* written by the Roman author Apuleius.[5] Most of the drama focuses on the misadventures of Lucius, a man who is accidentally turned into a donkey by a witch. Lucius stumbles from one problem to another, trying to regain his human form and struggles with various female figures. His misfortunes are reminiscent of Odysseus' wandering and Fedot's quest to go "I know not where." Lucius is eventually restored to his human form by the Great Goddess Isis, and he is initiated into her cult. Symbolically, he honors the archetypal feminine, the way Fedot befriended his mother-in-law, the Great Mother Goddess. At the end of his tale, Lucius enters the cult of Osiris, a god the story says is the greatest of all. Like Odysseus and Fedot, Lucius' final task is to move from the inner feminine to the deep masculine.

A third illustration of the masculine-feminine-masculine sequence comes from Dante's *Divine Comedy*. At midlife, Dante lost his positions of authority and honor and was forced to give up conventional patriarchal roles, as mentioned before. Confused and disoriented, he described himself as being lost in a wilderness. He wandered he knew not where, like Fedot and Odysseus. In this crisis, the beautiful Beatrice sends Dante help, first through Virgil, who leads him through the Inferno, and then appearing in person to guide him through Paradise. But at the very end, it is a man, St. Bernard, who initiates Dante into the ultimate mystery, a direct encounter with God. In Christian tradition, of course, God is wholly masculine. So Dante moves from conventional heroic male roles to an experience of the anima, but arrives finally at the deep masculine.

Significantly, the masculine-feminine-masculine theme survives in the oldest known written epic, the saga of Gilgamesh. The first half of the myth focuses on Gilgamesh and his warrior-comrade, Enkidu, as they play out conventional, heroic masculine roles. (They undertake a quest to kill a monster.) When Enkidu dies, the heroic motif fades. Gilgamesh despairs over Enkidu's death, devastated not only over the loss of his friend, but from the realization that he, too, will die, like all other humans. (This is a classic male midlife crisis.) Gilgamesh then goes in search of his ancestor, Utnapishtim, who reputedly knew the secret of immortality. Gilgamesh has no success until he meets Siduri, a woman innkeeper, and she sets him on the right path. Like Beatrice in Dante's *Divine Comedy*, or Zakia in "The Sultan's Handkerchief," Siduri is an anima figure who guides a man in a dire predicament. But his ultimate goal is to find Utnapishtim, a male figure. As a secret, immortal man, Utnapishtim symbolizes an indestructible male vitality and personifies the deep masculine. Gilgamesh thus shifts from conventional heroism in the first half of the epic, to Siduri, the anima, in the middle of the saga, and arrives finally at the deep masculine, symbolized by Utnapishtim. His saga recapitulates the male life cycle.

These tales from different cultures and historical epochs offer several important lessons for men today. The stories emphasize that men's development does not end in youth with heroic and patriarchal roles. There are specific tasks left for midlife. The first is giving up heroic roles and learning to honor the feminine. This is men's initiation into the goddess. Difficult as it is, the task is not the final step in male maturation. Immersion in the deep masculine comes next. Yet the masculine mysteries are open only to men who have first served the goddess. This sequence, I might add, ensures that the deep masculine and the wild man are not primitive rejections of the feminine, code words for a male backlash against feminism. The deep masculine appears only after men have come to terms with their fear of and fascination for the feminine.

So important are these lessons that they appear in men's mature initiations celebrated by aboriginal cultures. An example comes from the island of Malekula in Melanesia. Malekulan tradition holds that after death, a man's soul is initiated into the spiritual realm through a series of steps. First the dead man meets a female ghost, who guards the entrance to the "cave of the ancestors." On the ground before her is a sacred design, and as a test, she obliterates half of it. The dead man must complete the rest or be destroyed. Success here initiates the man into what is called "low Maki." In psychological terms, the specter of death destroys a man's traditional masculine identity, forcing him to confront the primordial power of the feminine, personified in the Malekulan myth by the female ghost. By passing the test, the initiate shifts from conventional male roles to the archetypal feminine. This parallels Fedot's evolution from a conventionally masculine marksman to a pilgrim who meets the Great Goddess. The Malekulan legend also resembles the Gilgamesh epic, where death—Enkidu's passing—destroys Gilgamesh's comfortable, heroic way of life, prompting him to seek immortality and grapple with the anima.

In the Malekulan myth, a man's soul moves from the female ghost to a lonely seashore. He lights a fire to summon a guide and a helpful spirit leads the man to a powerful god on a tall, fiery mountain. Encountering this male deity is the final step of initiation when the dead man becomes a "high Maki."[6] The second half of the Malekulan initiation echoes Fedot's drama. The dead man in the Malekulan myth requires a guide, analogous to how Fedot needed the old frog. The Malekulan guide then leads the spirit of the dead man to a masculine god on a fiery peak, exactly the way Fedot meets Shmat Razum in a mountain surrounded by fire. Malekulan men thus shift from the female ghost to a male deity, the way Fedot moves from his female in-laws to Shmat Razum. The similarities between the Malekulan myth and the Russian tale are astounding. Clearly, the double transition, from conventional male roles to the inner feminine and then on to the deep masculine, cuts across cultures and history. The pattern reflects the deep structure of the masculine psyche.

ALCHEMY AND THE DEEP MASCULINE

The Malekulan myth has a Western counterpart in medieval European alchemy. Alchemy may seem esoteric, but like myth and fairy tales, it expresses unconscious symbolism and reveals the male psyche in particular. I will discuss alchemy at some length because it represents an indigenous Western approach to the deep masculine. Exotic secret initiations from far-off aboriginal cultures are not the only means of gaining access to the deep masculine. Furthermore, as Jung pointed out, alchemy provides a model and metaphor for psychotherapy especially applicable to men. Therapy, in turn, offers men today one of the more accessible forms of initiation into the deep masculine.

Alchemy focuses on the deep masculine for several reasons. First, most alchemists were men, and their writing reflects masculine concerns. Second, alchemists dealt with flasks, flames, tubes, and chemicals. The technological focus is a typically masculine interest. Third, alchemists cultivated a meditative attitude when working, and such an altered state of consciousness fosters the spontaneous emergence of archetypal images, ordinarily hidden behind social convention. (The noxious chemicals that alchemists used may have enhanced the altered states, because the compounds can produce hallucinations.) Finally, alchemists worked alone and secretly, and this solitude is archetypally masculine, recalling Native American vision quests. The isolation also nurtures unconscious symbolism.

The explicit goal of alchemy was to produce "the philosopher's stone," which could turn lead into gold, confer immortality, bestow wisdom, and work other miracles. Jung suggested that the philosopher's stone is really a symbol for self-actualization or enlightenment. Turning lead into gold, for example, is a good metaphor for transforming base instincts like lust or anger into sublime wisdom. The real aim of alchemy, Jung concluded, was the alchemist's psychological and spiritual development. In a sense, alchemy represents a medieval version of therapy, and the stages of the alchemical process, which its practitioners described in great detail, symbolize men's individuation.

Alchemists described two helpers crucial to their work. The first is the "mystical sister." She is a classical anima figure, and alchemical manuscripts provide many charming pictures of her aiding the alchemist on his search for wisdom. She symbolizes the initial challenge for men, which is to learn about the feminine. But the mystical sister eventually yields to an even more powerful male helper, the spirit Mercurius. European alchemists considered Mercurius the essence of transformation and explicitly identified him as a Trickster figure. He was unpredictable and as likely to kill as to help. (This was literally true, because alchemists used liquid mercury extensively to dissolve other compounds and mercury produces toxic vapors.) Life-giving but deadly, instructive but dangerous, Mercurius represents a paradoxical union of opposites, like all Tricksters. As the alchemist's helper, Mercurius represents the Trickster Companion in a new guise, analogous to Shmat Razum in Fedot's tale, the ghoul in "The King and the Ghoul," and St. Peter in "Brother Lustig." So when alchemists describe a shift from the mystical sister to Mercurius in their work, they recapitulate the drama of men's tales, where the focus moves from the anima to the deep masculine.

A seventeenth-century illustration summarizes the stages in alchemical work and emphasizes the parallels to Fedot's tale.[7] The portrait depicts several scenes, drawn within three concentric circles. In the outermost circle reclines a mermaid, half human and half fish. She can be interpreted as an anima figure, like Fedot's wife, who was also half human and half animal. The next inner circle portrays the alchemist with his mystical sister. They sit together in a pastoral setting and fish in a river. Psychologically, this represents a man delving into the unconscious with the help of his anima, like Fedot going on his quest aided by the female frog, or a man wrestling with his feminine side in therapy, grappling with intuitions and emotions. In the innermost circle of the drawing, the mystical sister sits in a boat and fishes for a male figure who is underwater. Located at the center of the whole picture, the man represents the core of the male psyche, namely the deep masculine. He corresponds in Fedot's tale to Shmat Razum, whom Fedot reaches only with the help of the female frog.

Another alchemical drawing strengthens the parallels to Fedot's story.[8] The portrait shows an alchemist dressed like a pilgrim entering a mountain. There he discovers a temple with a fiery phoenix on top. Inside the sanctuary is the philosopher's stone, the goal of alchemy. The setting recalls Fedot's encounter with the old men and Shmat Razum in the secret recesses of the fiery mountain. Moreover, Shmat Razum turns out to be the goal of Fedot's quest, the way the philosopher's stone was for alchemists. Symbolically, men must make an inward journey at midlife to reclaim their souls.

One last analogy between European alchemy and Fedot's tale is striking. Alchemy frequently portrayed Mercurius as a magical stag.[9] This suggests that the golden stag in Fedot's tale is symbolically connected to Mercurius. As a Trickster, Mercurius explicitly parallels Shmat Razum. In a sense, the stag represents an undeveloped, mute, inarticulate form of the deep masculine, who later becomes Shmat Razum. The stag thus resembles the magic dove that turns into Fedot's anima-wife: the dove symbolizes the anima in an unconscious state, and as Fedot becomes more conscious of the inner feminine, the dove becomes human. The deep masculine goes through the same evolution.

FROM INNER FEMININE TO DEEP MASCULINE
IN MEN'S LIVES

Men's tales portray the same drama, the journey from conventional masculine roles to the inner feminine and on to the deep masculine. The same process appears in men's lives, and Jung provides a striking example. As discussed earlier, after his break with Freud, Jung suffered a severe midlife crisis. He was unsure of his life's direction and felt adrift. Like Fedot, Jung went he knew not where, seeking he knew not what. During this period, Jung picked out two "big" dreams that were turning points in his life. In the first dream, described in his autobiography, Jung sat with his children around a table in a beautiful palace. A small white bird flew in, a dove or a sea gull, and the bird changed into a little girl with blond hair about eight years old. She started playing, later resumed her bird form, and then flew off. The parallel between Jung's bird-girl and Fedot's dove-wife is immediately apparent. Both female figures represent the anima. Indeed, the bird-girl helped Jung formulate the concept of the anima and was the first of many such figures in his inner life.

Some time later, Jung had another pivotal dream that heralded a whole new creative phase in his development. In this second "big" dream, Jung walked down a lane of ancient sarcophagi. Dead men lay on stone slabs, like the statues of knights placed over their tombs in medieval crypts. As Jung passed the sarcophagi, he looked at the dead men, and they came to life, one by one. Each successive sepulcher contained a man from more ancient eras. Jung puzzled over the dream for some time and finally concluded the men represented something from the unconscious that went beyond his personal experiences. Although Jung did not use the term, the men can be interpreted as symbols of the deep masculine. Their resurrection dramatizes the emergence of long-neglected masculine energies from the unconscious. Significantly, Jung dreamed of these men *after* his dream of the bird-girl. So the anima preceded the deep masculine, just as in Fedot's tale.

Robert Bly, the poet-leader of today's men's movement, provides another example of the shift from inner feminine to deep masculine. Although Bly celebrates the deep masculine today, for many years he extolled the virtues of the feminine and honored the goddess. Like Jung and Fedot, Bly focused on the anima and the inner feminine, before embracing the deep masculine.

A case described by Sherry Salman, a Jungian analyst, provides another illustration of men's shift from conventional masculinity to the inner feminine and then to the deep masculine.[10] During analysis a man in his thirties dreamed that he met two women. They were his mother and sister in the dream, although they did not resemble his family in real life. The women told the man to find his "father" and pointed to a building with stairs that went down into the earth. When the man approached the entrance, he found it was lined with animal horns. Although brief, this man's dream is highly symbolic. The first character is male, namely the dreamer himself, but the focus quickly shifts to female figures when the man dreams of his "mother" and "sister." The man's task, though, is to descend into the earth, into the unconscious, in search of his "father." This would presumably not be his real father, just as the "mother" and "sister" in the dream were not his real ones. In seeking a masculine figure hidden in the earth, the dreamer searches for the deep masculine. The dream highlights the point in a small detail: the entrance into the underworld is lined with animal horns, an archetypally masculine symbol that recalls Fedot's stag with golden antlers. The dream thus begins with the male dreamer, shifts to the feminine figures, and then points to a hidden masculine archetype yet to emerge.

The same sequence appeared in a dream of my own. In the dream, I heard an announcement that an important figure would appear and save the world. He had been living incognito among humanity, but would now reveal himself. In the next scene, I had magical powers and could control the wind, flying where I wished. At one point, several criminals attacked me, but I used my wind power to blow them away. I then wondered if I was the person who was supposed to save the world, finding that hard to believe, but hoping it was true. In the next moment, I heard another declaration that indicated an even more important figure would appear and replace the first savior. This second person was an actress, developing a new form of opera. I was annoyed by this announcement, thinking that my wind power was more significant than her acting talent. Then came a final revelation, proclaiming that a third savior would appear and he would be the most important of all. This third figure would be a male spirit that would fill everyone with knowledge and vision.

My dream begins with an announcement that a savior will soon appear. When I discover that I control the wind, can fly, and defeat criminals, I wonder if I am that hero. This is, of course, a question most men ask themselves in youth, secretly believing the answer is yes. But the dream makes a second announcement and introduces a more important figure. This turns out to be a woman, an anima figure, and her talent lies in opera, in emotional expression. The dream illustrates how the anima supplants the hero in men's development, and how feeling displaces power as the focus in men's lives. A final announcement reveals that the ultimate helper will be a male spirit who will inspire everybody with wisdom. This alludes directly to the Christian image of the Holy Ghost, who is masculine in Christian theology. So the dream portrays a shift from the traditional hero to the anima, and then on to a divine masculine spirit.

REASONS FOR THE SEQUENCE

Why do men deal with the deep masculine after the inner feminine? The deep masculine, I think, is more unconscious than the anima. This may sound surprising, but most men take their masculinity for granted, and assume that manliness is simply what society says it is, namely being the hero and the patriarch. Men do not explore the foundations of masculinity. On the other hand, since feminine traits in a man are considered shameful in most societies, men quickly attend to the anima and the inner feminine when it emerges at midlife, if only to repress it.

Fedot's story graphically symbolizes the theme by having him contact his mother-in-law, the Great Goddess, fairly easily. Meeting Shmat Razum, however, requires a journey to a mountain ringed by fire, "at the end of the world." The deep masculine is farther away in the unconscious. Corroboration for this point comes from two intriguing psychological studies in which researchers used a variety of tests to determine a man's conscious and unconscious sense of masculine identity.[11] Three distinct groups of men emerged. In the first category were men who consciously saw themselves as masculine, but who had an unconscious feminine identity, reflected in strong feelings of emotional dependence on their mothers, for instance, or an identification with their mothers rather than their fathers. These men behaved outwardly in "macho" ways and actively disavowed and derided feminine activities. They tried to be tough and cool, playing the traditional role of the hero. Inwardly, however, they doubted their masculinity, wrestled with feelings of inadequacy, and struggled to suppress their "feminine" impulses. The second set of men were consciously and unconsciously masculine. Outwardly, they acted in traditional male roles and were independent and autonomous in love and work. Inwardly, they identified with their fathers and felt confident of themselves as men. The researchers expected to find these two types of men, so they were surprised when they came across a third category.

Men in this last group were unconsciously masculine but consciously feminine. They intentionally affirmed the importance of the feminine and focused on relationships, emotions, and intuitions. Yet the men maintained a strong, unconscious sense of masculine identity and did not harbor doubts about their manhood. This third group included the most mature, creative, and successful men of all. Mature manhood thus involves a conscious affirmation of the feminine, combined with a deeper masculine identity.

Aboriginal shamans dramatize the observation. Men who become shamans at midlife frequently dress as women and adopt feminine ways, as mentioned before. Yet in their trances, male shamans usually appeal to masculine deities or spirits.[12] A Siberian Chukchi shaman, for instance, dressed like a woman, yet at the height of his ecstatic trances, he spoke in a deep voice, proclaiming he was the "bull of earth," chosen to be the agent of a god on earth. While he consciously honored the feminine, this shaman retained access to the deep masculine. Shamans, as Roger Walsh points out in *The Spirit of Shamanism*, are also psychologically mature individuals. So once again we have the suggestion that male maturity involves an affirmation of the feminine, concealing a deeper celebration of the masculine.

One reason the deep masculine remains hidden in the unconscious and appears relatively late in men's development is that it is personified by the Trickster, who is easily confused with the shadow. As discussed earlier in Chapters 5 and 6, meeting the Trickster requires that men come to terms with the dark side of life, with evil, suffering, vulnerability, tragedy, and death. This demands maturity and depth of experience. Moreover, the Trickster is suppressed by patriarchal tradition, so that men gain access to him only if they overthrow social conventions. While adolescents engage in such rebellion, they are usually not ready for the primordial energies of the deep masculine. Youthful rejection of convention also gives way after a few years to more conventional worldly ambitions to take a place in society. So young men usually do not reach the deep masculine.

RETURN TO THE FEMININE

Men's shift from the anima to the deep masculine is not the final step in masculine development. "Go I Know Not Whither" portrays two further events. First, Fedot returns home with Shmat Razum and rejoins his wife. The story thus puts the anima back on stage and reaffirms the importance of the feminine. In returning home, Fedot embraces the ordinary human realm of marriage, relationships, and domestic life. He thus moves from his archetypal experiences with Shmat Razum to everyday reality, and this prevents him from becoming inflated or grandiose. A hint of such inflation appears at the end of both "Brother Lustig" and "The King and the Ghoul." Recall that the King in the Hindu story is honored by all the gods, while in the German tale, Lustig cheats his way into Heaven. These endings struck me as incomplete and dissatisfying. The reason, I think, is that both stories lack any significant feminine presence at the end. In focusing so exclusively on the deep masculine, they become unbalanced. Fedot's tale restores harmony by having him return to his wife.

The same emphasis on everyday life and the feminine appears

in the *Divine Comedy.* Whenever Dante addresses an archetypal theme, dealing with God, Eternity, Salvation, and so on, he always ends his discussion with a human example from his life, as Helen Luke points out in *Dark Wood to White Rose,* her analysis of Dante's classic. Dante's everyday experience provided him grounding, even on his journey into Hell, Purgatory, and Heaven. Writing this chapter gave me a very personal experience of the theme. As I researched Trickster tales, I became excited by the deep parallels in stories across the world. For several weeks, I had trouble sleeping, as ideas and images poured through my mind. Yet when I discussed my work with colleagues, they gave me blank looks: I had flown off somewhere into outer space. The archetypal material was too much for me to handle! I therefore turned to visualization for help. A familiar figure quickly appeared, but one with whom I had not talked for a long time, and whom I knew simply as the Lady of the Woods. A beautiful woman who lives in the wilderness, she is, of course, an anima figure. When I described my situation to her, she smiled. The solution, she said, was simple. Instead of writing about the Trickster and all his archetypal symbolism, becoming intoxicated by abstract ideas, I should look inward to my own personal experience. Where did the Trickster appear in my life and work? I took her advice and began reviewing my dream journals over the years and my notes from psychotherapy cases. My overwrought soul immediately cooled down. Reflecting on particular experiences with real people in everyday situations was grounding.

When a man returns to the inner feminine after his encounter with the Trickster, he relates to the anima in a different manner. The deep masculine changes him. In their first encounters with the anima, most men are usually no match for her because she is so powerful and fascinating. But after contacting the deep masculine, men have an ally as powerful as the anima, the Trickster Spirit. Strengthened by the deep masculine, men no longer need to dominate women or feel threatened by them. Fedot's tale illustrates the point. At the outset, his wife is clearly more powerful than he is, possessing a magic book with two spirits to do her bidding. Baba Yaga, the Russian witch, also says that Fedot is easily disposed of, but his wife is another matter. And Fedot's wife's mother is the Great Goddess herself! After meeting Shmat Razum, however, Fedot is equal to his wife. Indeed, Fedot switches from receiving aid offered by his wife and her family to giving them gifts. With Shmat Razum's help, Fedot puts on a feast for his in-laws, where the Great Mother Goddess dances with joy. And later, Fedot defeats the tyrant King, something his wife apparently could not do, even when she was persecuted by the monarch.

With his new masculine power, Fedot does not try to dominate his wife or her family, trying to be a patriarch. He continues to honor and respect the feminine. This is a fundamental trait of Tricksters that is often overlooked: they favor equality between men and women, unlike the patriarch and the hero. Tricksters like Legba in Africa do not battle the Great Mother, yet they maintain their independence from her.[13] Loki and Raven even change sex and voluntarily become women to carry out their pranks! They do not share the horror and repudiation of the feminine typical of heroes and patriarchs.

If Fedot's tale is inspiring and insightful for men, it also promises comfort and challenge to women. For wives, mothers, and daughters who fear they will lose their men to the deep masculine and the men's movement, Fedot's story offers the reassurance that men will return to them. (Men, of course, have a similar fear of losing wives and daughters, as women become involved in the feminist movement.) If men do not return home to relationships, Fedot's tale suggests, there is a problem, a developmental block. How long a man needs to remain in the deep masculine varies with each individual. Fedot's wife did not know how he could go "I know not where," but she specifically said it would take eighteen years. This is a long time and it can be trying for women to wait for their men to deal with the deep masculine. But women have their own mysteries to attend to, namely the deep feminine. Fedot's story hints at this by saying that Fedot's wife spent her time in the wilderness, in the form of a dove, a bird closely associated with Great Goddess figures.

The final event in Fedot's tale is his overthrow of the evil King. On one level, this conclusion can be interpreted as an Oedipal victory: Fedot defeats the tyrannical older man who tried to kill him off earlier in the story. There is a deeper level of symbolism, however, which comes out if we compare the conclusion of Fedot's tale with that of "The King and the Ghoul." In both stories, an evil patriarchal figure is killed and a new order established. These two tales portray the overthrow not just of a patriarch, but of the patriarchy itself. Society is transformed, and not just a man's private life. Once again, men's tales emphasize that the Trickster ultimately seeks the common good, and his emergence as the deep masculine is a communal event, not simply a personal psychological experience.

SUMMARY

Fedot's tale is unusually complete and integrates themes from previous stories. His drama in turn summarizes men's tasks in maturity. Fedot's tale starts when he meets his anima and marries her. Symbolically, he honors the feminine and integrates it in his life, like the monarch in "The Sultan's Handkerchief." This is men's first step in the journey beyond the hero. Jealous of Fedot's wife, the King plots to kill the soldier. As a greedy tyrant who tries to steal everything and dominate everyone, the King represents a shadow figure, and specifically the dark side of the patriarchy. He vividly recalls the tyrant in "The Wizard King," and both monarchs dramatize what happens when men cling to the heroic and patriarchal tradition. In persecuting him, Fedot's King also resembles the monarch in "Brother Lustig," who abandons Lustig after twenty-five years of service. Symbolically, the heroic and patriarchal paradigm betrays men at midlife.

Thinking the task impossible, the King sends Fedot on a quest for a magic stag, but Fedot's anima-wife helps him. She illustrates how the inner feminine rescues men at midlife, like Zakia in "The Sultan's Handkerchief." On Fedot's second quest, though, his wife is helpless. The marksman must wander "I know not where." His mission sums up men's plight at midlife: after the collapse of heroic and patriarchal ideals, they grope in confusion for new convictions, roaming the world like Lustig or pacing back and forth in a cemetery like the King carrying the corpse.

On his journey, Fedot meets his mother-in-law, representing

the Great Goddess, and their friendship illustrates how thorough his integration of the feminine has become. But even the Nature Goddess does not know how to "go I know not where," emphasizing the limits of the feminine in helping men at midlife. Vital as the anima is, she must yield to a new, specifically masculine helper. In Fedot's story, this is Shmat Razum. Like St. Peter in "Brother Lustig" and the ghoul in "The King and the Ghoul," Shmat Razum becomes Fedot's Trickster Brother. He aids the soldier and initiates him into the deep masculine. An archetypal reality in men's lives, the Trickster Teacher appears through dreams, fantasies, and therapy, the way Jung encountered Philemon and Dante envisioned Virgil. The Spirit Companion introduces men to a new paradigm of manhood, centered around the Trickster's hidden wisdom, not the hero's glory or the patriarch's power.

After Fedot contacts the deep masculine, he returns to his wife, reaffirming the importance of the feminine and everyday life. As an initiated man, Fedot is now her equal. With his newfound power, Fedot overthrows his evil monarch and establishes a new social order. He does not settle for private happiness but moves society beyond the hero and the patriarch. This is the final step in the mature male initiation, working for the common good.

One last theme of great importance remains in "Go I Know Not Whither"—men's spiritual quest at midlife. The theme becomes clearer when we compare Fedot's adventure with the legend of Parsifal, because there are profound and unexpected parallels between the two soldiers.

CHAPTER TEN

Go I Know Not Whither: Part 2. Parsifal Revisited and Men's Spiritual Quest

PARSIFAL PARALLELS

As I reflected on "Go I Know Not Whither," I was struck by the deep parallels between it and the medieval legend of Parsifal. Both tale and legend focus on a man's post-heroic odyssey and reveal the spiritual dimension of the deep masculine. I shall summarize Parsifal's story, particularly as discussed by Robert Johnson in his book *He: Understanding Masculine Psychology.* I will then compare Parsifal's drama to Fedot's and discuss the practical lessons in both tales for men today.

Chrétien de Troyes, a twelfth-century poet, gives us one of the earliest known versions of Parsifal's story. According to the tale, Parsifal grew up in a forest with his widowed mother. In his adolescence, he met a knight and was so inspired by the sight that he went to King Arthur's court and became one himself. After finding a mentor in a man named Gournemond, Parsifal embarked upon many heroic adventures. On one such journey, Parsifal traveled through a devastated wasteland and met an ailing King, fishing on a river. The Fisher King, as the monarch was known, invited Parsifal into his castle, where the aged father of the Fisher King also lived. In the castle, Parsifal beheld a magical Grail, or vessel, which fed the Fisher King and his father. Although curious about the Grail, Parsifal remained silent, following the advice of his mentor Gournemond not to talk too much.[1] Parsifal was expelled from the castle and later learned that he had seen the Holy Grail and that if he had asked about it, he would have healed the wounded King and restored the barren kingdom to fertility.

Despite his failure in the Grail Castle, Parsifal went on to become one of the premier knights of King Arthur's Round Table. At the height of his fame, a hideous woman appeared before Parsifal and the nobles of Camelot. She berated Parsifal for his failings, especially for wronging many women without even knowing it and for not asking about the Holy Grail when he saw it the first time. As penance, she told Parsifal to seek the Grail a second time. Parsifal embarked upon a midlife quest, and after years of fruitless efforts he met a hermit in the forest who offered to tell him where to find the Grail. Unfortunately, Chrétien's version of the story ends in the middle of a sentence without revealing whether Parsifal succeeds. Chrétien stops just where men need the most guidance—in the midst of the midlife quest. This is the importance of Fedot's tale. To my mind, it completes Parsifal's drama.

The parallels between the two stories run deep. First, Parsifal embarks upon his search for the Holy Grail in maturity, after successfully becoming a warrior, just like Fedot the marksman-soldier. Parsifal had no idea where to look for the Grail, so like Fedot he ventured "I know not whither." The hideous woman who sent Parsifal on his quest also recalls the frog that led Fedot: ugly females, not beautiful princesses, guide men at midlife! Second, on his mature Grail quest, Parsifal succeeds where other knights of the Round Table fail. Some versions of Parsifal's story even say that his name means "right through the middle," referring to Parsifal's skill in hitting a target with a lance, and, by extension, his ability to do things right.[2] Similarly, Fedot is a marksman who always hits his target and does everything correctly. Finally, the Grail Castle is secret and sacred, just like the mysterious mountain where Fedot meets Shmat Razum. The two old men in Fedot's tale also parallel the main residents of the Grail Castle, the Fisher King and his aged father. For his part,

Shmat Razum magically feeds the old men in the mountain, the way the Holy Grail feeds the Fisher King and his father.

Since Chrétien de Troyes stopped in the middle of his story, we do not know what the mature Parsifal would do when and if he enters the Grail Castle a second time. Many poets wrote continuations of Parsifal's tale, but these versions are contradictory and unsatisfactory, as Grail scholars have pointed out. Fedot's tale fortunately picks up where Parsifal's ends and Fedot shows how Parsifal and other men on midlife quests can succeed.

When Fedot arrives at the fire-ringed mountain, the frog tells him to go inside, observe the two old men carefully, wait till they leave, and then do exactly what they did. Fedot obeys the frog. He watches the two men until they depart, and then calls out for Shmat Razum, just like the old men. But the marksman next disobeys the frog. Fedot does something the old men did not do. He asks Shmat Razum to sit down and eat with him, and this "deviation" prompts Shmat Razum to befriend Fedot. The marksman's actions contrast with Parsifal's behavior during the knight's first encounter with the Holy Grail. Young Parsifal remained silent, obeying his mentor's advice not to talk too much or ask questions of strangers. The youthful Parsifal was consequently expelled from the Grail Castle, and later had to seek the Grail a second time. By contrast, the mature Fedot disobeys the advice of his mentor, the frog, and speaks to Shmat Razum. As a result, the invisible spirit allies himself with Fedot, and the marksman completes his quest. The older Fedot succeeds where the younger Parsifal fails.

Fedot's example suggests that Parsifal—and other men on midlife quests—must complete two specific tasks to succeed. The first challenge is disobeying instructions from mentors and teachers, the way Fedot ignored the frog's advice in the mountain. More generally, men must break free from traditional heroic and patriarchal ways of thinking and acting. The second task is making contact with a Trickster Brother, the way Fedot befriends Shmat Razum, or Jung encounters Philemon. The two tasks—breaking with convention and meeting a Trickster—are related since the Trickster delights in breaking rules.

As I looked more deeply into Parsifal's legend, I found that two Jungian analysts, Emma Jung and Marie-Louise Von Franz, arrived at a similar conclusion after their detailed study of Grail legends. They noted that Parsifal struggles with the feminine and the shadow on his midlife quest, trying to integrate male and female, spirit and instinct, good and evil. He has trouble with this because he follows the patriarchal rules of medieval chivalry, which splits the world into two separate camps: the luminous, masculine, spiritual world of God, and the dark, feminine, instinctual domain of the Devil. Parsifal's first task is to abandon his patriarchal ethics. For this, Emma Jung and Von Franz theorized, he needs the help of a Trickster-teacher. The two analysts based their conclusion on the Celtic lore behind Grail legends. The fact that the same themes appear in Fedot's Slavic story emphasizes the cross-cultural nature of the men's spiritual quest at midlife. Even more significantly, the same two tasks appear in other men's tales. In "The King and the Ghoul" from India, the monarch meets a Trickster in the form of the ghoul, and the demon forces the King to abandon logos and patriarchal thinking. In "Brother Lustig" from Germany, St. Peter is the Trickster, and he teaches Lustig how to lie and steal. Violating conventions and meeting a Trickster are two archetypal tasks for men on mature quests, visible in tales around the world.

THE DIVINE TRICKSTER AND THE SACRED MASCULINE

Emma Jung and Von Franz added an intriguing point in their discussion of Parsifal. They concluded that the Trickster whom Parsifal would meet is the Holy Ghost. Their suggestion is startling, but Fedot's story repeats the theme by linking Shmat Razum the Trickster with the Holy Ghost. Fedot's tale does this in two small details. First, as noted before, "Shmat Razum" means "a bit of reason." But in Christian doctrine, reason is associated with the divine Logos, the eternal Word, and specifically identified with the Holy Ghost. Shmat Razum can thus be considered a "bit of Logos," or "a bit of the Holy Ghost." The second detail involves Shmat Razum's relationship to the two old men in the mountain. The three male figures constitute a male trinity, analogous to the Christian Trinity. The two old men also parallel the

Fisher King and his aged father in the Grail Castle. Because the Fisher King is wounded, he is often interpreted as a Christ-figure, or as God the Son. This makes his father equivalent to God the Father. By analogy, the two men in Fedot's mountain should be equivalent to God the Father and God the Son. As the third party in the subterranean trinity, Shmat Razum would parallel the Holy Ghost. And Shmat Razum is an invisible spirit, just like the Holy Ghost.

The assertion that the Holy Ghost is a Trickster borders on blasphemy in Christian tradition, and this may be one reason that Parsifal's legend was never satisfactorily completed by medieval poets. The notion would have been unthinkable. To modern readers, the link between the Holy Ghost and the Trickster may seem esoteric or obscure. As I discovered, though, the association is profoundly symbolic. First of all, the link reveals the spiritual side of the Trickster, and the tricky side of spirituality. Tricksters like the Holy Ghost illuminate the sacred face of the deep masculine and men's spiritual tasks in maturity. Second, the association emphasizes the cross-cultural breadth and archetypal power of the deep masculine. Even in its abstract form, the Christian concept of the Holy Ghost resembles aboriginal Tricksters from across the world. In the rarefied sanctuary of patriarchal theology, the Trickster pops up! These two points become clear if we compare the Christian image of the Holy Ghost with aboriginal Tricksters. The comparison essentially summarizes the major tasks men face in maturity.

First of all, as mentioned before, Tricksters like Hermes, Legba, and Eshu are mediators and communicators, linking humanity and the gods. Tricksters are also linguists, and both Hermes and Legba are credited with inventing language. (Legba still remembers the original language of the Creator, which is why he can communicate with the Creator and charges a fee for his service.) In Christian theology, similarly, the Holy Ghost is Logos, the Divine Word, and acts as God's messenger, bringing revelations to saints, mystics, and prophets. The mediating role of Tricksters and the Holy Ghost symbolizes a vital challenge for mature men, shifting from the hero's focus on conquest to a new emphasis on communication.

Second, aboriginal Tricksters are founders of human culture and community, giving humanity basic foods and social customs. Yet the Trickster is also an iconoclast, who constantly challenges convention. He stresses the creative and inventive aspect of human culture. The Holy Ghost plays the same paradoxical role in Christian lore. The Holy Spirit is considered the animating and unifying spirit within Christian communities, and the descent of the Holy Ghost upon the Apostles at Pentecost traditionally marks the establishment of the Christian Church. At the same time, individuals dissatisfied with the dogmas of the established church invoked the authority of the Holy Ghost in challenging those doctrines, like Martin Luther contesting the Pope's authority. So the Trickster and the Holy Ghost both emphasize the social dimension of the mature male quest and men's need to work for the common good rather than personal enlightenment or salvation. The task reappears in another trait of the Trickster and the Holy Ghost. Both are generative. Just as the Trickster favors creativity and fertility, the Holy Ghost is considered a spirit of life, and its heraldic color is green, for vegetation and fertility. The parallel reminds men that their ultimate task in maturity is to foster life, creativity, and the human condition, not merely their own individual development.

Third, men's tales make clear that the Trickster aids, advises, and comforts men in crisis. The Holy Ghost does the same and is called the "Paraclete," or the "Comforter." Here the Trickster and the Holy Ghost join in a promise of support and wisdom for men walking the road of ashes, lost in the middle of a midlife quest. The aid, moreover, is uniquely masculine because the Trickster Spirit replaces the anima as a source of comfort and advice.

Finally, the Trickster brings fire to humanity, like the Polynesian Maui, the Brazilian Exu, the Native American Raven, and the Greek Prometheus. The Holy Ghost, in its turn, is often depicted as fire. Medieval paintings depict the descent of the Holy Ghost upon the Apostles at Pentecost as fire falling from Heaven, and in paintings of holy communion, the Holy Spirit is often portrayed as fire emanating from the Eucharist. The fiery nature of the Trickster and the Holy Ghost symbolizes the fierce passion that lies at the core of the masculine soul, recalling the wildness of the North Wind or the lusty love of life embodied by Brother Lustig. The deep masculine, the sacred face of the male psyche, is wild and fierce, not pale and ascetic.

The similarities between the Holy Ghost and aboriginal Tricksters are surprising. Even after Christian theology eliminated all reference to instinct and shadow in the concept of God, the Trickster sneaks in, disguised as the Holy Ghost—just like Lustig tricking himself into Heaven. Clearly, the Trickster takes many forms and if men do not look carefully, they can easily miss him.

The similarities between the Trickster and the Holy Ghost also highlight the spiritual aspect of the deep masculine. The religious nature of the Trickster may seem surprising, because Tricksters are usually scandalous and scatological. Yet in most cultures, Tricksters are *gods,* and they often represent the original, primordial deity, like Raven in Northwest America, or Gao in Africa. Moreover, as discussed in Chapter 8, the Trickster is related to the shaman, and the shaman is intensely spiritual, perhaps the original spiritual figure in human culture. So the Trickster's sacred dimension is an ancient one, which survives even in abstract Christian theology.

The divine aspect of the Trickster offers a new paradigm of spirituality for men, distinct from the familiar patriarchal image of the Divine King or the Father God. (The divine Trickster is specifically a male archetype, and fairy tales about women show that they have their own unique image of spirituality, the deep feminine. I leave this topic for another time.) As discussed before, the Trickster appears in men's lives after they move beyond the hero and the patriarch. This means that the Trickster's divine aspects specifically offer a post-heroic and post-patriarchal paradigm of spirituality. Joachim of Fiore, a medieval Christian mystic, suggested this around the time of the Parsifal legends, yet his concepts are surprisingly relevant today. Joachim divided history into three periods, the first governed by God the Father, exemplified by the patriarchal Jahweh of the Old Testament, and the second ruled by God the Son, reflecting the Christian focus on Jesus, the son of God. The last age, still to come, would be inspired by the Holy Ghost. Psychologically speaking, Joachim suggests that the patriarchal and heroic models of spirituality will be replaced by a new masculine archetype, symbolized by the Holy Spirit. Parsifal's legend and Fedot's tale add that this Holy Spirit will be a Trickster, like Shmat Razum.

The nature of the Trickster's spirituality is dramatized by Zen masters, Sufi teachers, and Taoist poets.[3] These "holy fools" reject conventional teaching or logic and insist that each individual attain a direct, personal experience of spiritual illumination. Their goal is "crazy wisdom." Zen masters, for instance, do outrageous things to force their pupils to abandon rationality and convention for the sake of direct spiritual insight. This is exactly what the ghoul does to the King in "The King and the Ghoul." In a similar way, the Kdir, a divine Trickster in Islamic tradition, plays pranks on unsuspecting individuals, trying to initiate them into religious truths. The same applies to Nasruddin, the Trickster in Sufi folklore, and to Don Genaro in Carlos Casteneda's books. These prankster-teachers parallel St. Peter in "Brother Lustig" and Shmat Razum in Fedot's tale. Significantly, one version of Parsifal's legend interprets his name to mean "Holy Fool," and this is another term for the divine Trickster. (This interpretation of Parsifal's name recalls the meanings of Lustig's, as discussed in Chapter 7: "lustig" connotes foolishness and thus conjures up the image of the Fool. In German, I might add, the word for silly is "selig," which derives from "holy" or "blessed," as Jean Collins notes in her essay on the Trickster.) Men's tales reveal that a central spiritual task for mature men is to find "crazy wisdom," a new, authentic, unconventional, and often scandalous connection to the divine.

This discussion may seem abstract, and the divine Trickster merely a psychological theory. But he is not. He is the stuff of men's lives and appears in men's dreams and fantasies today. Two wildly different examples demonstrate the point.

THE DIVINE TRICKSTER IN MEN'S LIVES

The first example came to me in a Tricksterish way. Before working on men's tales, I found an intriguing autobiographical essay which I later realized dramatizes the sacred face of the Trickster.

The report comes from John Battista, a psychiatrist, who described a dream that was a turning point in his life. Although Battista does not indicate the exact age at the time of his "big" dream, it occurred after he was married and became a physician, placing him in the middle third of life. His dream parallels Fedot's tale and Parsifal's legend.

In the dream, Battista drove along a highway with his wife and turned onto a side street. They stopped at a beautiful house, and his wife led him into the basement. There a choir sang an ancient Christian song while a monk recited holy texts. Moved by the music, Battista walked alone to another building, where he heard a choir singing even more beautifully. The music was so mystical, Battista felt he was about to meet God face-to-face. Just as the chorale neared its climax, a cardboard angel floated down from the sky and fell at Battista's feet. Behind him, someone laughed. Astonished, disappointed, and furious, Battista turned around and saw his brother chuckling. Battista cried out, "Don't laugh, that could have been me." Here his dream ended.

In his comments, Battista interpreted his wife as an anima figure, playing the classical role of the inner feminine: she leads him on a journey into the unconscious, symbolized by their entry into the basement of the beautiful house. This is analogous to Fedot following the female frog to the mysterious mountain, and the hideous damsel sending Parsifal on his second quest for the Holy Grail. As Battista's dream proceeds, he goes on to another building without his wife. Similarly, Fedot leaves the female frog when he enters the sacred mountain, and Parsifal travels alone on his second Grail quest. Battista then encounters more and more religious symbols in his dream, from a choir singing ancient Christian hymns, to monks chanting holy scriptures. (Monks, of course, are spiritual brothers and bring up the theme of fraternity.) Battista anticipates meeting God face-to-face, but his hopes are rudely dashed. Instead of the Supreme Being, a cardboard angel flutters down from Heaven! The dream shifts from the sublime to the ludicrous, from religious revelation to sacrilegious humor. This is characteristic of Tricksters, and the dream elaborates on the theme when Battista's brother appears, laughing at the whole situation. There is no reverence or awe here, only hilarious farce. Battista's brother plays the role of the sacred clown, an important form of the Trickster. Instead of meeting God or beholding the sublime Grail, Battista meets a Trickster Brother. This is exactly what occurs with Fedot when he befriends Shmat Razum, and what Emma Jung and Von Franz predict will happen to Parsifal when he finds the Grail the second time and meets the Tricksterish Holy Ghost. Battista's dream thus demonstrates that the divine Trickster appears spontaneously in the dreams of men today, just as it does in fairy tales and medieval legends. (Notice also how Battista's dream shifts from conventional masculinity to the anima, and then moves to the Trickster Brother and the deep masculine, a theme prominent in Fedot's tale.)

The second example of the divine Trickster comes from a man named Sam, with whom I worked for a number of years. Sam suffered a series of psychotic breakdowns and had many religious preoccupations focused on the Holy Ghost. Although reluctant to reveal his inner world, over several years Sam gradually did so, and one session was dramatic. Sam declared, "The Holy Ghost is like 'The Three Stooges.' " Befuddled by what he said, I asked Sam to explain, and he described an episode of the television comedy series "The Three Stooges," during which the comedians had their feet encased in concrete. The cement blocks had rounded bases, so that when one of the stooges leaned too far, the block would roll over and the comedian would fall down. But then the block would right itself, rolling back to its original position and pulling the man into a standing posture. The stooges thus resembled old-fashioned clown dolls which stand up again when knocked down. This episode, Sam said, explained why the Holy Ghost is like the Three Stooges. Sam could not elaborate further, prompting me to reflect on his startling assertion.

The idea that the Holy Ghost is similar to the Three Stooges may seem merely crazy. The only apparent connection would be the number three, since there are three stooges, paralleling the Holy Trinity. As Jung noted, though, psychotic individuals often have direct access to archetypal insight, and Sam was no exception. The deeper meaning of his comment emerges with a bit of reflection. As discussed with "The Little Peasant" and "Brother

Lustig,'' the Trickster is intimately linked with clowns. The farcical humor of the Three Stooges and the pranks they play on each other qualify them as Trickster figures. In comparing the Three Stooges with the Holy Ghost, Sam simply asserted that the Holy Ghost is a Trickster. In this light, the image of the Three Stooges with their feet encased in concrete takes on new symbolic meaning. When the stooges are knocked down, the concrete blocks pull them upright again, and this dramatizes an important trait of Tricksters: no matter what happens and how foolishly they act or what disasters befall them, Tricksters recover. Knocked over by their own impulsiveness or bad luck, they pop back up. Even when they are killed, Tricksters return to life. The Trickster's resilience reflects his link to a deep center. In Jungian terms, the Trickster is connected to the Self. In religious terms, the Trickster is rooted in God. Japanese Buddhism, in fact, uses knock-down dolls to represent spiritual enlightenment, because no matter what pushes the enlightened individual down, he or she recovers, laughing at the experience. The divine Trickster personifies this profound spiritual wisdom, which Sam summed up by saying the Holy Ghost is like the Three Stooges. The amazing analogy, abstract and odd though it seems at first, repeats a fundamental message of men's tales: no matter how bleak a man feels on the road of ashes or how foolish he seems with his goat's ears, a source of healing awaits him deep within his soul, an abiding center beyond despair, shame, and confusion.

THE DIVINE TRICKSTER AND HEALING THE FATHER-SON WOUND

The sacred aspect of the Trickster often appears in men's lives in a particularly important way: the divine Trickster helps reconcile fathers and sons, healing the wounds they inflict on each other. The Trickster does this by revealing the elusive but enduring bond between fathers and sons. Christian theology expresses the theme in very esoteric and abstract terms: the Holy Ghost represents the "spiritual essence" common to God the Father and God the Son, connecting the two. But Tricksters in aboriginal cultures also mediate between fathers and sons. Ananse, for instance, reconciled

Nyame the High God with his favorite son, the Sun God, when the two were estranged.[4] Other Tricksters, like the alchemical Mercurius, play similar roles. An illustration from a seventeenth-century manuscript even portrays an "alchemical trinity," where Mercurius sits between God the Father and God the Son, mediating between the two.[5] Parsifal's drama develops the theme further. In Robert de Boron's version of the legend, which takes up where Chrétien de Troyes' story ended, Parsifal finds the Grail Castle the second time with the help of the Holy Ghost. When he meets the Fisher King, Parsifal follows the advice of the Holy Ghost, and asks questions about the Grail. This heals the ailing Fisher King, who then tells Parsifal an earth-shattering secret. Parsifal's dead father, of whom Parsifal knew nothing, was the son of the Fisher King! This means Parsifal is the grandson of the Fisher King and the heir to the Grail Castle. Parsifal thus reclaims his long-lost paternal heritage, healing the deep wound he suffered from his father's premature death. At the same time, Parsifal cures the ailing Fisher King. Father and son are healed through the agency of the Holy Ghost, advising Parsifal.

A man I shall call Bruce provides a real-life example of the divine Trickster reconciling a father and son. Bruce started therapy with me because of a midlife depression. Successful in his career and happy with his marriage, Bruce did not understand why he suddenly felt uncertain and sad. In therapy, the precipitant for Bruce's depression became apparent. His father had suffered a heart attack a year before and nearly died. The event brought up many painful issues about his father for Bruce. He had spent most of his adolescence rebelling against his father and categorically rejected the older man's way of life. The two had a strained relationship for many years, so Bruce was surprised at the effect of his father's illness on him.

As therapy progressed, Bruce realized how much he yearned for a closer relationship with his father. At the same time, Bruce discovered how similar he was to the older man. Bruce had become a lawyer precisely because his father was a doctor and wanted Bruce to become a physician, too. Yet Bruce chose a career as a relatively low-paid public defender, dedicated to helping the poor. In just the same way, his father worked in public clinics to serve the needy. Bruce was also shocked to find himself laughing the same way his father did and even using some of the same gestures as his father. The two men never talked about these similarities or their personal lives, although Bruce tried for a time. His father had grown up in a different generation and was not given to speaking about his feelings or even reflecting on them. Yet Bruce recognized for the first time how much he was his father's son. The insight was profoundly healing to Bruce and his depression lifted.

At the same time, the tense and distant relationship between father and son gradually melted and became warmer and more fulfilling, although neither man spoke openly about the change. The link between father and son remained secret, silent, sacred, and yet substantial. This is the invisible bond that the divine Trickster symbolizes, the inarticulate connection that endures even through silence, hostility, or absence. As Robert Bly eloquently notes, it is as if fathers give their sons invisible sustenance merely from being together, without talking to each other. The genetic substance of the son is half from the father, after all, and what is uniquely masculine in the son, the Y chromosome, comes entirely from the father. The Trickster's unspoken bond does not excuse fathers and sons from trying to communicate verbally, but the Trickster Brother reminds men there is masculine communion deeper than words. Men err if they seek only verbal communication with their fathers. Expressive, emotional conversations, after all, reflect the feminine mode of communication, and not the Trickster's primordial masculine spirit.

SPIRIT AND INSTINCT

The sacred aspect of the Trickster contrasts sharply with his earthy, instinctual, sexual, impulsive, and greedy nature. While Christian theology has eliminated the paradox by suppressing any shadow element in the Holy Ghost, men's tales like "Brother Lustig" preserve the theme. Lustig steals, breaks promises, and spends his money foolishly, yet he also gives to the poor and ends up in Heaven. The very title of his story conveys the polarities: "Brother Lustig." "Brother" is usually a religious title, and Lustig befriends St. Peter himself, highlighting the spiritual theme. Yet the root of "Lustig" in German is "Lust," which refers to lust, desire, or passion. The Latin version is "libido," the term Freud used to refer to instincts. So "Brother Lustig" combines spirit and instinct. Tricksters emphasize the paradox by taking animal forms. Ananse, the Ashanti Trickster in Africa, is a spider, while the Trickster in Native American tradition is a coyote, a hare, and a raven. Yet the Trickster is also a god. He unites instinct and spirit. Shamans, for their part, repeat the duality. Shamans are profoundly spiritual, particularly with their visions. Yet their trances are intensely physical, produced by dancing, drumming, fasting, or hallucinogens, all somatic means. Many shamans even compare their ecstatic states with sexual fervor. Shamans also have animal helpers or claim to take the form of animals in their spirit travels.

The spiritual and beastly nature of the shaman-Trickster sums up another major task for mature men: reclaiming instinct and integrating it with insight, reuniting body and spirit. This reverses the heroic and patriarchal paradigm, which splits thought from emotion, mind from body, and spirit from instinct. Such splitting helps young men control their impulses and develop consciousness. It also reflects the heroic paradigm, the effort to *conquer* the body and subjugate instinct. Once men master the division between mind and body, however, the next step is to reintegrate the two. Like Tantra, the Trickster reveals the sacred aspect of the body and the embodied aspect of the sacred. He celebrates ecstasy in all its forms, sexual, sensual, aesthetic, and spiritual. Here the divine Trickster overthrows an insidious patriarchal prejudice, the belief that the body is the domain of evil and the feminine, while spirit is good and masculine. The Trickster reminds men that their bodies are *masculine* and divine. Athletes know this instinctively and celebrate the male body, relishing the sensuality of swiftness, strength, and skill. But the experience is usually eclipsed by the hero's focus on competition and conquest. The Trickster reminds men of the spiritual, sensual foundation of sports, deeper than mere winning.

MEN'S CALLING AT MIDLIFE

The divine Trickster has one final trait that is of vital importance to men at midlife. The Trickster has a sacred vocation or calling. Christian tradition makes this clear when the Holy Ghost inspires mystics, saints, and prophets and gives them their sublime calling. Yet the same emphasis on a divine mission appears in aboriginal tales of the Trickster. In Winnebago folklore, Wakdjunkaga the Trickster was sent to earth by Earthmaker, the supreme deity, to fight demons and evildoers and make the earth safe for humanity. As would be expected, Wakdjunkaga often forgot and ignored his mission, but in the end he remembered and fulfilled the divine calling. Tricksters from other cultures, like Big Raven among the Koryaks of Siberia, have the same sacred summons.[6] Eshu of Africa, for his part, received his charge directly from Olodumare, the supreme being, and Eshu's mission was to overcome the demons and disease that plagued humanity, clearing the way for humanity on earth, hence Eshu's title, "roadmaker." "Brother Lustig" reflects this aboriginal vocation of Tricksters in a small detail when the soldier clears a castle of demons and makes it safe for human habitation again. (The farmer in "The Little Peasant" did something similar in evicting the devilish parson from the miller's house. The theme is archetypal.)

The Trickster's sublime vocation clashes with his greed, cunning, pranks, and foolishness. The combination of divine calling and material instinct is the central paradox of the divine Trickster: he is sublime but also sneaky. The contradiction baffled me, but as I puzzled over it an explanation came to me in a Tricksterish way. I remembered a fortune cookie I received some years ago at my favorite Chinese restaurant. The message, which moved me deeply at the time, said, "Genius does what it must. Talent does what it can." I was young then and like most young men, I hoped that "genius" applied to me. Sobering years in the real world quickly disabused me of that vanity, and eventually I forgot the fortune cookie. Then writing this chapter, I realized that the comment explains the essence of the Trickster's calling.

The "genius" mentioned by the fortune cookie does not refer to extraordinary talent or intelligence, but rather to the genie or spirit in each individual. This is what the ancient Romans called the *daimon,* the divine spirit responsible for a man's destiny. It is the source of a man's calling, summoning him to a purpose beyond himself, to his vocation and mission. When heard, the inner voice is preemptory and must be answered. To ignore the calling or turn away from the inner genius is to betray oneself and the world. Hence the oracle from the fortune cookie: "Genius does what it must." The story of Jonah from the Bible dramatizes the point. When Jonah refused God's summons to be a prophet, he was swallowed by a whale until he obeyed the divine calling. Native American tradition reiterates the warning. When a man has a vision of a Thunderbeing, it means he is summoned to be a heyoka, a contrary or Trickster figure. This is an odious, onerous profession, and most men would rather refuse the calling. But they dare not, because refusal means death or insanity.[7] The divine vocation cannot be ignored.

The experience of a man's preemptory inner calling has its roots in shamanism. Across cultures, the shaman is summoned by a spirit which demands obedience. In Siberia, this is the "tutelary spirit," in Australia, the "totem spirit," in Tibet, the "yidam spirit." By any name, it is the *daimon,* the inner calling, which is ignored only at great risk. Although Joseph Campbell advised people to "follow your bliss" and answer the calling, he neglected to mention the coercive, terrifying, tormenting aspect of a divine summons and the catastrophes that occur when the vocation is ignored.

In youth, a man's calling takes the form of a noble vision, a specific ideal to fight for, a dogma to believe in without reservation, or a cause to die for.[8] At midlife, heroic ideals fade, and men wander without direction for a time. Then from the rubble of the old vocation, a new calling arises, which is vague and formless, more like a haunting song heard faintly on the wind. It is a summons to abandon familiar beliefs, to explore new horizons, to "go I know not where, and bring back I know not what." The calling is no longer tied to a particular dream or belief or cause or group, as it was in youth, only to a sense of pushing forward, seeking goals that are not yet clear. Heeding the summons can be terrifying, as the Biblical story of Abraham illustrates. At the height of Abraham's power and happiness, God commanded him to sacrifice his beloved son, Isaac. This was the son for whom Abraham had waited many years and who was to be the beginning of a new nation. Yet God now demanded Abraham slay Isaac and destroy everything Abraham believed in and worked for. Abraham was called to go "I know not where."

Parsifal's legend illustrates the male midlife calling in a subtle detail. When Parsifal enters the Grail Castle the second time, according to the various continuations of the legend, he asks several questions, and his action heals the Fisher King and redeems the land. The questions vary depending on the version of the story, but they are usually something like, "What is the Holy Grail?" "Whom does the Grail serve?" and "What ails you, Fisher King?" The variation in the questions indicates that the specific content is not crucial. What is fundamental is the *asking*. The whole point of the Grail quest is to raise questions. The answer lies in the questioning, and it is this spirit of inquiry and doubt which distinguishes a man's midlife calling from the idealism and fanaticism of youth. The mature calling is the summons to seek, to ask, to explore, and to go "I know not where," not to make edicts or proclaim absolute truths. As Joseph Campbell concluded after his analysis of Grail legends, the Grail Quest is "the unprecedented sense of yearning and striving towards an unknown end, not knowing what to look for or how to look for it."[9]

An old adage goes, "Many are called, few are chosen." I disagree and would say, "All are called, but few listen." Reclaiming the calling is a major task for mature men because the divine summons is so often buried under practical concerns, the need to earn a living and provide for one's family. After years of labor, cynicism and world-weariness eclipse men's sense of vocation. Yet renewing the calling is crucial because it reawakens the divine spark in men's hearts, redeeming their souls.

James Fowler confirms the importance of the haunting midlife call in his book *Stages of Faith*. He studied how religious belief develops over the life cycle and found several distinct phases. At midlife, he noted, individuals abandon familiar religious dogmas to explore new perspectives. The process is often prompted by personal crises, but the end result is remarkable psychological openness: individuals venture spiritually they "know not where." A feeling of curiosity, wonder, and awe results. In a separate study, Larry Cochran looked at the sense of vocation experienced by a number of highly successful men. In youth, these individuals had a specific vision or dream they pursued, such as earning a million dollars, reforming society, or becoming a famous writer. But in maturity, the calling became indefinite. Cochran concluded, "Far from ending in certitude, persons seem to experience or seek uncertainty."[10] Jung expressed the point succinctly, summarizing his own midlife transformation: "My whole being was seeking for something still unknown which might confer meaning upon the banality of life."[11] This is the midlife summons to "go I know not where."

EXAMPLES OF MEN'S MIDLIFE CALLING

The film *Field of Dreams* dramatizes the mature male calling and parallels Parsifal's story. In the movie, a middle-aged corn farmer in Iowa, played by Kevin Costner, hears a voice that says, "If you build it, he will come." The farmer also sees a vision of a baseball field in his fields and fears he is going crazy. When he hears the voice and sees the vision several more times, he obeys it, encouraged by a tolerant wife. The farmer plows under his cornfields and builds a small baseball stadium, using all his savings. Baseball stars from the past then appear magically and start playing on his field. Without his crops, however, the farmer faces financial ruin, but he refuses pressure from the bank to sell. He then hears a voice saying, "Ease his pain," and among the spirits playing on his field, the farmer recognizes his own dead father. His father had dreamed of being a professional baseball player, but only made it to the minor leagues. Failing his dream, the father had gradually become a bitter, sad man. The farmer had been estranged from his father for years before the older man's death, but on the magical baseball field, father and son meet and reconcile. The film closes with the two men playing catch, throwing baseballs to each other. Meanwhile, hundreds of people arrive at the field, paying for tickets to see the other magic baseball players and solving the farmer's financial crisis.

Outwardly the story is nothing like Parsifal's drama or Fedot's tale, but the underlying drama is the same. *Field of Dreams* begins with a man in the middle of life, who suddenly hears voices and has visions telling him to do something crazy, to build a baseball diamond in his cornfields. This is his midlife vocation, calling him to do something he cannot understand, analogous to Parsifal's second quest for the Holy Grail and Fedot's journey to "I know not where." The farmer's vocation also resembles the midlife summons of the Thunderbeings in Native American lore, who command a man to be a contrary and do crazy things. In the film, the farmer has a vision of a baseball diamond in his cornfields just before a thunderstorm. After he builds the small stadium, the farmer also hears the voice tell him, "Ease his pain." His father then appears, a man wounded by the failure of his youthful dream to become a major-league baseball player. Father and son are reconciled, repeating a central theme from Parsifal's tale: the grown son heals the wounded father and contact with the father heals the son. Although there is no explicit Trickster figure in the film, the farmer's mysterious voices, dreams, and visions represent the equivalent of Shmat Razum guiding Fedot, or the Holy Ghost helping Parsifal.

A real-life example of a midlife calling resembling the movie comes from the life of Emanuel Swedenborg.[12] An eminent seventeenth-century Swedish scientist, Swedenborg began having dramatic dreams and visions when he was fifty-five years old. He recorded these in his diary, one of the first known dream journals, and they reveal his struggle with raw, unconscious material. He had visions of Heaven and Hell, dreams of cannibalism, and encounters with demons and angels, reminiscent of "The King and the Ghoul." Swedenborg feared he was going insane, but from his ecstatic, horrifying, scandalous, and blissful experiences, he experienced a divine calling: to record his visions and convey them to others, offering people a deeper spiritual life. He abandoned his many scientific and administrative posts and devoted his life to mystical, theological writings. Many of his dreams and visions resemble those of Jung during Jung's midlife crisis, and the images that Dante preserved in his *Divine Comedy*. The three men each experienced a terrifying, divine calling in the middle of midlife crises. Swedenborg's images, I might add, contain many Grail themes, emphasizing the link between Grail legends and men's mature spirituality.[13]

TRICKERY AND THE CALLING

A man's midlife vocation is only half the picture. When Joseph Campbell advised individuals to follow their bliss and pursue their vocation, he implicitly promised that practical, material realities would take care of themselves. Others have put the point more bluntly, like Marsha Sinetar in her book *Do What You Love: The Money Will Follow.* These maxims reflect the optimism of youth. Any middle-aged individual, accustomed to struggling with the world, will find the advice naive. And this is where the second prophecy of my oracular fortune cookie comes in: "Genius does what it must. Talent does what it can."

Unlike genius, talent preoccupies itself with the possible and the practical, not the visionary and the ideal. Talent does whatever it must to get a job done and to survive in a difficult world. This is the counsel of the divine Trickster. Cunning, clever, opportunistic, and even ruthless, he takes each situation and exploits it to the maximum. His aim is practical, to seize the day. The Trickster laughs at those who pursue pie-in-the-sky schemes, because he wants concrete results, and true to his scandalous intent, he often seeks the crudest rewards of all: food, sex, or money. What distinguishes the Trickster's machinations from that of a sociopath or a selfish tyrant is his divine nature and his ultimate service to the inner *daimon,* to generativity and a higher calling. Conversely, what separates the Trickster's calling from idle dreams and impractical idealism is his cunning and practicality, his trickery. This is the Trickster's paradox: he unites divine inspiration with clever pragmatism, genius with talent. Almost miraculously, the Trickster integrates calling and calculation. Ordinary English reflects his paradoxical spirit because the word "vocation" means both a divine calling, as in a priest's vocation, and a humdrum, everyday job, focused on practical survival, as in "vocational training."

Each man hears the Trickster's midlife summons in a different way. For one, the calling may lie in devotion to his work, for another, dedication to social action, and for a third, love for his children. A father cannot know what his sons and daughters will become when they grow up, yet he will "go I know not whither, and bring back I know not what," for their sake. Whatever is necessary to protect and nurture them, that he will do. It is this spirit that prompts fathers to labor at boring jobs and to stand up after each defeat. It is the cunning and perseverance of the Trickster, righting himself after being knocked down, like the Three Stooges.

My discussion risks becoming sentimental. This is anathema to the Trickster, so a story about Ananse, the Trickster from Africa, provides a useful corrective here. The tale parallels Fedot's story and Parsifal's legend in a dramatic way.

One day, Wulbari, the High God, became tired of all the boasts that Ananse made. So Wulbari decided to teach the Trickster a lesson. Ananse was Wulbari's Captain of the Guard, so the High God told to him go on a journey and bring back "something." Wulbari would not explain what he wanted, leaving Ananse in the lurch. The Trickster secretly dressed up in feathers, pretended to be a bird, and climbed up a tree next to Wulbari's residence. The High God saw the strange bird, and asked if anybody knew its name. Nobody did, but everyone suggested that Ananse would know. Wulbari sighed and explained that he had sent Ananse to bring back "something," without telling him what that was. Everybody laughed at Ananse's predicament, and wanted to know what Wulbari had in mind. The High God explained that he desired the sun, the moon, and darkness. After everyone departed, Ananse climbed down the tree, took off his bird suit, and went in search of the sun, the moon, and darkness. After considerable effort and more clever tricks, he returned with all three, to the astonishment of Wulbari![14]

In this tale, Ananse is the Captain of the Guard for the High God, analogous to Fedot's position as the best marksman in the King's army or Parsifal's fame as a knight. Such success symbolizes the honor and achievement of men at midlife. Ananse also boasts continually, reflecting the pride typical of men in the heroic and patriarchal phase. Wulbari, the Sky God, decides to put Ananse in his place and tells the Trickster to bring back "something." This is the same charge Fedot receives, to "go I know not whither and bring back I know not what." It is men's undefined summons of midlife, the haunting, perplexing call. In Ananse's case, the summons comes from the High God, emphasizing the divine, spiritual origin of the midlife calling. To fulfill the summons, Ananse resorts to trickery, dressing up as a bird and eavesdropping on Wulbari. Through this practical, clever, and hilarious ruse, Ananse divines the High God's intention and then fulfills it. Shmat Razum, similarly, helps Fedot through trickery, and Parsifal receives the help of the Tricksterish Holy Ghost. These tales emphasize how the Trickster's pragmatism and cunning is essential in answering the divine summons of midlife. In the end, Ananse returns with the sun, the moon, and darkness, as Wulbari wanted. Since Wulbari is the Sky God, the sun, moon, and darkness symbolize his essence. Psychologically speaking, Ananse is initiated into the mysteries of the divine masculine and deep manhood. Moreover, he succeeds only because he united a sublime calling with practical cunning, genius with talent, divinity with trickery.

MEN'S INITIATION INTO THE SACRED MASCULINE: A CASE HISTORY

After this long discussion, we need a real-life example of a man's spiritual quest at midlife. Such an illustration comes from Edward Edinger, a Jungian analyst. In his book *The Living Psyche: A Jungian Analysis in Pictures,* Edinger describes the inner journey of an artist at midlife. Although commercially successful, the artist started analysis because he felt his life had no meaning. During the process, he created an extraordinary series of paintings which depict his dreams and fantasies and trace out his midlife odyssey. The paintings parallel Fedot's tale, Parsifal's legend, and Ananse's adventure. The painter was well versed in Jungian psychology, and his works reflect many classical Jungian concepts, such as the anima and the shadow. What is striking is the appearance of themes *not* addressed either by Edinger or orthodox Jungian literature, but which are clear in "Go I Know Not Whither" and Parsifal's legend. The paintings portray a midlife initiation into the deep masculine, a spiritual journey beyond the hero. (I cite a case from another therapist to emphasize how the drama of men's tales emerges spontaneously in men's therapy. An illustration from my own practice would be less persuasive, since my biases would undoubtedly shape the course of therapy.)

The artist's works fall into three chronological groups. The first involves images of suffering, violence, conflict, imprisonment, and oppression. These paintings reflect the collapse of his youthful hopes and convictions and the resulting inner turmoil. This is the proverbial male midlife crisis that follows the disintegration of heroic and patriarchal ideals. The tone of this first series of paintings is hellish and melodramatic, filled with images of torment. They depict the "road of ashes" men take at midlife, and reflect men's initiation into the shadow and the dark, tragic side of life. This stage parallels Fedot being persecuted by his King or Parsifal berated by the hideous damsel.

A thematic shift occurs after the first thirty paintings, and the anima now appears prominently, offering guidance and support. This parallels Fedot's marriage to his anima-wife and his meeting with the Great Goddess. In the artist's paintings, initiation themes also become explicit, and one work is particularly poignant: it depicts the suicide of the artist's father, a trauma the artist had previously avoided dealing with. The painting brings up a central issue in men's midlife journey, the encounter with a father's failings. This is the archetypal theme of the wounded father, so clear with the ailing Fisher King in Grail legends. But the wounded father symbolizes more than a father's personal failing. The injured father also personifies the collapse of the whole patriarchal paradigm which men experience in the middle years. Confronting a father's failures and giving up the patriarchal paradigm force men to seek something beyond conventional manhood.

For the artist, the replacement emerges dramatically in a painting inspired by a dream. The art depicts a newborn infant crawling and smiling. Near the child hangs a poster for the Equal Rights Amendment, and beneath the poster sits the artist, sucking on two red phallic forms. In explaining the scene, the painter identified the infant as Hermes, a classical Trickster figure. The appearance of a Trickster in the midst of a midlife initiation is exactly what men's tales show, with Fedot meeting the tricky Shmat Razum, Lustig befriending St. Peter the Trickster, and Parsifal being aided by the Tricksterish Holy Ghost. The details of the artist's painting elaborate on the Trickster theme. In the portrait, for instance, the artist holds two red phallic forms. Around the world, Tricksters are represented by similar phallic symbols, and Eshu, the Yoruba Trickster, is often portrayed sucking on his finger, a candy, a pipe, or other phallic objects. The Equal Rights Amendment in the painting initially seems odd, but it sums up three basic features of the Trickster: his role as cultural gadfly, his instinct for social reformation, and, as will become clearer in the next chapter, his affirmation of women and the feminine.

The portrait of Hermes ushers in the artist's third phase of paintings, which emphasizes death and rebirth, successful journeys, reconciliation with parents, and the union of opposites. The themes are prominent in men's tales. The death and rebirth motif, for instance, is clear in the resurrection episodes of "Brother Lustig," while the reconciliation of father and son is central to Parsifal's legend. Tricksters like Shmat Razum or St. Peter also personify the union of opposites stressed in the artist's paintings. The artist's final three works are particularly significant because they revolve around a new image: the artist sailing on a ship in the night, following a distant star. The painter explained that the sea journey symbolized his voyage of life, while the guiding star referred to his destiny and calling. The artist dramatizes the theme of a divine calling in another painting, where he portrays God's hand descending from Heaven, holding a long stick. The artist reaches for the stick and describes it as "my vocation." The painting offers a graphic illustration of a divine summons, a direct link between God and a man. The goal of the artist's calling remains unclear, as does the destination of his sea voyage, so the painter is essentially summoned to "go I know not whither." This divine calling marks the climax of the artist's series of paintings and represents the ultimate goal of men's initiation into mature manhood.

The artist's experience recapitulates the themes of men's tales, like Fedot's story and Parsifal's legend. The paintings dramatically trace out men's midlife quest. The saga begins with a crisis, when heroic dreams collapse. Men grapple with the anima, then, learning to honor and embrace the feminine, reversing the heroic and patriarchal denigration of the goddess. Men also walk the "road of ashes," coming to terms with the shadow, with their faults, failings, and wounds, together with those of their fathers. In this painful time, the Trickster Companion materializes, offering help and counsel. He introduces a new form of male energy, focused on healing rather than heroism, communication instead of conquest, and generativity rather than glory. Ultimately, the divine Trickster reminds men of their sacred calling, a summons into the unknown. This is the divine aspect of the Trickster and the sacred face of the deep masculine, hidden in the shadows of the patriarchal paradigm. Men's task is to follow the Trickster's summons, crazy though it may seem, with all the cunning and pragmatism they have learned from their experience with the world.

Each tale we have discussed so far sketches out different aspects of men's midlife odyssey. The full story comes out only when men's tales are assembled together. One final saga remains to be told. This is the epic of the deep masculine itself, the origin and history of the shaman-Trickster. Where did he come from? And why does he take so many forms? To that epic, pieced together from anthropology, archeology, prehistory, and paleontology, I now turn.

CHAPTER ELEVEN

A Tale of the Deep Masculine: Part 1. From Stone Age to New Age

a tale of the deep masculine

Long ago, when humanity first awoke in the mists of time, people roamed the world in small bands of families, moving with the seasons. Men were hunters and stalked reindeer, mammoth, and bison, using stone-tipped spears. Women were gatherers and harvested fruits, nuts, and roots in woven baskets. Arrows and pottery were yet unknown. But humanity had fire, language, art and ritual, and these four gifts lifted humankind above the animals. Men and women also adorned themselves, and they buried their dead with offerings in the hope of an afterlife.

When men went hunting they first met secretly for a sacred ritual. They danced, drummed, and sang, praising the animals they hunted, asking the beasts for a gift of food and life. In the rite, men became shamans, and they painted pictures of their quarry showing spears hitting the animals or the creatures caught in traps. The images were enchanted and ensured a successful hunt: what the paintings portrayed would magically come to pass. To protect the supernatural power, the hunters kept their paintings secret, hiding them in sacred places or erasing them after each hunt. Yet the hunters did not rely only on magic. When they set out after their quarry, they disguised themselves in clever ways, wearing bison skins to stalk bisons, and mammoth fur for mammoths. From downwind, they crept stealthily toward the herds, until they were near enough to use their spears. Or the men hid beside river fords, ambushing migrating herds when the animals were most vulnerable, struggling through water.

After bringing down their quarry, the men danced and sang once more, this time to thank their quarry for giving its life to them. Then the hunters brought their game back to camp, and everyone shared in the bounty. Nobody went hungry, even the old and infirm. After the feasting, the hunters gathered for another ritual. They collected the bones of their quarry and secretly buried them. They honored the creature who sacrificed itself to give them the gift of life, and called upon the animal spirits to raise a new creature from the remains of the old.

Often hunters returned from their forays empty-handed, their quarry too swift and strong for them. Yet no one starved, because women gathered ample fruits, roots, and vegetables. Edible vegetation was always reliable and filling. Without the bounty of women's work, the band would starve. Yet without meat from hunters, which provided essential proteins, the group also would perish. Men and women were both essential for survival, so they were equal. At the dawn of humanity, neither gender dominated the other; they honored each other.

Each group of families traveled widely, and when they met other bands, the occasion was joyful and exciting, a time for dancing and celebration. Hunters told each other where game might be found, while women shared their knowledge of ripening fruit and roots. The groups also exchanged gifts and traded goods from far-off places. A band just arrived from the mountains might offer amber, while another group from the seashore might give shells. Young men and women met at these gatherings, fell in love, and married. Sometimes the newlyweds remained with the husband's group or the wife's, and sometimes they joined a new one.

In their leisure time, men, women, and children played games, told stories, made music, and danced. Artists carved exquisite figures of women just large enough to fit the hand. Made of stone, ivory, and wood, the figurines brought blessing and luck, and people carried them as they traveled. Groups often returned to favored campsites year after year, especially in sheltered areas overlooking rivers. At these locations, artists engraved larger portraits of women, and the stone images blessed the hearthfires and protected the tribe. The artists also painted in caves with the light of oil lamps and resin torches, filling limestone caverns with magnificent animals. People came to these hidden galleries from time to time, gazing in awe at the vivid images. On certain occasions, men gathered secretly in the deepest chambers of the caves. There they engraved and painted images of themselves as hunters and shamans, dancing in animal disguises, sometimes wounded by the great beasts. In these hidden chambers, young men were initiated into the way of the hunter and the shaman. The youths went on vision quests in the underworld darkness, seeking the images that would give meaning to their manhood.

In the sanctuaries, older men instructed young initiates in the secret lore of manhood. By the flickering light of torches, the senior men spoke of their patron, the Trickster, part animal, part human, and part spirit. Elusive and secret like the hunters themselves, the Trickster was the master of disguises and hunting ruses, the inventor of spears and traps. He watched over the hunters and carried their prayers to the animal spirits.

The Trickster was not alone. Equal to him were the patrons of women, the sacred Sisters, who knew the art of basket weaving, the secrets of plants, the timing of the seasons, and the mystery of fertility. Neither Trickster nor the divine Sisters dominated, because men and women were equal.

In this time long ago, being a man meant being a hunter, a shaman, and a Trickster. Manhood was a venture into the unknown, a contest with creatures more powerful and swift than any man could hope to be. Only by wits, trickery, and prayers to the animal spirits did men survive and bring food back for their people. Yet the world was rich then, with an abundance of game and edible plants never again seen on earth. Men and women did not labor long to provide food or shelter for their families, and they had more leisure than their descendants would ever know. This was the paradise of Eden. But the golden era would not last forever.

As hunters and gatherers, humanity flourished. Men and women were fruitful and filled the world. Then, over the millennia, the climate changed, the land became less fertile, and the endless herds of animals vanished. Hunting became more difficult, animals scarcer, and there were more and more mouths to feed. Fortunately, women discovered the secret of growing grain. With their knowledge of wild plants and the cycle of the seasons, women began sowing and reaping wild cereals, doing by conscious plan what nature had done before only by accident. Soon men and women settled down amidst cultivated fields, and they learned to tame wild animals. Goats, cows, and pigs filled the new farms, providing a constant source of meat. The hunter was needed less and less, and he receded into the background. With him went his divine source of inspiration, the shaman-Trickster, whose disguises and hunting rites were now superfluous. Once a numinous figure, secret and sacred, the Trickster became an anachronism.

In the new agricultural era, fertility of the fields was paramount, and for the first time, motherhood became precious. Many children were an asset to the new farmers because children can do many simple chores. To the ancient hunters, having many children was a liability, because infants must be carried when the band travels, and children cannot hunt. With fertility so important to farmers, the feminine gradually eclipsed the masculine. The sacred Sisters, once the equal of the Trickster, soon overshadowed him. The Mother Goddess emerged and soon reigned over the world, governing the fruitfulness of fields and families. Humanity appealed to her for help in time of need, and the Trickster became secondary, merely the consort of the Mother Goddess. At the same time, shamans were replaced by priestesses and priests. The wild dancing and ecstatic visions of hunter-shamans gave way to ordered rituals and collective dogmas. Religion became reliable and predictable, like the cycles of the seasons so vital to farming. The Mother Goddess became so important that men were sacrificed to appease her wrath or to guarantee the fertility of the earth. Being a man no longer meant being a hunter, a shaman, or a Trickster, but rather a servant of the Great Goddess, a consort and helpmate to women.

As people settled in permanent villages, they began to collect possessions. Where their nomadic ancestors kept only a few objects which could be carried from camp to camp, farmers began to amass stores of grain and pottery, herds of animals and buildings. Great inequalities between rich and poor appeared for the first time in human history. Social tensions increased, aggravated by an ever-increasing population, an uncertain climate, and periodic famines. When their crops failed, farmers could not move on to richer lands, like their hunting ancestors, because all territory was now claimed and occupied. Land could only be taken by force, and the stage was set for a frightening new invention—warfare. No longer was fighting a matter of two individuals arguing and coming to blows, as it was among the ancient hunters. Battle became organized, planned, and cold-blooded. The intent was to take land, herds of animals, or hoards of precious goods. With the domestication of the horse and the appearance of mounted warriors, war spread like a plague.

To survive, farmers moved into fortified villages, and men became warriors. Male instincts, honed by millennia of hunting and neglected in the early agricultural era, were bent toward a new use: to kill people rather than reindeer or bison, and to seize wealth and power instead of food. Warriors organized themselves around charismatic leaders, and the leaders became chiefs. The chiefs, in turn, took control of village life, marshaled supplies, and directed men and women for the sake of defense.

A hierarchy of power emerged for the first time, with the chief at the top, warriors just below, and everyone else beneath. Kings soon appeared, wielding the absolute authority of war chiefs even in peacetime. Slavery was invented, too, as war captives and their descendants were forced to labor against their will. The rich art of the peaceful farming period, with its intricate ceramics and delicate jewelry, was replaced by swords, shields, and spears. A siege mentality soon dominated all aspects of culture.

In these perilous times, the warrior became an ideal of manhood. The archetype of the hero was born: boys from an early age were taught to be fearless, aggressive, and merciless in battle. Boys were now favored over girls for simple reasons of survival: boys became warriors, warriors were lost in battles, and new warriors were constantly needed. Slowly and insidiously, women lost ground to men. In times of siege, fighting men were fed, not women. Warriors also began treating their own women like the slaves captured in war. The patriarchy took shape, replacing the feminine culture of early farmers, just as the farmers had displaced the earlier, egalitarian hunter-gatherers. From this time on, being a man meant being a warrior, killing without fear or remorse, dominating women, and aspiring to be a ruling chief.

In the realm of mythology, warrior-gods dethroned the great Mother Goddess. Once beneficent and beloved, the Mother Goddess was recast as a malevolent, destructive being. The warrior-king became the source of light, goodness, and glory, and he killed off the Mother Goddess. Myth mirrored reality, because in real life warriors conquered peaceful farmers. As the Mother Goddess was pushed further into the darkness, so was the Trickster. Perhaps even more than the Great Mother, the hunter-Trickster threatened the new patriarchal order. He opposed war, inequality, and hoarding. But he was too fierce, strong, and independent to be dismissed as a coward. So the patriarch made the Trickster into a demon and banished him.

Yet the Trickster was bred too long in men's bones to be forgotten completely. He surfaced in tales and dreams, welling up spontaneously from the unconscious. Taking many disguises, he escaped the censorship of the patriarch and emerges in men's tales today. The Trickster's language is difficult to understand after millennia of disuse, but his words are vital to men and women. He recalls humanity to an earlier time where men were clever hunters, not deadly heroes, shamans rather than slavemasters, and partners of women, not their overlords. He is the original model of manhood and personifies the deep masculine in a literal sense—deep in time and deep in the masculine soul.

Part 1. From Stone Age to New Age

THE ORIGIN OF THE TRICKSTER

Unlike the other tales in this book, this story of the deep masculine is not a fairy tale. The saga is consistent with facts from anthropology, archeology, prehistory, and paleontology. Yet the story is not pure history either, because we do not know the exact details of life in the unrecorded distant past. So my history is partly dramatized. It is less than science but more than myth. I tell it because of its importance to people today. The story explodes several false myths about manhood that oppress both men and women today.

My tale of the deep masculine makes five basic claims. The first is that the archetype of the shaman-Trickster arises in nomadic hunting cultures and specifically reflects the hunter's way of life. The second is that the hunter differs from the warrior-hero. The two are often considered the same since they both kill, but this is a false myth. The hunter and the warrior reflect two entirely different cultures and two separate ideals of manhood. In fact, I argue that the hunter and the Trickster offer modern men an alternative to the hero and the patriarch.

Third, hunting cultures represent the original form of human society. The hunter-Trickster is one of the earliest archetypes. This claim contradicts a myth that is popular today—the theory that the Great Mother Goddess dominated the earliest mythology. But Mother Goddesses arise among *agricultural* communities, which evolved many millennia after hunter-gatherers. This is the fourth point in my tale of the deep masculine: the shaman-Trickster is older than the Mother Goddess. Yet he has an equal— the ancient archetype of the deep feminine, embodied in myths and legends as the divine Sisters. Like the hunter-Trickster, the wild Sisters reflect the way of the hunter-gatherer and antedate the Great Goddess. The fifth and final point in my saga is one that feminists have made: patriarchal culture arose *after* the Mother Goddess. This explodes another myth, that the hero and patriarch represent the foundation of the male psyche. Actually, the way of the warrior-king represents the newest and shortest chapter in the history of manhood.

These five points have profound practical implications for men and women today. I will discuss my claims one by one, presenting the evidence for them, their relevance to men's tales and male psychology, and the resulting vision of men and women in a new kind of society.

HUNTING AND THE TRICKSTER

Anthropology makes the first point clear: the archetype of the shaman-Trickster animates nomadic hunting cultures, like the Kung of Africa, the Inuit of North America, and Australian aborigines.[1] This means that the shaman-Trickster is not an abstract invention. The archetype reflects a particular way of life and is thoroughly practical. The traits of the shaman-Trickster, in fact, closely mirror the features of nomadic hunters. Hunters, first of all, are almost always men, like Tricksters. Women typically do not hunt, but gather fruits, vegetables, nuts, and roots. Hunters and Tricksters are archetypally masculine. Second, aboriginal hunters must be Tricksters to succeed. Australian aborigines masquerade as emus when hunting those giant birds, the way the Bushmen of Africa use feather disguises when pursuing ostriches. Similarly, before the Spanish brought horses and guns to America, Plains Indians disguised themselves as buffalo to approach the herds close enough to make a kill. Lacking powerful weapons, aboriginal hunters have to be Tricksters. They also prefer to attack large quarry, like walruses and bears, when the animals are sleeping or hibernating (something a warrior-hero would disdain to do). The hunter resorts to trickery in order to survive, and this, I suggest, is the original reason for the Trickster's deceptions. His knavery does not originate in a criminal spirit, but in the hunter's contest with animals larger, faster, and more fearsome than he. Tricksters resort to ruses out of necessity, as we discussed in Chapter 5. At the heart of the Trickster's spirit and at the core of the male psyche lies a creative instinct for survival.

Yet the hunter is not concerned only with his own survival or gain. Hunters provide food for their people, and in almost all nomadic hunting cultures, successful hunters share the bounty with everyone in their tribe. No one is allowed to go hungry.[2] To their people, hunters are sources of nourishment, abundance, and life. The theme is clear in men's tales like "Brother Lustig," in which the ex-soldier gives away almost all his food and money to three beggars. Similarly, the North Wind's first gift to the poor peasant is a magic box that provides food. And Shmat Razum constantly feeds people. The emphasis on nurturing in men's tales was surprising, but it makes sense when the Trickster is linked to hunting cultures. The male role, first and foremost, is that of provider, and the Trickster's deceits serve a generative purpose: feeding his people.

Hunting is uncertain and often dangerous, so hunters typically resort to magic. This is where the shaman half of the shaman-Trickster comes to the fore. Although less well known than their healing practices, a major function of shamans among aboriginal cultures is to guarantee successful hunting.[3] Among the Ojibway of North America, before hunters left on an expedition, a shaman would draw a magic picture of the quarry being sought and paint an arrow flying into the animal's heart to guide the weapon to its target. In the Arctic, Inuit shamans appealed to the spirit guardians of animals, asking for abundant game, while in South Africa, the San Bushmen used ecstatic dances to ensure hunting success. During these dances, some men entered a shamanic trance and claimed to turn into lions. As man-lions, the shaman-hunters would help their human comrades find and kill animals for food.

The hunter and the shaman-Trickster are linked together in an ancient way of life. So closely related are the three roles that we can speak of a combined archetype, the "hunter-shaman-Trickster." The term is awkward, so I will use "Trickster" as a general term, or "hunter-Trickster," or "shaman-Trickster." The three represent different aspects of an integrated, masculine way of life, a coherent model of manhood. The archetype is also distinct from that of the hero and the patriarch, and this brings me to the second point in my tale of the deep masculine.

THE HUNTER VS. THE WARRIOR

The hunter is not a warrior. Traditionally, the two are considered to be the same, because they both kill intentionally. But this view is profoundly wrong and deeply harmful to men and women alike. First and foremost, hunters kill animals, not people. Nomadic hunters, in fact, tend to be pacifists and avoid human bloodshed.[4] The claim may seem surprising since many aboriginal cultures emphasize hunting and also extol warrior virtues, for example, tribes in Africa, America, or the Pacific. These warrior-hunter societies, though, are usually cultures under attack, like Native American societies in the nineteenth century which resorted to warrior ways to defend themselves against European colonists. In other cases, especially in Africa, South America, and New Guinea, hunter-warrior cultures actually depend on gardening and animal husbandry for survival, not hunting. Tied to their land and animals, farmers go to war to defend their property against other tribes. Nomadic hunters, by contrast, have no farms, crops, or domesticated animals to steal. The large game animals that hunters prefer, like buffalo and antelope, are highly mobile and move in huge territories that are impossible to defend or claim as private property. Nomadic hunters also favor pacifism for very pragmatic reasons: cooperation with other hunting bands is the best strategy for survival.[5] By sharing food, water, and information with each other, mobile hunters ensure that any group suffering a run of bad luck in finding food can count on help from other bands. Cooperation provides a safety net and contrasts with the competition characteristic of heroes.

Men's tales mirror the distinction between the hunter-Trickster and the warrior. "Go I Know Not Whither" is particularly clear here. At the beginning, the story *says* that Fedot is a soldier, but *shows* him hunting for a living. He also hunts for the golden stag and then for the "I know not what." He acts like a warrior only at the very end, when the King attacks him directly. So although he is said to be a warrior, Fedot is really a hunter.

Other Trickster stories make the distinction even clearer, because Tricksters typically make fun of warrior ways and favor pacifism. Wakdjunkaga, the Winnebago Trickster, for example, once called a war feast. All the warriors in his tribe attended, bringing choice foods, as was the custom. After Wakdjunkaga ate his fill, he destroyed his war bundle, an unbelievable act of sacrilege. His war feast was a ruse to obtain free food and to mock warrior customs! Similarly, Odysseus, "the wily Greek," opposed the Trojan war and feigned insanity to avoid being drafted into the Greek armada. (His ruse was uncovered, forcing him into war.)

As a pacifist, the hunter-Trickster opposes the hero-warrior. The word "hero," after all, derives from the ancient Greek word for "warrior."[6] The original function of heroes is to make war and kill people. The hunter-Trickster offers men an alternative to this bloodstained tradition. In particular, he breaks the traditional heroic dichotomy between "real men" who fight each other, and "wimps" who avoid battle. Although it sounds paradoxical to men raised in a heroic tradition, the hunter is fierce and yet peaceful. He bravely pursues dangerous game, but remains gentle with people. The hunter-Trickster personifies a long-neglected form of male fierceness deeply relevant to modern society.

Hunters maintain peace among themselves with a variety of ingenious techniques that offer intriguing suggestions for men today. When disputes between hunters break out, as they inevitably do, men keep the fights on a personal level, involving only the individuals arguing. For this purpose, hunters often use ritual battles, like wrestling or boxing matches, but such combat is stopped before serious injury occurs to either man. By contrast, when disagreements erupt in patriarchal, warlike cultures, fighting typically escalates to mortal duels in which one man is killed. Family "honor" also becomes involved, and clans take up the battle, generating long-running vendettas. Hunter cultures dampen disputes, while warrior cultures glorify them. The hunter-shaman relies on mediation and negotiation, while the hero-patriarch resorts to combat and conquest.

The hunter-Trickster also uses "fission" to resolve disagreements. When two people in a band of hunter-gatherers cannot stand each other, one will simply leave and join another group. Individuals are not forced to obey others or to accept group decisions they disagree with. Farmers, by contrast, are tied to their land and cannot easily move away. They are forced to use authority and coercion to maintain social harmony. "Brother Lustig" illustrates the hunters' approach when Lustig and St. Peter part ways because the soldier keeps taking rewards: instead of St. Peter using his patriarchal authority and trying to dominate Lustig, the two men split up amicably.

Nomadic hunters tolerate many different views and practice an early form of pluralism. This helps explain why the Trickster is a pluralist, as discussed with "The King and the Ghoul." In today's multicultural, multiracial society, such tolerance and pluralism are essential. Patriarchal insistence on one authority and one viewpoint does not work. The aboriginal hunter-Trickster offers better advice.

Hunters also use ingenious trance techniques to resolve conflicts, relying on the power of the shaman-Trickster. Among the Kung of Africa, when two men argue, a shamanic celebration is held, and the disputants are forced to dance next to each other until they enter an ecstatic trance. When they return to normal consciousness, their hostility is spent. Similarly, when strangers arrive at a camp, the Kung hold a trance dance and the ecstatic experience helps defuse the fear and suspicion provoked by strangers.[7] The Mbuti, another hunting culture, also use dancing to reduce interpersonal tensions, as do many Australian aborigines. By contrast, warrior cultures use dances to provoke murderous frenzy. War dances, common among warrior cultures, incite young men to overcome their natural qualms over killing, the better to slay their enemies. The hunter-shaman's peaceful use of trance states is deeply instructive for men today. The purpose of altered states of consciousness, the hunter-Trickster insists, is not private entertainment or personal indulgence, as is commonly thought today. Psychedelics, dancing, drumming, meditation, or sweat lodges were originally methods of *communal conflict resolution*. They aim at social harmony, not private pleasure, and the precedents offer healing for society today.

The hunter-Trickster differs in another way from the hero-warrior. Hunters kill their quarry with reverence and gratitude.[8] Like the Kung of Africa or the Inuit of North America, hunters "negotiate" with their game, asking permission and forgiveness before killing the animal. They also thank the creature afterward, and treat the remains with reverence. To the hunter, animals are sentient beings, equal to, if not wiser than, themselves. By contrast, the warrior demeans his enemies. Soldiers dehumanize their opponents and treat the enemy as an inferior, subhuman creature. (This is clear in wartime propaganda, which portrays "the enemy" as a terrifying beast.) The dehumanization eliminates any limitations on aggression, and war brutality results. Warriors often gloat over their victims, mutilating them, taking scalps, or keeping heads as trophies. They do not revere their victims the way the hunter honors his quarry.

In respecting the sacrifice the animal makes for them, hunters recognize that their gain comes from the animal's loss. They live because the animal dies. This is the zero-sum outlook, which is characteristic of the Trickster, as discussed with "The Little Peasant" and "Brother Lustig." The hunter-Trickster recognizes the cost to everybody of his personal gain. To the warrior, on the other hand, personal triumph and glory are everything. The enemy's defeat, humiliation, and death are ignored or rationalized away. The warrior looks at only his half of the equation, unlike the hunter, who sees the whole picture. The holistic, zero-sum outlook of the hunter-Trickster is essential in today's shrinking world, where smokestacks in one community cause acid rain elsewhere, and the privileges of one ethnic group rest on the disadvantages of another. The hero's focus on his personal advantage endangers human survival, whereas the hunter's zero-sum realism promotes sustainable growth.

THE SPIRIT OF THE HUNTER-TRICKSTER:
EQUALITY AND SHARING

Other features of the hunter-Trickster distinguish him from the hero-patriarch. The warrior-king, for instance, typically denigrates the feminine and dominates women. By contrast, the hunter-Trickster respects the feminine and treats women as his equals. The Trickster's egalitarian attitude reflects the spirit of nomadic hunters, in which men and women are both essential to survival.[9] Men's hunting is unpredictable, so women's gathering of fruits and wild grains actually provides the bulk of food in terms of weight and calories. Yet hunting is vital because meat supplies essential proteins absent in vegetation. Moreover, meat is prized above all other foods: male and female hunter-gatherers consider themselves hungry if they have eaten their fill of vegetable food but lack meat.[10] Hunter-gatherers also typically trace their kinship through both parents, rather than just through the father's line, as in patriarchal cultures. The mother's side is equally valued.[11] Although nomadic hunting cultures are often considered "primitive," their egalitarian spirit is surprisingly modern and fits well with both feminism and the men's movement. The hunter-Trickster respects women while affirming masculine fierceness.

Among nomadic hunters, equality also holds between men. There is usually no single "chief" who runs all tribal affairs. This contrasts with the hero and patriarch, who habitually create hierarchies ruled by a single man. Among hunters, one man may lead hunting forays because of his skill in tracking, another may take charge in judging disputes because of his diplomacy, and yet a third person may oversee the move to new campsites because of his pathfinding talent. The Bushmen of Africa enforce equality among men in a particularly Tricksterish way—with humor. When a hunter successfully kills an antelope, other hunters customarily describe the quarry as a scrawny old sick thing, hardly worth bringing back to camp. The successful hunter is expected to agree, and go along with the joke. Similar teasing can be seen among Alaskan Inuits, Australian aborigines, and African Pygmies, not to mention in men's locker rooms today. The humor counteracts unequal status among men and is a form of the

Trickster's satire. The Trickster makes fun of heroes and authorities to level out differences in power and prestige.

Today the hunter's spirit of equality and pluralism is particularly important. With the Baby Boom reaching midlife, a large number of men compete for a few positions of traditional patriarchal authority. Most men will be left out, feeling frustrated and dissatisfied. The hunter-Trickster offers an alternative, a vision of many leaders in different domains, using specific talents, and not one patriarch dominating everybody else. This spirit of pluralism is equally important to women. As long as organizations have a hierarchy of power, the masculine way of the patriarch and the warrior will dominate. To be successful in this context, women must adopt male attitudes. Remove the hierarchy and new worlds open up. Feminists like Riane Eisler have therefore offered alternative models for organizations, based on horizontal networks typical of women's relationships among themselves, rather than masculine hierarchies. Many men unconsciously oppose these feminine paradigms, fearful of losing their masculinity in such systems. The hunter-Trickster offers help here, because he personifies a *male* spirit of equality, negotiation, and pluralism, a paradigm of masculine cooperation and fierceness, consonant with feminine traditions.

Although Tricksters steal, they typically give away their booty. They do not hoard wealth, and this reflects another dramatic difference between hunters and heroes. Constantly on the move, hunter-gatherers cannot accumulate much property. Marked differences in wealth therefore do not develop. By contrast, heroic and patriarchal cultures focus on hoarding, and a major motive for warfare is to take territory and possessions from other tribes, to accumulate more wealth. Modern capitalism continues the theme, and today a man's masculinity is often judged on how many possessions he owns. Men's tales like "Brother Lustig" dramatize the hunter-Trickster's aversion to hoarding: Lustig steals two geese but gives one to the two hungry young men. Moreover, Lustig does not use his magic knapsack to accumulate wealth for himself. He also turns down the grateful lord who offers him a secure position at his castle after Lustig clears the place of demons. Lustig prefers to wander the road and is closer to the generous, nomadic hunter, than to the acquisitive, territorial hero.

Nomadic hunter-gatherers do not hoard possessions, because they cannot afford to carry heavy loads as they travel from place to place. Today, we cannot afford to hoard objects, either, for a different reason: the earth is running out of resources, and our wastes foul the planet. We need to travel more lightly, like nomadic hunter-gatherers. The hero's hoarding has become deadly, while the Trickster's generosity is life-preserving.

THE HUNTER-TRICKSTER AND THE GREAT MOTHER

Scholars of pre-history generally agree that humans were nomadic hunter-gatherers in the Paleolithic period, the era of the Old Stone Age (from "paleo," meaning "old," and "lithic," meaning "stone").[12] This is the third thesis in my saga of the deep masculine: hunter-gatherers represent the original form of human culture. The Paleolithic Era stretches from the dawn of the human race, perhaps 75,000 years ago, to the invention of agriculture, some 10,000 years ago. It is the first chapter in the human drama and the longest by far. Humans were hunter-gatherers for some 65,000 years, and farmers for only about 10,000. Because the shaman-Trickster is so important to nomadic hunter-gatherers who survive today, the archetype was probably equally vital to Paleolithic hunter-gatherers.

Here we run against a theory that has become popular today, the view that early human culture focused on the Mother Goddess and the feminine, and that mothers and women ran society, not men. This is the "matriarchal" theory of human origins (from "mater," or "mother," and "archein," or "rule"). Jungians are much taken with this theory, and I was, too, when I began my work on men's tales. As I looked into the evidence, however, it became clear that the matriarchal view is incorrect.

The point is vital to understanding men's psychology, because it clears up a persistent and pernicious error. If human culture was originally matriarchal, then maternity and the feminine are the fundamental principles of the psyche. Hence, the masculine must be derivative and secondary. For men to maintain any sense of masculine identity and independence, they must actively reject the maternal and the feminine. So men will inevitably fear, flee, and fight the feminine, according to the matriarchal theory.

However, anthropology has failed to turn up any example of a truly matriarchal society where women rule men.[13] If matriarchy were fundamental to human culture, it should show up in some society. Moreover, a closer look at the cultures that were once considered matriarchal, the Iroquois of North America, the Timorese of Indonesia, and some Australian aboriginal tribes, for instance, reveals that those societies are actually "matrilineal." That is, they trace inheritance through the mother's line, rather than the father's (hence the term "matrilineal"). But women do not rule men. Although women control certain domains, like the household, and have great influence in some political matters, men typically exercise greater authority. Property, for instance, is inherited through the mother rather than the father, but it is the mother's *brother* who controls the wealth. Even in cultures in which feminine figures dominate mythology, like in eastern Indonesia or among the Aranda of Australia, men still control tribal life and look down on women.[14]

Given this new evidence, matriarchal proponents revised their theory. According to the new view, the earliest human cultures focused on maternity and Mother Goddesses, but women did not rule men: the sexes shared power. Human societies were originally "matrifocal" not matriarchal, mother-focused not mother-ruled. Archeological evidence confirms the revised theory. As Marija Gimbutas points out, cities like Catal Huyuk in Turkey, or Minos on Crete, apparently worshiped a Mother Goddess rather than a patriarchal god, and the feminine seems to have been honored more than the masculine.[15] However, it is vital to distinguish between the Paleolithic or "Old Stone Age," and the Neolithic or "New Stone Age." The Paleolithic was the age of hunter-gatherers, while the Neolithic was the era of farmers. And *the evidence for matrifocal cultures comes from the Neolithic, not the Paleolithic.*[16] Catal Huyuk and the Minoan civilization were agricultural, Neolithic societies. The crucial question is whether Mother Goddesses also reigned over Paleolithic hunter-gatherers.

Anthropology suggests that the answer is no. Existing hunter-

gatherer tribes are not matrifocal and do not worship Mother Goddesses (or patriarchal gods).[17] Of course, we cannot assume that
contemporary hunters are accurate models of Paleolithic culture.
But existing hunter-gatherers are the closest living model for prehistoric humans.[18] Some Eskimo and Siberian hunting tribes speak
of a "mother of the animals." Although widely equated with Mother
Goddesses, this "mother of the animals" differs in significant ways
from the Great Goddesses of agricultural societies.[19] The Eskimo
mother of animals, for instance, does not generate or give birth to
the creatures. In some tales, she is simply the spirit of a dead woman
who descended to the bottom of the sea and somehow gained control
over its animals. Nor is she the main mythological figure, because
the same cultures describe a Supreme Being who lives in the sky
and is male (although he does little that affects humans). The mother
of beasts is better considered a guardian spirit of animals. The
guardian is explicitly male among other hunter-gatherers, like the
Pygmies of Africa, the Yukaghir and Chukchi of Siberia, and the
Yaghan of South America.

Existing nomadic hunter-gatherers are also egalitarian, and as
discussed earlier, neither men nor women are considered more
important. This is a second reason to believe that Paleolithic
hunter-gatherers were neither matrifocal nor patriarchal. They
were presumably egalitarian. Direct evidence supports the point.
Burials of fully modern humans (that is, "Cro-Magnon" humans
as opposed to Neanderthals) first appear about 35,000 years ago,
and include similar funeral goods for women and men. This suggests that men and women had equal social status.[20] (In Neanderthal burials, men had more offerings than women.) Modern
humans also apparently shared food equally from the beginning,
just like recent nomadic hunter-gatherers.[21] Telltale signs of social inequality multiply during the Neolithic age, after the invention of agriculture. Women in certain Neolithic cultures were
buried with more goods than men, implying greater status. In
later patriarchal cultures, of course, men had spectacular collec-
tions of wealth compared to women. The Paleolithic was perhaps
the most egalitarian period in human history.[22]

Faced with this evidence, those who favor the matrifocal theory
retreat to a different line of reasoning. They argue that maternity

is easy to understand, but paternity is not. Many "native" cultures today apparently do not understand paternity, so prehistoric hunters presumably did not either. Mothers would therefore be more important than fathers, and women more respected than men. This theory of prehistoric sexual ignorance is probably wrong. Paleolithic humans apparently understood the importance of the male in animal procreation. Several Paleolithic caves, like that of Montespan in France, contain animal sculptures which were probably part of fertility rituals used to foster plentiful game animals.[23] The animals are explicitly paired, male with female, even though they do not travel that way in real life. The deliberate linkage suggests that Paleolithic humans recognized the necessity of both males and females in reproduction. The claim that many aboriginal tribes do not know about sexual biology also has become suspect.[24] Such allegations in early anthropological accounts often reflect nineteenth-century colonial prejudice more than scientific observation. Moreover, most primates display an instinctual understanding of paternity. Male primates, for instance, protect their offspring and not those of other males.[25] Prehistoric humans presumably had a similar unconscious understanding of paternity.

Proponents of the matrifocal theory appeal finally to the observations that originally inspired the matriarchal theory: women are much more common and prominent in Paleolithic art than men. These ancient female portrayals include the famous "Venus" statuettes, carved of bone and ivory, depicting women with exaggerated breasts and buttocks, like the celebrated "Venus of Willendorf."[26] The figurines look pregnant, so early scholars regarded them as Mother Goddesses. A closer analysis of the "Venus" figures, however, reverses the conclusions.[27] Most are *not* pregnant. Although they all have large breasts and hips, this apparently was an artistic convention (the Paleolithic equivalent of the flat, stiff style of Egyptian art from many millennia later). Many of the Venus statuettes are actually of very young or old women, before or after childbearing years. They are not simply pregnant mothers. In fact, it is only in the agricultural, Neolithic period that female figures are portrayed as mothers, either holding infants or giving birth to them, as Marija Gimbutas notes. Paleolithic art contains no such maternal themes. The gradual evolution of Neolithic images of women confirms the point. The oldest Neolithic portrayals give women huge hips and breasts but no faces, just like the Venus statuettes of the Paleolithic. Later Neolithic art adds faces or masks to women, along with clothes, and finally thrones and shrines. These later symbols of individual identity and power are absent from Paleolithic portrayals of women, suggesting that women and mothers gained prestige only in the Neolithic.

FROM THE SECRET HUNTER-TRICKSTER TO THE MOTHER GODDESS

If Paleolithic humans were not matrifocal, how do we explain the greater frequency of female figures in prehistoric art? The reason is probably that the male image was taboo. Judging from recent hunter-gatherers, the basic assumption behind hunting magic is that depicting an animal being killed magically ensures that a real animal would be killed.[28] Portraying animals controls them magically, and the same applies to the hunter. So hunters avoid being portrayed or keep their likenesses hidden away. The principle is clear in voodoo: making an effigy of the victim gives the magician control over the person. In a similar spirit, many men and women from aboriginal cultures refuse to have themselves photographed, because capturing their image on paper would mean that their souls were trapped. The theme persists in modern culture, since we speak of ''shooting'' people when taking their picture, as if to kill them.

The taboo on male figures helps explain a striking fact about Paleolithic portrayals of men: the images are almost invariably disguised, represented by schematic stick-figures or given fantastic, grotesque faces, reminiscent of masks. Since prehistoric artists were extraordinarily skillful in their depictions of animals and women, these distorted images of men must have been deliberate. Moreover, Paleolithic male and female figures are typically segregated and found in different types of places.[29] (This contrasts with Neolithic art, which commonly presents men and women together, often with women being more prominent.) Images of Paleolithic women are found at living sites, while male figures were placed in caves that are very difficult or dangerous to reach.

Perhaps the most famous Paleolithic example of a male figure is the dancing shaman of the Trois Frères cave in the French Pyrénées, and he can be seen only after an arduous journey, crawling through a long, muddy subterranean passage. Similarly, the male figure in the "sanctuary" of the Lascaux cave in France is accessible only by climbing down a vertical shaft, using ropes. Even in these secret locations, male figures could often be seen only from a certain angle.

The predominance of female figures in Paleolithic art, I conclude, does not appear because the feminine was more important than the masculine, but because hunting magic made male portraits taboo. The practices of the hunter-shaman, not the Mother Goddess, make up the explanation here. The original culture of humanity, therefore, did not focus on the Mother Goddess. Men honored the hunter-Trickster, while women followed his counterpart, the sacred Sisters. Neither the deep masculine nor the deep feminine dominated the other because of the egalitarian spirit of hunter-gatherers.

Once agriculture was invented, a slow, steady cultural revolution took place. With farming, grain and bread became staples, while meat was provided by domesticated pigs, cows, oxen, sheep, and goats. Hunting and its patron, the Trickster, became less important. Agriculture also depends on steady, cyclical work, similar in spirit to the labor of raising children. So feminine and maternal values gradually eclipsed masculine ones. The virtues of the hunter, on the other hand, became faults: the hunter's willingness to take risks in hunting, for instance, had no outlet and degenerated into male gambling and thrill-seeking. Female fertility became a priority to farmers, because the more children farmers have, the more helping hands there are. For hunters, by contrast, having many children is a burden.[30] On a hunt, after all, unskilled children are likely to scare game away.

In mythology, Great Mother Goddesses appeared and soon dominated the Trickster. He became her consort or son, and was no longer equal to the divine feminine. Cerunnos, the Celtic Horned God of the Forest, dramatizes the point. He wears horns, dances, and hunts, like the Paleolithic hunter-shaman. But in Celtic lore, Cerunnos serves a more powerful female figure, a Mother Goddess.

He is secondary, she primary. In African folklore, similarly, Legba the Trickster is the son of a ruling Mother Goddess.

The Navajo illustrate the shift from a hunter-gatherer tradition to a matrifocal, agricultural society.[31] Originally part of the Athabascan hunter-gatherer culture, the Navajo long ago migrated from Alaska and Canada to their present position in the American southwest. In settling their new homeland, the Navajo adopted agriculture from the nearby Pueblo Indians, and shifted to a matrilineal society, typical of farming cultures. The Navajo also began celebrating seasonal rituals emphasizing the fertility of the earth. But Navajo mythology retains ample traces of an earlier hunter-gatherer period: the Trickster, in the form of Coyote, prowls through their folklore. However, he has become more comical and less awesome, compared to Tricksters like Raven, from the Kwakiutl tribe and other Athabascans who remained hunter-gatherers.

FROM HUNTER TO GODDESS AND GODDESS TO HERO

The final point in my account of the deep masculine is one that feminist historians have documented well: patriarchal tradition arose after agriculture.[32] Starting from perhaps 6,000 years ago, patriarchal cultures displaced matrifocal farming cultures. Several forces fueled the shift. First, the population increased steadily, while the climate deteriorated, making food harder to obtain. Skeletons from Neolithic burials reveal telltale signs of malnutrition, infection, and severe episodic stresses, suggestive of periodic famine. Skeletons of Paleolithic hunter-gatherers do not exhibit such traumas.[33] Competition for fertile land became keen. At the same time, farmers accumulated property, and this wealth made a tempting target for raids. Warfare was invented—deliberate, planned battle, involving organized groups of men. Of course, earlier hunter-gatherers, like anybody else, no doubt came to blows. But their fights were spontaneous and probably limited to the individuals' disagreeing with each other, judging by the example of existing hunting cultures. Moreover, there are no images of war in Paleolithic art. Battle scenes, in which groups of men fight each other, appear in art only at the end of the Paleolithic.

The invention of war dramatically changed human culture. Warriors become necessary for a culture's survival. Because of their greater strength and size, men were sent out to the battlefield to protect mothers and children at home. To ensure that they made good warriors, boys were taught from an early age to deny fear and pain. Harsh, mutilating puberty rites were invented to force boys into the heroic mold. (Such ordeals are less common among nomadic hunters.)[34] Only girls and women, boys were told, cry out in fear or pain, so the worst insult to a male in a warrior culture was comparing him to a female. Men were thus taught to reject the feminine and denigrate women, in order to be fearless warriors. (This is ironic, because the whole reason to be a brave warrior was to protect women and children!) The heroic ethic was born as a desperate means of survival. Warriors who survived battle also brought the brutality of war home with them. Although many warrior cultures have rituals to "decontaminate" a warrior upon his return, it is impossible for men to be fearless killing machines on the battlefield, yet gentle and loving at home. Killing enemies makes it easier to strike wife and children in anger. Preoccupied with defense, warriors turned over family responsibilities to women and looked down upon domestic chores. In warrior cultures, husbands and wives are much more distant from each other, compared to hunter-gatherers.[35] Children in heroic cultures are also raised primarily by women and have less contact with their fathers. So boys initially have a feminine identity, and in order to develop a masculine one, young men reject all things feminine. This heightens male denigration of women.[36]

Prompted by the invention of warfare, the patriarchy evolved. What began as a means of survival soon dominated virtually every aspect of society and almost every culture. Societies which rejected the warrior way were overrun by more warlike neighbors. Archeology documents the grim process, as Gerda Lerner, Riane Eisler, and Marija Gimbutas have pointed out. Although these scholars focus on Mesopotamian and Middle European civilizations, the same pattern appears elsewhere in the world.[37] Scandinavia offers a unique illustration, because peat bogs there have preserved religious offerings deposited in lakes. The oldest sacrifices involve animal bones and were probably associated with shamanic rituals in a hunter-gatherer culture. Later offerings were made to goddess figures related to agriculture, while the most recent sacrifices were made to war gods. Meso-America repeats the pattern. The earliest artifacts are petroglyphs which focus on hunting magic. After agriculture supplanted hunter-gathering, cities appeared, and the art in these early civilizations emphasizes peaceful scenes with many female figures. Only later do war images appear, along with the glorification of warrior-kings.

Native Americans in North America experienced a similar evolution. The Comanche, for instance, were apparently peaceful hunter-gatherers, like the Shoshone, until the Spanish introduced horses and European colonists began encroaching on traditional Comanche territory. The tribe mastered the use of horses and firearms in an astonishingly short time, shifted to a heroic ethic focused on the mounted warrior, and fought back against the European invaders. In the cultural upheaval, Comanche women lost many of their traditional rights and were soon treated as chattels, less valuable than a good horse. The peaceful, egalitarian way of the hunter-gatherer was overrun by the warrior-hero, as he vainly tried to resist the destruction of his people.

Within mythology, patriarchal warrior-gods displaced earlier goddesses. In Greece, for instance, Gaia and Demeter, two Great Goddesses, were displaced by Zeus, the patriarch. In ancient Babylonia, Marduk the warrior-hero killed Tiamat, the original creator-goddess and took her place. And in Scandinavia, the Aesir, who were the warrior-gods like Thor, demoted the Vanir, who had been the older farming-gods like Frey. Along with the Mother Goddess, patriarchal gods also suppressed the ancient hunter-Trickster. With Zeus paramount, Hermes the Trickster became his mere messenger. When Yahweh took center stage in Semitic tradition, the Trickster was banished to the dark fringes and became Satan. Similarly, under Odin's rule, Loki the Trickster was treated as an outlaw. Two figures from Greek myth dramatize this patriarchal suppression of the Trickster: Prometheus and Sisyphus.

Prometheus was a Titan, older than the Olympian gods, and a consummate Trickster. He stole fire from the gods to give to man, as is typical of Tricksters around the world. To punish Prometheus, Zeus chained him to a rock and sent an eagle to devour his liver every day. Zeus also made Prometheus' liver grow back each night to make the torment endless.

The same patriarchal persecution of the Trickster appears in the story of Sisyphus. Most readers will be familiar with Sisyphus as the man condemned after death to push a stone uphill, only to watch the rock roll down again, and have to force the stone up once more. What is less well known is the reason for his torment. Sisyphus was the King of Corinth and an accomplished Trickster, whose very name means "the clever one." Sisyphus ran afoul of Zeus by witnessing the god's rape of Aegina, the daughter of Asopus, a river spirit. When Asopus went looking for his daughter, Sisyphus struck a bargain with the river god. In return for revealing his daughter's location, Asopus gave Sisyphus a reliable spring of water that the city of Corinth badly needed. Zeus retaliated by giving Sisyphus the futile task. Like Prometheus, Sisyphus was a Trickster who defied a patriarch to help his people, and who then paid a terrible price.

The evolution of the masculine, from hunter-gatherer culture to farming societies and finally to patriarchal warrior traditions, is hinted at in engravings made on prehistoric megaliths in Portugal.[38] On one monument at Vale de Tejo, a man with an erect phallus holds a dead stag, and the figure has been interpreted as a shaman, similar to the dancing men of the Paleolithic caves. However, at another Portuguese site, Cueva de los Letreros, a male figure with a phallus wears what appear to be horns on his head and holds a sickle in each hand. Above him is a circle and crescent, suggestive of the sun and moon. He seems to reflect the transition from a hunting culture focused exclusively on game animals to an agricultural tradition centered on the seasonal, solar, and lunar cycles, so important in planting and harvesting. The celestial theme becomes more prominent with megaliths located at Fratel and Ficalbo, which depict men with phalluses holding up sunlike designs, emanating rays. These figures resemble a masculine sun god, usually associated with patriarchal warrior cultures. The rock engravings thus hint at an evolution of masculine images from the hunter-shaman to an agricultural seasonal god, arriving finally at a patriarchal sun god.

CONCLUSIONS

From all evidence, the Paleolithic Era of hunter-gatherers was an affluent and tranquil period, with few people, abundant resources, and no organized warfare.[39] There has been no comparable period of peace and plenty since. The Paleolithic thus comes closer than any subsequent era to the Biblical image of Eden, or "the golden age" described in many mythologies. War came later and the Bible summarizes the drama in a poetic way: Cain murdered Abel *after* Adam and Eve were expelled from Eden. Murder and mayhem followed humanity's exile from the Paleolithic paradise. Moreover, Cain was a farmer, and Abel a shepherd, and this is consistent with the historical evidence showing that warfare arose after agriculture and animal domestication.

Traditionally, the warrior-king is considered to be the foundation of the masculine psyche. But I believe this is false. The heroic and patriarchal ideal is a new invention and represents a superficial layer of the masculine psyche. Many also believe the Great Mother Goddess is the original mythic core of human culture. Yet this, too, is mistaken. Preceding her by uncounted millennia were the shaman-Trickster and the divine Sisters, the deep masculine and the deep feminine, reflecting the wisdom of egalitarian hunter-gatherers.

The earliest records of the hunter-Trickster and the deep masculine lie in Paleolithic images of men painted in caves. The art is of great significance because it represents one of humanity's oldest known symbolic expressions. Like dreams and fairy tales, cave art presumably reveals unconscious meanings. The cave paintings, in fact, are prehistoric equivalents to men's tales: both contain complex symbols and tell stories. Of course, we cannot be sure about the meaning of Paleolithic art, since there are no prehistoric hunters to interview. But many existing hunter-gatherers cannot explain the significance of their rituals and sacred art either. The meaning is unconscious and must be inferred, as is the case with fairy tales. Paleolithic cave paintings, in fact, parallel men's tales to an astonishing degree. The ancient art represents the first chapter in the long saga of manhood and the deep masculine.

CHAPTER TWELVE

A Tale of the Deep Masculine: Part 2. The Evolution of the Trickster

The Paleolithic Story

Unlike the Greeks who left us the written story of Odysseus, or the Sumerians with their epic of Gilgamesh, Paleolithic hunters had no writing in which to record their tales. But the ancient hunters did have art, and their portrayals of men tell a story of manhood, just like men's tales. Although there are significant sites in Africa, India, and the Americas, the most intensely studied examples of Paleolithic art come from Europe, and particularly from France, with its spectacular and well-preserved caves. It is impossible to discuss every male image of Paleolithic art, but several basic themes run through the masculine figures. Together the motifs outline the original chapter in the saga of the deep masculine.

Paleolithic caves contain portraits of animals, women, and men, usually placed over each other in what seems to be a jumble. Scholars originally thought the order of figures was random, but André Leroi-Gourhan, an authority on prehistoric art, discovered otherwise. After analyzing data on all known Paleolithic caves, he found a common organization to cave art.[1] The images follow a pattern, which hints at a story. Certain animals like bears, lions, and stags are associated with male figures. Others, like bison and oxen, cluster around female figures. Typically, as one enters a cave, animals associated with men appear first, and more rarely, male figures themselves. Once inside the main chambers, figures of women or signs and animals associated with women are prominently displayed. These areas of the cave were accessible and frequently visited, judging by the many artifacts left in them.

Going deeper into the caverns, explicit depictions of men appear in remote areas. These almost-inaccessible sites were apparently used as secret sanctuaries. While Leroi-Gourhan did not rely on statistics, statistical analysis confirms his general findings.[2] Paleolithic caves demonstrate a specific sequence of images, moving from the entrance to the innermost areas: "masculine" animals appear first, followed by portraits of women and "feminine" animals, arriving finally at male figures in the secret and deepest chambers.

This pattern is basic to men's tales. As discussed in Chapter 9, men's stories begin with conventional masculine themes, shift to anima images, and only then turn to deep masculine. "Go I Know Not Whither" starts off with Fedot as a marksman and soldier, then focuses on his magical anima-wife and her family, before moving to Shmat Razum and the deep masculine. The pattern reappears in the *Odyssey,* in which Odysseus starts off as a victorious warrior, loses his ships, and then grapples with powerful anima figures, like Circe and Athena. Finally returning home, Odysseus makes a sacrifice to Poseidon, symbolically honoring the deep masculine. In the *Divine Comedy,* similarly, Dante starts off as a powerful patriarch, loses everything at midlife, and then meets the divine Beatrice, who guides him through Hell and Purgatory. But at the end, it is St. Bernard who leads Dante to a face-to-face meeting with God, the sacred masculine.

Cave paintings repeat the pattern as one moves through the caverns. The first images to appear, located at the entrances, are animals associated with men, such as lions or stags. The animals probably reflect the hunter's preoccupation with predators and prey, the desire to be like lions, or to control powerful quarry like stags. In the middle of the caves, female figures and animals specifically associated with them appear. Visited frequently by Paleolithic individuals, these middle chambers were apparently considered feminine, just like living sites, which were associated with engravings and statuettes of women. The abundance of animals painted near feminine figures also hints at a link between food, nurture, and the feminine. In modern psychological terms, the feminine imagery in the middle of Paleolithic caves reflects anima themes. Finally, in the most remote parts of Paleolithic caves, male figures appear. They presumably represent secret, sacred images of the masculine. Paleolithic cave art thus begins with images of the hunter's conventional masculine role and then shifts to feminine motifs, before arriving at the deep masculine. This is the core drama of men's tales and suggests that the pattern originates in the dawn of human culture. The stories preserve the very first archetype of manhood.

Men's tales use the masculine-feminine-masculine shifts to depict an initiation into the deep masculine, as discussed in Chapter 9. Paleolithic cave art may have been used for similar initiatory purposes.[3] A few underground sites have footprints of youths, preserved in mud, suggestive of dancing and initiation rites. Certainly, the darkness, danger, and isolation of cave sanctuaries lend themselves readily to vision quests, like those central to male initiations among Native Americans. The Shoshone and Coso tribes of North America, in fact, depicted their initiation visions in rock art, and their engravings are remarkably similar to Paleolithic cave paintings. Among tribes like the Crow, moreover, a man seeking an initiatory vision often cut off a finger joint as a sacrifice to the spirits. Many Paleolithic caves have outlines of hands with missing finger joints. Other caves contain images that have been retraced repeatedly, suggesting some kind of ritual use of the art. These Paleolithic engravings are reminiscent of the sacred images used in many Australian aboriginal initiations, where the same portraits are ritually repainted year after year.[4]

THE DEEP MASCULINE IN THE PALEOLITHIC

Images of men in the deepest chambers of Paleolithic caves take three forms, according to André Leroi-Gourhan and Henri Breuil, the leading authorities on the subject.[5] These three types of male figures reveal the original concept and image of the masculine.

The first category includes half-men, half-animal figures who are usually dancing. The most famous illustration is the "dancing shaman" of the Trois Frères caves, but other magnificent examples occur at Gabillou, Fontanet, and Labastide. Prehistoric rock art from India also portrays dancing men with horned heads and masked faces.[6] So the image of the dancing shaman is not restricted to Paleolithic Europe.

The second type of male figures includes grotesque, "ghostly" faces, particularly prominent in the caves at Font-de-Gaume, Rouffignac, Les Combarelles, and Marsoulas. The final group involves wounded men, and the example in the "sanctuary" of the Lascaux cave is especially significant because long spears and beautifully sculpted lamps were found nearby, suggesting some kind of ritual was enacted in front of the portrait. Older examples of the wounded man can be found at Pech-Merle and Cougnac, both dated to about 20,000 years ago.[7]

The three types of male figures reflect the basic traits of the shaman-Trickster archetype. In fact, the first group of Paleolithic male images, half-animal and half-human dancers, are usually interpreted today as shamans.[8] The stag-headed man in the Trois Frères cave is often called "the dancing shaman." Support for this interpretation comes from contemporary hunter-gatherers who portray half-men, half-animal dancers in their art, identifying the beings as shamans. The San of Africa, as mentioned before, believe that a man can take the form of a lion during shamanic hunting dances, and an ancient site of rock art in the San area depicts a half-man, half-lion figure, engraved some 26,000 years ago. This suggests that the San belief originated in the Paleolithic.[9] (European dancing shamans often have lion traits, too, like lion legs or lion phalluses, emphasizing the archetypal nature of the half-man, half-animal theme.) The bestial aspect of Paleolithic male figures anticipates the Trickster's habit of taking animal forms, like Coyote of North America, or Ananse the Spider from Africa. Tricksters also continue the dancing theme from Paleolithic images. Legba, the African Trickster, was made chief of the gods because he alone could play the flute and the drum while simultaneously dancing. (The dancing shaman of the Trois Frères cave, I might add, appears to be playing a flute. And flutes have been found at a number of Paleolithic sites.) Eshu was also portrayed dancing. Moreover, Paleolithic dancing men almost invariably have erect penises. (Some cave sites, like that of Bedeilhac in the Pyrénées, use stalagmites as penises for male figures!) Similarly, Tricksters like Hermes, Legba, Eshu, and Shiva are often symbolized by sacred phalluses and carry on the phallic theme.

The second type of Paleolithic male figures, the ghostly or grotesque images, probably represent animal spirits, dead people, creatures from the spirit world, or shamans in a trance journey.[10] These interpretations again come from parallels between Paleolithic images and the art of existing hunter-gatherers. The Bushmen in Africa portray bizarre male figures in their rock art, and tribesmen interpret the images as spirits of the dead or as shamans traveling in the spirit world. The same applies to the secret, sacred art of Native Americans. Similarly, Australian aborigines paint grotesque figures which represent the spirits of the original clan ancestors.[11] In portraying spirits or the dead, the ghostly male figures in Paleolithic art reflect the role of the shaman-Trickster as a spiritual messenger, communicating between the living and the dead, the spirits and humanity. The Paleolithic ideal of manhood is part animal, part human, and part spiritual, just like the Trickster. The original male image thus combines animal instinct with sublime insight, rampant sex, and deep spirituality. From the beginning the shaman-Trickster integrated opposites.

The final category of male figures in Paleolithic caves, the wounded man, is perhaps the most intriguing. There is a simple, practical meaning to the image: Paleolithic men were probably injured frequently when hunting large animals like mammoths. However, shamanism offers a deeper level of interpretation. In shamanic tradition, a wound or an illness initiates an individual into being a shaman, as discussed in Chapter 8. Many scholars therefore suggest that Paleolithic images of wounded men allude to shamanic initiations.

Hunting magic provides a third level of symbolism. As mentioned earlier, the aboriginal hunter feels that his quarry makes a sacrifice in allowing itself to be killed. Among many existing tribes, hunters believe they must return the sacrifice by being wounded themselves. (Prehistoric petroglyphs in the Guyanas appear to portray this type of exchange.)[12] Consequently, many hunters identify themselves with their quarry. This means that the hunter sees himself as both hunter and hunted, wounder and wounded. The injured man of the Lascaux cave illustrates these multiple meanings. The figure, located in the "sanctuary" of the cave, is a man lying on the ground before a wounded bison and a nearby rhinoceros. (Similar scenes involving a bison and a wounded man occur in other sites, like Le Roc de Sers, and Villars, so the theme is archetypal, not accidental.) There are two commonly accepted interpretations of the Lascaux scene.[13] The first is that the man is a hunter who was injured by the bison or the rhinoceros. The second is that the man is a shaman in a trance. This latter interpretation relies on the fact that a staff topped by a bird figure lies beside the man. Such staffs are commonly used by shamans in hunting cultures even today, suggesting that the Paleolithic figure is a shaman. The man also has an erect phallus, indicating that he is in an excited, ecstatic state, like a shamanic trance. These two traditional interpretations do not contradict each other: the man may have been wounded in a hunting accident, but the wound led to a trance, which initiated him as a shaman.

The wounded theme is clear in classical Tricksters. As discussed earlier, Tricksters are commonly killed and resurrected repeatedly. Besides their physical wounds, they also suffer blows to their pride and fall into hilarious predicaments. Unlike the hero or patriarch, who denies his vulnerability, the Trickster accepts his. The shaman-Trickster recognizes his weakness and pain, but also knows his fierceness and power.

We probably will never know for sure whether Paleolithic images of men were used for male initiations. But the evidence is intriguing, and the profound parallels between cave art and men's tales today emphasize the continuity of masculine archetypes from prehistoric times to the present. At the center of the male psyche, now and 20,000 years ago, is a secretive, elusive spirit: the hunter-shaman-Trickster. He is literally the deep masculine, deep in caves, deep in time, and deep in the male soul.

TRICKSTER TRACES

Originating in the Paleolithic, the shaman-Trickster was later buried under the goddess traditions of agricultural societies, and then the patriarchal conventions of warrior cultures. Yet the Trickster is too powerful to be banished permanently, so he surfaces in many subtle, symbolic, and often baffling ways. Residues of the shaman-Trickster, for instance, appear prominently in three Greek gods: Hermes, Hephaestus, and Dionysus. Hermes is well known as a Trickster, of course, but a small detail also links him to hunting: the moment he was born, Hermes hungered for meat. He did not desire milk, like an ordinary infant, but wanted meat, like a hunter. Hephaestus, for his part, is associated with fire and metalworking, and he gave crucial inventions to humanity. These are traits of Tricksters like Raven of North America, Maui of Polynesia, and Legba of Africa. Moreover, Hephaestus was often represented by a phallus, analogous to Hermes, Eshu, Legba, and Shiva. As the only crippled Olympian, Hephaestus also carried the wounded aspect of the shaman-Trickster. Significantly, Hephaestus was injured by Zeus, who threw him off Olympus in a fit of rage. Like Prometheus and Sisyphus, Hephaestus is a Trickster figure wounded by a powerful patriarch.

Dionysus is not usually considered a Trickster, but he has many features of one.[14] He often went about in disguises, like Hermes and other Tricksters. As the god of wine, Dionysus was associated with uninhibited impulses, analogous to the Trickster's lustfulness, hunger, and greed. In rituals honoring Dionysus, a sacred phallus played a central role, as it does with Tricksters like Eshu in Africa or Wakdjunkaga in America. Yet Dionysus does not denigrate or abuse females, unlike Zeus or other patriarchal gods. Like his fellow Hermes, Dionysus also had to fight for recognition, which is also true of the Polynesian Trickster Maui and the African Legba. (Patriarchal pantheons normally reject Trickster figures.) Killed and torn apart by Titans, Dionysus came back to life, just like the Native American Coyote or the Celtic Cerunnos.

Finally, Dionysus was associated with satyrs, half-animal, half-human figures, and Tricksters typically take such half-animal forms. In fact, Dionysus was often depicted as a half-man, half-animal figure, reminiscent of the Paleolithic dancing shaman.

Traces of the Trickster can be found in other Greek gods. Eros, in some areas of Greece, was worshiped in the form of a sacred phallus, just like Hermes. In later lore, he was identified with the creative force that generated the world, and Plato even described Eros exactly like a Trickster: Eros was homeless, inventive, high-strung, and brave—a sorcerer, philosopher, seeker of wisdom, and a great hunter.[15] The link between Eros and the hunter is surprising, but it makes sense when we recognize the Trickster's tie to hunting. The personification of relationship, Eros also reflects the Trickster's role as mediator and communicator. Proteus, an ancient Greek sea god, exhibits other traces of the Trickster. Proteus had the power to change his form at will and was associated with prophecy. This link between disguise and divination is odd, but typical of the shaman-Trickster. Legba and Eshu of Africa are the patrons of divine oracles, yet they continually invent disguises, tricks, and schemes.

Ares offers another instructive example of Trickster traces. Although he was the Greek warrior god, Ares learned to *dance* before he learned to fight. This is surprising, but the same sequence appears in male initiation rites from many warrior cultures, like the Gisu of Africa.[16] These puberty ceremonies require boys to dance almost continuously, night and day, in the week preceding their initiation ordeals and circumcision. Dancing precedes warriorhood. The pattern is archetypal, I suggest, and reflects the origin of the masculine psyche in the shaman-Trickster: male initiations probably first focused on hunting and shamanic dancing, and the heroic theme was added on much later. There is some evidence for this. Bullroarers are carved bone or wooden implements which create an eerie noise when whirled. In historical times, they have been used almost exclusively in male puberty rites among hunter-gatherers, like Australian aborigines and Native Americans. Remains of such bullroarers have been found in Paleolithic sites dating to 17,000 years ago in the Ukraine, and 13,000 years ago in France,[17] suggesting they were used in ancient initiations.

Ares was famous for his battle frenzy, and this brings up another trace of the original Trickster. War madness is widely romanticized among warrior cultures. German and Scandinavian warriors, for instance, often went "berserk," and the term comes from the German for "bear shirt." The warrior, it was thought, actually became a ferocious bear in the frenzy of battle. Other people, like the Celts, the ancient Greeks, and many Native American tribes, explicitly associate frenzied energy with the warrior. Such a state, I suggest, derives from the older, dancing trance of shamans and hunters. The San of Africa provide a precedent here. As mentioned before, San men dance prior to hunting, and some enter a trance in which they believe they become lions. The lion is the most ferocious animal in the San environment, just like the bear in German forests. The San lion-trance thus resembles the German bear-frenzy, but with one crucial difference: berserker madness aims at killing people rather than animals. The shaman's frenzy is for hunting, healing illnesses, and resolving differences between people. The word "shaman," I might add, comes from the Tungus people of Siberia, and derives from the word for "excited."[18] Shamanic energy is life-preserving, unlike the warrior's fury.

Trickster traces also appear in patriarchal gods like Yahweh and Zeus. Both were originally wind gods, as discussed in Chapter 5. And wind gods, like wind in reality, are notoriously unpredictable, elusive, and invisible. They are Tricksters. The Tricksterish nature of Yahweh is clear in the Book of Job, where God and Satan play cruel tricks on Job to test the poor man's faith. For his part, Odin, the Norse patron of warriors and heroes, was also a magician, a god of poets, and closely associated with runes and prophecy. The last three traits are more typical of the Trickster than the warrior. The unsuspected tie between Tricksters and patriarchal gods leaves us with the scandalous suggestion that the latter derive from the former, the way humans descend from apelike ancestors. The shaman-Trickster is the primordial form of the masculine, not the warrior or the patriarch.[19]

The Trickster's greater antiquity can be inferred from language. The Pope is officially called "the Supreme Pontiff" in the Catholic Church, yet "pontiff" derives from the Latin term "pontifex'' which means "bridge-builder" ("pontis" for bridge, and "fex" from "facere," to make). The Pope's original function is to build bridges, chiefly between God and humanity. But this is the Trickster's primary role around the world, to communicate messages between humanity and the gods, like Hermes connecting Olympus and earth, or Legba carrying messages to the High God. The pontiff's original Tricksterish role as mediator and messenger, however, has been hidden underneath layers of patriarchal pomp and power. The same fate occurred to the Chinese term for Emperor, which translates into "Son of Heaven." The title reflects the Emperor's role as the one who mediates between Heaven and earth, a shamanic function normally carried out by Tricksters. However, the mediation has been eclipsed by patriarchal domination.

Other words convey the same insight, such as "authority." Although patriarchs emphasize authority as power, the word derives from the Latin for "originator," or "progenitor." The primordial meaning of "authority" is thus generativity and creativity, and the Trickster, lustily phallic and wildly inventive, personifies this more basic masculine energy. Finally, the word "jovial" today means jolly or funny and points to the Trickster. Yet the word derives from "Jove," or Jupiter, the Roman version of Zeus. Behind the patriarch lies a clown!

These Trickster traces in mythology and language reiterate two points relevant to men today. First, Trickster themes emerge in complex, elusive ways which are easy to overlook. In practical terms, this means that men often miss Trickster motifs in their dreams and fantasies and lose the insights and wisdom the Trickster has to offer. Second, although suppressed by patriarchal tradition, the Trickster constantly reappears in both folklore and men's dreams. His repeated resurrections reflect the power and importance of the archetype. He truly is the deep masculine, the primordial image of manhood.

Trickster tales underscore the primordial nature of the Trickster. Native American stories, for instance, call the Trickster "First Born." Recall also that the Trickster Prometheus was a Titan, older than the Olympian gods, and Loki, the Norse Trickster, was a primeval giant, antedating Odin and the gods of Valhalla. Similarly, Hopi Trickster-clowns are considered the original human beings, and Kaggen, the Trickster of the African Bushmen, is described as the first man on earth. For his part, Raven, the Northwest American Trickster, created the earth out of the primal ocean, before other living things appeared. The primordial nature of the Trickster explains his many contradictory qualities: he is kind and cruel, cunning and stupid, altruistic and selfish at the same time, precisely because he is prior to conventional distinctions between good and evil, life or death, dark or light. He defies tradition, particularly patriarchal ones, because he is older and more important. Indeed, Tricksters are often placed above warriors and patriarchs in a very literal sense. The Chamamcoca of South America describe five worlds, of which the middle belongs to humanity. Beneath that is a vacant world, and at the bottom the realm of the sun, to which the sun descends each night. Above the human world is the realm of the jaguar, who is usually associated with warriors and kings. But highest of all is the world of the fox, the Trickster!

TRICKSTER TRACES AND GRAIL LEGENDS

Men's tales reflect the long history of the deep masculine. The stories are like archeological sites, with older layers of meaning hidden under more recent ones. This is the major reason why the Trickster theme is so subtle and complex in men's tales: the archetype is covered up by more recent goddess and patriarchal traditions. The Grail legends, discussed in Chapter 10, illustrate the multiple levels of symbolism. On the surface, the Grail drama is about the adventures of noble warriors like Parsifal, Gawain, and Galahad. The tales are heroic, full of fighting and gallant victories, reflecting patriarchal values. Underneath this drama, however, Grail scholars have unearthed a distinctly different stratum of symbolism, which emphasizes the feminine and the maternal.

In one version, when Parsifal reaches the Grail Castle the second time, he learns that the Grail King is his mother's brother. This kinship makes him, according to the tale, the rightful heir of the Grail King. This version invokes inheritance through the *mother's* line, reflecting the matrilineal and matrifocal traditions of ancient Celts.[20] Grail legends also associate the Grail with a magic sword and spear, which were said to be part of the sacred treasures of the Tuatha de Danaan. The latter were the mythical ancestors of Celts, ruled by a Queen, not a King. The Grail itself was carried by a maiden, rather than a man, emphasizing the importance of the feminine.

Underneath the matrifocal Grail themes lies yet a deeper layer of meaning. As discussed in the last chapter, after their exhaustive study of Grail legends, Emma Jung and Marie-Louise Von Franz concluded that the Grail is linked to the Holy Ghost, and the Holy Ghost is something of a Trickster. In fact, Celtic tradition associates magic vessels, like the Grail, specifically with Tricksters. Bran, for instance, was a Celtic magician and Trickster who possessed a cauldron which could resurrect the dead. Cerunnos, the Celtic horned god and a Trickster figure, was brought back to life in a miraculous vessel after he was killed, while Mananna MacLir, a Tricksterish sea god, owned a cauldron which contained an ambrosia of immortality. The Trickster theme, in turn, points back to ancient hunting cultures and the shaman-Trickster, antedating goddess tradition. Almost all versions of the Grail legend also feature a magic spear or lance, associated with the Grail, while only some describe a magic sword. The spear, of course, was the original weapon used by Paleolithic hunters. (Swords were invented only after metalworking was discovered, since stone is not strong enough to make long blades.) At the core of the Grail legends, then, lurks the hunter-Trickster, hidden beneath images of a Mother Goddess and the even more recent heroic tradition.

If Trickster traces are subtle in Grail legends, they are explicit in another figure, popular around the time of the Grail legends. This is the Fool, who typically wore animal skins or a cap with the ears of an animal. He resembles the archaic half-man, half-animal dancing shaman. Fools were often deformed individuals, too, recalling the image of the wounded shaman. The Fool's link to animal ears and physical deformity, incidentally, offers a deeper interpretation to the goat's ears in "The King's Ears." The embarrassing animal ears point to the Fool, and back to the shaman-

Trickster, hidden behind the patriarch. The Fool's link to hunting reappears in the harlequin, another form of the court Fool. But "harlequin" derives from the old French "hellequin," which means "demon huntsman."[21]

TRICKSTER TRACES IN MEN'S TALES AND MEN'S DREAMS

The hunting motif surfaces in subtle ways in men's tales. As mentioned before, "Go I Know Not Whither" specifically says that Fedot hunted for a living, and hunting is a basic metaphor in his story. This theme reappears in "Brother Lustig" and provides deeper meanings for odd details in the story. St. Peter, for instance, resurrects the dead Princesses by manipulating their bones, and the procedure parallels shamanic rites, as mentioned in Chapter 9. But the ritual also resembles *hunting* ceremonies. Among Siberian and Native American tribes, hunters extract, clean, and then ceremonially bury the bones of their quarry, believing that new animals will arise from the skeleton.[22] Lustig's magic knapsack provides a subtler allusion to hunting. He first uses the magic pack to obtain two geese, rather than something more practical, like gold. So he uses his pack like a hunting trap rather than a wallet or money bag.

Hunting motifs likewise materialize in "Iron John," one of Robert Bly's favorite fairy tales about men. In the story, a hairy wild man personifies the deep masculine. He is discovered specifically by a *hunter*. Similarly, in the epic of Gilgamesh, Enkidu, who is initially a hairy, wild man, is also discovered by a hunter. Many other men's tales begin with hunting references. In the story of "Gromer Somer Joure," King Arthur loses his way during a hunt and then has his fateful meeting with Gromer Somer Joure. "The King Who Would Be Stronger Than Fate" from India follows a similar plot. Hunting sets the stage for men's dramas, although the theme is usually eclipsed by heroic themes.

As would be expected, the theme of the hunter-Trickster can be found in the dreams of modern men, but in highly disguised form. One of Jung's "big" dreams, discussed earlier, dramatizes the point. Recall that during his midlife crisis, Jung dreamed of murdering Siegfried, the archetypal hero of Germanic tradition. Jung was accompanied in the dream by a "brown-skinned savage" who helped him kill Siegfried. They did this with a treacherous ambush, hiding behind a rock and shooting Siegfried from safety—something no self-respecting warrior would do. The "brown-skinned savage" represents an archetypal hunter, and the ambush reflects the hunter's trickiness.

A similar reference to hunting appeared in a dream of a psychologist who came for therapy shortly before his fortieth birthday. Albert suffered a midlife crisis and felt depressed despite his successful professional career. As we worked together sorting out the issues involved in his "burnout," Albert had a series of "big" dreams which were deeply healing for him. One is particularly noteworthy. In the dream, Albert was a pallbearer at the funeral of a soldier who had been decorated for bravery. The procession carried the body of the hero past a forest, and a group of hunters waited impatiently for the funeral to pass, because the mourners blocked the way into the wilderness. On the other side, under the trees, a fox sat, watching everything with an amused grin. Although brief, the dream is highly symbolic. The soldier symbolizes heroic masculinity. But the soldier is dead, reflecting the collapse of the heroic paradigm. As discussed before, this calamity often precipitates a man's midlife crisis. In Albert's dream, hunters and a fox wait for the dead soldier to be carried past them. The hunters reiterate the importance of hunting to the masculine psyche, while the fox is an archetypal Trickster figure. So Albert's dream sums up, in a nutshell, the drama of men's tales: after men leave the hero's path or the hero dies, the way of the hunter-Trickster awaits.

In encountering the ancient image of the hunter-Trickster, men come face-to-face with the original form of the masculine from the dawn of human culture. Long before the hero, the patriarch of the Great Goddess, and for a far longer period, the Trickster personified manhood and male energy. In going beyond the warrior and the king, men do not have to invent something new, or grope toward unfamiliar ways of life. Men need only reclaim the essence of the masculine psyche, laid down long ago and transmitted over generations through stories and images.

THE DEEP MASCULINE AND MEN'S EARLY
PSYCHOLOGICAL DEVELOPMENT

If the shaman-Trickster reflects the masculine as it emerged at the dawn of the human race, he also represents the earliest form of male energy for individual men. The Trickster personifies typical traits of the immature male psyche. Boys and adolescent males, for instance, are impulsive, awkward, rebellious, and boastful, just like the Trickster. Men normally repress these juvenile impulses as they grow up and take their place in society, but the Trickster traits reappear in maturity and demand to be integrated into conscious life. In a sense, the Trickster presides over each man's personal history, just as the Trickster animated early human society. Furthermore, Trickster themes appear and vanish throughout the male life cycle in predictable ways.

The Trickster is clear in boys. From birth, boys are more active, impulsive, difficult to control, and slower to be "civilized," compared with girls. Tricksters, of course, are also impulsive. Their gluttony, sexual appetite, and greed get them into humorous predicaments. Boys also master their own bodies later than girls, and are uncoordinated early on. This recalls the Trickster's awkwardness and lack of a coherent body sense. (In some tales, the Trickster's left hand fights with the right, and Tricksters commonly misplace body parts!) Boys more commonly break rules than girls, and this rebelliousness is characteristic of the Trickster. Psychoanalysts also have noted a phase in male development when boys are fascinated by their penises and take delight in showing them to anyone interested. Tricksters from Coyote to Ananse do the same. Finally, boys are more susceptible than girls to accidents, learning disabilities, and hyperactivity. Tricksters, in turn, fall into the most ridiculous and hilarious predicaments, and are frequently injured and killed: they are painfully vulnerable just like boys. The Trickster mirrors, trait for trait, the features of the early male psyche.

After four or five years of age, Trickster traits normally go underground in boys. Patriarchal rules force young males to control their impulsiveness. Boys become "civilized." This discipline is particularly important in modern society because agricultural and industrial civilizations provide little room for wild adventures. (Hunter-gatherer cultures are much more lenient with their children.) After several years of relative peace, puberty shatters boyhood discipline. With adolescent surges in sexual energies, boys become moody and impulsive like the Trickster. As they undergo the normal growth spurt, teenagers feel clumsy, no longer at home in their own bodies, once again like the Trickster. Teenage boys also alternate between bravado and collapse, boasting about their achievements and overestimating their abilities, only to be crushed and dejected by small insults from friends or dates. Such bragging and collapse are typical of the Trickster, who now dramatizes the wild confusion of adolescent boys.

As young men mature, the Trickster once more goes underground. Following the heroic and patriarchal paradigm, men learn to suppress wayward impulses and channel their energies into career and family. The result is focused consciousness, disciplined will, and self-reflective awareness, shining virtues of the heroic and patriarchal tradition. Then at midlife, youthful dreams collapse. Heroic discipline breaks down, or men often simply abandon the effort. Long-suppressed impulses come to the surface, making the Trickster once more relevant to men. At this time, men act more like adolescents, plunging into affairs or ill-advised business ventures. Fortunately, the Trickster offers a model of how to balance resurgent impulses, consciously integrating instincts rather than suppressing them. Through the Trickster's pluralism, playfulness, creativity, and generativity, men consciously assimilate wild juvenile impulses.

THE FATHER AS TRICKSTER

The Trickster symbolizes another early experience of the masculine. He represents the boy's first encounter with the father. This is a surprising claim and requires some explanation. In most cultures, fathers have a role distinctly different from that of mothers. Normally the mother is constantly available to the infant, relatively reliable, and soothing. The father, by contrast, comes and goes episodically. Across different societies, fathers also tend to play with their children in spontaneous, unpredictable ways that are exciting and stimulating for the child.[23] To the child, then, the father represents a novel source of fun, excitement, and challenging situations. These are the central qualities of Tricksters, who are playful, mercurial, and elusive. In the infant's experience, *the father is a Trickster.* That is, the infant's first experience of a masculine archetype involves the Trickster.[24] Only much later does the father play the role of patriarch and disciplinarian. So the Trickster is prior to the patriarch in boys' experience, and would therefore be located deeper in the unconscious.

The way infants learn language corroborates the father's role as a Trickster. For the majority of infants in different cultures, the first word used is the term for father, like "dada" or "papa" in English. The word for mother comes later.[25] Moreover, when infants are presented with photographs of their mothers and fathers, they are able to pick out their father's picture several months before they recognize their mother's. These observations are surprising, since the infant spends most time with the mother and would be expected to name her first or recognize her picture before the father's. The father's frequent absences, however, apparently force the infant to develop some kind of memory or symbol for him. Since the mother is present more of the time, the infant has less need to remember her or internalize her. The infant, therefore, symbolizes the father first, using language and pictorial memory. So it is the father who introduces the infant to the world of symbols, and whom the infant first symbolizes. Metaphorically speaking, the father brings language and symbolism to the infant. This is precisely what Tricksters do in mythology: they bring language and speech to humanity, the ability to symbolize the world. As Robert Pelton put it after his study of Tricksters, "the trickster embodies the very process of symbol creation."[26] Because symbols and language are central to consciousness and culture, the Trickster is the founder of human civilization in both a mythological and psychological sense.

Given the father's basic role, he should be as important in the child's development as the mother. The father's effect, though, is subtle, and only now do psychologists appreciate it. Across cultures, infants usually become attached to *both* mother and father by six to eight months and protest separation from the father as much as from the mother.[27] This finding puzzled researchers since the mother spends far more time with the infant, and it was assumed that the infant would be more attached to her. But the quantity of time the father interacts with the infant does not seem to matter so much as the quality. (In various cultures, much of the time mothers spend with their children involves doing household chores rather than interacting with the children.) Dramatic evidence for the father's importance to the infant comes from cases when the father is missing. The earlier the absence, the greater the impact, and the effect remains for years afterward. When boys are tested in adolescence, those without fathers during the first two years of life have less intellectual competence, decreased self-confidence, fewer traditionally masculine interests, and a more feminine pattern on tests of cognitive ability. (Males typically do better on mathematical rather than verbal tests. Those without fathers early in childhood show a reversed pattern.) Father-deprived boys also tend to be more dependent, hostile, and delinquent, as well as less industrious, assertive, or trusting. This effect is not due to economic or social problems that result from a missing father, because researchers took those factors into account. The damage was specifically psychological. Clearly, fathers exert an early, important, and profound effect on their children, equal to the mother's influence. But the father's impact is often subtle. This brings up an intriguing analogy with Paleolithic art. Although male hunters were vitally important in Paleolithic culture, images of men were secret and hidden, like the father's influences on his children.

The observation that the Trickster-father exerts a profound influence early in boys' lives is liberating for men and women. It offers a way out of the nasty impasse that plagues traditional views of men's psychology. According to these theories, mentioned earlier, and which I believed until my work on men's tales, men begin life under the domination of the mother. Enfolded within a feminine world, boys develop a masculine identity by rejecting the maternal and the feminine. Thus, hostility, fear, and ambivalence toward women are inevitable, according to this theory. The Trickster-father radically changes the situation. Men do not need to repudiate the maternal and the feminine to protect themselves, retreating into machismo and male chauvinism. They can turn instead to a masculine energy as powerful and primordial as the mother's, but more elusive. Instead of resorting to the hero's violence to prove their manhood, men can embrace the humor and ingenuity of the Trickster.

THE TRICKSTER FROM PAST TO FUTURE

As the archetype of the deep masculine, the shaman-Trickster probably draws its power from hereditary factors. Just as male traits like beards and balding heads are determined by genes, I suspect that male behavior personified by the shaman-Trickster also reflects genetic factors. Hereditary influences are usually ignored by psychological theories of development, which generally assume that children are shaped by their environment. References today to genetic influences also suffer from a bad reputation, because in the past hereditary arguments were based on faulty research and questionable statistics. Even when scientific errors were corrected, worse problems remained, because genetic arguments were often used to defend patriarchal and racist traditions. Men (or whites) were said to be aggressive and dominant by nature, while women (or minorities) were considered childlike and dependent, so (white) men were supposed to run society. This view assumes that men are warriors and patriarchs by nature. As discussed in the last chapter, the assumption is probably incorrect. Patriarchal and warrior cultures are relatively recent, having arisen perhaps less than 6,000 years ago. For most of human history—at least 25,000 years—men and women lived as hunter-gatherers, and were probably egalitarian and cooperative. Natural selection was also more intense in the hunter-gatherer period, compared to later agricultural or patriarchal epochs. This is because in the small groups typical of nomadic hunters, the incompetence of one hunter could lead to starvation and death for everybody in the band. In larger agricultural settlements, the ineptitude of one farmer or warrior can be compensated by many others in the village.[28] So human genes were probably shaped more by the hunter-gatherer way of life.

Indirect confirmation for the biological primacy of the hunter-shaman comes from male puberty initiations in warrior cultures. David Gilmore analyzed these masculine rites of passage in his book *The Making of Manhood*. He argues that the initiations are necessary to force boys into the strenuous and dangerous way of the warrior, despite the boys' natural tendency to avoid pain and risk. Simply put, a warrior personality is not normal, and the arduous, mutilating nature of puberty rites reflects just how much effort is needed to inculcate the warrior's way and maintain it. What is more natural, instinctual, genetic, and primordial, I suggest, is the spirit of the hunter-gatherer, symbolized by the shaman-Trickster.

In a surprising twist, the ancient image of the hunter-Trickster offers modern society help and healing. Today the world is threatened by ecological collapse, sectarian strife, and a widening gap between rich and poor. As many have pointed out, feminist or not, behind these problems lies the spirit of the hero and the patriarch, with their drive to fight enemies, "conquer" nature, gain power, and hoard wealth, while ignoring the cost of those ambitions to other people. The hunter-Trickster offers an alternative vision of male energy. The Trickster's zero-sum perspective and his respect for animals, for instance, are deeply ecological. He recognizes that he can take only so much from nature without giving something in return. Neither does he hoard possessions. Yet he is not an ascetic altruist, because he steals what strikes his fancy. What sets the hunter-Trickster apart from the thief or the hero is that the Trickster gives away his loot. He does not value booty or trophies so much as the excitement of inventing ruses and playing pranks. He also delights in the experience of exchange and trade, not in accumulating wealth. The Trickster, in fact, is a traditional patron of trade and marketplaces, and he would do a better job, I think, presiding over modern economies than the patriarch and hero. The latter two see the market as another arena for conquest and domination, one more vehicle for hoarding wealth, power, and fame. The hunter-Trickster, by contrast, favors interchange instead of accumulation, exchange rather than exploitation, communication over capital, the process of trade more than the possessions traded.

As an inventor, the hunter-Trickster is the true patron of technology. Furthermore, he does not use inventions to dominate nature, like the hero, but rather to celebrate human creativity and cleverness. As the god of chance, the shaman-Trickster is also the sponsor of statistics, the foundation of modern science. Ironically, as scientists peer into quantum physics or chaos theory, the aboriginal shaman-Trickster grins back, the master of luck and chance. As a mediator, the shaman-Trickster also fosters the exchange of ideas and experiences. He is the natural benefactor of workshops and retreats, modern versions of the ancient Greek forum, where people gathered to trade opinions. As a messenger, the Trickster is likewise a sponsor of computer networks, cellular phones, and satellite television, linking the diverse people of the world. With his spirit of curiosity and exploration, the shaman-Trickster does not see strangers as enemies or competitors, the way the hero and patriarch do, but as potential friends and comrades. The hunter-Trickster especially affirms equality between men and women, and his attitude is the ultimate in conservatism, recalling the original culture of humanity. Ironically, by reaching back to the past and embracing the archaic hunter-Trickster, men find hope for the future.

Before concluding this tale of the deep masculine, a caveat is in order. I will be the first to admit that my epic of the deep masculine is really another myth, and that I am inventing a story. For one thing, we probably will never know definitely what Paleolithic hunter-gatherers were like. Although I believe my comments are consistent with the available evidence, there are other possible interpretations of Paleolithic art and artifacts. This pluralism will no doubt please the Trickster! I think it important to set forth a history of the deep masculine to integrate the many different themes in men's tales and to counteract several erroneous myths about manhood: the myth that the hero and patriarch are basic to the masculine psyche or that matriarchy is fundamental to human nature. Myths are not simply fantasies or superstitions. They influence belief and behavior and infuse meaning into our lives. With the decline of the heroic and patriarchal myth, we need alternative images of the masculine. That is what the archetype of the hunter-shaman-Trickster offers. The deep masculine emerges in the beginning of the human drama and constitutes the primordial image of manhood. Long before the warrior-king or the Great Mother Goddess, men were hunters, shamans, and Tricksters. And for each man the Trickster represents the first image of the masculine, through the infant's contact with the Trickster-father, the elusive, exciting figure who opens up the world of language and symbols.

Men's tales from "The Wizard King" to "Go I Know Not Where" depict a search for manhood beyond the hero. The stories also reveal the path that men must take: as they mature, their task is to reach back into the past to the archetype of the hunter-Trickster, reclaiming prehistoric archetypes and long-repressed playful impulses. The result is a new vision of manhood and new hope for the future of humankind.

Epilogue

Our sojourn through men's tales comes to an end, and with it our journey beyond the hero.[1] The drama begins when men arrive at positions of responsibility somewhere in their middle years, becoming fathers, mentors, and community leaders. As men assume the role of patriarch, they confront younger men, and the reaction between senior and junior, as "The Wizard King" makes so clear, is often envy and competition. This is the age-old Oedipal drama, the male rivalry between father and son, boss and employee, teacher and student, mentor and protégé. Ultimately it is the battle between hero and patriarch, in which the irresistible force of a young man meets the unmovable authority of a senior male. This is the secret weakness hidden behind the glory of the hero and the patriarch: there is room for only one of them. Tragedy results unless mature men move beyond heroic and patriarchal roles. For that, men require three initiations.

The first rite of passage introduces mature men to the healing power of the feminine. Some cultures retain a formal ritual for this, like the Yoruba tribe of Africa and their Ogboni cult, or the Bimin-Kuskusmin tribe of New Guinea and their secret tale of the goddess Afek. For Western men, initiation into the feminine often involves psychotherapy and usually begins with mysterious women appearing in dreams and fantasies. These women are anima figures, personifying a man's feminine side—the sensitivity, vulnerability, and intuition which men learn to ignore and deny in youth. Men's task in meeting the anima is to honor her and the realm of the feminine, affirming the importance of relation-ships, feelings, and hunches. At first the challenge seems humil-iating or ridiculous to men, like Zakia's demand that the Sultan learn a menial trade in ''The Sultan's Handkerchief.'' But men must eventually give up the pride of the patriarch and the glory of the hero to serve the goddess. The experience is ultimately renewing and lifesaving because feminine wisdom rescues men at midlife, just as Zakia saves the Sultan from the cannibal cook and Beatrice guides Dante in the *Divine Comedy*. The process is liberating for women, too, because as men develop their inner feminine side, they learn to deal with their own feelings and depend less on women to do so for them. This frees wives, lov-ers, mothers, and daughters to pursue their own development.

Men's journey beyond the hero involves a second rite of pas-sage. This is the initiation into the shadow, in which men come face-to-face with their vulnerability, fear, and sorrow. As they look to the future, their own mortality and the inevitability of death stare back at them. When men review their past, they grap-ple with forgotten traumas, broken dreams, and abandoned loves. Like the monarch in ''The King's Ears,'' they confront their de-formities, faults, and secret shame—their goat's ears. Men take the ''road of ashes'' at this time, journeying into the land of death, tragedy, evil, suffering, and helplessness, the way the monarch in ''The King and the Ghoul'' walked back and forth in the cemetery. A man's enemy is no longer a witch or a mon-ster, such as the young hero faces in fairy tales. It is now death, or the blackness in his own heart, or random misfortunes. This is the stuff of tragedy, not romance. Inevitable and invincible, death and the limitations of the human condition shatter the rem-nants of the hero's glory and the patriarch's power.

With the patriarchal paradigm in ruins, men wander in confu-sion and often become impulsive, doing things that would have seemed outrageous to them a few years earlier. Tales like ''The Little Peasant'' show men lying, cheating, stealing, and most shocking of all, being rewarded for it. Gentle, accommodating men suddenly become wild and unpredictable, like the farmer in ''The North Wind's Gift.'' While the change is frightening, men do not degenerate into sociopaths, criminals, or savages. A deeper truth appears in the form of the Trickster.

Although he initially appears to be evil, like the ghoul in "The King and the Ghoul," the Trickster becomes a companion, therapist, teacher, and friend to men who have lost their way in the middle years. The Trickster Brother helps men break free from masculine logos and patriarchal thinking, and teaches them the virtues of pluralism and paradox. Like the ghoul for the King, or St. Peter for Lustig, the Trickster Companion overthrows convention and leads men into fresh, new worlds. In real life, the Spirit Brother appears in dreams and imagination, the way Philemon guided Jung, and Virgil inspired Dante. Today, many men encounter the Trickster Brother through therapy. Contact with the Spirit Companion helps men become more tolerant of differences in opinion, the novel ideas of the younger generation, and their own inner complexity. Freed from patriarchal conventions, men experiment with new ways of life.

The Trickster also guides men through ever deeper levels of the unconscious. He replaces the anima and helps men understand their own inner depths. Ultimately, the Trickster introduces them to a wild, fierce, nurturing, provident, and divine masculine energy. Hidden behind conventional masculine roles, this primordial male vitality is the deep masculine, and it is the Trickster who initiates men into its mysteries. This is the third rite of passage for men in the middle years.

As "Brother Lustig" and "The King and the Ghoul" reveal, the deep masculine takes the form of the shaman and the Trickster. They are two aspects of one archetype, just as the hero and patriarch are two sides of one mythic image. Furthermore, the shaman-Trickster offers an alternative to the hero-patriarch, a new vision of masculine energy. The shaman-Trickster fosters communion instead of conquest, fraternity over hierarchy, and healing rather than heroism. He affirms women and does not denigrate the feminine. He acknowledges his wounded humanity while affirming his wildness and freedom.

The senior ranks of many men's lodges celebrate the Trickster's masculine energy. Secret societies like the Newekwe of the Zuni, the Masonic order of Europe, and the Bohemian Club in America are composed of men who have proven themselves as heroes and patriarchs. They assemble under the tutelage of the Trickster, play pranks on each other, defy patriarchal conventions, and pur-

sue spiritual brotherhood. Men's immersion in the deep masculine may make women feel threatened, fearful that they will lose
the loyalty of their husbands, fathers, and sons. But the ultimate
result of a man's encounter with the Trickster Brother is a deeper
ability to relate to others, male or female. Initiated men return
home, the way Fedot returns to his wife in "Go I Know Not
Whither," and the men now know how to balance masculine and
feminine, light and dark, instinct and spirit.

Initiated men also discover their divine vocation, a haunting,
wordless summons to go "I know not whither and bring back I
know not what." To carry out this calling, men need all the
discipline, perseverance, and courage they learned from their heroic struggles in youth, and all the cunning and calculation the
Trickster can teach them. Yet the aim of the trickery is not personal reward or private indulgence, but rather generativity, creativity, the common good, and ultimately the enrichment of
humanity.

The roots of the deep masculine reach far back in time to the
dawn of history. Older than the hero or the patriarch, the shaman-
Trickster dances on the walls of Paleolithic cave sanctuaries. He
is the spirit of the hunter—masked, wounded, and ghostly:
masked because he loves disguises and inventions and celebrates
human ingenuity; wounded because he pursues game fiercer than
himself and repays the animal's sacrifice with his own suffering;
and ghostly, because he communicates with the unseen and im-
material, uniting instinct and soul, this world and the next.
Hunter, shaman, and Trickster, he reflects the first symbolic expression of manhood, long before warriors or kings arose. He is
literally the deep masculine, deep in caves, deep in time, deep
in the male psyche.

After initiation into the deep masculine, one final task remains:
to return to the ordinary world, to real people in real communities. The shaman-Trickster demands that men take action in the
world, making their divine calling practical. In fact, the shaman-
Trickster offers a specific, concrete vision of a post-industrial,
post-modern society. With his zero-sum perspective, the hunter-
shaman honors the balance of nature and champions a masculine
spirit of ecology. As the patron of the marketplace, he empha-

sizes exchange over exploitation, and communication rather than competition. He avoids hoarding and accumulation in favor of exploration and experimentation. As a messenger and mediator, he sponsors forums, workshops, and retreats. As a pluralist, he celebrates a diversity of opinions and perspectives. He insists on the equality of men and women, and between men as well, countering the hero's focus on hierarchy and the patriarchs' denigration of the feminine.

This new vision of manhood, personified by the hunter, the shaman, and the Trickster, has already been hinted at by many writers. In his recent book, *Knights Without Armor,* Aaron Kipnis calls for a masculinity that is "irresponsible, unpredictable, silly, inconsistent, afraid, indecisive, experimental, insecure, visionary, lustful, lazy, fat, bald, old, playful, fierce, irreverent, magical, wild, impractical, unconventional." This is the shaman-Trickster. Edward Whitmont in *Return of the Goddess* and Sam Keen in *Fire in the Belly* likewise describe a new vision of manhood based on the image of the explorer, the seeker, and the pilgrim. This is the hunter-shaman, open to the new and the unexpected. He is also "the wild man" that Bly so eloquently describes, fierce and gentle, fiery and nurturing.

If men's tales focus on men at midlife, the deep masculine often emerges earlier. This is particularly true today. Many men, moved by feminism, abandon the chauvinism of the hero-patriarch early in life—only to flounder, unsure of any alternative. Men are caught in the middle between paradigms, and that is really what men's tales are about, the painful betwixt and between, the limbo after the reign of the warrior-king ends, but before the shaman-Trickster appears. Yet the warrior-king has his part to play in men's lives. From the hero-patriarch, men learn discipline, perseverance, and courage. In the heroic period of life, men develop a strong ego, a sturdy sense of identity, and consciousness freed from instincts. After gaining those psychological skills, men are finally ready to deal with the primordial energies of the unconscious and the deep masculine. Men's tales are clear on this point: only individuals who have already mastered the way of the hero and patriarch embark upon the quest for something beyond. Lustig, Fedot, Parsifal, and Odysseus are post-heroic.

The trail of the deep masculine has taken us on many unexpected turns. I certainly did not anticipate ranging so far into archeology and anthropology, but men's tales are so similar and so intriguing that they demanded extensive research. The venture, appropriately enough, became a hunt, with an elusive and wily quarry who leaves only scattered clues behind. The goal is the hunter himself, the shaman-Trickster. Rooted in the prehistoric past, the hunter-Trickster is the key to a deeper, more vibrant and vital manhood. Mediator not monarch, wanderer not warrior, healer not hero, his ideal is exploration rather than exploitation, dialogue not domination, and integration instead of imperialism. Beyond hero, patriarch, or goddess, and before all of them, he is the deepest, truest masculine self, as important today as he was at the dawn of the human race. The hunter-Trickster recalls men to their original vocation, older than the warrior's or the patriarch's, the mission of Wakdjunkaga, Eshu, and Raven. From Paleolithic hunters to modern scientists and businessmen, as it was in the beginning, so it is now: men's summons is to go forth "I know not where" to clear the way for humanity.

Endnotes

PROLOGUE

[1]In presenting examples from men's lives, I have altered names and small details to protect their privacy.

CHAPTER ONE. *The Wizard King: Hero/Patriarch, Father/Son*

The story is from Lang (1966a).
[1]Gewertz (1988), Gilmore (1990), Lamb (1982), Sanday (1981).

CHAPTER TWO. *The Sultan's Handkerchief: Men's Initiation into the Feminine*

The story is from Gilstrap and Estabrook (1958).
[1]I discuss the research cited in *Once Upon a Midlife*.
[2]Chinen, Spielvogel, Farrell (1985).
[3]Kolbenschlag (1988), Stein (1983).
[4]Eliade (1958), Friedman and Lerner (1986), Gewertz (1988), Hendersen (1967).
[5]Morton-Williams (1960), Pelton (1980), Pemberton (1975).
[6]Welbourn (1984).

CHAPTER THREE. *The King's Ears: The Shadow of the Patriarch*

The story is adapted from the Welsh tale, "March's Ears," in Sheppard-Jones (1978), and the Yugoslav tale, "The Tsar's Ears," in Curcija-Prodanovic (1957). The story is Type 682 in the Aarne-Thompson (1961) fairy tale index.
[1]I discuss this in *Once Upon a Midlife*. See also Mussen and Haan (1982), Vaillant (1977), Vaillant and Milofsky (1980).

CHAPTER FOUR. *The North Wind's Gift: Men's Oppression and the Wild Man*

The story is from Calvino (1980). An almost identical tale comes from Africa, the Ashanti story, "How It Came About that Children Were First Whipped," in Radin (1952).
[1] A similar case comes from Gustafson in Mahdi et al. (1987).

CHAPTER FIVE. *The Little Peasant: Shadow and Trickster*

The story is from the Grimms' collection. Cf. "The Peasant Pewit," "The Woman in the Chest," and "A Peasant Sells a Cow as a Goat" in Ranke (1966), and tale Types 1535, 1355A, 1358A, 1358C, 1359C, and 1360B in the Aarne-Thompson index.
[1] Jung (1960).
[2] Gove (1985), Oldham and Liebert (1989).
[3] Tricky youths are common in fairy tales, e.g., in "Tom Thumb," "The Brave Tailor," or Types 1539 and 1542 of the Aarne-Thompson index. But simple trickery does not make a Trickster. In youth tales, trickery is a *means* to heroic victory, and the latter is the end. By contrast, for Tricksters trickery is the end, not heroic victory. Similarly, many women in middle tales resort to tricks, but as a means to reach their goals, not as an end in itself. See *Once Upon a Midlife*.
[4] Fauth (1988), Jung (1967), Lorenz and Vecsey (1986), Messer (1982), Pelton (1980), Radin (1972), Williams (1979).
[5] Jung (1972, 1967), Henderson (1967), Layard, (1958), Metman (1958), Moore and Gillette (1990), Samuels (1989), Sandner (1987), Whan (1978).
[6] Grottanelli (1983), Messer (1982), Pelton (1980), Radin (1972), Toelken (1990), Williams (1979).
[7] Crossley-Holland (1980), Williams (1979).
[8] Combs and Holland (1990), Layard (1958), Pelton (1980).
[9] Sekaquaptewa (1979). Cf. Brown (1979), Tedlock (1979), Lorenz and Vecsey (1986).
[10] Janus (1975).

CHAPTER SIX. *The King and the Ghoul: The Trickster Teacher*

The story is adapted from Emeneau (1934), Bhavan (1960), Tawney (1956), and Riccardi (1971). The most accessible version is Zimmer (1956), but his retelling is incomplete.
[1] The necromancer appears to be a worshiper of Shiva, the god of destruction. This highlights the shadow theme.
[2] The necromancer has other features of classic Trickster figures. He works in a cemetery with corpses, mediating between the living and the dead, like Hermes and other Tricksters. The necromancer is also a liminal figure, occupying a no-man's-land, at the outskirts of society. This is again typical of Tricksters.
[3] The use of sub-stories in "The King and the Ghoul" creates a complicated

narrative structure. This is typical of Trickster tales, like those of the Native American Wakdjunkaga or the African Ananse.
⁴Gilligan (1982).
⁵Davis (1991).
⁶McAdams (1985). See also Friedman and Lerner (1986), Samuels (1989), Thompson (1991). Feminists like Eisler (1987) argue that pluralism is feminine. This is mistaken, because the Trickster personifies a masculine form of pluralism.
⁷Radin (1952) and Pelton (1980).

CHAPTER SEVEN. *Brother Lustig: Part 1. The Spirit Brother*

The story comes from the Grimms' collection and is Type 785 in the Aarne and Thompson (1961) fairy tale index. Cf. Types 330, 753A, 1525K.
¹Lorenz and Vecsey (1986), Pelton (1980), Radin (1972), Tedlock (1979), Toelken (1990).
²An example even comes from Brazil, where St. Peter and Eshu the African Trickster are equated. See Williams (1979).
³Pelton (1980) and Radin (1972).
⁴Frye (1957).
⁵See Brod (1987), Hammond and Jablow (1987), Lewis (1981).
⁶Cf. the notion of the "double." Walker (1976) and Hopcke (1990).
⁷Mahdi et al. (1987), Thompson (1991).
⁸Eliade (1964), Jung (1953), Lorenz and Vecsey (1986), Radin (1972), Samuels (1989), Toelken (1990), Williams (1979).
⁹Pelton (1980) and Pemberton (1975).
¹⁰Pelton (1980, 50). See also Radin (1972).

CHAPTER EIGHT. *Brother Lustig: Part 2. Secret Societies and Men's Initiation into the Deep Masculine*

¹Boas (1897), Heckethorn (1965), MacKenzie (1967), Webster (1968).
²Lowie (1970), Tedlock (1979).
³Heckethorn (1965), Jones (1967).
⁴Eliade (1958), Gregor (1985), Henderson (1967), La Fontaine (1985), MacKenzie (1967), Morton-Williams (1960), Pelton (1980), Webster (1968).
⁵MacQuade (1985), *Newsweek* (August 2, 1982, 21).
⁶Hays (1963), Pelton (1980), Radin (1972).
⁷See also Kerenyi (1986), Stein (1983), Pearson (1986), Whitmont (1987).
⁸I will focus on men, although women can become shamans, too. See Halifax (1982), Eliade (1964), Walsh (1990).
⁹Campbell (1959), Fuller (1991), Hays (1963), Nicholson (1987), Radin (1972), Salman (1986).
¹⁰Kramer (1989), Riegel (1973).
¹¹The Trickster is not the only originator of human culture, since female figures play an equally important role in mythology. Unlike the patriarch, the Trickster does not try to steal credit from women!
¹²See also Downton (1989), Henderson (1967).

CHAPTER NINE. *Go I Know Not Whither: Part 1. From Inner Feminine to Deep Masculine*

The story comes from Afanas'ev (1973, 504–520). Three other versions (Downing, 1989; Raduga, 1981; Wolkstein, 1991) differ substantially from Afanas'ev's although they all cite him as their original source. I have therefore relied upon Afanas'ev's version. The story is related to Type 465, 465A, and 571B in the Aarne and Thompson (1961) fairy tale index.

[1]Cf. Gimbutas' discussion of the toad (1982).

[2]I am indebted to John Boe for this insightful and charming point.

[3]I am indebted to Vassily Barlak for this interpretation. See also Wheeler (1984).

[4]Several other episodes within the Odyssey recapitulate the theme of meeting the anima and then the deep masculine, like the encounter between Menelaus and Proteus (Hanna, 1977), or Odysseus' confrontation with Circe (Stein, 1983).

[5]Heckethorn (1965), Von Franz (1980), Wyly (1989).

[6]Gewertz (1988), Henderson (1967).

[7]Figure 132, Jung (1953).

[8]Figure 93, Jung (1953).

[9]Salman (1986), Emma Jung, Von Franz (1986).

[10]Salman (1986).

[11]Miller and Swanson (1966), Sanford (1966).

[12]Eliade (1964), Hays (1963), Peters (1990).

[13]Pelton (1980), Radin (1952).

CHAPTER TEN. *Go I Know Not Whither: Part 2. Parsifal Revisited and Men's Spiritual Quest*

[1]Robert Johnson's discussion of Parsifal, which is otherwise invaluable and impeccable, errs in saying that Parsifal followed his mother's advice. Chrétien de Troyes says it was Gournemond's counsel (de Troyes, 1991).

[2]Matthews (1990).

[3]Emma Jung and Von Franz (1986), Jung (1953), Nisker (1990), Qandil (1970), Wilson (1991).

[4]Hermes, the Greek Trickster, is often portrayed as an old man and a son, prompting Karl Kerenyi (1986) to argue that Hermes is simultaneously father and son.

[5]Figure 179, Jung (1953).

[6]Hays (1963), Radin (1972), Pemberton (1975), Davis (1991).

[7]See Combs and Holland (1990), Brown (1979).

[8]Levinson et al. (1978), Cochran (1990), Kolbenschlag (1988).

[9]Quoted in Matthews (1990, 198).

[10]Cochran (1990, 172).

[11]Jung (1965, 165).

[12]Swedenborg (1977, 1979), Sigstedt (1952).

[13]Robert Monroe (1971) offers a modern parallel to Swedenborg, with out-of-body experiences that began in midlife.
[14]In Radin (1952).

CHAPTER ELEVEN. *A Tale of the Deep Masculine: Part 1. From Stone Age to New Age*

[1]Campbell (1959, 1988), Lewis-Williams and Dowson (1988), Hays (1963), Radin (1957), Walsh (1990).
[2]Here I refer to mobile or nomadic hunters, like Australian aborigines, or the Kung of Africa. Hunters with fixed residences, like Northwest Native Americans, differ dramatically.
[3]Anati (1983), Davis and Reeves (1990), Hays (1963), Hoffman (1891), Lewis-Williams and Dowson (1988), Maringer (1956), Schrire (1984).
[4]Hadingham (1979), Glantz and Pearce (1989), Lee and Devore (1968). Cf. fishing cultures, which developed later.
[5]Dickson (1990), Glantz and Pearce (1989), Ingold et al. (1988), Lee and DeVore (1968), Pfeiffer (1982), Price and Brown (1985), Schrire (1984).
[6]Evans (1988).
[7]Campbell (1988), Dickson (1990), Ingold et al. (1988), Price and Brown (1985), Schrire (1984).
[8]Baynham (1991), Hays (1963), Nelson (1991), Radin (1957), van der Post (1991).
[9]Campbell (1959), Dickson (1990), Ingold et al. (1988), Lee and Devore (1968), Lerner (1986), Pfeiffer (1982), Price and Brown (1985), Sanday (1981). Note that relative equality occurs mainly among *nomadic* hunter-gatherers. Moreover, when nomadic hunter-gatherers gather in large groups for rituals, they temporarily follow a hierarchical pattern.
[10]Dickson (1990), Lee and Devore (1968).
[11]There are some exceptions, of course. Many Australian aborigines and Eskimo tribes are less egalitarian than the Kung. This inequality, though, may be a recent development (Lamb 1982).
[12]Campbell (1988), Dickson (1990), Ehrenberg (1989), Fagan (1990), Gamble (1986), Glantz and Pearce (1989), Hadingham (1979), Ingold et al. (1988), Lee and DeVore (1968), Maringer (1956), Pfeiffer (1982), Price and Brown (1985), Schrire (1984), Wymer (1982).
[13]Gewertz (1988), Lerner (1986), Sanday (1981).
[14]A modern analogy is helpful: advertising today is filled mainly with images of women, so an archeologist from the future might conclude that women dominated today's culture. See Ehrenberg (1989), Lerner (1986).
[15]Eisler (1987), Ehrenberg (1989), Gewertz (1988), Gimbutas (1982, 1989), Lerner (1986), Maringer (1956).

Many scholars speak of THE Mother Goddess. However, Mother Goddesses were local deities, and it is not clear that prehistoric cultures identified them all with a single Mother Goddess. The latter notion may actually derive from patriarchal tradition, which unified different cultures and tribes under one rule.

[16]Writers sometimes overlook the distinction between Paleolithic and Neolithic. McCully (1984), for instance, cites archeological research on Catal Huyuk as evidence for a Paleolithic matriarchal cult. But Catal Huyuk is *Neo*lithic.

While Gimbutas (1989) does distinguish between the Neolithic and Paleolithic, she offers idiosyncratic interpretations of the latter. For example, she claims that the famous scene depicted in the "sanctuary" of the Lascaux cave represents a vulva and signifies the dominance of the feminine. To my knowledge, no student of prehistoric art has offered a similar interpretation. Moreover, such female figures and signs are extremely rare in inaccessible cave sites like the Lascaux sanctuary and what Gimbutas sees as a vulva is not the typical Paleolithic vulva pattern.

Eisler (1987) argues that prophetic or oracular powers were first associated with goddesses and women, rather than gods and men, and cites the Delphic oracle as a good example. Eisler overlooks the prophetic, oracular function of shamans in hunter-gatherer societies, which antedated Neolithic agricultural settlements.

The situation here is ironic. As feminist historians have demonstrated, early researchers, trained in patriarchal traditions, naively assumed that men always dominated women, and so ignored or suppressed evidence of ancient goddess cultures, where women were powerful. In trying to redress the imbalance, feminists sometimes commit a similar error, and overlook evidence from an even more ancient period—that of the Paleolithic hunter-gatherers.

[17]Ehrenberg (1989), Hays (1963), James (1957).

[18]Dickson (1990), Ingold et al. (1988), Schrire (1984).

[19]Eliade (1964), Ehrenberg (1989), Hadingham (1979), Hays (1963).

[20]Dickson, (1990), Ehrenberg (1989), Harrold (1980), Ingold et al. (1988), Lee and Devore (1988), Maringer (1956), Pfeiffer (1982), Price and Brown (1985).

[21]Sharing food is suggested by the location of storage pits for food. In Paleolithic sites, pits are equidistant from shelters, implying equal access. This changes over time, particularly in the Neolithic. See Glantz and Pearce (1989), Price and Brown (1985).

[22]Dickson (1990), Eisler (1987), Hadingham (1979), Martin (1985), Maringer (1956), Miller and Tilley (1984), Pfeiffer (1982), Price and Brown (1985), Wymer (1982).

[23]Campbell (1988), Hays (1963), Leroi-Gourhan (1974).

[24]Frayser (1985), Hays (1963).

[25]Glantz and Pearce (1989), Lamb (1982).

[26]While Venus figures receive more attention, male figures are equally ancient, with examples from Terme-Pialet and Laussel in France, dated to the so-called Aurignacian period, roughly 35,000 years ago. Examples also come from Hohlenstein-Stadel and the Kostienski site in Russia, also dated to the Aurignacian. Dickson (1990), Gamble (1986), Hadingham (1979), Hahn (1972), Leroi-Gourhan (1974), Sieveking (1979).

[27]Dickson (1990), Hahn (1972).

[28]Anati (1983), Campbell (1988), Dickson (1990), Fagan (1990), Gamble (1986), Hadingham (1979), James (1957), Maringer (1956), Pfeiffer (1982), Sieveking (1979), Wymer (1982). Hunting magic, I might add, probably antedates art. Neanderthal hunters apparently practiced various rituals involving cave bear skulls, which were most likely related to hunting.

[29]Campbell (1988), Dickson (1990), Leroi-Gourhan (1974), Maringer (1956), Sieveking (1979).

[30]Ehrenberg, (1989), Hays (1963), James (1957).

[31]Hays (1963), Sanday (1981), Toelken (1990).

[32]Eisler (1987), Lerner (1986).

[33]Ingold et al. (1988), Lee and Devore (1968), Price and Brown (1985).

[34]Lee and DeVore (1968), Sanday (1981).

[35]Gewertz (1988), Lamb (1982), Sanday (1981).

[36]Chodorow (1987), Gewertz (1988), Glantz and Pearce (1989). Among hunter-gatherers an extended family takes care of children so that the mother is not the all-important, single nurturer, as in modern families.

[37]Glob (1969), Hays (1963), Lerner (1986), Sanday (1981).

[38]Gomes (1983).

[39]Dickson (1990), Gamble (1986), Glantz and Pearce (1989), Hadingham (1979), Ingold et al. (1988), Lee and DeVore (1968), Schrire (1984), Sieveking (1979). Even today, though, existing hunter-gatherers work fewer hours for food and shelter than men and women in agricultural or modern societies.

CHAPTER TWELVE. *A Tale of the Deep Masculine: Part 2. The Evolution of the Trickster*

[1]Dickson (1990), Leroi-Gourhan (1974), Schrire (1984), Sieveking (1979).

[2]Statistical contingency tables were calculated as follows:

> 1. For the five most commonly portrayed animals at six different positions within caves: the chi-square is 65.3, with 20 degrees of freedom, $p < .001$; that is, the probability that different types of animals are placed in a purely random fashion in a cave is less than .001.
> 2. For men appearing at six different positions within caves, the chi-square is 15.6, with 5 degrees of freedom, $p = .01$.
> 3. For women portrayed at six different sites within caves, the chi-square is 163.2, with 5 degrees of freedom, $p << .001$.
> 4. For the 4 different "male" signs at six different cave positions: the chi-square is 53.5, 15 degrees of freedom, $p < .001$.
> 5. For the six types of "female" signs at six locations in cave: the chi-square is 43, with 25 degrees of freedom, $p < .02$.

Another way to look at the male-to-female-to-male pattern is to see how many caves demonstrate it. From his exhaustive atlas of cave art, Leroi-Gourhan (1974) gives good descriptions of twenty-four Paleolithic caves with human figures. Only three of these twenty-four sites had clear depictions of women in them—Le Gabillou, Pech-Merle, and Les Combarelles, all in France. These three caves had male symbols at the entrance, female figures in central chambers, and male figures at the rear of the cave. Thirteen other caves had no definite female figures in them, but still depicted men at the rear of the caves, or in remote areas. These sites include Lascaux, and Trois Frères, already mentioned, as well as Pergouset, Los Hornos, Niaux, Villars, Cougnac, and Le Portel. The cave at Villars is noteworthy because the man at the end is associated with a bison, just like in Lascaux. Although these thirteen caves did not have explicit female figures, they did contain animals and signs usually associated with female figures. And those animals and signs appeared in the central chambers. So once more, the masculine-feminine-masculine pattern holds. The remaining eight caves with human figures were ambiguous or unclassifiable because of damage or incomplete records.

[3]Cameron (1983), Dickson (1990), Hadingham (1979), Hays (1963), Kubler (1985), Lewis-Williams and Dowson (1988), Maringer (1956), Pfeiffer (1982).

[4]Fagan (1990), Hadingham (1979), James (1957).

[5]Breuil (1979), Leroi-Gourhan (1974). Cf. Hadingham (1979).

[6]Wakankar (1983).

[7]Sieveking (1979), Leroi-Gourhan (1974). The Lascaux and Pech-Merle caves are quite similar, although they are probably 3,000 years apart in age. Wounded men also appear on small engravings. A reindeer antler from Laugerie Basse depicts an injured man behind a wounded bison, while a carved stone slab from Le Pechialet portrays another wounded man, stretching his hands toward a bear.

[8]Campbell (1959), Dickson (1990), Lewis-Williams and Dowson (1988), Sieveking (1979).

[9]Schrire (1984). Modern individuals encounter similar images in shamanic experiences. See Matthews (1990), Walsh (1990).

[10]Anati (1983), Campbell (1988, 1983).

[11]Campbell (1988), Hoffman (1891).

[12]Anati (1983).

[13]Campbell (1988), Dickson (1990), Maringer (1956).

[14]Collins (1991), Combs and Holland (1990), Doore (1988), Evans (1988), Gimbutas (1982).

[15]Hopcke (1990).

[16]La Fontaine (1985).

[17]Gregor (1985), Hadingham (1979).

[18]Peters (1990).

[19]Radin (1957) suggested this earlier, and considered the divine king to be a fusion of two earlier roles, the shaman and tribal chief.

[20]Emma Jung and Von Franz (1986), Matthews (1990).

[21]Collins (1991).

[22]Hays (1963), Maringer (1956). As Eliade (1958) and Campbell (1959) note, hunters associate renewal with bones, while farmers associate rejuvenation with seeds.

[23]Cath et al. (1989), Lamb (1982).

[24]Of course not all fathers are Tricksters, since there are many individual variations. I speak of a general, archetypal pattern. Moreover, mothers have Trickster features, since they, too, come and go. However, mothers also have many other roles, like that of caretaker, whereas the father is usually experienced predominantly as a Trickster.

[25]Lamb (1982).

[26]Pelton (1980, 254).

[27]Lamb (1982), Cath et al. (1989).

[28]Glantz and Pearce (1989), Lee and Devore (1968).

EPILOGUE

[1]After completing the first draft of this manuscript, I came upon the work of Northrop Frye (1957) and realized that he independently corroborates the themes of men's tales. Frye observed that there are four basic genres of literature written by male authors. These parallel men's tales from oral folk tradition. Frye's first two categories involve young men who undertake adventures and battle evil patriarchs. These dramas reflect the paradigm of the hero-patriarch, and correspond to fairy tales of youth. Frye's third genre of literature is tragedy, in which a man at the height of fortune is thrown down, humiliated, and ruined. These men are forced to confront the shadow side of human existence—helplessness, suffering, and the evil in the human heart. The fourth and final category is irony. From satire to farce, irony makes fun of established social conventions and reflects the Trickster's spirit.

Bibliography

Aarne, A., and S. Thompson. 1961. *The Types of the Folktale: A Classification and Bibliography.* Academia Scientarium Finnica: Helsinki.

Abrahams, Roger. 1983. *African Folktales.* Pantheon: New York.

Afanas'ev, Aleksandr. 1973. *Russian Fairy Tales.* Tr. Norbert Guterman. Pantheon: New York.

Anati, E., ed. 1983. *International Symposium on the Intellectual Expressions of Prehistoric Man: Art and Religion.* Edizioni del Centro: Brescia, Italy.

Bain, R. Nisbet. 1895. *Cossack Fairy Tales.* Frederick Stokes: New York.

Battista, John. 1980. "Images of Individuation: A Jungian Approach to the Psychology of Imagery." In J. E. Shorr, G. E. Sobel, P. Robin, and J. A. Connella, eds., *Imagery: Its Many Dimensions and Applications,* 122–132. Plenum: New York.

Baynham, Benjamin. 1991. "Mukushan." *Parabola 16:* 44–46.

Bettelheim, Bruno. 1976. *The Uses of Enchantment: The Meaning and Importance of Fairy Tales.* New York: Knopf.

Bhavan. 1960. *Stories of Vikramaditya.* Bhavan's Book University: Bombay.

Bly, Robert. 1990. *Iron John: A Book About Men.* Addison-Wesley: Reading, Massachusetts.

Boas, Franz. 1897. "The Social Organization and the Secret Societies of the Kwakiutl Indians." *Annual Report of the Smithsonian Institution 1894–1895.* Smithsonian Institution: Washington, D.C.

Breuil, Henri. 1979. Tr. M. E. Boyle. *Four Hundred Centuries of Cave Art.* Hacker Art Books: New York.

Brod, Harry, ed. 1987. *The Making of Masculinities: The New Men's Studies.* Allen & Unwin: Boston.

Brown, Joseph Epes. 1979. "The Wisdom of the Contrary." *Parabola 4:*62.

Bushnaq, I. 1986. *Arab Folktales.* Pantheon: New York.

Calvino, Italo. 1980. *Italian Folktales,* Pantheon: New York.

Cameron, Thomas. 1983. "The Rock Art of Writing-on-Stone, in the Milk River Valley, Southern Alberta, Canada." In Anati, 457–466.

Carlson, Roy. 1983. "Expressions of Belief in the Prehistoric Art of the Northwest Coast Indians." In Anati, 187–200.

Campbell, Joseph. 1959. *The Masks of God: Primitive Mythology.* Penguin: New York.

Campbell, Joseph. 1968. *The Hero with a Thousand Faces.* Princeton University Press.

Campbell, Joseph. 1988. *Historical Atlas of World Mythology. Vol 1: The Way of the Animal Powers. Part 1: Mythologies of the Primitive Hunters and Gatherers.* Harper and Row: New York.

Cath, Stanley H., Alan Gurwitt, and Linda Gunsberg. 1989. *Fathers and Their Families.* Analytic Press: Hillsdale, New Jersey.

Chinen, A. B. 1989. *In the Ever After: Fairy Tales and the Second Half of Life.* Chiron: Wilmette, Illinois.

Chinen, A. B. 1992. *Once Upon a Midlife: Classic Stories and Mythic Tales to Illuminate the Middle Years.* Tarcher: Los Angeles.

Chinen, Allan, Anna Spielvogel, and Dennis Farrell. 1985. "The Experience of Intuition." *Psychological Perspectives 16:*186–197.

Chodorow, Nancy. 1987. "Feminism and Difference: Gender, Relation and Difference in Psychoanalytic Perspective." In Mary Walsh, ed., *The Psychology of Women: Ongoing Debates,* 249–264. Yale University Press: New Haven. Originally published 1979.

Clatterbaugh, Kenneth. 1990. *Contemporary Perspectives on Masculinity: Men, Women and Politics in Modern Society.* Westview Press: Boulder.

Cochran, Larry. 1990. *The Sense of Vocation: A Study of Career and Life Development.* Albany: State University Press of New York.

Collins, D. Jean. 1991. "The Trickster and Creative Illness." *Gnosis 19:*27–31.

Combs, Allan, and Mark Holland. 1991. *Synchronicity: Science, Myth and the Trickster.* Paragon House: New York.

Courlander, Harold, and George Herzog. 1978. *The Cow-Tail Switch and Other West African Stories.* Henry Holt and Co.: New York.

Crossley-Holland, Kevin. 1980. *The Norse Myths.* Pantheon: New York.

Curcija-Prodanovic, N. 1957. *Yugoslav Folk Tales.* Oxford University Press: New York.

Davis, Erik. 1991. "Trickster at the Crossroads: West Africa's God of Messages, Sex and Deceit." *Gnosis 91:*37–43.

Davis, L. B., and B. O. K. Reeves, eds. 1990. *Hunters of the Recent Past.* Unwin Hyman: London.

de Troyes, Chrétien. 1991. *Arthurian Romances.* Tr. W. Kibler. Penguin: New York.

Dickson, D. Bruce. 1990. *The Dawn of Belief: Religion in the Upper Paleolithic of Southwestern Europe.* University of Arizona: Tucson.

Doore, Gary, ed. 1988. *Shaman's Path: Healing, Personal Growth and Empowerment.* Shambhala: Boston.

Dorson, R. 1982. *Folk Legends of Japan.* Charles Tuttle: Tokyo.

Doty, W. G. 1978. "Hermes Guide of Souls." *Journal of Analytical Psychology 23:* 358–365.

Downing, Charles. 1989. *Russian Tales and Legends.* Oxford University Press: Oxford.

Downton, J. V. 1989. "Individuation and Shamanism." *Journal of Analytical Psychology 34:* 73–88.

Edinger, Edward. 1990. *The Living Psyche: A Jungian Analysis in Pictures.* Chiron: Wilmette, Illinois.

Ehrenberg, Margaret. 1989. *Women in Prehistory.* University of Oklahoma Press: Oklahoma City.

Eisler, Riane. 1987. *The Chalice and the Blade: Our History, Our Future.* Harper and Row: San Francisco.

Eliade, Mircea. 1958/1975. *Rites and Symbols of Initiation. The Mysteries of Birth and Rebirth.* Harper: San Francisco.

Eliade, Mircea. 1964. *Shamanism: Archaic Techniques of Ecstasy.* Tr. Willard Trask. Princeton University Press.

Emeneau, M. B. 1934. *Jambhaladatta's Version of the Vetalapancavinsati: A Critical Sanskrit Text in Transliteration with an Introduction and an English Translation.* American Oriental Society: New Haven.

Evans, Arthur. 1988. *The God of Ecstasy: Sex Roles and the Madness of Dionysos.* St. Martin's Press: New York.

Fagan, Brian. 1990. *The Journey from Eden: The Peopling of Our World.* Thames and Hudson: London.

Fauth, Wolfgang. 1988. "Hermes." In *Spring: A Journal of Archetype and Culture,* 108–111.

Fogel, Gerald, Frederick Lane, and Robert Liebert, eds. 1986. *The Psychology of Men: New Psychoanalytic Perspectives.* Basic Books: New York.

Fowler, James. 1981. *Stages of Faith: The Psychology of Human Development and the Quest for Meaning.* Harper and Row: San Francisco.

Frayser, Suzanne. 1985. *Varieties of Sexual Experience: An Anthropological Perspective on Human Sexuality.* HRAF Press: New Haven.

Frazer, James. 1978. *The Illustrated Golden Bough.* Doubleday: New York.

Freud, S. 1928/1961. "Humour." Tr. J. Strachey. *Standard Edition, Vol 21.* Hogarth: London.

Friedman, Robert, and Leila Lerner. 1986. *Toward a New Psychology of Men: Psychoanalytic and Social Perspectives.* Guilford Press: New York.

Frye, Northrop. 1957. *Anatomy of Criticism: Four Essays.* Princeton University Press.

Fuller, Fred. 1991. "The Fool, the Clown, the Jester." *Gnosis 19:*16–21.

Gamble, Clive. 1986. *The Palaeolithic Settlement of Europe.* Cambridge University Press: Cambridge.

Garfinckel, Perry. 1985. *In a Man's World: Father, Son, Brother, Friend and Other Roles Men Play.* New American Library: New York.

Gerzon, Mark. 1982. *A Choice of Heroes: The Changing Faces of American Manhood.* Boston: Houghton Mifflin.

Gewertz, Deborah, ed. 1988. *Myths of Matriarchy Reconsidered.* University of Sydney, Australia.

Gilligan, Carol. 1982. *In a Different Voice: Psychological Theory and Women's Development.* Harvard University Press: Cambridge.

Gilmore, David. 1990. *Manhood in the Making: Cultural Concepts of Masculinity.* Yale University Press: New Haven.

Gilstrap, R., and I. Estabrook. 1958. *The Sultan's Fool and Other North African Tales.* Henry Holt and Co.: New York.

Gimbutas, Marija. 1982. *The Goddesses and Gods of Old Europe: Myths and Cult Images.* Thames and Hudson: London.

Gimbutas, Marija. 1989. *The Language of the Goddess.* Harper and Row: New York.

Glantz, Kalman, and John Pearce. 1989. *Exiles from Eden: Psychotherapy from an Evolutionary Perspective.* Norton: New York.

Glob, P. V. 1969. *The Bog People: Iron-Age Man Preserved.* Tr. Rupert Bruce-Mitford. Cornell University Press: Ithaca.

Gomes, Varela. 1983. "Aspects of Megalithic Religion According to the Portuguese Menhirs." In Anati, 385–401.

Gove, Walter. 1985. "The Effect of Age and Gender on Deviant Behavior: A Biopsychosocial Perspective." In Rossi, Alice, ed., *Gender and the Life Course,* 115–144. Aldine: New York.

Gregor, Thomas. 1985. *Anxious Pleasures: The Sexual Lives of an Amazonian People.* University of Chicago Press.

Grimm, Jacob, and Wilhelm Grimm. 1972. *The Complete Grimms' Fairy Tales.* Pantheon: New York.

Grottanelli, Christiano. 1983. "Tricksters, Scapegoats, Champions, Saviors." *History of Religions 23:* 117–139.

Gurian, Michael. 1992. *The Prince and the King.* Tarcher: Los Angeles.

Hadingham, Evan. 1979. *Secrets of the Ice Age: The World of the Cave Artists.* Walker: New York.

Hahn, Joachim. 1972. "Aurignacian Signs, Pendants and Art Objects in Central and Eastern Europe." *World Archeology 3:* 252–266.

Halifax, Joan. 1982. *Shaman: The Wounded Healer.* London: Thames and Hudson.

Hammond, Dorothy, and Alta Jablow. 1987. "Gilgamesh and the Sundance Kid: The Myth of Male Friendship." In Brod, 241–258.

Hanna, Barbara. 1977. *Jung: His Life and Work: A Biographical Memoir.* Michael Joseph: London.

Harrold, Francis. 1980. "A Comparative Analysis of Eurasian Paleolithic Burials." *World Archeology 12:* 195–211.

Hays, H. R. 1963. *In the Beginnings: Early Man and His Gods.* Putnam: New York.

Heckethorn, Charles. 1965/1975. *The Secret Societies of All Ages and Countries. Vol. 1.* University Books: New Hyde Park, New York.

Henderson, Joseph L. 1967. *Thresholds of Initiation.* Wesleyan University Press: Middletown, Connecticut.

Hoffman, W. J. 1891. "The Mide'wiwin or 'Grand Medicine Society' of the Ojibwa." In *Seventh Annual Report of the Bureau of Ethnology 1885–1886.* Government Printing Office: Washington, D.C.

Hogenson, George B. 1991. ''The Great Goddess Reconsidered: Recent Thinking About the 'Old European Goddess Culture' of Marija Gimbutas.'' *The San Francisco Jung Institute Library Journal 10:* 5–24.

Hopcke, Robert. 1990. *Men's Dreams, Men's Healing.* Shambhala: New York.

Ingold, T., D. Riches, and J. Woodburn. 1988. *Hunters and Gatherers 1: History, Evolution and Social Change.* Berg: Oxford.

Jacobs, J. 1890. *Indian Fairy Tales.* Putnam: New York.

James. E. O. 1957. *Prehistoric Religion.* Thames and Hudson: London.

Janus, Samuel S. 1975. ''The Great Comedians: Personality and Other Factors.'' *American Journal of Psychoanalysis 35:*169–174.

Johnson, R. 1976. *He: Understanding Masculine Psychology.* New York: Perennial Library.

Jones, Mervyn. 1967. ''Freemasonry.'' In MacKenzie, 152–177.

Jones, Trevor, ed. 1977. *Oxford-Harrad Standard German-English Dictionary, Vol III.* Clarendon Press: Oxford.

Jung, C. G. 1953a. ''Two Essays on Analytical Psychology.'' *Collected Works Vol 7.* Princeton University Press.

Jung, C. G. 1953b. ''Psychology and Alchemy.'' *Collected Works Vol 12.* Bollingen: Princeton University.

Jung, C. G. 1960. ''Stages of Life.'' *Collected Works Vol 8.* Princeton University Press.

Jung, C. G. 1965. *Memories, Dreams and Reflections.* Vintage Books: New York.

Jung, C. G. 1967. ''The Spirit Mercurius.'' *Collected Works Vol 13.* Princeton University Press.

Jung, Emma, and Marie-Louise Von Franz. 1986. *The Grail Legend.* Sigo Press: Boston.

Kast, Verena. 1991. *Sisyphus: A Jungian Approach to Midlife Crisis.* Daimon Verlag: Switzerland.

Kerenyi, Karl. 1986. *Hermes: Guide of Souls. The Mythologem of the Masculine Source of Life.* Tr. Murray Stein. Spring Publications: Dallas.

Kipnis, Aaron. 1991. *Knights Without Armor: A Practical Guide for Men in Quest of Masculine Soul.* Tarcher: Los Angeles.

Kluger, Rivkah. 1991. *The Archetypal Significance of Gilgamesh, a Modern Hero.* Daimon Verlag: Switzerland.

Kolbenschlag, Madonna. 1988. *Kiss Sleeping Beauty Goodbye: Breaking the Spell of Feminine Myths and Models.* Harper and Row: San Francisco.

Kramer, D. 1989. ''Development of an Awareness of Contradiction Across the Lifespan and the Question of Post-formal Operations.'' In Commons, M. L., J. D. Sinnott, F. A. Richards, and C. Armon, eds., *Beyond Formal Operations II: Comparison and Applications of Adolescent and Adult Developmental Models,* 133–159. New York: Praeger.

Kubler, George. 1985. ''Eidetic Imagery and Paleolithic Art.'' *Journal of Psychology 119:*557–565.

La Fontaine, Jean. 1985. *Initiation: Ritual Drama and Secret Knowledge Across the World.* Penguin Books: New York.

Lamb, Michael E., ed. 1982. "The Role of the Father in Child Development." Wiley: New York.

Lang, Andrew. 1966a. *The Yellow Fairy Book.* Dover: New York.

Lang, Andrew. 1966b. *The Violet Fairy Book.* Dover: New York.

Lawlor, Robert. 1989. *Earth Honoring: The New Male Sexuality.* Park Street Press: Rochester, Vermont.

Layard, John. 1958. "Note on the Autonomous Psyche and the Ambivalence of the Trickster Concept." *Journal of Analytical Psychology 3:* 21–28, 26–27.

Lederer, Wolfgang, and Alexandra Botwin. 1982. "Where Have All the Heroes Gone? Another View of Changing Masculine Roles." In Solomon, Kenneth, and Norman Levy, eds. *Men in Transition: Theory and Therapy,* 241–246. New York: Plenum.

Lee, Richard, and Irven DeVore, eds. 1968. *Man the Hunter.* Aldine: Chicago.

Lerner, Gerda. 1986. *The Creation of Patriarchy.* Oxford University Press: New York.

Leroi-Gourhan, A. 1974. *Treasures of Prehistoric Art.* Tr. N. Guterman. Abrams: New York.

Levinson, Daniel, Charlotte Darrow, Edward Klein, Maria Levinson, and Braxton McKee. 1979. *The Seasons of a Man's Life.* Ballantine: New York.

Lewis, Robert A., ed. 1981. *Men in Difficult Times: Masculinity Today and Tomorrow.* Englewood Cliffs, New Jersey: Prentice-Hall.

Lewis-Williams, J. D. and T. A. Dowson. 1988. "The Signs of All Times: Entopic Phenomena in Upper Paleolithic Art." *Current Anthropology* 29:201–245.

Lorenz, Carol, and Christopher Vecsey. 1986. "Hopi Ritual Clowns and Values in the Hopi Life Span." In Nahemow, Lucille, Kathleen McCluskey-Fawcett, and Paul McGhee, eds., *Humor and Aging.* Academic Press: New York.

Lowie, Robert A. 1970/1924. *Primitive Religion.* Liveright: New York.

Luke, Helen M. 1989. *Dark Wood to White Rose: Journey and Transformation in Dante's Divine Comedy.* New York: Parabola Books.

MacKenzie, Norman, ed. 1967. *Secret Societies.* Crescent Books: New York.

MacQuade, Walter. 1985. "The Male Manager's Last Refuge." *Fortune 112:* 38, August 5, 1985.

Mahdi, Louise Carus, Steven Foster, and Meredith Little, eds. 1987. *Betwixt and Between: Patterns of Masculine and Feminine Initiation.* Open Court: LaSalle, Illinois.

Malinowski, Bronislaw. 1929. *The Sexual Life of Savages in North-Western Melanesia.* Harcourt, Brace and World: New York.

Maringer, Johannes. 1956. *The Gods of Prehistoric Man.* Weidenfeld and Nicolson: London.

Martin, E. 1985. "Mémoire collective et préhistoire de l'homme." *Révue Française de Psychanalyse 49:* 111–126.

Matthews, John, ed. 1990. *The Household of the Grail.* The Aquarian Press: Northamptonshire.

McAdams, Dan P. 1985. *Power, Intimacy and the Life Story: Personological Inquiries into Identity.* Dorsey: Homewood, Illinois.

McCully, Robert S. 1984. "Sorcerers as Masculine Protest Symbols in Upper Paleolithic Times." *Journal of Psychoanalytic Anthropology* 7:365–378.

McLeish, John. 1976. *The Ulyssean Adult: Creativity in the Middle and Later Years.* New York: McGraw-Hill Ryerson.

Messer, Ron. 1982. "A Jungian Interpretation of the Relationship of Culture Hero and Trickster Figure Within Chippewa Mythology." *Studies in Religion* 11:309–320.

Messner, Michael. 1987. "The Meaning of Success: The Athletic Experience and the Development of Male Identity." In Brod, 193–209.

Metman, Philip. 1958. "The Trickster Figure in Schizophrenia." *Journal of Analytical Psychology 3:* 5–20.

Miller, Daniel, and Christopher Tilley, eds. 1984. *Ideology, Power and Prehistory.* Cambridge University Press, Cambridge.

Miller, Daniel, and Guy Swanson. 1966. *Inner Conflict and Defense.* Schocken Books: New York.

Monick, Eugene. 1987. *Phallos: Sacred Image of the Masculine.* Toronto: Inner City Books.

Monroe, Robert. 1971. *Journeys Out of the Body.* Doubleday: New York.

Moore, Robert, and Douglas Gillette. 1990. *King, Warrior, Magician, Lover: Rediscovering the Archetypes of the Mature Masculine.* Harper San Francisco: San Francisco.

Morton-Williams, Peter. 1960. "The Yoruba Ogboni Cult in Oyo." *Africa* 30:362–374.

Mussen, P., and N. Haan. 1981. "A Longitudinal Study of Patterns of Personality and Political Ideologies." In D. Eichorn, J. Clausen, N. Haan, M. Honzik, and P. Mussen, eds., *Present and Past in Middle Life,* 393–414. New York: Academic Press.

Nelson, Richard. 1991. "Exploring the Near at Hand." *Parabola 16:* 35–43.

Newsweek. 1982. "The Elite Meet in Retreat." *Newsweek 100:*21, August 2.

Nicholson, Shirley, ed. 1987. *Shamanism: An Expanded View of Reality.* Quest Books: Wheaton, Illinois.

Nicoloff, A. 1979. *Bulgarian Folktales.* Nicoloff: Cleveland, Ohio.

Nisker, Wes. 1990. *Crazy Wisdom.* Ten Speed Press: Berkeley.

O'Collins, G. 1978. *The Second Journey.* New York: Paulist Press.

Oldham, John, and Robert Liebert, eds. 1989. *The Middle Years: New Psychoanalytic Perspectives.* Yale University Press: New Haven.

Osherman, Samuel. 1986. *Finding Our Fathers: How a Man's Life Is Shaped by His Relationship with His Father.* Ballantine: New York.

Oxford University Press. 1971. *The Compact Edition of the Oxford English Dictionary: Vols 1 and 2.* Oxford University Press: Oxford.

Pearson, Carol. 1986. *The Hero Within: Six Archetypes We Live By.* Harper and Row: San Francisco.

Pelton, Robert D. 1980. *The Trickster in West Africa: A Study of Mythic Irony and Sacred Delight.* University of California Press: Berkeley.

Pemberton, John. 1975. "Eshu-Elegba: The Yoruba Trickster God." *African Arts 9:* 21–27, 66–70, 90–91.

Peters, Larry. 1990. "Mystical Experience in Tamang Shamanism." *Re-Vision 13:* 71–85.

Pfeiffer, John E. 1982. *The Creative Explosion: An Inquiry into the Origins of Art and Religion.* Harper and Row: San Francisco.

Price, T. Douglas, and James A. Brown. 1985. *Prehistoric Hunter-Gatherers: the Emergence of Cultural Complexity.* Academic Press: New York.

Qandil, Barbara. 1970. "A Comparative Study of a Near Eastern Trickster Cycle." *Southern Folklore Quarterly 34:* 18–33.

Radin, Paul. 1972. *The Trickster: A Study in American Indian Mythology.* Schocken Books: New York.

Radin, Paul. 1952. *African Folktales.* Schocken Books: New York.

Radin, Paul. 1957. *Primitive Religion.* Dover: New York.

Raduga Publishers. 1985. *The Three Kingdoms: Russian Folk Tales from Alexander Afanasiev's Collection.* Raduga Publishers: Moscow.

Ranke, K. 1966. *Folktales of Germany.* Tr. Lotte Baumann. University of Chicago Press.

Riccardi, T., Jr. 1971. *A Nepali Version of the Vetalapancavimsati: Nepali Text and English Translation with an Introduction, Grammar and Notes.* American Oriental Society: New Haven.

Riegel, K. F. 1973. "Dialectical Operations: The Final Period of Cognitive Development." *Human Development 16:* 346–370.

Roberts, Moss. 1979. *Chinese Fairy Tales and Fantasies.* Pantheon: New York.

Rowan, John. 1987. *The Horned God: Feminism and Men as Wounding and Healing.* Routledge & Kegan Paul: New York.

Sabo, Don. 1987. "Pigskin, Patriarchy and Pain." In Abbott, Franklin, ed., *New Men, New Minds: Breaking Male Tradition.* Crossing Press: California, 47–50.

Salman, Sherry. 1986. "The Horned God: Masculine Dynamics of Power and Soul." *Quadrant 19:* 6–26.

Samuels, Andrew. 1989. *The Plural Psyche: Personality, Morality and the Father.* Routledge & Kegan Paul: New York.

Sanday, Peggy Reeves. 1981. *Female Power and Male Dominance: On the Origins of Sexual Inequality.* Cambridge University Press, Cambridge.

Sanford, John, and George Lough. 1988. *What Men Are Like.* Paulist Press: New York.

Sanford, Nevitt. 1966. *Self and Society: Social Change and Individual Development.* Atherton: New York.

Schrire, Carmel, ed. 1984. *Past and Present in Hunter Gatherer Studies.* Academic Press: New York.

Schwartz, Howard. 1985. *Elijah's Violin and Other Jewish Fairy Tales.* Harper Colophon: New York.

Sekaquaptewa, Emory. 1979. "One More Smile for a Hopi Clown." *Parabola 4:* 6–9.

Sharp, Daryl. 1988. *The Survival Papers: Anatomy of a Midlife Crisis.* Inner City Books: Toronto.

Sheppard-Jones, Elisabeth. 1978. *Stories of Wales.* Cardiff: John Jones Cardiff.

Sieveking, Ann. 1979. *The Cave Artists.* Thames and Hudson: London.

Sigstedt, Cyriel. 1952. *The Swedenborg Epic: The Life and Works of Emanuel Swedenborg.* Bookman Associates: New York.

Stein, Murray. 1983. *In Midlife: A Jungian Perspective.* Spring Publications: Dallas.

Swedenborg, Emanuel. 1977. *Swedenborg's Journal of Dreams.* G. E. Klemming and W. Ross Woofenden, eds., J. J. G. Wilkinson, tr. Swedenborg Foundation: New York.

Swedenborg, Emanuel. 1979. tr. *Heaven and Hell. G. F. Dole.* Swedenborg Foundation: New York.

Tamir, Lois M. 1982. *Men in Their Forties: The Transition to Middle Age.* Springer: New York.

Tawney, C. H. 1956. *Vetalapanchavimsati.* Bombay: Jaico.

Tedlock, Barbara. 1979. "Boundaries of Belief." *Parabola 4:* 70–77.

Thompson, Keith, ed. 1991. *To Be a Man.* Tarcher: Los Angeles.

Toelken, Barre. 1990. "Ma'ii Joldlooshi la'Eeya': The Several Lives of a Navajo Coyote." *The World and I.* April 1990, 651–660.

Vaillant, G. 1977. *Adaptation to Life: How the Best and the Brightest Came of Age.* New York: Little, Brown.

Vaillant, G., and E. Milofsky. 1980. "Natural History of Male Psychological Health: IX. Empirical Evidence for Erikson's Model of the Life Cycle." *American Journal of Psychiatry 137:* 1348–1359.

van der Post, Laurens. 1991. "The Song of the Hunter." *Parabola 16:* 14–19.

Von Franz, Marie-Louise. 1980. *A Psychological Interpretation of The Golden Ass of Apuleius.* Spring Publications: Dallas.

Wakankar, V. S. 1983. "The Dawn of Indian Art." In Anati, 497–502.

Walker, Mitchell. 1976. "The Double: An Archetypal Configuration." *Spring: A Journal of Archetype and Culture:* 165–175. Spring Publications: New York.

Walsh, Mary, ed. 1987. *The Psychology of Women: Ongoing Debates.* Yale University Press: New Haven.

Walsh, Roger. 1990. *The Spirit of Shamanism.* Tarcher: Los Angeles.

Wasson, Will. 1979. "How Salmon Got Greasy Eyes." *Parabola 4:* 66–69.

Webster, Hutton. 1968/1932. *Primitive Secret Societies: A Study in Early Politics and Religion.* Octagon Books: New York.

Wehr, Gerhard. 1987. *Jung: A Biography.* Tr. David Weeks. Shambhala: Boston.

Welbourn, Alice. 1984. "Endo Ceramics and Power Strategies." In Miller and Tilley, 17–24.

Whan, Michael W. 1978. " 'Don Juan,' Trickster, and Hermeneutic Understanding." *Spring: A Journal of Archetype and Culture:* 17–27.

Wheeler, Maurice. 1984. *Oxford Russian-English Dictionary.* Clarendon Press: Oxford.

Whitmont, Edward C. 1987. *Return of the Goddess.* Crossroad: New York.

Williams, Paul, ed. 1979. *The Fool and the Trickster: Studies in Honour of Enid Welsford.* Brewer, Rowman & Littlefield: Norfolk, Great Britain.

Wilson, Peter. 1991. "The Green Man: The Trickster Figure in Sufism." *Gnosis 19:22–26.*

Wolkstein, Diane. 1991. *Oom Razoom or Go I Know Not Where, Bring Back I Know Not What: A Russian Tale.* Morrow Junior Books: New York.

Wyly, James. 1989. *The Phallic Quest: Priapus and Masculine Inflation.* Toronto: Inner City Books.

Wymer, John. 1982. *The Palaeolithic Age.* St. Martin's Press: New York.

Zimmer, Heinrich. 1956. *The King and the Corpse: Tales of the Soul's Conquest of Evil.* Joseph Campbell, ed. Princeton University Press.

Zweig, Connie, and Jeremiah Abrams, eds. 1991. *Meeting the Shadow.* Tarcher: Los Angeles.

Index

Fool
>animal ears, 42
>crazy wisdom, 189
>divine calling, 196
>hunters, 245
>Parsifal, 189
>patriarch, 114
>shamans, 244
>Tricksters, 72, 109

Fraternities. *See also* secret
>>societies, Spirit Brother
>midlife, at, 117
>youthful vs. mature, 116

Freud, Sigmund
>break with Jung, 26, 173
>humor, 71
>Oedipal complex, 14

Generativity, 69
>authority, 242
>male lodges, 133
>phallos, 119
>pluralism, 89
>Holy Ghost, 187
>Trickster, 120, 146, 201, 215
>zero-sum perspective, 122

Gerzon, Mark, 1, 47

Gilgamesh
>deep masculine, 168
>hunter theme, 245
>masculine-feminine-masculine
>>shift, 168
>warrior comrade, 116

Gillette, Douglas, 1, 73

Gilmore, David, 51

Great Goddess, 47
>agriculture, 213
>anima, 161
>deep masculine, 175
>evolution of, 210
>Grail legends, 244
>hero, 32, 162, 212
>hunter-gatherers, 224
>matriarchy, 222, 223
>men's development, 162
>men's initiation into, 7, 34,
>>169, 255
>Mesoamerica, 230
>Neolithic vs. Paleolithic, 223
>Robert Bly, on, 174
>sacred sisters, 210
>"soft males," 47
>suppression of, 212
>Tricksters, 120, 211, 214, 227

Gurian, Michael, 16

Hermes, 63, 65
>culture-bearer, 131
>fire, 145
>hunting, 239
>linguist, 186
>messenger, 115, 140
>phallus, 119, 237
>psychopomp, 125
>Trickster, 204, 230, 239
>wandering, 110

Hero
>adapatation to warfare, 229
>body, attitude to, 195
>deep masculine, 4, 9
>derivation of term, 217
>dualism of, 91
>equality, 179, 220
>father-son relations, 18,
>>229
>feminism, 19, 25, 220
>great goddess, 162
>history of ideal, 212
>hoarding, 66, 221
>humor, 70
>hunter, 213, 216
>initiation into, 8, 125, 134,
>>229
>Jung's dream, 26, 246

ABOUT THE AUTHOR

Allan B. Chinen, M.D., is a psychiatrist in private practice in San Francisco and is on the clinical faculty of the University of California, San Francisco. He is also the author of *In the Ever After: Fairy Tales and the Second Half of Life* and *Once Upon a Midlife: Classic Stories and Mythic Tales to Illuminate the Middle Years.*